An Old Affair

ISBN 9798327131569

This publication is a work of fiction. All names, characters and events in this publication, other than those clearly in the public domain, are fictitious and any resemblance to real persons, living or dead, or actual events is purely coincidental.

Copyright © 2024 by G J Bellamy. All rights reserved.

The moral right of the author has been asserted.

No part of this publication may be reproduced, stored in a retrieval system, or transmitted in any form or by any means, without the prior express written permission of the publisher.

Contents

Note to new readers — V
Cast of Characters — VII
Prologue — 1
1. The old is new again — 11
2. Travel plans — 22
3. Local customs — 37
4. The Mundays — 50
5. The Eldreds — 61
6. Minor difficulties — 72
7. Decks, dots, and dashes — 84
8. Sun, sea, and superstition — 95
9. Scouting party — 105
10. The Swan by the river — 125
11. Waterloo to Wynbourne — 135
12. Dumond Hall — 148
13. The Fête — 157

14.	Tripping the light fantastic	174
15.	The breaking of silence	184
16.	The morning after the night before	198
17.	Around the pool	208
18.	Conspiracy	218
19.	Telling conversations	236
20.	Getting ready	245
21.	Enemies in the house	255
22.	The Masquerade	266
23.	And the band played on	278
24.	Under the cover of darkness	286
25.	It's all over	294
26.	A quick change of plan	307
27.	Running Rabbit, Flying Dragon	315
28.	The cautious and the cautioned	327
29.	Archie ties a bow	342
Epilogue		353
Other books by G J Bellamy		360

NOTE TO NEW READERS

If you're new to the series, or it has been a while since you read an installment, here's a brief introduction or refresher to the background and setting of Burgoyne's and the secret agency hidden within it.

Sophie, in her early twenties, started her domestic service and typing firm within the last twelve months. During that time, she and her staff have been involved in several 'special' cases. These operations have usually divided into two parts.

Penrose, Superintendent of Special Duties, acts as the co-ordinator for Scotland Yard in the cases, and employs Burgoyne's staff members to work as domestic servants while they are spying for the police. In the field, Sophie reports to Detective Inspector Morton or Detective Sergeant Gowers.

Often, Archie Drysdale of the Foreign Office (FO) — Sophie's cousin — has Burgoyne's investigating foreign spies.

Penrose and Drysdale work together within a small, loose network of agents that can react quickly to foreign or domestic threats. Drysdale is a spymaster. Sophie reports to him, keeping him informed on their foreign spy intelligence-gathering efforts. The police and spy cases often overlap.

Sometimes, the Home Office (HO) is also involved because its jurisdiction differs from that of the FO. Purely concerned with threats within the British Isles, the HO does, however, possess more assets and personnel than the FO, and so takes the lead in any domestic operation. Lord Laneford of the Home Office is Archie Drysdale's counterpart within the network.

Sophie's core spy team comprises herself, Ada (a trained servant), and Flora (an actress and Sophie's school-friend). Frequently assisting are Lady Shelling (Sophie's aunt) with whom Sophie lives when in London, and Elizabeth, a researcher, who works in the agency's office.

During a case, Sophie still has the headache of running her typing and domestic service business, while trying to keep her secret work hidden.

Cast of Characters

Family & Friends
Sophie Burgoyne / Phoebe King
Henry Burgoyne, vicar - Sophie's father
Lady Shelling (Elizabeth Burgoyne) - Auntie Bessie
Ada McMahon / Nancy Carmichael - Sophie's friend
Flora Dane / Gladys Walton - Sophie's long-time friend
Archie Drysdale - Sophie's second cousin

The Agency
Miss Jones, typist and office manageress
Elizabeth Banks, researcher and office helper
Douglas Broadbent-Wicks, footman and spy
Nick, errand boy

The Mundays of Dumond Hall
Viscount Gerald Munday, an invalid
Basil Munday, business man, 47
Clare Munday, his wife, 43
Luke Munday, 24, the eldest of their five children
Audrey Munday, 22
Clive Munday, 20
Violet Munday, 19
Julia Munday, 13
Todor Minkov, a guest

The Eldreds of Capel House
Viscount Pascoe Eldred, 38
Viscountess Shelagh Eldred, 35
Edward Eldred, 13
Harriet Eldred, 11
Myra Eldred, 9

Scotland Yard and Government Departments
Superintendent of Special Duties (Inspector) Penrose
Detective Sergeant Gowers, CID
Ralph 'Sinjin' Yardley, Foreign Office agent
Sir Hoël Llewellyn, Chief Constable Wiltshire Constabulary
Detective Inspector Haddock, Wiltshire Constabulary

Prologue

August, 1781

It was mid-afternoon when the horses crossed the old Fulham Bridge at Putney. The heat was so cloying and, although there had not been rain for a week, even the dust seemed too lazy to rise. Indeed, there was not a breath of wind, and the Thames looked thick and viscous, more like a river of oil than of water.

"Mortlake's no more than a mile," said Martin Eldred. He was twenty and angry.

The groom leading the third horse remained silent. He did not answer his master because it was not his place to do so. Today, on this ride, his habitual respectful attention was heightened because Eldred was in a foul, reckless mood, and he was armed.

They rode in the heat at a walk to spare the horses. If Eldred had believed a quarter hour would make any difference, he would have spurred his mount into a gallop. Instead, in his mind, he spurred a red horse of hatred for James Munday.

To cut off a loop in the tidal river, they took the Richmond Road to rejoin the Thames by the White Hart in Barnes. From there, they followed the path by the river, because this was not the tavern Eldred sought. Cows stood knee deep in the water, and rowing boats were pulled up on the shore between the banks and the river. The heat turned the distant western sky into nothing but a grey haze supporting an unmerciful sun. The horses shuffled along — heads bowed and their manes lank.

At Mortlake, they came to the high ancient walls of the palace of Thomas Cromwell — he who had been chief minister to Henry VIII. The sprawling complex on the river had long since gone, having fallen down, and the materials taken for other buildings. The sun was striking old Tom's wall, and the riders felt the reflected heat pouring off it. To their right, a small sailing barge waited, its topsail hanging limp and of no more use than a string until a breeze came to stir it.

The Ship tavern was next, but neither was this the one wanted. Fields and a farm were to their left, the river to their right, but straight ahead was the ferry. The Ferryman tavern came into view. Eldred did not take his eyes off it until he dismounted outside the old ramshackle building.

"Water the horses," said the young master to his groom.

Eldred lifted his tricorne hat to mop his brow with a handkerchief. Then he pushed open the door of the inn. The long, low main room was sparsely furnished with chairs and tables and little else. It was cooler inside than he had expected. He saw several patrons sitting alone, but it was to the group of four that Eldred directed his steps.

"Why are you here!?" James Munday stood up, overturning his chair in so doing. The other three turned — the young woman among them looked at her approaching brother in horror.

Eldred ignored Munday. "Susanna, come with me. I shall take you home."

"We're to be married... How dare you interfere?" said Susanna.

"You are not married yet. And this is not how it shall be done. Come."

"Martin," said Munday. "Wait, just wait a moment..."

"Be quiet, sir, if you know what's good for you. Consider our friendship forever broken."

"Be reasonable..."

"Cease yapping, you cur."

The two men glared at each other. Munday was twenty-five and, although younger, Eldred was the more forceful man of the two.

One of Munday's friends named Devon spoke up. "I believe we can settle the matter amicably." He was conciliatory, and rightly so, because Eldred was a good swordsman, and he was carrying a sword. He was also an excellent shot, and there was a pistol in his belt.

"Susanna, come away."

"I'll not go with you," she replied defiantly.

"You see?" asked Munday. "You're not needed here."

"She is not of legal age to decide the matter."

"We're going to Gretna Green, and you shan't stop us," protested Susanna.

"An anvil marriage! Have you no decency!? No thought for your parents!? Shall you bring ignominy upon those dear heads? You shame them. You shame the family name. Susanna, I implore you, turn from such a wicked course."

The young woman looked amazed. "How can you say…? How dare you say that my love for James is wicked?"

"We shan't discuss it in public. Come, and we can put all this behind us."

Eldred seized his sister's arm as if to pull her from her chair. Munday restrained him, saying,

"She's not your property that you may drag her about where you please."

Eldred gripped her arm a moment longer before roughly releasing it. With studied care, he took a glove from his belt, then slapped Munday hard across the cheek with it.

"Where!?" hissed Munday.

"Anywhere you please, I care not… The Great Pagoda is as droll a place as any."

"Tomorrow, then. First light."

"Agreed."

"Pistols?"

"Agreed."

"Then I will arrange everything," said Munday.

The dawn's cloudless sky could only promise the same weather as the day before, yet it started off cool. When sunlight first touched the exhausted, yellowing grass in Kew Park, it revealed precious little dew. What there was would be gone in an hour but, for now, the passage of two different parties had imprinted dark marks in the silver coverlet. The parties met at the end of a colonnade of trees which bordered a grass-covered drive. Towering, overshadowing, and solitary in the nearby open space, was the majestic tan-bricked, red-painted, and many storied pagoda. Its gold dragons were bright even in the early morning. Several looked down at the gentlemen below.

The duel was supposed to be conducted according to established custom. The duellists, in their shirt sleeves, would choose their weapons from a velvet-lined case, and then stand back to back. Upon a signal, they would cock their pistols, each walk their ten paces, turn, present, and fire. If the combatants so wished, further attempts would be permitted. In the event of a satisfactory conclusion, a doctor would be on hand to tend the wounded. Today, the difference was, there was no doctor. Half a dozen friends accompanied Munday. Eldred had only his groom with him.

Susanna had slept alone at another inn. She had given all her money, barring a few coins, into James's safe-keeping. Before dawn and frantic to reach the pagoda, she gave her few remaining shillings to the inn's uncooperative ostler, begging him to give her a horse. Reluctantly, he gave in to her entreaties, but only after she had pledged all her luggage against the horse's safe return. Knowing just the direction in which Kew Park lay, she set off on the slow, dispirited animal.

In the park, she lost her way, because she could not see the pagoda which was to guide her. She searched in this direction and that, her desperation mounting as the fateful sun rose and, all the while, the horse was unwilling to go above a trot. What drew her in the end was the sound of two pistol shots close together, soon followed by a third. The loud and sudden noises set the rooks a-cawing.

She found the place, and the two bodies stretched out with no one else present. Her brother was dead, and so was his groom. Susanna could not comprehend or take in the scene. She had imagined it would be James she would find lying there, and so what she saw disordered her mind. Susanna stooped by her brother's side; then she held him. The shining dragons leered down, making the tragedy seem an even greater nightmare as she looked about for help. Two bullet wounds were in his back and the blood was sticky. His groom lay close by, shot through the heart. All their possessions and their horses were gone. James Munday, whom she loved and was to marry, had murdered her brother.

It was October two years later and, as was widely said, James Munday had gone to the devil. He went everywhere in London and did everything. Munday visited respectable houses and social gatherings, and frequented all the other places. Living somewhere near the Strand, one never really knew where he would turn up next — a Royal garden party or a brawl in the street. Even his friends thought him difficult, unpredictable, and unreliable, for he rarely would commit to anything, preferring to drift wherever his whim suggested. But if one studied him patiently, deeming such an occupation worth one's while, the address of his apartments, the whereabouts of his favourite haunts, and such regularity of his movements as existed would become plain.

He was often in the Strand because, on purpose, he lived nearby. It was a street lined with both respectable and derelict buildings; a street filled with money and the want of it — all jostled together. During the day, it was a place for one to be seen. At night, and unless one had specific business, it was a place to avoid. Although the Strand itself was fashionable while the light lasted, the alleys and side streets were reservoirs of every ancient vice a city has ever possessed. After the sun had set, the contents of those reservoirs flowed out.

It was dark enough for the link boys to light their torches and ply their trade, accompanying pedestrians and sedan chairs to and from the Strand. The road itself was better, if sporadically so, lit by the oil lamps and candles in shop windows, and the lanterns suspended outside the more prosperous properties. Munday left the Grecian Coffee House because he would find no amusement there this evening. He stood on the step and wondered which way to go. Go east, and there was gambling. Go west, and there lived a certain lady. Instead of choosing, he decided upon a chop house first, then a pint of sack at The Crown. Afterwards, he would consider the matter again.

Sometimes others know us better than we know ourselves. And so it was with the person concealed in a hooded cloak who was now watching indecisive James Munday. As soon as Munday set a foot forward, the person knew to which chop house and then tavern he was going. Although his friends found him unpredictable, his enemy, who had studied well, did not.

When Munday left The Crown, he believed himself too stupefied with wine to risk gambling, so he turned west. The person waiting in the shadows followed him.

A quarter-mile of walking in the cool night air somewhat sobered Munday. The paving was uneven in front of the old Savoy Barracks. Fire had gutted the main building, leaving only a stone shell, although the rest of the complex was still in use. Whoever used it now had no money for lamps, and so the open area by the road was dim, with only the weak lights from the other side of the road keeping it from complete darkness.

Munday heard no approaching step. He only knew of his peril when the muzzles of two pistols were pressed hard into his back. He stopped and began trembling.

"Don't shoot me!"

"Be quiet," whispered the woman.

"Yes, yes. I'll be quiet... I have money."

"Shhh... Why did you murder Martin?"

Munday was silent as he strove to comprehend the question. "Susanna?"

"Answer me."

"Put the pistols down and I'll explain everything."

"Why did you do it?" She poked him with the muzzles.

"Look, you must understand, I loved you... I still do." He received no answer. "Let us talk this over sensibly."

Susanna brought a muzzle up to his ear. "Answer me."

"All right, I will... He was a much better shot than I. You know I've never been very good with pistols. Don't you see? He would have killed me straight off. We all knew it, and so..."

"Yes?"

"And so the *others* came up with a plan and I agreed and went along with it. I was too scared to do otherwise."

"Ah, is *that* what happened? Walk ahead of me."

"You won't shoot?"

"Walk, sir, and mark you this. I'm as good a shot now as Martin ever was."

Within a minute, they entered an alley. A single lantern outside a closed shop revealed two loitering men.

"I have a bullet for each of you," said Susanna, clearly and fearlessly, as the men straightened themselves up, preparing for some dirty work. She kept a pistol on Munday and pointed the other towards the two cutpurses.

"Take off your rings," said Susanna, "and give them to these men. They must not go away empty-handed tonight."

Munday pulled off several rings. Susanna signalled and the smaller of the two thieves came forward to get them.

"Now go." At her command, they hurried through the alley away from the Strand. "Tell me, James. Be exact. Whose plan was it?"

"Well, Devon's, of course. You must remember how he was."

"I do, indeed. Then it was all Devon's idea, was it? How comical. Indeed, it is, James. For it was just last night that he told me it was *your* idea. Can you see the humour in the situation?

"You've seen him?"

"Yes. It is so extraordinary how muddled you both are, and how unhesitatingly you each betray a friend. But then, James, you set little store by honour, loyalty, duty, and courage. I also once lightly considered such things. But, oh, how I have learned the errors of my ways. Dreadful lessons they were, too. Shall I whisper them? A broken heart, a stricken family, a betrayed and murdered brother, and a vile coward, whom I nearly married, who lives free — seemingly free of even a guilty conscience."

"No matter what he said, it was all him. He killed Martin. You must believe me. I wanted no part of it."

"Of course, James. But then I also believe Devon. He said it was you who snatched up the pistols and shot Martin while his back was turned, and it was you who killed his groom, though he pleaded for his life. Such *bravery*... I gave you my money once. Give me your purse and we shall consider that particular score settled. Be careful how you do it."

His hand shook as he passed the purse behind him to Susanna.

"After all, Devon proved to be an honest soul. We spoke at length... Then he died. Now it is your turn to do the same. Tell me the truth, omitting nothing. And remove your vestments down to your shirt, sir. I wish to relive that August dawn as nearly as possible."

When the loud reports came, they barely disturbed the Strand. Several people looked out of their windows, but they saw no one, and believed it safer to enquire no further. The official discovery of Munday's body had to wait until morning. By that time, others had stripped his corpse of everything except the valueless bloody shirt, the back of which was ruined by powder burns and two bullet holes.

Chapter 1

The Old is New Again

Friday, 6th of May, 1921

It was mid-morning and hot for the time of year. Two old men, retired farm labourers, sitting on the settle in front of the Swan in the village of Wynbourne, had, of course, mentioned the unusual heat to each other. Weather permitting, they always sat outside and so, in their way, they were by default a seasonal yet persistent feature. Their conversation now had extended to more rousing topics.

"It don't matter who you vote fer, you'll not get a second pint," declared Ben Tubb, local-born septuagenarian.

They each sat in a corner of the worn wooden settle which stood against the outside wall of the pub. With a glass of beer in hand and a walking stick propped close by, they each stared across the dusty road at a row of thatched-roofed and white-washed cottages.

"Arrh... Loike as much," replied Fred Gardner, also a native, who knew the day of his birth but not the year. However, they both acknowledged he was the elder of the two. The men could have settled the matter of Fred's birth year had they looked in the church baptismal records, but it would never occur to either man to trouble the vicar on such a point.

Through their daily discussions, the two men had boiled down to their very essence all domestic political policies and how such things applied to them personally. They had reached the stage where they could reduce matters no further. At present, and the situation had been unchanged for some time, they both received five shillings a week. From this sum, each man found he could just about afford a daily half pint of beer. By taking turns at collecting empty glasses and keeping ashtrays clean, they both could earn another half pint a day each from the landlord. What Ben and Fred truly hoped to find was a political party guaranteeing them a second daily pint.

"For all their talk about the welfare o' the common man," opined Ben, "Labour will never gi' us a second pint."

"But they *moight*," said Fred. "You just never can tell. So, I'll vote for 'em next toime."

"See here. Who's talking about increasing pensions, I'd loike to know? Not Labour, and not no one, that's who."

"But Labour *moight* put a shillin' on the pension," insisted Fred. He sipped his ale. "Drat. I've been nursin' me beer for so long it's gone warm."

He held up the pint glass to his near-sighted gaze to study the contents. Ben and Fred always drank their half pints from pint glasses because that meant extra beer. The landlord always pumped over the half, because if he served under or right on, he would never hear the end of it.

"That's because it's hot for this toime o' May," said Ben. "Reckon there'll be a drought this year... Arhh."

"That's what I said to you yesterday, so course there'll be a drought. It's as plain as the nose on your face."

"That's not roight. I said that to *you* yesterday."

"You did *not*. I said it first, just now."

"Ohh, 'ave it your own way. You always do. But you'll not never get a second pint, not from Lloyd-George, and not from Labour neither."

"I *moight*," said the implacable Fred.

They sat and studied the unvarying scene. Birds chirped. A sparrowhawk hung momentarily overhead before flapping once to glide away. The breeze stirred the treetops, but little else. From their perch, the men could see the church within its stone wall at the other end of the village, while the Swan stood at the bridge end of Wynbourne, close to that small, humped stone structure that spanned the Wynnet. It was a small river which joined the nearby River Kennet further north. Wynbourne lay on a gentle slope in open, undulating farmland on the south side of a shallow valley. From atop the plateau on the southern ridge, while looking south across a band of large fields, the border of Savernake could be seen. This was a forest of ancient oaks, managed by its Hereditary Warden. At one time, a man named Seymour occupied the office, and he had a daughter named Jane. Henry VIII took notice of youthful Jane while visiting her home, Wolfhall. So much notice did the king take that she eventually became his third wife.

Ben and Fred gave little thought to long departed kings and their doings. Neither did they discuss the old Roman town of Cunetio. This once important town had stood a scant three hundred yards from The Swan, but its remains were all buried. Ben still possessed three small Roman coins he had discovered at different times while working in the fields as man and boy. Fred, every time he found one of his five coins, quickly sold it in the nearby town of Marlborough.

The men heard a motor car descending Loxie Lane — a narrow road running through a green tunnel of trees.

"Who be that?" asked Ben before the car could be seen.

"Comin' from Chopping Knife Lane," said Fred.

"Has to, seein' as Loxie don't lead nowhere else."

The dark blue, two-door car drove past them. Two men were sitting in the front. The old men stared at the car from the moment it crested the hump of the bridge until it disappeared around the bend just past the church.

"Is that Lord Eldred?" asked Fred.

"Yes. But I wonder who that wor' with him?"

"Dunno."

"Where they be goin'?"

"Who cares?" Fred spoke gruffly. "Benefittin' themselves, no doubt."

"Argh. That's what the Eldreds and the Mundays do, and how they go about it is beyond the ken of us'en."

Wynbourne returned to its quiet ways. No sooner had it done so, the peace was shattered by the harsh cracks of two quick-fired pistol shots. They seemed to originate from the road beyond the church. The village came out of doors to see what the noise was about. Ben and Fred left their comfortable seats and walked as fast as their old bones allowed.

The man lying face-down in the road was dead. The dazed and appalled villagers were certain of this, because they all could plainly see the two bullet wounds in his back.

Sophie frowned. While sitting in her office, she read again the perplexing letter in her hand. It was an insistent reminder from the Foreign Office that she must go to Malta at her earliest convenience, and the FO would pay for her passage. The reason for the unusual request was that in the not too distant past, Sophie had discussed with the Foreign Office, represented by her cousin Archie Drysdale, how best they would pay her for her ongoing services. After much back and forth, Sophie received a modest, but acceptable, salary for which she was expected to act as the liaison officer to a recently recruited spy. That recently recruited spy, no longer useful, had long since departed. The salary, however, remained. Now, to fulfil some baffling governmental requirement among the terms of her employment, she must go to Malta as an interpreter. Adding to the surreal nature of the arrangement was that the length of her stay was entirely at her discretion, as long as she delivered her letter of introduction to the Governor of Malta. To top it all, she did not know a word of Maltese. Still, as long as she complied with the request, her salary would continue. Although the money was welcome, she felt somewhat guilty for being paid while not earning it. She looked at her list of things to do and added, 'Talk to Archie.'

Sophie called from her office door.

"Elizabeth. May I see you for a moment, please?"

"Yes, Miss Burgoyne."

Elizabeth Banks was an intelligent woman in her sixties and, besides being a very pleasant receptionist, she was the secret agency's researcher and chief car mechanic. As the agency possessed only a single car in its fleet — a new Austin Twenty named Rabbit — and as Elizabeth had instructed Sophie in how to maintain the car, Elizabeth now acted more in the role of a consultant master mechanic, with Sophie as her apprentice. Somehow, Nick, the fourteen-year-old office boy, was another such apprentice. In this way, Rabbit always shone because of the eager attention lavished upon it. Elizabeth, certain of one reason she was being called into Sophie's office, took several files with her.

"Ah, good. You brought them," said Sophie, espying the files.

"Yes, Miss Burgoyne."

"Please, sit down."

"Thank you."

Elizabeth settled herself and took several documents from the top file.

"The history of the murders is quite fascinating," said Elizabeth.

"I should think it is," said Sophie.

"Here's a summary of all killings and deaths under suspicious circumstances." Elizabeth handed the list to Sophie. Elizabeth's writing was a little idiosyncratic, but perfectly legible. Sophie read it.

Legal disputes over the Tongue,
& the tally of untimely deaths
between the
Munday and Eldred families.

The Tongue is an irregular tract of land of one and one-quarter acres, situated between the forks of the River Wynett, a northerly flowing stream that joins the River Kennet. Both tributary branches and the co-joined river are all named Wynett, which forms the dividing line between the neighbouring Eldred and Munday properties. Hence the confusion in the title deeds for both estates.

1741 Ownership of the Tongue tried at court - no settlement. Munday and Eldred agreed to share the Tongue. Peaceful co-existence.

1781 Death No. 1 Shooting of Martin Eldred by James Munday. He used a brace of pistols at short range in Kew Gardens.

1783 Death No. 2 Murder of James Munday by Susanna Eldred in the Strand. (Never brought to trial, as there was no evidence against her.)

1804 At court to settle ownership of The Tongue. No decision.

1811 Death No. 3 Lieutenant Munday, believed to have been murdered with a bayonet on the Spanish peninsula during the battle of Fuentes de Oñoro.

1815 Death No. 4 Captain Eldred shot twice in the back at the battle of Waterloo.

1840 Death No. 5 Clive Munday shot dead in York.

1857 Death No. 6 James Eldred murdered with a knife near Oxford University.

1880 Death No. 7 Martin Eldred murdered with a knife at Paddington Station.

1881 Death No. 8 Robert Munday shot dead outside Cardiff.

1904 Deaths No. 9/10 Alfred Eldred and Stephen Munday both died from wounds after a duel on Hampstead Heath.

1915 Death No. 11 Major Ian Eldred gave orders to Lieutenant David Munday to lead a detachment on a suicide mission at the battle of Festubert. Lt. Munday killed in action.

1915 For reference only. Viscount Martin Eldred, wounded in battle at Loos, died three days later.

1917 Death No. 12 Major Ian Eldred (now Viscount Eldred) killed during an artillery bombardment but was subsequently found to have died from two bullet wounds in the back.

1920 August. Death No. 13 Allan Munday shot in the back by a shotgun in The Trossachs, Scotland. Although there were some suspicious details noted, the Coroner's jury eventually ruled it was an accidental death.

1921 February. Death No. 14 Bartholomew Munday killed in a knife attack in Hyde Park.

(Miss Burgoyne has extracts from Scotland Yard police files for numbers 13 and 14.)

NB. In no instance has anyone been charged by the police or faced a court-martial, etc.

The Death Toll:
Eldred family - 7
Munday family - 7

"How absolutely ghastly," said Sophie, looking up. "Have these people finished, do you think? Or will they continue until they've obliterated each other?"

"The Mundays are quite numerous, but not so the Eldreds. As to your question, I cannot say, Miss Burgoyne."

"Well, whoever killed Bartholomew Munday in London must still be alive. Who's capable among the Eldreds of carrying out such an attack?"

"Unless further research proves otherwise, there are only two male persons. Lord Pascoe Eldred and his son, Edward Eldred, who is only thirteen."

"As ridiculous as it seems, we can't ignore Edward. Come to think of it, we can't exclude any of the women, either. Susanna Eldred's behaviour makes that abundantly clear. How did she get away with it?"

"There is no clear account of the murder in the Strand. The London newspapers of the time implied the murder was a crime of passion, but they named no names. The newspapers mentioned that all of Munday's possessions were taken, but they assumed the body was despoiled separately from the murder. They only way I can see they would state that is if they got wind of something close to the truth, but hesitated to print it without facts in case of a libel action. I'm sorry for such imprecision."

"Don't apologize, Elizabeth, it's not your fault... So, everyone believed she did it, but no one could *prove* that she did. Is that the idea?"

"I believe so, Miss Burgoyne. With regards to the present day, there are several women who could have murdered Bartholomew Munday, but I'm unable to find out more than a few scant details about them."

"Hmm... Do you think a trip to the Wynbourne area is necessary?"

"I'm hesitant to suggest such a venture with all the expenses it will incur. You see, Miss Burgoyne, although public records will fill in some details, I can't see how they can help in the current situation. Of course, one never knows, something might turn up."

"It might. What puzzles me is how these families have got away with such wholesale slaughter for so long. It requires explanation and, perhaps, if we can find the right people to interview, we might learn something concrete about the more recent killings."

"But the police will have interviewed many people for that purpose."

"Yes. I'm sure they have. They've also spoken to many, many people over the last hundred and forty years, but it hasn't got them anywhere. I want to know why. Therefore, we shall go.

Would two or three days be sufficient time? That's all I can spare, really."

"It will have to be."

"Good. We need to return before the eighteenth of May, which is when the agency starts its duties for the Munday family at Dumond Hall. So... that means," Sophie consulted a calendar, "we'll drive down on Sunday and find a place to stay, then we can start first thing Monday morning. Is that convenient for you?"

"Yes, and may I say how exciting it all is, Miss Burgoyne? There's just one thing..."

"Your cats!"

"Precisely."

"I'm sure Nick can be persuaded to look after them. Send him to see me as soon as he appears."

"Very good. Um, there's one other thing. Will your aunt, Lady Shelling, be accompanying us?"

"Good grief. I hadn't even thought of her. She's bound to want to come."

"Lady Shelling is very insistent sometimes."

"That's putting it mildly. I'll ask her and see what she says, because should she find out and I haven't told her, then I'd never hear the last of it." Sophie leaned forward and lowered her voice. "Thank you for reminding me. I'll telephone her right away. Leave the files so I can look them over. Is that all for the present?"

"Yes, Miss Burgoyne."

Sophie smiled and reached for the receiver. Before she touched it, the phone rang, but the noise no longer startled her. Elizabeth left the room.

"Burgoyne's Agency, good morning."

"Good morning. Is that you, Soap?"

"Hello, Archie."

"You're about to receive a letter from us concerning a foreign matter."

"Aha! I've received a letter concerning a foreign matter this morning."

"Excellent, excellent. Toddle over right away because there are a few details to be thrashed out."

"I agree, but is there something else of which I'm not aware?"

"Yes. So come round, and I'll tell you all about it."

"I shall toddle immediately."

Before going out, Sophie called her Aunt Bessie.

"Hello, Auntie?"

"Hello, Sophie. You'll have to be quick. I'm going out to lunch."

"Right. Elizabeth and I are going down to Wiltshire to investigate a series of murders that have spanned generations. Elizabeth will conduct her research, and I'll be finding out what I can about two local families. There's room in the car if you wish to accompany us."

"When is this? One moment, I'm putting the receiver down to get my appointments book."

After a minute, she returned.

"What days did you say?"

"We'll drive down on Sunday the fifteenth and return late on the eighteenth."

"Oh. How late?"

"If we leave about four, we should be back about eleven. It's about eighty miles."

"Whereabouts are we going in Wiltshire?"

"A village called Wynbourne, but we must find a hotel in nearby Marlborough or further away so as not to be seen near Dumond Hall — that's the place we'll be working at as spies. Elizabeth will conduct her research, and I'll be interviewing anyone who might know about the recent murder."

"Marlborough... Marlborough... Oh, of course. Dot Callan lives close by. She's an old friend, and sure to know something useful. Also, she can put us up and that will be far more comfortable than any hotel or inn. Shall I telephone her?"

"We shan't be able to mention anything, Auntie."

"On the contrary, you could tell her practically everything because she is excellent at keeping secrets. Horses, dogs, gardening, and other people's failings are her areas of interest, yet she's no idle gossip and never has been."

"I don't think I can permit it."

"Sophie, do you trust me, yes or no?"

A frantic argument broke out in Sophie's mind, with the alarmed nay side shouting loudest.

"Yes, Auntie."

"I am in *earnest* when I say I have a friend who can be trusted. I shall inform Dot that what we might tell her must never be repeated, and it won't be. It's as simple as that, my dear."

"Very well, Auntie."

"Good. I will speak to her at once."

Chapter 2

Travel plans

Sophie sat facing Archie at his desk in the Foreign Office. She could not quite believe what he had just finished explaining.

"Just to confirm I have it all straight. I'm no longer going to Malta, but to Gibraltar, despite the instructions I received in the letter today?"

"That is correct. By doing so, you will fulfil the terms of your employment when you deliver a letter and get a receipt for our records here."

"Understood. But I'm not travelling by boat, which you say takes about a week to Gibraltar, or two weeks to Malta, although I'm no longer going there, of course."

"Yes."

"Instead, I am travelling by plane to Gibraltar, which you mentioned will take about sixteen hours."

"That's right. Go to Gib by plane and return by boat."

"How is that even possible? Aeroplanes can't fly eleven hundred miles, can they?"

"You'll make the journey in a series of short, co-ordinated hops."

"Co-ordinated? I'll have to take your word for that part, because I'm very unclear on how all of this works. As soon as I arrive, I'm to see Mr Bishop at the government offices. Then,

I'll board the SS Rangoon, which will have left Porto Valetta but puts in at Gib en route for Southampton. As I'm about to board, I'll be met by an agent who will point out Mr Todor Minkov of Bulgaria. From then on, I'm to keep Minkov under observation until we reach England."

"That's right. And don't forget this part — you're to send a telegram should anything of significance occur."

"No, I won't forget."

"Is something still troubling you?"

"Yes, and it's hardly surprising, really. I've never flown, although I want to try it. But this sudden announcement is rather unsettling. I need to get used to the idea first. When do I leave?"

"Tomorrow, at sunrise."

"*Tomorrow!* You *must* be joking."

"Far from it. The Rangoon, with Minkov aboard, set sail from Malta five days ago."

"Then why haven't you sent someone before now? And what about the agent aboard the ship? Why doesn't he see the job through to Southampton?"

"Minkov used to be a German agent and now occasionally works for Russia, or anyone willing to hire him — except for Britain, that is. He doesn't seem to like us very much. We know he has been invited to Dumond Hall, and we need to know if he communicates with anyone during the voyage. Somehow, we must find out the underlying purpose of his visit.

"Now, there are two specific reasons why you are the right and, indeed, the only person to go on this mission. Firstly, we're short-staffed and there simply isn't anyone else available. Secondly, Minkov as Basil Munday's friend, has been invited to the celebrations at Dumond Hall. That much we already knew, but his turning up in Malta was a bit of a surprise. We believed he was in Germany. Naturally, as soon as Malta was mentioned, I thought of you."

"Archie, I'm not quite seeing the urgency of my, indeed of anyone's, following him, seeing as he's coming to Britain, regardless."

"Minkov can turn his hand to anything in the espionage line, and that includes rough stuff, so be careful. In this instance, I suspect he's acting as a courier, but I don't know the parties involved or what he's carrying, if anything."

"Am I to find out what he's doing?"

"No. Only observe his movements and who communicates with him. If he makes an exchange of documents, for example, it's highly unlikely you'll witness the event. Now, if you can get the names of anyone to whom he speaks, *that* would be most helpful."

"I'll do so."

"One benefit of a week at sea watching the man is that you'll recognize him anywhere. So, if he uses an assumed name at Dumond Hall, it won't mislead you into thinking he hasn't shown up. Naturally, you'll be very careful he doesn't identify you as an agent — on the ship or later."

"This is getting rather difficult."

"It's unavoidable, Soap. Keep your distance from him while aboard."

"How do Basil Munday and Minkov know one another?"

"We're not sure how they met, but they are business associates. I'll brief you on what you need to know when you return. As for the agent currently following him, I'm not allowed to mention him. All I can say is that he's unable to land in mainland Britain. He is, however, free to land in Gibraltar, which he must do in the course of his work. The chap is more or less doing us a favour."

"Can I have a moment to think this over?"

"Um, I'm sorry, but I need your answer immediately."

"Oh." Sophie puffed out her cheeks. "Very well, then. I suppose I'll have to be at Croydon Aerodrome in the middle of the night."

"You're not departing from Croydon. You will depart from a private residence near Worthing."

"Worthing?" She was momentarily baffled. "You surely don't mean Sinjin?"

"I certainly do. He's in the next room awaiting your decision."

"But I can't fly with him. We're not married!"

"I assure you, he will be fully occupied flying the aeroplane."

"I hope so! Ah, but wait a moment. His plane, Celia, is a single-seater. I've seen it."

"He has a few planes, and one of them is a Bristol fighter named Biffy. It's a two-seater reconnaissance plane. Don't worry, though. He's removed the machine guns."

"That's a relief." She shifted in her seat. "Why does he have numerous planes?"

"Partly hobby, partly to keep a few war-time mechanics employed, partly his business interests, and partly for the work he does."

"That's a lot more than I knew before. Why is everything so terribly, terribly top-secret?" She put up a hand. "You needn't answer *if* you were even going to. Good grief, I suppose this is an open plane, exposed to the elements... and for eleven *hundred* miles."

"Yardley's an excellent pilot. I'm sure you'll be dozing in the back."

"It's more likely my head will get blown off in the wind."

"May I bring him into the discussion?"

"You might as well."

Archie left the office and returned with Sinjin Yardley.

"Miss King," said the beaming Yardley, "as always, you look radiant. Adding to the lustre of your radiance today is your noble sense of duty and thoroughly sporting attitude. With you as my flying companion, I could neither be happier nor more content."

"Hello, Sinjin," and she smiled despite herself. "You may be pleased, but I have a sinking feeling about the whole mission. I've never flown before, and I'm finding the idea rather alarming."

"Understandable," said Yardley. "Modesty forbids I commend myself to you, but please allow me to say this much. I possess some skill and a great deal of experience — amounting to over two thousand hours of flying time. The plane is one of the finest to be produced by Britain, and the best mechanics the Royal Flying Corps has ever seen maintain it in perfect working order. So, in technical matters, the craft which shall convey you is of and kept up to the highest standard."

"Thank you for that. It's very reassuring. But we still must fly across the Channel... All that open water is a horrific prospect."

"A mere matter of fifteen minutes' flying and we've crossed the sea. Then you will laugh at how easy it was."

"We'll see about that. What about the weather?"

"Everyone says it's fine and dry for the next few days."

"And we're to fly from Elflund Hall?"

"That's correct," said Yardley, "although you shan't be meeting the family, of course. They're used to my coming and going at odd hours, but we must sneak you in and fly out without your being noticed. There is also an unbreakable commandment to be observed. You must travel light — a small single suitcase, and that's all. I'll supply the necessary flying kit, including a leather coat, which I'll bring back on the return flight."

"You seemed to have thought of everything. What is it you *haven't* thought of that I should worry about? Anyway, Sinjin, what are all these short hops? Archie mentioned them. He also mentioned you call your plane Biffy."

"Well, Biffy has a range of four hundred and fifty miles because of an extra fuel tank I've installed. Even so, the route is tricky because of the different borders we'll be crossing. It restricts us to landing at aerodromes or only those smaller airfields that we can warn in advance about our needing a quick refuel and turnaround. So, the route shall be Le Bouget-Limoges-Bilbao-Madrid-Seville-Gibraltar."

"Just think of that. France, Spain, *and* Gibraltar." For several moments Sophie's face was aglow with delight. "Oh, my goodness! I don't have a passport."

She and Yardley turned to Archie, who had largely been forgotten during their exchange.

"Fortunately for you, my dear Soap," said Drysdale, "I know a chap two floors down who can provide you with the necessary in a matter of an hour. Is the mission on?"

Sophie nodded. Archie picked up the receiver.

On one end of the rug in front of the desk was an overturned wastepaper basket. At the other end stood a man hunched over. He held a putter and was ready to tap a golf ball. With intense concentration, he studied the line of the ball, as if he were a recently qualified surgeon about to make the first solo incision of his surgical career. He lifted the putter a matter of two inches and, as he initiated the delicate swing, the telephone rang.

"Con-*found* the wretched instrument!" exclaimed 'Sock' Blackwool, a tall man about thirty.

The ball had hit the rim of the wastepaper basket only to ricochet and come to rest under an immovable cabinet of great size and age.

Disgusted, he answered the call.

"Hello, who's this?"

"Drysdale, here," said Archie.

"Archie, what do you think you're doing? You've ruined my putt!"

"Well, you shouldn't be playing golf in the office. I have a special for you. Must be done at once, old boy."

"The reason I play golf in the office is that all this dry weather is ruining the greens at me club. Sandy soil, you see, and the greenkeepers are virtually moribund. It's an awful state of affairs which keeps me up at night."

"I'm sure it does. One individual coming down to you pronto, two passports wanted."

"Very well. Bainesy will see to everything. Do you know that blessed woman now stops me from doing a stroke of work? She's an absolute tyrant when one comes to think of it."

"Probably because she has good cause to be one."

"Meanin'?"

"Meaning this: she fills out the forms properly while you don't."

"That's all rot. I've got the hang of the entire process now. Despite that, she continues fussing over me like an old hen. There's nothing more annoying for a fella."

"You'd be lost without her."

"Oh, absolutely, but it's most undignified being treated like a child."

"I must go."

"You busy chaps have all the fun. What's the name of the party?"

"Phoebe King."

"Oh, she's a woman. She wouldn't happen to be young and pretty, eh?"

"She's a relative of mine, and you'll remember your manners. But be warned. She'll savage you if you're not careful."

"Modern type, I suppose. Does she play golf?"

"I have work to do."

"I wish I had. Cheerio."

After he replaced the receiver, Sock put his head around the door to speak to Miss Baines, who was a small woman of about forty.

"Drysdale's sending a Double Special by the name of Miss King. Show her in as soon as she arrives. Thank you."

"Yes, Lord Blackwool." She called him by his honorific because he was the third son of the Marquess of Wisbech.

Within a few minutes, Sophie entered the ante-room where sat Miss Baines.

"Good morning. Am I addressing Miss Baines of Extraordinaries?"

"You are, indeed. Are you Miss King?"

"I am."

"Excellent. Please take a seat. I have the forms here and they're simple to fill out. Am I correct in assuming Miss King is your real name?"

"No, it isn't," said Sophie.

"Ah. If you could give me the particulars of your real identity first. I'll fill in that form for you. Then you will fill in the false application. We don't want the same handwriting on both documents, you understand. You will, however, sign both. I mustn't be involved in the fraud, you see." Miss Baines gave a short and rather loud laugh.

"Very well. I was wondering about the photographs."

"We do them here. Lord Blackwool will take the pictures, and then we send everything next door to be made up. Miss Fawcett is very efficient, and it will only take her twenty minutes to finish both passports. You may as well wait — it will save you having to come back. Excuse me a moment." Miss Baines took a small wooden mallet from a drawer and approached a nearby radiator. She tapped the mallet on it repeatedly.

"Incoming double special?" asked Sophie.

"Do you know morse code, Miss King?" Miss Baines was delighted. "Miss Fawcett and I were both telegraphists during the war, and we like to keep up our skills. Where did you learn?"

"I was a supervisor in the Land Army."

"Oh, right, right. Now, let's get down to business, shall we? I have an extensive list of false addresses from which you can select something appropriate."

They quickly completed both forms, and Sophie had just finished signing them when the door to the inner office was flung open.

"I heard you tapping ten minutes ago," said Lord Blackwool, who ignored Sophie to bestow his mild irritation at being left out upon Miss Baines.

"This is Miss King," said Miss Baines, completely unruffled. "She is now ready for her two sets of photographs, Lord Blackwool."

He turned his attention to the visitor. "Good morning, Miss King. Step this way, if you please."

Inside his office was a corner dedicated to taking photographs. He guided Sophie to a chair in front of a plain screen and then went over to the camera tripod.

"This won't take a moment." He began loading a film. "Do you play golf, Miss King?"

"Occasionally, Lord Blackwool."

"Occasionally, eh?" He brightened. "Where do you play?"

"I've played at several clubs in Hampshire, although I'm not very good. I've been told I pull and hook the ball. All I know is the ball never goes near where it's supposed to."

Lord Blackwool tutted as he bent over and fiddled with the camera. "Pull *and* hook. That's very bad, very bad. Still, as I always say, no golf swing problem is incurable. Practise, Miss King — that's the answer. You should have a session with Johnson at my club. Such a marvellous chap. What he don't know about golf, ain't worth the knowing. Cured me of a dreadful slice." He stood upright with a sparkling look as a novel idea occurred to him. "I say! Why don't I take you to meet him? It'll do wonders for your game. Go on, say you will. You won't regret it."

Sophie, forewarned by Archie, replied, "I'm afraid I can't, despite the generosity of your offer. I'm going abroad, you see."

"Oh, what a thick head I've got. That's why you're here, of course. What about when you return?"

"I might not return."

"Dear me, Miss King. Don't put it like that. Sounds altogether too final."

"Then I'm going for an extended period of indeterminate length."

"That's much better." He attended to the camera again. "Nearly ready." He fiddled some more. "There. Please compose yourself. Try not to smile. I'm sure you smile beautifully, but the powers that be prefer one looks as if a gust of wind has dropped one's otherwise perfectly driven ball into a sand bunker... Watch the little birdie." The moment he looked through the viewfinder, he produced and waggled a small shapeless, fluffy, yellow thing which was meant to be either a baby duck or a canary, but its beak and one eye were missing, so it was hard to tell.

Sophie smiled, and he took the picture. He took a dozen more photographs — half with Sophie wearing a hat.

"Right, that should do it." He removed the camera from the tripod. "I'll have these developed in ten to fifteen minutes. You may as well sit with Miss Baines. Excuse me." He abruptly disappeared through a door and into a small darkroom.

When Sophie left the Foreign Office, she possessed two smart-looking navy-blue passports. In one of the beautifully taken photographs, Phoebe King, looking quite serene, wore a hat, while, in the other, hatless Sophie Burgoyne was smiling. Lord Blackwool was pleased with the results and said the one with her smiling was the best of the lot. He took his time explaining the merits of both his photographic skills and Sophie's excellence as a sitter. He then asked what she was doing for dinner. Sophie regretfully informed him she needed to pack because of her early morning start, and hurriedly left before he had any more ideas.

Sophie returned to the agency office and convened an emergency meeting with Elizabeth and Miss Jones. Could they hold the fort while she was away? It was decided that they could, so Sophie left immediately, only to discover that she kept remembering things she should have mentioned at the meeting.

She alighted from a taxi in Regent's Street. Dickins & Jones, she recalled, were rumoured to be moving further up the road and had reduced their prices to sell slower-moving stock. Sophie hoped that wear suitable for a cruise on a ship was included in these reductions. Inside, she found the right area only to be intercepted by an elegant being, one with a frightfully superior voice, who was patrolling the frontier of the women's clothing department.

"Good afternoon. May I assist Modom in hah selections?"

Sophie was unsure if it was an affectation or if it was how the woman was constructed, but the assistant definitely tilted her nose in the air to a lofty angle. It gave Sophie the impression that her inquisitor was all nostrils.

"Yes, you may. I'm looking for two summer dresses and a light jacket suitable to be worn aboard ship."

"We have several cruise-wh-are collections. With which shipping line shall you sail?"

"I don't know. Does it matter?"

"Oh, yace." The assistant spoke faintly, implying that Sophie was foolish even to think of such a question and certainly displayed naïvete in expressing it. "Third class cabin on the *Cunard* line exceeds first class on some smaller lines in all matters of refainement and distinc*tion*."

"Well, let us assume it's a middling sort of ship." Sophie found the woman exasperating.

"As you wish, Modom." The assistant immediately seemed much less interested. "And *wh-are* is this vessel bound?"

Sophie could hardly say England without introducing a confusing difficulty.

"The Mediterranean."

"Then you really should considah the purchase of suitable swimming costumes and evening gowns. For day *wh-are*, we have some very jaunty ensembles with a nautical theme.

These are very populah at present. Have you considahed such things, Modom?"

"Not particularly."

"*Ohh.*" She implied Sophie was so far out of vogue it was piteous. "If you would be so kind as to follow me, I'm sure we can find you s*omething*."

The assistant set off but, as she did, Sophie caught sight of a dress on display that looked just the thing. Because it lay in a different direction, and the assistant, in a world of her own, had moved several paces away, Sophie left her to it.

Another, more helpful, assistant approached Sophie as she stood studying the display dress. When Sophie explained her choices were limited by economics and weight, the assistant became thoroughly invested in finding exactly what 'Madam' wanted to fit in her small suitcase.

"Perhaps it will close if I sit on it," said Sophie.

She and Mary, her maid while she stayed at her aunt's residence in White Lyon Yard, had struggled and failed to close the suitcase. Success eluded them even when Sophie kneeled on it.

"Shall I fetch Mr Marsden to sit on it?"

He was Lady Shelling's footman.

"No, Mary. We're very close and we shall conquer this ourselves."

"If you took something out, it might close then."

"But I can't. Everything in it, I need. The suitcase must close... I know! Go and find some rope."

"Yes, miss."

As she went, Mary thought that nothing in the world could ever induce her to get in an aeroplane, and yet now Miss Sophie was flying to Gibraltar. The maid was convinced that

Miss Sophie was doomed, and that's all there was to it. She was never coming back. Mary also considered it was all very well folding everything so nicely but, no matter what, Miss Sophie was going to have a sight of ironing to do once she was on the ship. And why was she doing all this rushing about, anyway? It made no sense at all. She found the rope and returned.

Mary watched as Sophie tied a noose around the suitcase and then, with a supreme, combined effort, one latch was pressed home. The second side now went all the easier. When it was closed, Sophie tightly bound the suitcase with the rope to prevent it bursting open.

"There. All done." Sophie smiled. "Thank you for your help. Now, where is Auntie at present?"

"I believe Lady Shelling's still in the garden, Miss."

Sophie found her aunt in the shade in her pleasant but tiny rear garden, which was much improved by overlooking a shared private garden area with benches. She looked up from her reading when Sophie came down the steps.

"What are you doing back so early? Come and sit down. The weather's lovely for this time of year."

"Isn't it just? The reason I'm back early is that they've sent me on another mission, and it starts in the small hours tomorrow morning. Would you like to hear about it, Auntie?"

Lady Shelling set aside her book. She listened patiently and asked a few minor questions, but she saved her most important observation for when Sophie had finished.

"I suppose, in the end, everything will turn out for the best. He'll have to marry you, of course."

"Auntie, I said something similar at first, but then Archie explained Sinjin will only be flying the aeroplane. So everything's above board."

"Rubbish. You cannot fly off into the night..."

"Day, Auntie."

"Day, then. But you're still starting off in the middle of the night with a man."

"Len, the chauffeur, is driving me down to Elflund Hall. All Sinjin will do is fly the aeroplane at first light."

"What does his family say about all these goings on?"

"They don't even know, and never shall."

"Don't even *know*! This sounds dreadful... Oh, the shame of it."

"Stop it at once. It's a secret mission, and nothing more than that."

"It may well be a secret mission, and all be as you say, *but*, when everyone finds out, they shan't believe that. Oh, no, not for a moment. And you shall never be able to explain what it is you are actually doing. Naturally, everyone, and I do mean *everyone*, will assume the worst. Believe me, I know how people's minds work."

"This is absurd."

"It is not."

"No one will ever know."

"You can't guarantee that, can you?"

"Yes, I can."

"Oh, no, you can't, for the simple reason that you do not control events. It would only take one person with a long tongue to see both of you together in Gibraltar, and then you're finished. Absolutely finished. I'm assuming Yardley behaves like a gentleman..."

"Of course, he does. And don't you say anything against him."

"I'll say what I please in my own garden and don't interrupt again. Assuming he's a gentleman, you must explain the situation to him. He shall either not fly the blasted aeroplane, and have someone else do it, or he'll behave decently and propose to you before witnesses. Tell him to do that and I'll be content."

"I can't believe you're saying this, Auntie. Nothing untoward is going to happen. He's decent, and just not that type of man, anyway. Archie's known him for years."

"The only person responsible for a woman's reputation is the woman herself. My dear, you cannot hand over such a precious commodity as that to a man's safekeeping without all the proper formalities being observed."

"I'm finding this very trying."

"It's all for your best. What would your mother have said?"

Sophie paused for a long time. "The same. In fact, she probably would have forbidden me to go."

"I like Mr Yardley, and I understand how all of this must be an exciting adventure for you, but one misstep and it will end in ruin." Having had her say, Aunt Bessie folded her hands in her lap.

"How about this?" said Sophie. "I'll tell him that as soon as we land in Gibraltar, we must not be seen together, not even for a moment."

It was Aunt Bessie's turn to consider.

"I don't like it, but I'll agree with your proposal. Promise me you'll do just as you've said."

"I swear it, Auntie. So, now there's nothing for you to be concerned about."

"I wouldn't say that, exactly. Aren't you at all worried about the aeroplane plunging into the sea?"

Chapter 3

Local customs

Sleep can be elusive, often occurring contrary to intention or desire. When needed most, it flees; when unwanted, it stalks. Sophie had gone to bed early, only to lie awake for hours. Now she was properly asleep in a corner of the dark, warm, leather-and-wood-scented interior of Yardley's Rolls-Royce. Len drove, knowing she was asleep, and had been so for two hours. He slid open the partition glass.

"Miss King." The Yorkshireman spoke softly, his voice sounding just above the purr of the engine, as if trying *not* to wake her. "Miss King."

The fresh air flowing through the partition dispelled the close atmosphere in the back. She stirred.

"I'm dreadfully sorry. I must have dropped off."

"Aye, you did that, miss."

"Rather rude of me, but I had meant to stay awake."

"Not at all rude, the way I look at it. I had to wake you up because we're only ten minutes away."

"That's very kind of you."

The moonless night hid the countryside. The car's headlamps only illuminated a short stretch of road ahead, and made the trees and hedges on either side look grey and ghostly. After a few moments, the trees petered out and there were no features to see except a brightening sky in the east above the darker, rounded, and undulating horizon.

"Where are we?"

"Crossing over some downs. During the day, you get a terrific view. Elflund Hall is south, just on t'other side."

Several minutes later, the road descended into more trees. Len slowed the car, then turned off the road and through an open pair of gates to pass by a darkened lodge. Sophie thought to herself how strange it was to be visiting Yardley's ancestral home at night while also at pains to avoid his family.

As the Rolls-Royce approached the house, Sophie could see it was made of stone and very old. Then the car swung away onto a different track. Here, there were lights ahead, and they soon came to a stop in front of a row of buildings. At the farther end were two hangars. From one, a group of men were pushing an aircraft onto the field.

"I didn't expect there to be so many people," said Sophie, as Len opened the door for her.

"It's often busy here, Miss King."

"But who are they all?"

"Some of them are gardeners. They work for Lord Ranemore in his greenhouses and what not. He's a very busy man, working to improve agriculture. He puts his heart into it, he does. The rest are mechanics or do other work for Mr Yardley. He's got 'em all up early. I bet there's a sight o' mutterin' amongst that lot."

"I'm sure there is," agreed Sophie with a laugh.

A figure — Yardley — detached himself from the group and came quickly towards them.

"Good morning, Miss King." He was as cheerful as ever. "And excellent timing, Len. Any problems on the way down?"

"No. It were easy, like. Is Biffy ready to go?"

"Yes, and is," he now addressed Sophie, "I'm assured, in splendid running order. Absolutely fit to make the trip."

"That's good to know," said Sophie. "Will this be the longest trip you've ever made?"

"Hmm, one of the longer ones."

"Oh, I no. You can't divulge anything. But tell me this much. How many planes do you have?"

"Six operational craft, two prototypes, and bits and pieces for spares."

"Have you really? Prototypes? Do you design aircraft?"

"Not personally, but a know a couple of clever chappies who do, and so we tinker and experiment here. Keeps us out of trouble, don't you know... Len, put Miss King's suitcase into the plane, and mind the whisky."

"Right you are, Mr Yardley."

"Whisky?"

"Gifts for friends. If you come this way, we'll get your kit for the flight. Take off is at twenty past five. The sun will be just cresting the horizon then."

They began walking towards a hangar.

"You never explain anything properly about what it is you do. It can't all be espionage related."

"It isn't."

"There. You just did it. Instead of being open, you're all closed-up. Not stand-offish so much as uncommunicative. I like full answers to my questions."

"Don't we all?"

"Then tell me more about yourself."

"Such as?"

"Why are you tinkering about with aeroplanes?"

"We're trying to develop a fast, reliable long-range craft for civilian use. It will be a dual-purpose machine, adaptable to carry six passengers or carry mail or both."

"How far have you got?"

"Not as far as we would like, unfortunately. Others are ahead of us, although we're catching up. The car improvements, by contrast, are coming along splendidly."

"You make cars?"

"No, we make parts. There are some cars we modify to improve the suspension, steering, and brakes, and increase engine power. But that's all I can say for now. We must look sharp if we're to get off on time."

They entered the hangar, and Yardley helped Sophie into a leather flying coat, then handed her a leather helmet, gauntlets, and a pair of goggles.

"Your feet shouldn't get cold," said Yardley, "but move them about and wiggle your toes if they do. If you feel sick, there's a receptacle. The way to avoid an accident is to lean into any turn, just as one does in a car."

"I can appreciate that. What about going up and down, though?"

"We'll fly at three thousand feet, and both the ascents and descents will be nothing for you to worry about."

"But I am worrying."

"I'll doubt you'll be sick, then. You're obviously not the type, because you'll be concentrating on where we're going, and that seems to be the cure for airsickness. Um, may I make a suggestion?"

"Please, do."

"If you wear your scarf like that, you'll lose it pretty quickly."

"Oh. I'll tuck it in, then." She rearranged her newly purchased white silk scarf that she had been wearing with one end jauntily thrown over a shoulder.

They started towards the plane. The sky was brightening, and Biffy stood in proper relief against the open fields and more distant trees. Nose to the sky, waiting, the aeroplane was ready. Sophie could see the runway of dewy grass ahead. She glanced towards Elflund Hall. It was a big place, rambling and ancient. *A friendly house*, she thought.

Yardley helped her up the steps and into the rear seat and explained how to secure the harness. She sat still. The seconds ticked away as he got into the cockpit, and the nervousness she should have had all along now made itself felt. Meanwhile, Yardley was checking the controls to see if everything functioned properly. At the angle she was sitting, she could see the great overhead wing, the dark blue fuselage, the back of Yardley's head, and nothing but sky beyond. She watched as the flaps moved and felt intimidated. A mechanic approached the propellor.

Yardley gave the man a thumbs-up signal. The mechanic grasped a wooden blade, then turned it with a sharp jerk. *Chok-chok-chok.* The engine failed to catch. Yardley signalled, and the man tried again. This time the engine roared into life, and the draft from the propellor sent trails of black exhaust smoke twisting and writhing far behind. The smoke turned grey and then became invisible as the engine warmed. They sat idling while the thrum of the machine made itself felt in every part of the plane. Sophie's nervousness turned to fear, and she wanted to get out. Yardley turned around to smile at her. She forced herself to smile back. He returned his attention to the controls, then waved to the onlookers. Willing hands removed the wheel chocks. The plane began moving, and Yardley opened the throttle. Sophie sank down into her seat.

She felt every bump in the field, heard the engine roaring louder and louder, imagined that it was about to explode or that they were going to hit the trees she had seen in the distance, and then everything changed. The bumping stopped. The noise from the engine diminished and became tolerable. She looked to her side and down. They were off the ground and rising steadily. Above the rooves and the trees, she watched as everything grew smaller — toy-like, then dot-like — as more and more of the world came into her view. She was so fascinated she forgot her fears.

Under power, Biffy was still climbing. The sun now struck the plane before it lit the land beneath. Sophie shivered a little as the cool dawn air washed over her. The plane banked and followed the coast for a few miles, before turning again to cross the Channel. Yardley turned around in his seat, smiled, and gave *her* a thumbs up. He shouted something. She smiled, believing he said, "See, there's nothing to worry about," but he might have said anything for all she had heard.

In the end, the sea held no terrors for Sophie. In fact, flying, she decided, was the apex of humanity's achievements and she even hoped to pilot an aeroplane herself one day. She looked up and wondered how far away heaven was. She looked down, and they were passing over the coast of France. Flight for her was an endless and effortless glide — a sliding through air under an unfathomable blue vault above, with a slowly changing patchwork pattern of fields, woods, lakes, and towns below. She marvelled and lost track of the time until Yardley raised his arm to point south-east towards the horizon. It took her a moment, but then she saw it. In the hazy distance stood the Eiffel Tour — a mere pin on a hill. Yet, more than anything she had seen so far, it made her sensible of being in the air of France. The plane started its descent.

The landing at Le Bouget seemed very bumpy to her but, as she learned later, Yardley considered it a smooth one. Sophie thrilled at the thought of being on French soil. There she was, on the outskirts of Paris, with a mild regret she would not be visiting the city. Men came running or walking quickly towards Biffy. Yardley cut the engine.

"We'll have time to stretch our legs," he said. "How was it?"

He was animated and looking slightly absurd in his goggles and helmet. Sophie supposed she must look equally absurd in hers.

"Absolutely exhilarating!" She shouted, even though the engine was off.

He laughed uproariously. "I *knew* you would love it. Once one gets over the initial jitters, there's nothing to beat flying."

"I'd say... I can't believe we actually *flew*. It's just amazing."

He helped her down from the plane. Then he issued instructions to a man in some of the most execrable French she had ever heard. The man understood, however, and relayed the information to others.

"Do you have your passport ready?" Yardley asked because two officials with clipboards were approaching them. "We can't do anything until we get their blessing."

Sophie had brought both her passports but, on this leg of the journey, she was travelling as Miss King. With great formality, an officer demanded their passports and then asked a few questions. Sophie answered in French, which pleased the official. He examined the documents carefully, and laid them on the lower wing of the plane. He made an entry in his report. Then, with great solemnity, he produced an ink pad and stamp, breathed on the rubber, inked it, and impressed the official stamp of France on a page of each of their passports. Yardley's had been franked so frequently it was almost full. When the ceremony was complete, he saluted them and left.

"Anything to declare, monsieur?" asked the second man, who spoke in English.

"Two bottles of whisky that are slowing us down. Could you take care of them for me?"

"With pleasure."

Yardley climbed up to retrieve two bottles from a crate in the cockpit. He returned and handed them to the customs official.

"Merci, monsieur." He put a bottle in each of his overcoat pockets.

"And how is your family?" asked Yardley.

"Very well. Madame Planchard is expecting our fifth child."

"Congratulations. Let me see... That's two boys and two girls. What are you hoping for this time?"

"I no longer worry about such things. All we can hope for is a safe delivery and an easy time for my wife, and may the good God grant them."

"I'm sure He will."

"Au revoir, mademoiselle, monsieur. May you both have a safe journey."

After waving to the head of the ground crew, he departed. The men pushed the plane to the nearby fuel pumps, with Sophie and Yardley following. Within twenty minutes, they were back in the air.

Landing on the small airfield at Limoges was such an informal affair, it barely created more of a stir than that of the refuelling of a car at a garage. Here, it cost Yardley another bottle of whisky plus a small, sealed envelope. The crew turned the plane around so promptly it really surprised Sophie.

And nothing could have prepared her for the reception at a small village close to Bayonne. They landed in a farmer's field in a narrow strip bordered by trees on one side and crops on the other. The landing was so bumpy she was sure the plane would be wrecked. However, it came safely to rest. Immediately, a horde of children and farm workers came running towards them. In the middle of the throng was a cart pulled by two horses. The old man, standing up to drive his team, waved his hat in exuberant welcome.

"What's going on?" asked Sophie.

"I should have warned you, but even I didn't expect such a turnout as this. I met a few of them during the war." He was not going to say more, that much was obvious.

The meeting was as effusive as any French citizen could hope for and as regrettable as every Englishman fears. Yardley was hugged and kissed until his face was scarlet. Sophie could not help laughing. Every child and several labourers got a hand on Biffy and turned it around ready for take-off. A labourer began pulling petrol cans off the cart to refuel the plane.

Under some shady elms, Sophie and Yardley were treated to a picnic lunch, and what a lunch it was! Several families from the village had contributed to the feast. It undoubtedly would have gone on for a very long time, except that Yardley insisted they must leave within the hour. The old farmer would not accept the two bottles of whisky Yardley offered. The impasse was only broken when the old man proposed Yardley should take two bottles of brandy in exchange. He had tried to add a case of wine but concerns over the weight of the plane compelled him to stop his entreaties without further demur.

While they all made such a fuss of Yardley, Sophie watched, intrigued as to the source of the obvious gratitude and affection. Knowing that Sinjin himself would be unlikely to satisfy her curiosity on this point, she was quick to steal a moment of his inattention and ask the farmer's wife about it. The worthy woman was overjoyed to discover Sophie could speak French.

"Capitaine Yardley, he was on a night raid in no-man's-land. At the edge of the British sector. It was lucky for us he was there. The day before, there had been a French attack, but the Boche beat it back. In a shell hole in the middle, there were eight wounded French soldiers just waiting to die. Just *waiting*... I cannot bear to think of it. Capitaine Yardley, he heard them. He disobeyed his orders and got into trouble. Instead of finding and bringing back a German soldier, he brought back the French wounded to the British lines. He himself carried my son, François. Poor boy lost his arm, but he's still alive, sitting there, right now. Then, the Capitaine goes out again alone because he had not enough men to bring back *all* the wounded at the same time. The Boche, they shoot at him and wound the Capitaine, but he brings the man back alive. Sadly, the wounded man died later. Three of the wounded and the man who died were all from this area. That is why we shall never forget Capitaine Yardley."

"I didn't know *any* of this," said Sophie, her eyes round with surprise, and welling with a few tears.

"He said nothing? That is how the men act with us, too... Is he your lover or your husband?"

"Oh, um... actually, I, um, know him quite well as a friend, but he's just taking me somewhere."

"Ahh, but you hope, yes?"

"A little."

"That is good. I ask no more questions. But the Capitaine, he took to flying, yes, and he was shot down, not once, but twice."

"Twice!"

"Yes. And he is thoughtful and kind. He wrote to us and sent money! Then, he wrote again, but after the war, saying how he needed a place to land his new aeroplane, and did we have a flat strip of land more than two hundred metres long? Well, we did. So, he comes and goes now and then. He always telephones the doctor in the village first so that we know when to expect him. The children love his visits in the aeroplane. Oh, they talk of nothing else for days afterwards."

"How often does he land here?"

"This is the second time this year... I think this is the ninth time. He will stop here on the way back. Perhaps he will stay the night. My husband and the Capitaine shall arrange everything. He comes this way to avoid going over les Pyrénées. Ice on the wings is a great danger to aircraft, so he says. It weighs down the plane."

"Oh, I see. I'd never even thought of that."

"Look, he is saying goodbye. I think it is time for you to go. I hope to see you again one day." The farmer's wife gave her a very knowing look.

"You just might. Thank you for such a lovely reception, madame, and the food was delicious."

After lunch, flying became gruelling. It was hot over Spain, and the land below was often brown, always rocky and, to Sophie's surprise, quite mountainous. Her clothes felt too heavy despite the rushing air. Bilbao near the Atlantic came and went. There, they did not even ask to see the passports. At the Cuatro Vientos airfield in Madrid, however, the plane was met by three officials, who all seemed in a state of high good humour. By the way they shook hands and greeted each other, Sophie could tell Yardley had met two of the men before. This time, three bottles of whisky changed hands. With the passports now stamped and the refuelling completed, the plane set off again. At the Seville airfield, there was no one to meet them because there were no flights expected for at least an hour. Yardley, annoyed at the delay caused by the Spanish taking a siesta, scouted around until he found an old man to pay and a young lad to help lug petrol cans across the baking surface of the runway.

Gibraltar, a British possession on the tip of a small Spanish peninsula, was a short hop away, and its majestic and dominating limestone rock soon came into view. As they neared the coast, Yardley had difficulty maintaining course because of a strong easterly breeze. Sophie learned afterwards it was a Levanter, a wind which blew in the Mediterranean, often bringing clouds and foul weather with it. The sky was still clear. However, the wind was problematic and needed to be worked around somehow. Yardley made a hand signal, but Sophie failed to interpret it and, therefore, was slightly alarmed as he turned the plane.

In a great arc, they swung eastward over the Mediterranean. Yardley lined up Biffy with the towering ridge of rock so that it was directly west of them. Then they flew straight towards it. He dropped in altitude until Biffy was about three hundred feet above the sea. The low sun created thousands of dancing lights on the water's surface while they seemingly skimmed along towards the looming mountain. At a certain point, the wind noticeably died away. The small plane had found shelter from the breeze on the leeward side of the peninsula. Yardley gunned the engine to maintain altitude. Within seconds, the ridge blocked out the sun. Yardley steered towards the Spanish side of the pinnacle. The agile craft responded, and as they came around the mountain, a powerful gust hit them and the aeroplane struggled against it.

In their descent to the old airfield in the navy yard, there were some moments in which Biffy seemed to float, feather-like, in mid-air, neither going forward nor moving side to side. The plane was dropping, but it was almost imperceptible. Sophie looked over the side, only to see docks, ships, warehouses, concrete structures, streets and houses, the sight of which caused her to shudder. The wind shifted and shifted again. Then, almost magically, they touched down with a bump, then bounced; bumped and bounced again. Finally, the aeroplane came to rest in front of an aircraft hangar, which was thronged with a crowd of navy personnel who had been watching the landing. Despite the stiff breeze, Sophie heard their raucous cheers and applause.

She was glad it was over, but received no time for further reflection. A lieutenant came running up to the plane before she was out of her harness.

"Well done, sir. Splendid landing," he said to Yardley, raising his voice above the wind. "Right on time, too." He then casually saluted Sophie.

"Yes. I thought to put down on the Jockey Club racetrack," said Yardley with a grin. "But that might have upset someone."

"It surely would have, sir. Old Smithereens would have blown his top, and we strive to keep him happy at all costs." He referred to Sir Horace Smith-Dorrien, Governor of Gibraltar.

Yardley laughed as he lifted his goggles. "Right. I need a few moments with my passenger. Then, if you could send someone to escort her to the government offices, I'd be very much obliged."

"I'll go myself, sir. It's not far."

"Thank you. Oh, before you go. Has the SS Rangoon docked?"

"Yes. A matter of an hour ago. You can see her funnel from here." The lieutenant pointed out the ship.

"Very good, that's very good."

Yardley took Sophie's suitcase, then helped her down from the aeroplane.

"We made it," he said with evident relief and pleasure.

"Did we nearly die back there?"

"No, of course, we didn't." He spoke airily.

"But the plane was all over the place, twisting, turning, and dropping. Then we just floated down."

"Wasn't that the loveliest part? We just hung there... then drifted to earth."

"You take too many risks," she said disapprovingly. Sophie studied his face and noticed his tired eyes. He was worn out but still going — that was obvious. She raised her goggles. They looked almost a matched pair in their flying outfits as they faced each other. She suddenly threw her arms around him and stood on tiptoe to kiss him on the lips. "Don't live so recklessly," she whispered in his ear. Then she picked up her suitcase. "We must *not* be seen together from now on... Which way do I go?"

Chapter 4

The Mundays

Dumond Hall sits on Loxie Lane and is the third house of that name built on the estate. The current incarnation began life as a modest, elegant, and symmetrical residence suitable for a Georgian gentleman and his family. Successive Georgian, Victorian, and Edwardian Mundays had each decided in their turn that they must enhance the property — to leave something for posterity. By 1920, posterity was convinced the Mundays had gone too far in their alterations, additions, reconfigurations, and remodellings, and that the family must immediately desist from fiddling with the place as it was beginning to look a mess.

The Mundays were wealthy, and it was not in their nature to refrain from 'improving' their country seat. Therefore, Basil Munday discussed building plans with his father, Viscount Gerald Munday, an invalid, in the autumn of 1920. Lord Munday had always wanted to tear down Dumond Hall and build anew, but a stroke had robbed him of the interest and energy required for pursuing major building projects. Instead, he came to a more minor decision with Basil's help. They would install a large and opulent swimming pool. Basil, sanctioned by his father, consulted architects on the matter and had the plans drawn up according to his father's fanciful ideas of classical antiquity. "There must be plenty of columns," insisted Lord Munday.

By early April 1921, the gaping hole disfiguring the south lawn had been concreted, and the tiling was well underway. When finished, it would be a Romanesque pool that, while no matter how glorious in its own right, would certainly be incongruous to every other part of Dumond Hall. The supplies for the project were already on site, strategically placed by the builder close to where the various buildings and features were to be constructed. However, the effect given by the neat piles of stones scattered about was that a demented family of giant, prehistoric moles were involved in the project. In one area, standing in a tight, motionless group near the raw hole of the pool-to-be, was a bevy of reproduction classical statues. Without having been deliberately arranged, they suggested they were plotting something dastardly and dramatic.

On May 10th, Basil Munday and his eldest son, Luke, stood in the drawing room of Dumond Hall. Basil Munday was a large, tall man and reminiscent of a friendly bear. At forty-seven, his luxuriant dark hair streaked with silver rendered his ruddy complexion more vivid. He had a small, clipped moustache, thick fleshy ears, and a snub nose, but it was his tolerant blue eyes one chiefly remembered. Through a window, he surveyed the ongoing work which marred the landscape.

"It's a pity it won't be entirely finished before the Fête, Father," said Luke, who was twenty-four, almost as tall as his parent and, although slimmer and more athletic in build, he would, in time, be very similar in general appearance. His features, however, were refined and his hair quite blond, thanks to his mother's contribution. It was said he was good-looking.

"There was never a hope of that. The builder assures me the pool and changing rooms will be completed and usable by the end of the week, but work upon Diana's Templet will hardly be started."

"I can't understand why they're so slow." Luke's impatient mannerisms betrayed his feelings, even if his words had not already done so.

"They are not unduly slow. In fact, they are proceeding according to schedule."

"But look here. There's a chap just staring down at the others. It's outrageous that he's idly standing about."

"That's Parsons, the builder. He's ensuring they do proper work."

"If you say so. Now, if it were my affair, I'd set him to work in short order. That loafer, Parsons, should have put more men on the job."

"Be patient." Basil often said this to his children. "I'm just as eager to see it finished as you, but these things take time. The main thing is that your grandfather gets to swim in it while he still can."

"Let us all hope he's strong enough for that. You should at least tell Parsons to set the statues out properly for the Fête. They look *ridiculous* where they are now."

Basil Munday smiled and turned from the window. He and his son wore black armbands in memory of Uncle Wilfred, Basil's older brother.

"Will they definitely release Uncle Will's remains to the undertaker today?" asked Luke.

"So I'm led to believe."

"I trust they do. The funeral's on Wednesday, and I simply must be back in London the following day. Autopsy, inquest — what an absolute waste of time it all is. Uncle Will was shot in the back by Pascoe Eldred, and those two old boys more or less saw him do it. We all *know* what happened, after all. The police should arrest him."

"We shall attend to Pascoe at a convenient time."

"But he's broken the rules, Father. No killings allowed on home ground. He's the first one ever to do such a thing. As he's forfeited all his rights, the police can have him, and they're welcome to him. It'll save us the bother."

"I disagree. Whatever *he* may do, *we* shall abide by the rules. Therefore, nothing can or shall be done during the next few weeks and, at all costs, we will keep the police out of it."

"I suppose he's coming to the funeral, as well?"

"Oh, yes. We must not break with tradition. He and his family are invited and expected at both. Whether he attends or not is his own affair."

"I don't know how I can face the cad. Such a filthy, scurrilous bounder and cheat. It's not even as though Uncle Will ever harmed anyone. *He* never went after the Eldreds. Had nothing to do with them. Why did Pascoe pick on him?"

"Enough!" Basil gave his son a severe look. "I shall ask him if I have the chance. You, however, are not to go near him. D'you hear?" Basil was on the threshold of an angry outburst, but he stopped and forced a smile. "Avoid the Eldreds altogether, my boy. But enough of them for now."

"Yes, Father." Luke knew well enough that, once warned, he should not bait his bear-like father anymore.

"Let us join your mother. She's rather upset at present."

The interior of Dumond Hall always surprises new visitors, even fastidious ones. Warned by the piecemeal exterior, they expect the worst inside. Instead of the anticipated hotchpotch of styles and regrettable furnishings that have long since had their day, there is to be found an aesthetically pleasing openness and devotion to comfort far exceeding expectations. In the past, Dumond Hall had certainly enjoyed its Victorian Mausoleum period contiguous with Queen Victoria lamenting the loss of Prince Albert for so many years, but that frozen style of overwrought grandeur underwent the indignity of a wholesale ejection. Lord Gerald wished to tear down the Hall but, thanks to Lady Alice, the departed wife of the extant Lord Gerald, the viscount's plans were derailed by her having said, 'No, it would take too long, Gerald dear, and neither of us is getting any younger.' She proposed an alternative project.

One fine day in 1902, the Mundays had a sale on their front lawn. The auctioneer worked hard for his commission. By the end of the session, more Munday furniture and bric-à-brac had gone to nearby houses or was being carted off to London than was left inside the Hall. Lady Alice had jettisoned everything she disliked, which was much. Remaining were the best pieces, better paintings, and only those portraits of bygone relatives deemed indispensable to family history. Lady Alice had swept out the old to bring in the new.

For several months, the marvelling inhabitants of Wynbourne beheld carts coming from the station in Marlborough laden with costly freight destined for Dumond Hall, and they believed there would never be an end to them. A frequent question was, "How much does all that lot cost, do you reckon?" Although never answered publicly, Lord Gerald knew the sum well. He did not overly object to the expense, because there was plenty of money. What riled him were the aesthetes, the paid designers, who gallivanted down from London, waltzed into his house, and floated from room to room, airily uttering blandishments on how they would redesign his interior if they could just get their hands on it. There was one woman he found particularly loathsome. She declared the house had a sympathetic spirit which had summoned her from afar, and this was patently untrue because it was an exchange of letters that had brought her. The person made many other similar declarations, which caused Lord Gerald fervently to wish once more to tear the place down but with the aggravating woman inside.

Lady Alice got on well with her coterie of designers, and the house certainly benefitted from their attentions. When every stick of expensive furniture and all the rare decorative objects were in their rightful places, nothing more needed to be added or taken away. The chosen colour schemes were durable ones, and there was no trace anywhere of faddish extravagance. When finished, Dumond Hall might not impress Royalty, but it awed the local lesser lights, and pleased the more distinguished visitors. In general, it was considered a comfortable and airy house, perfect for both the family and the honoured guest. And if the place lacked a proper hall, the several smaller reception rooms were at once dignified and welcoming. Inside, those who saw it all agreed that it was a beautiful house and home. Lord Gerald's idea to raze the Hall fell into abeyance, only to find resurgence after Lady Alice died in 1912, which was the same year he had his stroke.

Clare Munday, Basil's wife, was in the East Room, seated on a comfortable sofa covered in a timeless chintz. Sitting in silence in equally comfortable matching chairs were two of her three daughters. They were all dressed in mourning. The daughters had been listening to their mother's monologue, which now she brought to a close.

"As I have always said, and will continue to maintain, this feud business is absurd." Her look implied that her listeners had never heard her utter such a statement before, whereas they had heard it often. "Give them the Tongue and be done with it."

Clare had been told repeatedly by her family that the animosity would not end by setting aside their claim to the land, because the feud was absolutely no longer about the Tongue.

"They've killed Uncle Will, so now we shall kill one of theirs. That's what we do... Not too many of them to choose from now, really." Her eldest daughter, Audrey, spoke with a complacent drawl.

"How can you be so callous?"

A tall woman of forty-three, Clare was also fair-haired and delicately featured. If her husband was like a bear, then she was a swan — her neck gave that impression, although her long limbs also contributed to the effect. In fact, she had to angle her legs to sit comfortably, yet the effect, combined with her posture and her beautifully coiffed head, still and erect, imparted to her an immeasurable amount of grace. So she was a tall woman who, while standing in conversation, would express herself with small, gentle, yet unconscious sweeps of her hands. A few uncharitable people thought she only gestured in this way to display all the better her expensive bracelets and rings, but that was not true. The movement of her right hand just emphasized the question she had put to Audrey.

"I'm not callous, Mama. I've simply grown up with the status quo, and so I'm used to it — as we all are. You *married* into it. Therefore, you find our war absurd." Audrey, at twenty-two, was very similar to her mother, but with an indolent air — preferring to sprawl negligently with her legs stretched out, and to prop her head against the back of the chair.

"Your manner is altogether too glib... War? How can you even *think* such a thing with your Uncle Will not even decently buried?"

"It's just a word to express how we settle matters. *You'll* never accept the idea, whereas acceptance is not an issue for the rest of us. We've breathed it all our lives. There's no point in our talking about this, either. We shan't get anywhere. And as for Uncle Will," she leaned forward nonchalantly to take a cigarette from the box on the table, "he was a dear, and I'll always remember him. Just as I do Cousin Allan and Uncle Bart before him. Yes, it's sad that Uncle Will has gone, and I wish he were still with us. But we can't bring him back. All we can do is make the Eldreds pay. They have gone too far, and got away with too much for far too long."

"Stop it!" cried her mother. "You treat me as though I'm an outsider. I'm not one of your shallow London friends. You're talking of *murder*... I'm your mother!"

"Of *course*, you are, darling. You're upset, Mama." Audrey stubbed out the cigarette and went to Clare, giving every sign she intended to console her.

"No! Don't patronize me." Clare stiffened and put up a hand. "Your hard-hearted attitude is altogether foreign."

"Come *on*, don't be like this." Audrey stood looking down at her mother, smiling affectionately. She turned to her sister. "What do you say, Violet?"

"Leave me out of this." The nineteen-year-old took after her father. Dark-haired and quiet, she was shorter than her sister, and preferred home to anywhere else. "Neither of you will ever see eye-to-eye. But really, Audrey, you mustn't bring all that up now. Mummy's quite right, and she's very upset, as I am myself. You're only making things worse talking about the feud."

"Then I'll not say another word. I shall be very quiet and very good." Self-assured despite the rebuke, Audrey returned to her seat.

At that moment, Basil and Luke entered the room. Clare cast a look in their direction and decided it was best to say no more about the Eldred family.

"How are you, my dear?" asked Basil. He was brisk, which told her he wanted peace with no emotional displays. She supposed he and Luke had discussed what she and her daughters had been discussing.

"As well as can be expected," she said, her poise fully returned. To prevent an outburst, Clare intended they should talk of other matters, and therefore said, "I know now is probably not quite the right time to bring this up, but Surridge has informed me the price of coal has increased dramatically because of the strike."

"It has, indeed," said Basil, looking pleased. "Funny you should say that."

"Although this warm weather makes one think of almost anything but coal," said Clare, "should we be concerned about its availability?"

"Not unduly. I'm sure the strike will be over by the end of summer. If the worst happens, we can put in an oil system for heating and for running the generator. I might suggest that to father as a precaution."

Basil Munday preferred to stand and took up a position by the unused fireplace. He seemed in very good humour. A bushy maidenhair fern was in the grate, and he propped a foot on the brass rail. He unbuttoned his jacket, then rested an elbow on top of the ornate mantlepiece. They all knew he was about to speak about something important.

"You mentioned coal. You know that chap, Minkov? Well, he and I have had many dealings recently, as you're all probably aware."

"Excuse me," said Audrey. "Who is this Minkov?"

"You haven't met him, but you will at the Fête. He's a Bulgarian fella in the import and export business. Finds stuff for me around the Mediterranean to ship to Britain."

"Thank you."

"Yes. So, what with this miners' strike and the dock workers not handling imported coal at the ports, the whole situation puts the Royal Navy into a bit of a bind. They're having to draw down on their reserves to maintain the fleets at sea, otherwise they'll be forced to keep ships idle, which is the last thing they want. Now, although I said the strike would be over by summer's end, the Navy can't plan on guesswork of that type. Well, it just so happens the Bulgarians have good coal — semi-bituminous stuff, like the best Welsh coal, and highly suitable for burning in ships' furnaces. What's more, it's *cheap*." He enjoyed saying the word.

"Have you done one of your famous deals, Daddy?" asked Audrey.

"I most certainly have, and this is one of the better ones. What's more, I've got in ahead of everyone else."

"Well done, sir," said Luke.

"I thought Bulgaria was an enemy during the war," said Clare. "Aren't they also paying reparations to goodness knows whom?"

"The war's over, and it's time we looked forward. As for the reparations, the Bulgarians, just like Germany, have no money for anything, let alone paying their massive debts. They *should* pay, but that's beside the point. Consequently, being in a pinch, Bulgaria wants cash in a stable foreign currency, and that's what I'm giving them in exchange for their coal."

"And you're bringing it to Britain?" asked Violet.

"Can't, sweetie. The dockworkers won't allow it. But the British unions have nothing whatsoever to do with the Royal Navy's overseas coaling stations. In the Mediterranean, the Navy is now buying locally until the strike's over. My Bulgarian coal is being loaded onto several Greek ships that will deliver to the coaling stations at," he told off the places on his fingers, "Alexandria, Malta, Suez, Haifa, Gibraltar, and even as far away as Aden. The first two shipments have already arrived at Lemnos and Malta."

"I don't quite understand it all, but it sounds like you've done something extraordinary," said Clare. "Congratulations. I hope it's you the Royal Navy's paying."

"Naturally. I also chartered the Greek vessels."

"Then how's it worked with this Minkov chap?" asked Luke.

"He's handling the Bulgarian end. His family has excellent connections within the coal mining industry."

"You're looking very pleased with yourself," said Audrey, who playfully narrowed her gaze. "How good are the profits?"

"I ain't sayin'," said Basil archly, shifting away from the fireplace. "But I'll tell you this much. Bulgarian coal loaded onto a ship is thirteen shillings a ton. Add three shillings for freight and insurance and that makes sixteen shillings all in. The Royal Navy is paying twenty-nine shillings delivered."

"Good heavens!" exclaimed Luke. "You stand to make a fortune."

"Yes. Minkov gets a share of the profits, as does a Greek gentleman, but the bulk is coming to us."

"Then you'll be minting money as long as the strike lasts?" asked Audrey.

"The Navy gets through a lot of coal, so yes."

"It's a pity Uncle Will isn't with us to celebrate," said Violet.

"Yes… very sad," said Basil. "My thoughts fly to him often, and it gives me such a jolt. You know, my dears, it was inconsiderate of me to bring up the subject of business while we are in mourning. I simply forgot myself, and I apologize to you all."

"That was thoughtful of you, Basil," said Clare. She changed the subject to save her husband any further embarrassment. "Clive telephoned. He says he will be happy to stop at St. Mary's Colne to collect Julia on his way from Oxford. He says they will arrive here about five. Which reminds me. I must inform the headmistress about who it is who is coming to collect her. Miss Matthews might think that, in that car of his, Clive is Julia's swain and not her brother. Excuse me."

The family stood up as she left the room.

"Swain?" said Audrey. "That went out a hundred years ago."

"Don't," said Basil, raising a finger.

"No harm meant, Daddy. It's just terribly sweet and old-fashioned."

Basil smiled at his daughter. The family resumed talking.

Chapter 5

The Eldreds

To reach Capel House on the Eldred estate, it is necessary to use Parrish Row, which is one country lane east of Loxie Lane and the Mundays' estate. The two families are neighbours, enjoying the common boundary of the River Wynnet. They do not enjoy the most southerly section, for this is "the Tongue", that contentious acre, which has produced such bitter rivalry between the clans. Neither family uses it for anything or deigns to place a foot on that no man's sliver of land between the streams.

The Eldreds are farmers at heart and always have been. They out-produce the Mundays in terms of quantity and quality of crops and livestock, and this has been the case for as long as anyone can remember, notwithstanding that the Eldred estate is the smaller of the two and has the greater percentage of unusable acres. The Mundays do not farm; instead, they let out their fields to others. The Eldreds are children of the soil. Indeed, is not Lord Pascoe Eldred's wife also the daughter of a prosperous local farming family? She is, and Lady Shelagh cares for the estate's farming operations as much as his lordship does.

After passing through the gateless stone pillars, it becomes apparent that no money has been spent for some considerable time. The gravel in the tree-lined drive has worn thin in places and weeds are reestablishing themselves. This foretaste of the estate gives rise to the assumption that there must be a near-derelict house out of sight behind the trees, but this error is surprisingly refuted. Capel, in a green-treed and golden-field setting, is not the prettiest structure ever seen — although it is pretty — but it gives the impression of being the most fitting, and the absolute best one possible to be in this particular place. The house has so naturally settled into the landscape it is as if the place had always been there and always should be. Made of local stone, Capel is small and symmetrical, an oversized Queen Anne cottage without formal gardens. There are brilliant summer flower beds beneath the ground-floor windows, a few small lawns scattered about, and several stone paths, but little else.

Inside, not much has changed over the past fifty years besides the clothing styles worn by the current generation of inhabitants. The Eldred family had money once, and it shows in the tasteful furnishings and decoration. The house itself retains much of its original character and, throughout, everything is well kept, clean, and tidy.

One room, a study, is all that a Regency gentleman could have asked for in the way of refinement and elegance. Here at a desk, a man now sat writing with a fountain pen, one of the few modern conveniences in the room, and a gift from his wife, Shelagh. He signed a missive and replaced the top on his pen.

Viscount Pascoe Eldred was old at thirty-five. The tall man had no grey hair and his immobile features yielded no clue as to what was passing through his mind, yet he gave the impression he was burdened with a longstanding care that had robbed him of his energy. He stared across the room at a landscape painting without really looking at it. Sunlight, making the lace curtains glow, entered to touch its familiar places on the old red rug, infinitesimally bleaching out a little more colour, as it had done for generations.

He was absorbed in contemplating the family's circumstances. His father, Lord Alan, died in 1912 of natural causes. The death duties had been onerous for the land-rich but otherwise modestly wealthy family. Pascoe's eldest brother, Martin, inherited the title, but he died on the Western Front in 1915. Death duties and inheritance tax visited the Eldreds again with their inevitable swiftness. It was this blow that unequivocally left the Eldreds land rich and cash poor. The title passed to the second brother, Ian. In 1917, he was murdered in France during a German artillery barrage. The title passed to Pascoe, who was not ready, nor, indeed, had ever been groomed to be a peer. The weight of the responsibility and the changes it wrought in his life took away much of his happiness. When the tax bill came, it was Pascoe who was forced to decide which remaining investments must be sold and which could be kept to provide an income of some sort. He sought advice on the matter and, although it was good and reasonable, Pascoe ended by selling all the investments he should have kept, which left him with only those that, after the war, failed or faltered. There was no income now worth mentioning, except that which the estate produced. Farming, always a precarious and challenging life, provided food for the Eldreds, and employment for a few devoted local people, but little else. For example, there was insufficient money to educate properly his three children — a boy and two girls — let alone clothe them as befitted a viscount's family. The Eldreds were land rich and financially wiped out. One more round of death duties and that would be the end.

A breeze stirred the curtains. Pascoe got up to look through the window. He saw the fields, his fields, and, although still verdant, they needed rain. The area was thirsty and, according to the newspapers, this extended period of dry weather was affecting the entire country. Farming was his life and here, before his eyes, the land was on the brink of turning arid. As a farmer, he would fight the drought as best he could. If he were to lose the contest, Pascoe the farmer would have suffered the loss with little complaint, maintaining the hardy resolve to take off a bumper crop the following year. However, as a viscount, one lost harvest meant he would be forced to sell the already mortgaged estate.

For the almost four years of his viscountcy, the worry of failure had been always present, and now, with this dry spell, it threatened more ominously than ever before. Yet there was an additional care, a sudden and weighty one, thrust upon Pascoe's shoulders: what to do about the Mundays?

In 1915, Pascoe's brother, the then current viscount, Major Ian Eldred, had no choice but to send Lieutenant David Munday's company against a fortified German position, because he, himself, was under orders to do so. The major had also sent in two more companies to support Munday's effort, but the attack had failed, resulting in high casualties, with Munday among them. The Mundays blamed Major Eldred for this event, and it triggered the latest round of killings in the feud. Ian was subsequently murdered out of revenge. Pascoe could only surmise who did it. From what he knew, any of one of nine or ten members of the wider Munday clan could have done the deed, with several of them serving in France at the time. Although regrettable in the extreme, Ian's murder was unsurprising to Pascoe, who had believed throughout the interval that his brother's life was in serious jeopardy over and above the hazards of the trenches.

The situation worsened for the new Viscount Eldred when, in 1920, Allan Munday was killed in Scotland — shot in the back. Pascoe found it hard to believe and felt unwell for several days, trying to recall if he had ever been to Scotland. He was certain he had not, otherwise he would remember, surely? But who else, among the Eldreds, could be responsible? If that were not sufficient cause for him to worry about his own life, next came the news that Bartholomew Munday had been knifed to death in London. This time, Pascoe recalled being in London on that very day — he went up to town once a month for various reasons. The extraordinary thing was, he had liked

Bartholomew, always got on well with him, although they saw each other infrequently, and usually by accident, but always by design once a year at the Ball. Pascoe could not see why he would choose to kill Bart of all people if, indeed, he had.

Now came the third shocking blow. Pascoe considered the matter. It was widely supposed he had killed Wilfred Munday, simply because of the long-standing bitterness between the two families. But there were also reports of his having been seen driving through Wynbourne with a passenger just moments before shots were fired and Wilfred Munday lay dead in the road. Pascoe told the police only yesterday that it could not have been he who was driving, as he had not left the estate in the morning. Lady Shelagh Eldred had confirmed his statement. The police took notes and examined his car. Although it was a different make and shape to the one the witnesses had described, it was the same colour of blue. The police also removed two pistols belonging to Pascoe. While doing so, the Detective Inspector in charge said it was all just mere formality and no cause for concern. He spoke with a smile. Viscount Eldred detected the superficial tone in these reassurances but complied with the requests, all the while thinking the detective believed him to be the guilty party. After they departed, he wondered if he *had* gone out and driven the car without his wife seeing him leave. Had he, Pascoe, in some kind of funk or haze, killed Wilfred Munday without realizing it? He wished he could be sure on the point.

Returning to his desk, he felt he could decide the several pressing matters more easily while seated. Should the family attend Wilfred Munday's funeral? Pascoe decided they would. After all, the family had always attended Munday funerals, and he saw no reason to change the tradition now. The same logic, when applied to the question of whether or not to attend the Ball, yielded the same result. The Eldreds would go, as they always had. Next year, if there were to be a 'next year', he would likewise expect the Mundays to come to Capel House. Of them all, the next and last decision was the most difficult of the three, because it entailed a hard choice between two entirely different and life-changing courses of action. If only he could consult with someone on the matter, Pascoe may have seen another easier way. He was a farmer and, unexpectedly, a viscount yet to be reconciled with the idea of being one. Neither occupation prepared him for what he was facing. Should he continue the feud, or should he abandon the estate?

If he stayed, Pascoe reasoned, he must continue the feud, prosecuting it with a remorseless alacrity before *they* killed *him*. The Mundays would come after him — that was certain — *if* he stayed. Pascoe took from a drawer a list of eight names, each one possessing the potential of being his executioner. At the top were Basil and Luke Munday. To kill them, and the six other adults on the list, was his only recourse should he remain to fight it out. In the unlikely event he won such an unequal contest, the Munday viscountcy would not be extinguished, as there were minors in other branches who would inherit upon coming of age. The Mundays were far better placed to suffer losses. Conversely, they had only to kill him and his thirteen-year-old son for the Eldred viscountcy to cease to exist. There was no one else to fight the feud or inherit the title and estate.

The sad alternative was to settle up and leave the area. Superficially, it was the safer choice, but it also had severe drawbacks. Even if he sold everything, there would be little money left over once all the debts were settled. Perhaps there would be enough to buy a small farm that he and his wife could work. That part of the stratagem he did not mind so much as he perceived it as a way of escape. But it could never truly be an escape — one of the Munday family would pursue him regardless of what he now decided. Wilfred's death demanded vengeance, and whether they delivered it in Wiltshire, London, or elsewhere made little difference in the scheme of things.

Pascoe could accept his own death, but that his son should die in a conflict not of his own making was intolerable. The whole wretched, miserable thing should cease, but how? He did not know. Perhaps a parley with Basil at some opportune moment might put a stop to this endless string of senseless calamities. It was worth trying. But if it were not he who had killed Wilfred, then who was it? A knock came on the study door. It opened quietly to reveal a boy in a school uniform.

"Good morning, sir. I'm not disturbing you, am I?"

"Come in, Edward." Pascoe smiled.

The boy, although a good height, looked younger than his thirteen years. He clung to childish ways, too.

"Did the police really visit here yesterday?"

"They did."

"Why, sir? You would never do anything wrong. I think it's awfully bad of them."

"They were discharging their duties — nothing more than that."

"But you wouldn't kill anyone, sir. They shouldn't even think of such dreadful things."

"Enough, Edward. How is school this term?"

"Much better, thank you. A fellow named Saunders joined our form, and he's a frightful rip."

"A rip?"

"Sorry, sir. But he's ever so comical and says the most extraordinary things."

"I'm glad he keeps you amused. I was referring to your studies, however."

"Well, you know. I'm improving in Latin and mathematics, but Old Duffer gives us tons of work in history, making it so that a chap can't keep up with it all."

"I'm sure Mr Duffield gives you exactly what you need. History was also a heavy subject in my day."

"Then I shan't complain. May I go outside, sir? It's a lovely day."

"Yes, of course... I'll tell you what. Change out of your uniform, and we'll go down to the pond together."

"To feed the ducks? How splendid! Excuse me."

The boy eagerly rushed from the room. Pascoe intended to check the level of water in the artificial pond which was fed by the Wynnet. Useful against dry spells, Pascoe meant to see if the pond was as full as possible, and to check the sluice. Lady Shelagh entered the study. She was a healthy and energetic woman, thirty-four years old.

"I've just heard, so I'll accompany you to the pond," she said, then gave Pascoe a sharp look. "We can only do what we can, and trust in Providence for the rest." She was a lady in every sense, and one with a kind face and dark hair. Lady Shelagh, however, was never trained in the ways of a drawing room and the social graces. Her soft country accent betrayed this. She was and would always be a gentlewoman from a middle-class farming family, used to hard work, want sometimes, and one to put a proper value on diligence and thrift.

"Too true... Say nothing in front of Edward."

"No... although I think it toime he took on some responsibility. We can't shelter him forever."

"For my sake, then, let him be a child a while longer. He'll have plenty to deal with soon enough."

"I know that... And shall we all go to the funeral?"

"Yes. I'll talk to Harriet and Myra."

"If you wish to, Pass, but I've already set them straight on matters o' loife and death."

Pascoe smiled. "What would I do without you?"

"Fall to pieces, no doubt... They're going to come for you, aren't they?"

"They will."

"And the police?"

They stared at each other.

"Do you think I killed Wilfred?"

"Say you didn't and that'll be good enough for me."

"I didn't." Pascoe hoped it was true.

"Then if the police don't have a case, there's no need for us to worry what they think. What can we do about the other, though?"

"I've thought and thought, and the options are few and unpalatable."

"You can't kill anyone. You're not even to think of such a thing."

"Then we should sell up."

"Sell Capel House!? Oh, *no*. Whatever makes you say that?"

"Desperation."

They heard the quick approaching footsteps of several children, who soon burst into the room.

"Can Harriet and Myra come, too? I've got some bread." Edward held up a full paper bag as proof. By his side were two dark-haired, shy, smiling girls, eleven and nine years-old, respectively. They took after their mother.

"Perfect, and yes, of course, you can come, my darlings," said Lord Eldred to his daughters. "Now we can all feed the ducks together. And Edward, you'll not return to school until Monday."

"Hooray!" he shouted, before catching himself. "Sorry, sir." He did not look very sorry, but the sudden extension of a holiday from his boarding school, even though it included a funeral, was something for the child to shout about.

"Spare a thought for my poor eardrums," said Lady Shelagh.

"Forgive me, Mama." An affectionate boy, he hugged his mother.

The family's walk with a spaniel following was no simple affair of straight to the pond and back again. The children were in high spirits and played but, every so often, Lady Shelagh called them to her. She questioned each child to name a plant and tell the properties it held in fruit, root, and leaf. She taught her children what she had learned from her mother and aunts — the lore of the countryside. From the habits of birds and ways of animals to the plants and trees which surrounded them, she entrusted her children with what she knew, and that wisdom was ancient. Education, she maintained, was a fine thing in its way, but knowledge of the land from which they had sprung was equally, if not more, important.

Pascoe pushed back the straw trilby hat he wore to survey the fields, crops, and blue sky while listening to his wife's gentle voice guiding his children into a fuller understanding of their surroundings. He decided he was rich, after all. In that moment, he wanted more than anything that they could stay exactly as they were, particularly for the sake of Edward, who was safe as long as he was a child.

At the pond, they fed the ducks. Pascoe took a moment to examine the nearby river. He could tell the flow was diminishing, so he shut the sluice gate on the small channel that led to the pond in case the river dropped further and the pond water flowed back out. Lady Shelagh watched him as the small iron gate noisily dropped into place, and Pascoe stood up to brush the dirt from his hands. He went to her.

"The pond can't take a drop more," she said.

"If there's no rain in the next two days, we'll begin watering," he said.

"Don't leave it any longer. That part of the slope always dries fastest." She pointed out an area but told Pascoe nothing he did not already know.

"The day after the funeral, I'll have the men start first thing in the morning."

"Arh." She agreed with his timing. Shelagh knew Pascoe would work with the men to water the crops by hand pump and bucket, and she decided that, as the family had little money, she and the children could help as well. To her countrywoman's mind, the dry weather was too early and too long to be natural for that part of the country. Convinced the year was doomed, she determined to keep her pessimism to herself so as not to add to her husband's burdens. There was trouble enough and they would all work hard, come what may, even if defeat stared them in the face.

Chapter 6

Minor difficulties

Percival Penrose, Superintendent of Special Duties, Scotland Yard, got off the train in Devizes, a place he had never before visited. In the sunlight, he shielded his eyes to study the tunnel that the train had passed through before stopping at the station. Then he gazed upwards to the hill above.

"Superintendent Penrose?" said a burly man, equal in size and stature to Penrose.

"Hello, that's me." He turned around.

"Detective Inspector Haddock, Wiltshire Constabulary. Pleased to meet you."

"Likewise." They shook hands. "Tell me summat before we go. That railway tunnel goes right under that there castle on the hill?"

"It do, sir. But it's a Victorian castle, although there's a bit of an old Norman keep and a windmill incorporated into it somehow. It's beautiful on the outside and, I'm told, a rare treat on the inside, but I've never seen it. Private property, you see, sir."

"Ahh." Penrose was from the County of Somerset and, although his hometown of Taunton was less than fifty miles away from Devizes, his accent was noticeably different from that of Inspector Haddock.

"We can walk to headquarters. T'ain't far, loike."
"Lead on, MacDuff."
"That's Shakespeare, isn't it, sir?"
"So, I've heard."
"I thought so. He was a right smart lad."

Penrose smiled. "I've never heard him described like that before." They walked to the top of Station Road. Penrose halted to get his bearings. "Where are we exactly?"

"Well, the town's that way with all the shops and what not. Two hundred yards and you're in the middle of it all. We go this way, though, across the canal."

"Canal? That's right, you have Caen Hill Locks about here some place."

"We do, sir. Twenty-nine locks in a row, and the curse of every bargee that works 'em to get where he be going."

"I reckon that's right," said Penrose.

They crossed over a plain stone bridge that spanned the canal and walked past some houses.

"There are some nice places here," remarked Penrose.

"Yes."

"Red House." Penrose read the inscription on a pillar. "What type of man is your Chief Constable?"

"Colonel Sir Hoël Llewellyn is a fair-minded man, but what you moight call a stickler for the rules. A great organizer, he is."

"He was in the South African Police and he's ex-army," said Penrose.

"That's roight, sir. They made him a colonel, and he was knighted for his work during the war."

"They don't give out knighthoods for nothing, so he must have earned it. Ex-army, though. Doesn't always go well with police work."

"No, that's true. I think that's what contributed to the police strike in nineteen."

"Let's leave that be, shall we? Tell me about the latest Munday murder case."

"I haven't been officially handed the file yet, but I know it's a-coming. There are a few peculiarities I've been told. The surgeon who did the autopsy said Wilfred Munday wasn't shot in Wynbourne, because he was already dead, and had been for an hour or more. Not enough blood at the scene. They're always careful about committing themselves to toimes, though."

"That they are."

"So, someone pulled the corpse from the car just out of soight o' the village because of a bend in the road by the church. Before the car left, the driver fired two shots. None of us can understand why he did that."

"To attract attention," said Penrose.

"Well, yes, I s'pose he did. But why?"

"You'll have to ask him when you find him."

"I reckon we will, sir." Inspector Haddock smiled. "Anyway, there were two old boys a-sittin' outside of the Swan public house in Wynbourne. They both swear they saw Viscount Pascoe Eldred driving the car with a passenger they didn't recognize. But although they say it was him, we have found no corroboratin' evidence. His lordship don't have a vehicle exactly loike the old boys described and there was no blood in the car he does have. Then Lady Eldred says her husband was at home at the time of the murder. We took two revolvers belonging to his lordship, but they're the wrong calibre, and neither was fired recently."

"Then Lord Eldred borrowed a car. His wife gave him an alibi, and he threw the murder weapon away."

"Do you mean to say her ladyship loied?"

"Perhaps I've been working in London for too long."

"She wouldn't do that... At least, I don't think she would. But there, I never interviewed her. That's about all I know at present, sir."

"It sounds like an interesting case. And it's all connected with this feud that's been going on for over a century."

"That's roight. This is us, here."

"That fine stone archway does you proud," said Penrose, studying the entrance to the police station. It was more like a triumphal arch.

"We loike it," said Haddock, a satisfied note in his voice. "Used to belong to the militia before it were converted. Perishing cold in the winter, though."

"Having suffered in the past under similar circumstances, I can appreciate your agonies. Writing long reports with cold hands is excruciating, to say the least."

They passed under the impressive arch and into the small square beyond. Inspector Haddock pointed out features of interest as they went.

Colonel Sir Hoël Llewellyn, a spare old gentleman with a piercing gaze, could have had his career summed up in the motto, 'Get the job done'. Penrose could see who he was dealing with straight off.

"Thank you for coming, Penrose. I know you Yard fellows are busy, so I shan't waste your time. Having agreed to the inclusion of agents at the Fête and Ball, I was under the mistaken impression that they would be police officers disguised as servants. I have since had this impression corrected. They are not police officers, therefore I am reluctant they be employed as suggested."

The Colonel stopped abruptly. Penrose knew he must present his arguments effectively or Burgoyne's Agency would be pulled from the case.

"Well, Colonel, the team of agents in question has done excellent work. There is no doubt in my mind that they will be of much help in the investigation. If I may, I'll give you a couple of examples of what they have achieved in the past."

"Please, proceed."

Penrose did so by recounting several cases.

"Most impressive... They have more experience than I had imagined. However, I'm still not convinced on two points. The first is that they are, primarily, women from *London*. Therefore, they will be unacquainted with our ways here. The second is, how am I to integrate them with my men working on the case? My men have never employed freelance agents and are untrained in working alongside people outside of the force. I run this constabulary along very straight and clearly demarcated lines and come down severely upon those who break the rules. This proposed arrangement requires some latitude. Had they been women police officers, it would be a different matter entirely. Outsiders are not subject to disciplinary measures. I foresee potential dangers."

"I can set your mind at rest on the first point. I know for a fact that two of the ladies in the team are not from London and well understand rural life. They are all familiar with serving the landed gentry. The problem with them fitting in will not be from their lack of experience or ability, which brings me to your second point. I'll be sending a liaison officer with them, a detective sergeant by the name of Gowers. He's a good man, and thorough. He knows the agents well, because he's worked with them before."

"That's useful, particularly as we're short-handed at present. I've had to send a hundred officers to help police the miners' strike. They're in Wales as we speak." The Colonel clasped his hands together in front of him. "However, I'm still not completely convinced, although I'm very close."

"A part of the reason for my visit is something I could not explain by telephone. It concerns the Official Secrets Act."

"Ah, I thought there might be something more to it."

"We would have offered the services of the agents in any event, but there is a party who will almost certainly be present at Dumond Hall in the coming days. Certain departments in Whitehall have an interest in what this fellow gets up to. The agents we're discussing will watch him and report his movements."

"I see. Then say no more on the subject. I'm sure you're restricted about what you can reveal, in any event. My curiosity stops with local affairs. But tell me this much. Is anyone at Dumond Hall under suspicion in this other matter?"

"Not at present, and may never be, depending on what we discover."

"Good. You have allayed my concerns and the other matter makes it imperative you bring in these women."

"Thank you, sir."

"I shall now explain the feud from a policeman's perspective. There have undoubtedly been tit-for-tat murders for many years and, remarkably, no one has ever been brought to trial for them. Inspector Haddock, to whom I shall assign the case, will explain the history to you better than I can."

He stood up to walk slowly about the office as he spoke.

"We are hitting a wall of silence. The local villagers are reluctant to involve themselves in actions against either of the families. Some of this is due to partisanship. Individuals, sometimes entire families, are for the one and against the other. For all of them, speaking against titled persons runs contrary to their nature. The populace has adopted the attitude that as long as these two families perpetuate the violence at a distance, it views the matter almost as if it were entertainment or a sporting competition.

"Often, economic considerations affect a witness's behaviour. As a hypothetical example, a labourer hired by the Eldred family will not speak out against a member of the Munday family for fear of accidentally incriminating the person who employs him. He may also work for the Mundays or be related to someone who does. Therefore, the labourer will take the easier path and say he knows nothing, becoming evasive and unreliable when answering police questions. As for someone stepping forward to volunteer information — I don't believe that has ever happened. Without independent witnesses and with the families themselves bound by some extraordinary code, never to mention the feud publicly, the police are held back from doing their job."

"Then the local population just lets the Eldreds and Mundays have at one another and effectively shield them."

"That's what it amounts to... But it shall stop. All the murders have occurred in other jurisdictions, so I'm powerless to act in them, although we sent information to the Yard on Bartholomew Munday's murder in London. The murder of Wilfred Munday, however, is the first in Wiltshire since the feud began. Now we have our chance. All the principals live in the same area under my jurisdiction. I mean to have them, Superintendent Penrose. They shall not continue with these outrages any longer."

"Sergeant Gowers and the team of agents will likewise do their utmost to that end."

"Excellent. That's the spirit." Colonel Llewellyn approached Penrose with an outstretched hand. The Superintendent stood up, and they shook hands heartily. "Glad to have you join us," said Llewellyn.

Afterwards, Penrose and Haddock went to the Elm Tree for a pint and to discuss the case. On the way, Penrose suddenly declared that he had often said the best beer comes from Devizes, which unexpected disclosure very much pleased Inspector Haddock. Penrose did not elaborate that it had once been a signal used, among the secret network in which he worked, to identify a fellow agent.

Sophie became mesmerized, passing through the Strait of Gibraltar. With the SS Rangoon gliding past the coasts of Spain and Morocco, only seven or eight miles away on either side, she considered how such a whirl of events had contrived to place her where she was now. Cruising gave her the immeasurable luxury of being able to squander time without guilt. Usually busy, often overworking herself, she could now consider these ancient lands at her leisure. And if she did not have all the facts and dates of past civilizations in mind or at hand in a book, Sophie, having always been an avid reader, had something far richer — she had the flavour of them all while she gazed, dreamily resting on the ship's rail.

"Oh, hello," said a middle-aged woman with a bright voice. "You're new, aren't you? Did you get on at Gib?"

Wrenched from her drifting thoughts, Sophie turned to answer.

"Hello. Yes, I did."

"I thought you had. I'm Mrs Frank Talbot." She offered to shake hands.

As Sophie raised her hand in response, an alarming thought came to mind. She could not say 'Sophie Burgoyne', because she was travelling on her other passport. Neither could she say 'Phoebe King', because Minkov might hear the name on the ship and, if he heard it again at Dumond Hall, he would realize he was being followed. Then she would be truly sunk.

"Pleased to meet you," said Sophie.

"What's your name, dear?" asked Mrs Talbot. Sophie instantly knew she was faced with an arch-organizer, that species of middle-class woman who is determined to arrange everything and everyone in their proper place whether they liked it or not. She had often met the type before but, as this was her first time aboard a liner, Sophie was unsure how they functioned at sea.

"Miss Brown."

"Miss Brown, welcome aboard the SS Rangoon, although it's hardly *my* place to say that, seeing as it isn't *my* ship." Mrs Talbot let herself go with a gale of laughter. Just as suddenly as it had come on, it ceased. "We all go by our first names aboard. Absolutely throw convention to the wind. I'm

Roberta, but everyone calls me Bobbie, and I insist you do, too. Yours is?"

"Mary."

"Mary Brown... Which county?"

Here we go, thought Sophie. She had not expected to be pinned down so early in the voyage, yet she was not totally unprepared.

"One moment," said Sophie. "You wouldn't be one of the Talbots from Suffolk?"

"Oh, no. We're from Essex. Just returning from India, of course."

"I see. I'm from Hampshire," replied Sophie, believing herself safe with so many intervening counties between the two of them.

"Hampshire Browns... Hmm, I can't recall any. I don't think I know your family."

"I do, and they're very nice. But I must warn you, Bobbie," Sophie dropped her voice as if imparting a secret, "there are many, many Browns to be found in *every* county."

"Well, I suppose there are, aren't there?" She swept on. "Mary, do you play bridge? We all do, and it's how we survive this interminable voyage. What with a few drinky-poos and general light-heartedness, I can promise that you will have a marvellous time." She put her hand on Sophie's arm and spoke with intensity. "*Say* you play bridge, dear."

"I'm afraid, I don't."

"Uh, how *unfortunate*? Perhaps I could teach you before tonight? Are you a quick learner? It's very simple, apart from the bidding."

"No. I invariably put the wrong cards down, no matter what game I play. The others get very upset with me."

"Oh, well, they would. Are you travelling alone? Perhaps you're with a companion?"

"I'm travelling alone."

"Ah, all alone. Then I'm sure I shall see you at lunch or dinner." She looked along the deck. "Oh! Another newcomer.

I must find out if he plays bridge. Excuse me." Mrs Talbot, effusive and smiling, hurried away to corner her next unwitting victim.

After she had gone, Sophie went for a walk to think over how she needed to conduct herself during the voyage. She had brought a book — War and Peace — and her idea was to station herself in appropriately discreet places and, while pretending to read her book, oversee Mr Minkov's activities. She had glimpsed him twice now. The first time was when an Italian man, the agent following Minkov, pointed him out to her. He gave a few hurried words of explanation in English so heavily accented that she could barely understand them, before he abruptly left with her none the wiser about Minkov's habits.

The second occasion was as the SS Rangoon left the dock. While passengers lined the Promenade Deck rails and there were perhaps only thirty people standing on the docks to wave the ship off, Minkov scanned the people on the shore from the Boat Deck above. He did so surreptitiously, using a lifeboat as a screen. To watch a liner leaving a port was an unextraordinary action, but his self-concealment…? Sophie wondered what it signified.

Sophie, also on the Boat Deck, peered at *him* from behind another lifeboat. She rather thought Minkov, in his thirties, looked remarkably like Beethoven because of his exuberant hair; the only difference being Minkov's was jet-black.

Once through the Strait of Gibraltar, the land receded. Morocco disappeared when the ship steamed more to the north in crossing the Gulf of Cadiz. Ahead lay Portugal, but the ship was so far offshore, she could not see any details. She went to the port side of the Promenade Deck. Here she saw two ships farther out but heading in the same direction. Had she still been a child, she might have waited to see if those ships were faster than her ship — indeed, it crossed her mind to do so.

Yesterday's wind had died away and, if still breezy, at least the sun was warm. Far out to sea, the clouds seemed to be piled into one massive bank the size of a country. Two thoughts struck her almost simultaneously: how immense was the sea, and how small the world! She idly analyzed the conflicting ideas. The sea was boundless when compared to herself, while the world was made accessibly small by the ship sailing on it. Coming from India, the Rangoon could just as easily turn towards the West Indies as keep to the course for England. The other side of the Atlantic was only a matter of days away, and the other side of the world only weeks. Before going to her cabin, she dreamed a little of where she would visit, if she had charge of the Rangoon.

The SS Rangoon, an old P & O ship, was one that had narrowly escaped being torpedoed during the war, unlike many others owned by the line. It was a trim, well-built, single-funneled ship of eight thousand tons, designed to carry three hundred and fifty passengers, ranging from steerage to first-class, and carried cargo in holds fore and aft. Still showing residual evidence of its war-time service, the twelve-year-old Rangoon was, by this time, badly in need of a refit.

Whereas Sophie had envisioned herself travelling first class in delightful surroundings, engaging in an elegant and subtle spy-versus-spy battle of wits, the sight of her third-class cabin on the port side came as a crashing disappointment. It was a cramped, low-ceilinged cell, barely wider than its scuffed wooden door. Also, the porthole squeaked when opened. There were two narrow bunk beds, high-sided cots really, on one wall, and a washbasin with a cabinet opposite the door. What made her frown most were the wooden partition walls on either side, with gaps near the ceiling because of two girders. As she stood and realigned her expectations with the reality in front of her, she clearly heard a man and woman arguing a couple of cabins away. Her only solace was that her cabin was not near the engine.

Sophie studied her face in the mirror again and was dismayed at what she saw. Flying in an open plane wearing goggles and a leather helmet had produced an unwelcome effect. The sun had noticeably reddened her cheeks and nose, while her forehead and around her eyes remained woefully pale. In the matter of tanning, she always went red first before going brown, and now the world would know it for a fact, and might ask awkward questions about how she came to be parti-coloured. So far, she had disguised her all-too-evident affliction by the temporary and rather unsatisfactory measure of covering the red areas with her silk scarf. Now she meant to remedy the imbalance. Consequently, she ascended to the open Boat Deck and found a secluded bench. With her opera glasses and a pencil in her jacket pocket, she opened War & Peace, and held it abnormally high so that the sun struck her forehead, while the book shaded the lower part of her face. Sophie soon discovered that her book was a weighty tome in more ways than one.

Nothing was seen again of Minkov until lunchtime. Knowing that he occupied a second-class cabin meant he would dine in the second-class restaurant. Although she considered changing to second class, Sophie realized that Minkov would then see her at relatively close quarters some twenty-odd times over the coming days while leisurely eating. Her red and white face could so easily draw his attention, and that was to be avoided. Therefore, she left matters as they were, and sidled into the third-class restaurant as the lunch hour was ending, hoping to eat alone at a table with her face averted from the rest of the diners.

Chapter 7

Decks, dots, and dashes

To put the word Promenade before the word Deck was, Sophie believed, to create a falsehood. She was certain she could not be alone in her understanding that to promenade is to walk freely, without hindrance or obstacle. The verb also suggests gaiety, ease, and a certain amount of social pleasure derived from the exercise, and she had been looking forward to promenading in a circuit around the ship at will and, even if it rained, the deck would be sheltered. Instead, she found it to be sectioned by barricades and obstructions, deliberately erected to maintain Britain's class system. The first-class section had wooden screens to keep out all the other classes and to prevent gawking. From his own first-class section, the first-class traveller entered this first-class sanctum. Here, all the superior amenities were to be found, including, as Sophie learned, a gymnasium and Turkish baths.

Second and third classes were merely roped off from each another, but the rope was an inviolable red which meant that anyone crossing it would die a thousand social deaths, because no one from either class would ever again have anything to do with the malefactor who stepped over the boundary. If someone crossed the rope, third class would say quietly, 'What does he think he's doing? He can't do that.' The more practical, threatened, and nearly apoplectic second class would yell, 'Steward! Throw that bounder in the sea!'

The subdivisions did not end there. The Officers' PD and the Engineers' PD were built into the ship's superstructure and bounded by steel. However, all the sections had companionways up to the Boat Deck — an *almost* egalitarian space because, even there, steerage passengers were still not allowed. Here, on the roof of the ship, so to speak, one could actually promenade to one's heart's content. From here also, Sophie realized, she could descend unimpeded into whichever class she liked if she ignored the small 'First-class passengers only' warning signs.

On the second day, Sophie arose early. Reassured of her face's progress towards equilibrium and as the air was already warm, she went up to the Boat Deck. There were few people about as she passed a newly hung 'Ladies only' sign by the companionway to the deck above. Without a care, she ascended the steep stairs to take an undisturbed walk before breakfast. There was no wind; there was only the breeze made by the ship cruising at fourteen knots. The early sun was welcoming.

On top of the ship, she encountered the Women's Calisthenics Class, of whose existence she had previously been ignorant. It was just starting some warming-up exercises. Several of the fifteen women present were dressed like water nymphs, while the rest wore skirts and blouses or light dresses. The largest water nymph, a tall woman of about fifty with piercing eyes, and who was obviously not a crewmember, faced her class while gracefully standing on one leg with her arms outstretched. As anyone does, Sophie tried to go about her business without staring at the group, behaving as if they did not exist. She had barely gone five paces when the instructor noticed her. While still supported by a single limb, the woman bawled, as would a parade-ground sergeant. "You, thar! Come over hyar and join us! We'd be delighted to have you!"

The class turned to stare at Sophie, and several lost their balance.

"I'm not dressed for exercise!" shouted Sophie in return, giving the only excuse that came to mind.

"Don't worry about that! Just strip awrf and get stuck in! It's only us gels up hyar! No men allowed!"

"Come along, Miss Brown!" seconded Mrs Talbot, also a water nymph. "Don't be shy! We're not!"

There was no escape, and so, in stockinged feet and her new summer dress, Sophie wobbled with the others through the exercises and Greek 'airy-fairy' dancing, as she and her friend Flora had called it at school. By the end and feeling invigorated, she decided that, rather than avoiding these morning exercises, she would join the class.

Two days at sea proved Minkov to be a man of habit. He was travelling second class and always sat at the same table by a porthole. At every meal, the same fifty-year-old man joined him. Sophie, by walking across an entrance to the dining room, observed them, and once, she noticed their waiter in the act of removing a reserved sign. Minkov, who faced the entrance she used, had obviously paid a steward to reserve that table. She had to be careful, and so spied on Minkov infrequently, yet it was often enough for her to be surprised that she only saw the two men talking together once. When they were not eating, Minkov often stared through the porthole, while his companion usually read a magazine. Sophie pressed half a crown into their waiter's hand, which bought his discretion and the name of the unknown man. He was Foster, and something in the British government. When Sophie asked the waiter, he said the two men rarely spoke. However, he volunteered Minkov had tipped him several times with more than was customary.

By the third day, Sophie had written many marginal notes in her copy of War & Peace, but they related to Minkov's movements rather than the story. From her deck chair on the third-class PD, she could see Minkov's back. He spent much of his time reading, just as she did, or purported to. Occasionally he spoke to someone, more often it being they who initiated the conversation but, in either case, it only ever amounted to polite interactions. Sophie, on the other hand, was plagued with friendly people wanting to talk to her. Really, with a few of them, it was to talk *at* her.

It was a quarter to eleven, and the worst chatterbox in third class, a woman in her fifties whose husband avoided her and was always elsewhere about the ship, had pulled over a deck chair and plumped herself down next to Sophie. There was no getting rid of the woman until lunchtime. In a desperate bid to remain polite and yet continue her work, Sophie had happily discovered that she could still just about read her book, keep an eye on Minkov, and keep everything pleasant by throwing in a question or comment into the conversation every so often.

"Good morning. Ooh, I'm so glad you're here. What a delight it is to have someone to talk to. I mean that, my dear."

"Good morning, Mrs Clutterbuck. And how is your knee this morning?"

"That's funny. That's exactly what I want to tell you about. Last night, I put the liniment on it, as I always do, and I wrapped the bandage tighter than usual. Not really tight, because the last thing I'd want to do is to cut off me circulation. But just tight enough so I could get a finger in between the bandage and me flesh. But if I had tightened that bandage just that *little* bit extra... Well, that's very bad. Very bad, indeed. If I had done that, my leg would have turned *black* in the night, and there'd be nothing to do but have it *cut* off. And I wouldn't fancy having that done on a ship, let me tell you. Oh, no. Half of these ships' doctors are drunk when they do surgeries. And you'd better believe it."

"Surely not," said Sophie as she turned a page.

"Oh, yes, they are. You see, Miss Brown, when you get to be as old as I am, then you'll know a lot more about doctors and their peculiar ways. It's like this. A ship's doctor is not really a proper doctor. Not as well trained, you see. So, they have the habit of drinking to steady their nerves when they have to work. Everyone does in the navy, really, come to think of it. But what I say is this. Spirits might steady the doctors' nerves, all right, and I can see why they'd want a nip, 'cause it can't be very nice to go opening up someone's guts when you don't even know 'em. So, as I said, I can see how a nip, or two, might steady the nerves all right, but it doesn't steady the hand, now does it? Do you see what I mean?"

"Vividly," said Sophie, who glanced over at Minkov.

"Then there's the rolling of the ship to think about as well. Roll, roll... No, I don't think I'd like to have a surgery at sea. I'd chance it and wait until we docked, no matter what they wanted to cut off or cut out... Where was I?"

"You could get your finger between the bandage and your leg."

"Ha! It's a good job you're here, otherwise I'd have completely forgotten what we were talking about. Right, so I'd got the bandage just nice..."

Later, while Mrs Clutterbuck was recounting in a welter of detail the trials and tribulations her youngest sister was undergoing, a steward approached Minkov. It took Sophie a few moments to realize he was delivering a telegram. Minkov read it while the steward waited for a reply. She watched as Minkov took a stuffed notecase from an inside jacket and opened it. The steward, not wishing to appear inquisitive, gazed out to sea while he waited. Minkov used a pen to write his response on a slip of paper. Then he gave the steward the slip, and the two men spoke, after which Minkov handed the steward some money.

"Excuse me. I must go," said Sophie, interrupting Mrs Clutterbuck mid-flow.

"Where you off to in such a hurry?" asked the puzzled woman. Sophie, almost running, did not answer.

She caught sight of the steward on his way to the Radio Room and followed him around a corner and into the main passage. This led to the ship's offices and the companionway to the Bridge at the far end.

To send a telegram, passengers filled out a form at the counter of the Radio Room. It was a small opening, and blank forms, pens, and ink for use lay in a fixed tray to one side. Next to the counter stood a large sign painted in splendid alliteration which read, 'No passengers permitted past this point unless authorized.' Beyond the sign was the door to the Radio Room.

"Here, Sparky." The steward thrust his head through the opening to speak. "The bloke wants his reply sent immediate."

"Don't they all? Put it with the others and I'll get to it."

"Nah, mate. Send it now. He gi'us two bob."

"What? A tycoon, is he?"

At the corner where she stood listening, Sophie heard the radio operator's chair scrape on the floor.

"Don't know about that," said the steward. "He's second class, so can't be."

"Let's have a look... Seven words, that's 5s 6d. What did you charge him?"

"Five and six, of course, 'cause he's under the eight. He gi'us three half-crowns. Here you are."

Sophie watched as the steward handed over the money. There was a momentary delay, and she assumed the radio operator was sorting out the change.

"There you go," said the operator. "I'll send the message right away."

"Then I'll go back and tell him, to keep him sweet, in case he wants to send another."

"Do that. He's received before, but never sent."

Sophie retreated several paces, then made it appear as though she was just arriving at the main passage. The steward stepped breezily around the corner, smiled at Sophie, and continued on. When it was safe, Sophie, as noiselessly as possible, approached the counter, but kept out of sight of the opening. She risked a glance into the room. The operator was busy writing at his station. When finished, he put his headphones on. Sophie unobtrusively reached for a telegram form, then took out her pencil.

The operator turned a tuning dial on a board in front of him. He then used his Morse Key. The tapping was sufficiently loud for Sophie to hear. He sent the ship's call sign and other information. An answer came back after a few seconds' pause. The operator tapped out the recipient's details and message. He was quick, almost too quick, but she kept up, writing out the dashes and dots of Minkov's telegram. The tapping ceased. She heard the chair scrape and stuffed the form into her pocket before stepping up to the counter.

"Excuse me?"

"Yes, miss?" The operator was a wiry, ginger-headed man in uniform.

"Is this the right place for me to send a telegram?"

"Indeed, it is."

"Ah. How much do they cost?"

"That depends on the number of words used and where it's going. Britain, would it be?"

"Yes."

"Then the minimum is 5s 6d for the first eight words in the message, and a shilling for every word thereafter."

"That's very expensive… Why does it cost so much more for the extra words?"

With the resigned look of one who has explained the same matter countless times before, the operator replied,

"To send a telegram from a ship is expensive. The message is relayed through several systems before it reaches the recipient, and each system charges for its service. The ship's business is also conducted through the same systems, and so brevity in communication is highly desirable for all concerned. We must all share and share alike."

"That sounds fascinating, and I can see why you must have such a price scale. I wish I could learn more, but I'm sure you're too busy to answer my silly questions."

"I doubt very much they'd be silly questions, miss." Her interest visibly pleased the operator. Usually, his explanation did not completely banish the passenger's sour look over the cost, but only turned it into one of reluctant resignation. Here was a rarity. Someone who was actually understanding the shipping line's point of view. "I can spare you a minute. What would you like to know?"

"Are the same systems used no matter where the ship is in the world?"

"No, miss. From where we are now, we can communicate with the shore stations in Britain. All the North Atlantic is very well served, but our wireless transmission has limitations. A thousand miles is about our maximum range under the right conditions. We can, of course, send a message to another ship, who will then pass it on, but we only do that in an emergency. In other parts of the world, if we can't reach a British overseas station, we must rely on foreign services, and some of them are very slow."

"What type of messages does the ship receive?"

"Weather reports, announcements that might affect the Rangoon, messages from the owners or other ships, that sort of thing. Now some of it we get over the radio, but there's a lot of traffic by telegraphy."

"So, your work is vital to the ship's well-being?"

"Well, you know, you could say that." He looked abashed. "I'm just one of the crew, really."

"A very important one." Sophie beamed at him. "Now, tell me. If I sent a telegram today, when is the earliest it could reach its destination?"

"If I sent one for you now... Let's say the recipient is in an office in Central London, then they should get it mid-afternoon. The delay comes on the final leg, in getting the actual message into the recipient's hands. Now if the recipient has their own call sign, that's the letters which identify them within the service, then they'll have their own equipment. That telegram would be in the recipient's telegraphy room within an hour."

"Aren't modern advancements quite wonderful? Thank you. If I may, I'll take one of these." Sophie picked up a blank form. "I can see I'll have to keep my message to the bare minimum."

"When you're ready, miss, you just bring it back here, and I'll make sure it goes straight off."

"You're too kind."

"My pleasure, miss."

In her cabin, Sophie locked the door and set about deciphering Minkov's message. The translation from Morse to English went well, but the interpretation of English into something intelligible she found impossible. The message was addressed to Gavin Nuttall, 18 Garnet Road, Finsbury, London, and read as follows:

Unaccompanied enfreighted agreeable meeting urgentest redirect obliterate

She reviewed the Morse code to see if she had made a mistake. As far as she could tell, she had not. Sophie was familiar with one of the standard telegraphy codes used to shorten messages, but the words were unlike and, she assumed, did not conform to any of these other codes. It was English, and somewhat similar to the telegraphic language she knew journalists used in their messages, but she was not familiar with that, either.

Sophie began by adding faint commas to break the text into manageable parts, but soon erased them. She took a moment to clear her mind and think of the text logically.

Having seen Minkov receive a telegram, she knew he was replying to the sender, or he was informing another about the information he had just received himself. Gavin Nuttall would understand the message and was expecting to hear from Minkov. The message, then, was between parties who had prior knowledge of existing or expected circumstances and arrangements.

Next, she considered the word unaccompanied, and believed Minkov spoke of himself either by a plain statement or in answer to a question. Unaccompanied — no one travelling with him. That might be correct, but Sophie considered Minkov's antecedents. She knew nothing of him except he was a spy and his usual paymasters, according to Archie, were powers at enmity with Britain. Therefore, it was possible from his spying perspective, unaccompanied meant 'I'm not being followed.' *Oh, yes, you are*, she thought while grinning to herself.

Try as she might, she could not make sense of the rest, or derived too many possible meanings for anything to be useful. With the word 'obliterate,' she wanted to infer 'destroy this message' but was not definite about that interpretation. It became apparent she should quickly forward the message to Archie Drysdale so he could wrestle with it. At least he could find out about Gavin Nuttall, and that would go far to establish what the two men were doing. As this was the first telegram she had ever drafted, she carefully considered how she should express herself while encoding the message. It was most urgent — urgentest, even — to send it at once. She quickly composed the following, mindful of the cost:

Archibald Drysdale, Foreign Office, London.

Gavin Nuttall 18 Garnet Road Finsbury London received from observed following stop
Unaccompanied enfreighted agreeable meeting urgentest redirect obliterate

She foresaw a knotty problem. The telegraphist would transmit the same message he had sent only an hour earlier. It would raise questions in his mind — difficult ones for her to answer. Sophie wrote a fair copy on the form and set off for the Radio Room.

"Hello. It's me, again," said Sophie.

The operator turned around, then stood up, smiling.

"Do you have it ready?" he asked.

"I do. I totted up the number of words. There are nineteen, and so, per the rate scale, it should come to sixteen-and-six."

"Let's have a look, shall we?" He smiled once more, then counted. "It's twenty words, so that's seventeen-and-six."

"Nineteen, surely?" queried Sophie, who was not smiling now.

"No, twenty. See that number eighteen? You're charged for the one *and* the eight."

"But 18 is one number."

"They've always charged for each single number. Now, if you wrote in the word eighteen, then it's nineteen words."

"But that's ridiculous. Eighteen is much longer to send than the number 18, yet it's cheaper?"

"I don't disagree, but I must abide by the rules. Would you like to amend your message?"

"I certainly would."

She changed the text, then took out a pound note. He thanked her but returned her change in silence.

"Thank you," she said.

He was just turning away while studying the form when he stopped. The message had caught his attention. "Um…" It puzzled him, and he looked enquiringly at Sophie.

She put five shillings on the counter. He stared at the coins, then at her. Then he picked them up and cleared his throat. "No need to say any more. I'll get this off at once."

"Again, thank you."

She waited out of sight by the side of the opening. When she heard him tapping the Morse code for Archibald, she left.

Chapter 8

Sun, Sea, and Superstition

Day after day, the fine weather continued, and so it came to be taken for granted by the passengers aboard the Rangoon. The ship had entered the Channel the night before and it was now Friday, the thirteenth of May. If anyone considered it to be a day of ill-omen, they did not show it in public. Instead, the passengers were in that nothing-much-to-do frame of mind that descends on everyone, crew excepted, at the end of a long cruise and before the ship docks.

Along with walking under a ladder, or a black cat crossing one's path, so was a Friday the thirteenth superstitiously considered unlucky, even by the more rationally minded. The majority acknowledged the portent of the day even if they laughed off that anything bad could *possibly* happen. Owners of ladders and keepers of black cats consider neither unlucky. And the number of days in calendar months is a pure construct, completely unrelated to moon, sun, or season, thus rendering meaningless the numbering of a day as the thirteenth one. Therefore, nothing bad could *really* happen — so thought everyone, including Sophie.

It was, however, in the early morning of this Friday the thirteenth that Sophie, while descending the companionway to the foredeck, happy with the voyage, that it was nearly over, and with life in general, bumped into Todor Minkov for the first time just as he was ascending the same stairs.

"Ah, mademoiselle. We must not pass on the stairs today of all days." Minkov gallantly retreated to the bottom to allow her to come down.

Sophie became mute. A smile froze on her face. She gingerly put one foot in front of the other, believing herself about to fall while simultaneously thinking that her cover was blown and her real identity and intentions were apparent to him. Her position, she felt, was preposterous, which caused her to behave in sympathy with that feeling. For some unknown reason, she expressed herself in the arch-water nymph's manner, she who conducted the calisthenics class. At least acting out a deception gave her sufficient nerve to get through the ordeal.

"I am quaite superstitious myself," she started speaking upon reaching the last few stairs. "It is wayze to obsahve the powah of the day, mitigating by precaution any impending calamity wha-yre one can." She reached the deck. "I thank you, sah, for your *most* kind attention. Good day to you."

"Er, yes. Good day, mademoiselle." Minkov was bemused and his face showed it.

Instead of walking about the foredeck as intended, Sophie rushed back to her cabin, her face aflame. Uppermost in her mind was, *Why oh why, did I behave like such an idiot!?* Even once inside her cabin, it took a long time for rational thought to reestablish itself. There, she posed the question, *What must he think of me?* She answered, *That I'm a hideous fool.* She questioned herself again, *Will he recognize me at Dumond Hall?* To which she replied, *Minkov mustn't recognize me! That's all there is to that.*

At noon, the Rangoon drew abreast of the Isle of Wight. If there were no delays in Southampton Water, the ship would dock in two hours. An excited air of anticipation ran through the vessel. Passengers said their goodbyes to shipboard friends with promises of writing soon. Bags and trunks underwent the last stages of packing and errant items were hunted down. Forgotten was the serene idleness of the days and weeks of cruising — dispelled completely in those last feverish minutes. For some soon to disembark, especially those who had not seen Britain in years, the sight of the coast and the imminence of the homecoming made them quite emotional.

Sophie was becoming quite emotional with her suitcase, which refused to shut no matter how she tried. Her solution in the end was to carry two dresses and a nightgown carefully concealed within the coat she would carry. Fortunately, she had not the worry of the leather flying coat, because she had returned it to Yardley in Gibraltar.

The Rangoon waited in the bright sunshine, stationary at the mouth of Southampton Water, while the hands on a tugboat named Samson secured the ship's thick towing hawser. For large ships, the navigable channel leading to the harbour was narrow and required an experienced pilot with knowledge of the shoals to do the job safely. During this delay, and while passengers crammed the port side of the Promenade Deck knowing the ship would dock on that side, Minkov stood at the port rail between two lifeboats on the Boat Deck above, virtually hidden unless someone passed the gap he occupied. However, one person knew where he was. By standing on a lower step on a deserted starboard companionway, and with her line-of-sight inches above the deck, Sophie kept Minkov's lower legs under observation, which was only possible because the lifeboats were sitting in their cradles.

Despite her vigilance, all she discovered was that he had two pieces of hand luggage, his socks matched, his shoes were of excellent quality, and one turn-up of his summer trousers might be slightly wider than the other. All that was going into her report, and she recorded the details in War & Peace, which she had finished reading but still carried everywhere. Sophie believed that watching another person's stationary legs was, when considered as an occupation, too, too tedious for words. Suddenly, she had to crouch down lower because another man had come on deck. Without hesitation, the newcomer approached Minkov, and Sophie's eyes grew large.

They spoke, but she could not hear what passed between them. The newcomer was Foster, the man with whom Minkov daily sat at table. Foster looked around to see if anyone was about, and Sophie ducked down. When she re-emerged, Minkov had resumed his position while Foster was returning the way he had come, only now he carried a small case. She reviewed Minkov's legs and luggage. Minkov had given one of his cases to Foster. *What are they up to?* she asked herself.

Her own mission was about to end, yet now, with two people to follow, she sought for a way to get help. A telegram! She picked up her suitcase and rushed down to the Radio Room.

"Quick!" She set down her suitcase and coat. "I need to send a telegram." Sophie snatched a blank form and began filling it out.

The startled operator got out of his chair and came to the counter.

"You want to send a telegram?"

"Yes," said Sophie, a shrillness entering her voice.

"Sorry, but you can't, miss."

"Why? Because we're about to dock, or for some equally absurd reason?" She looked at him darkly.

"No, miss. I'd be happy to send your telegram, but there's something up with the system."

She looked at the alien apparatus behind the operator.

"Giving something a good thump might help," suggested Sophie.

"I wish it were just that. Radio's on the blink, as well, and the shore stations are having the same problems. Something's up with the atmosphere."

"What do you mean?"

"No one knows *what* it is, so I can't say. We're having to signal by semaphore to dock."

"Semaphore? Excellent! I want to send this message by semaphore." She waved the form. "Tell them it's *most* urgent."

The operator smiled. "I'm sorry, miss, but it can't be done."

"I'll speak to the Captain about this."

"He'll say no, even if you manage to get near him, which you won't. Should you get on the Bridge, they'd just escort you off again. If you were persistent, then they'd lock you in a cabin. Captains won't stand for any nonsense from the passengers."

"It is not *nonsense*, but a dire emergency."

"What emergency?"

"I can't tell you." Sophie straightened herself up and adjusted her sleeves. "Thank you very much for your help and please excuse my brusque manner. Goodbye."

"Goodbye, miss."

When she had gone, the operator opened a dictionary to look up the word brusque — a word he had never transmitted before.

At the dock, in the shadow of the Rangoon's hull, and inside the entrance of a cavernous shed where the passengers milled and surged, desperate to get away quickly, one of several Passport Officers seated at a row of tables asked Sophie questions.

"And this is the right address, is it, Miss King?"

"Yes," she said, even though she knew it was false. "I am in rather a hurry."

"I daresay you are." He answered with the disinterest of officialdom in action and went through her passport again. "Your passport was issued just over a week ago." He spoke accusingly. "The day after it was issued, you received a visa stamp from France and then Spain. That's on the same day, mind you. Today, you've just arrived here on the Rangoon, which came non-stop from Gibraltar." He was pleased with himself for noticing such things. "And yet... and yet there is *no* Gibraltar entry stamp." He gave her that 'I know you're guilty; I just don't know what the charge is yet,' type of look. "Would you mind explaining how all that is possible, Miss King?"

"Well, I went to France, then Spain, and then Gibraltar, and now, um, I am here." She was not sure if she had done something illegal, but she certainly felt as though she had.

"What did you do? *Fly?*"

"Yes."

He scowled at her and became more officious. "No, you didn't. I'd be obliged, Miss King, if you would answer my questions truthfully. There are serious consequences if you don't."

"I did answer truthfully."

He scowled again, then turned away abruptly. Sophie watched as he went to speak to another officer. She tried to quell the rising irritation she felt at this unnecessary delay. At any other time, she would have patiently endured the wait, but she had glimpsed Minkov ahead of her, and he was moving on to clear his luggage through customs.

The conference between the two officials seemed unduly long, and she felt the drag of every second. Next, unbelievably, a man dressed in a suit was brought into the discussion. The new man took her passport and looked at it, as they all did. He stared at Sophie; they *all* stared at Sophie. The man in the suit consulted a paper, nodded, then handed the document to the original officer, before resuming his unobtrusive position by an iron pillar.

"Everything seems to be in order," said the customs officer as if nothing had ever been the matter. He quickly stamped and returned her passport.

"Thank you," said Sophie.

"My pleasure... Next!"

Sophie, non-plussed but relieved, turned to go. She looked for Minkov in the customs shed. Instead, she spotted Foster close by, approaching another table where he was virtually waved through. The officer did not look at Foster's passport except to find the page in current use and stamp it.

"Excuse me!" Sophie called across an open table to the man in the suit by the iron pillar.

He was an older gentleman, precisely dressed, and looked surprised when hailed, but came over to her, nevertheless.

"Good afternoon, Miss King. Can I be of assistance?"

"Good afternoon, and yes, I trust you can." Sophie hoped what she was about to say did not sound strange. "Could you possibly recommend a good beer?"

The man made as if to answer, but a slight jolt made him pause. "My name is Canning. I'm from the Home Office. You must pardon me, but that is a code phrase with which I'm unfamiliar."

"Oh. Then how did you know to allow me through?"

"Your name was on my list of passengers who are not to be disturbed."

"I suppose I understand. Do you ever follow people?"

"I must apologize, but I can't answer that question."

"Then you do. That's very good. That man at the customs table over there. His name is Foster. I think he's very suspicious. Is he on your list?"

"I'm obligated to keep secret the names on my list."

"Then, just suppose, if he *were* on your list, and I'm not suggesting he is, but if he were, what could you tell me about him?"

"If he *were* on my list — again, I could say nothing... However, it is public knowledge that he's in the Diplomatic Corps."

"Mr Canning, in a single breath, you have proved yourself an absolute marvel of discretion while being tremendously helpful. Thank you. I'm very sorry to have troubled you."

"No trouble in the slightest. Goodbye, Miss King, and I wish you every success." He smiled.

Sophie rushed away with her suitcase and coat, hoping to catch up with either Minkov or Foster before they disappeared. At the Customs table, she spoke to a grizzled officer.

"Hello, I'm in a frightful rush. I have only the one little suitcase and, I assure you, there's really nothing of interest in it."

"If you would just put it on the table, please."

"Am I to open it? It's ever so difficult to shut. That's why I had to tie it with a rope — as a precaution against the case bursting open. It will be a lot of trouble to tie it up again."

"Could you untie the rope, please?"

"I could but... Oh, *very* well." She hauled the suitcase onto the table. "Why can't you take a person's word for what's inside? I'm obviously honest."

As she complied and started untying the knot, Mr Canning approached to speak privately to the Customs officer. The man frowned at the interruption. Then he ungraciously chalked her case.

"A thousand times, thank you." She spoke with heartfelt gratitude to Mr Canning. Then she rushed away.

Now she saw a curious thing — several curious things, and all at once. Minkov's luggage was being inspected with a fine-toothed comb by two customs officers. In sharp contrast, and because of his diplomatic immunity, Foster was cleared through customs without an examination. Sophie saw Foster was carrying the case given to him by Minkov, while a porter followed him through the shed with the rest of his luggage. As she watched, she noticed a man standing and reading a newspaper, as though oblivious to his surroundings. He, too, stood by a pillar, and this idle pursuit amid such an incessant whirl of activity struck her as very odd. But she had no time to investigate and so walked briskly to find a telephone. Just as she was about to leave, she looked back and was in time to observe the man with the newspaper casually fold it and move away. Out of the corner of her eye, she also noticed a supposed passenger stir and pick up his suitcases. She looked back again along the length of the shed. This time, she saw Minkov approaching. She now understood that agents were at the ready to follow him, and her part was truly over.

Directed to the nearby South Western Hotel, Sophie entered the glorious marble foyer. At the desk, and conscious of the carpet's thick pile, she asked,

"Where is your public telephone?"

"In the alcove behind you, madam," replied a smart and pleasant young man.

"Thank you. By the way, do you know if the telegraph is working?"

"No, it isn't. It's been out of commission for some hours. They say the atmosphere is to blame, although, whatever it is, it has done nothing to the telephones."

"Rather alarming, isn't it?"

"Very, madam, and we have never experienced the like before. Makes one wonder what's coming next."

"It most certainly does."

There were two wooden telephone booths. One was occupied, and she could see the outline of a seated woman through the opaque glass. The other was empty, but an elderly gentleman was unmistakably walking towards it. Sophie, rather ungraciously, she could not help but feel, made a dash to get in ahead — but this was an emergency.

"Oh, I'm terribly sorry," she said engagingly to the gentleman as she grasped the door handle. "I shan't be a moment." She stepped inside and shut the door, not daring to look at the man in case he was glaring at her, which he was. Flustered and feeling ashamed for being so rude, she laid out all her coins on top of the telephone directory.

It took some minutes, but she got through without a hitch to Archie Drysdale, who was at his flat. Sophie poured out her coded story as succinctly as she could, racing against the operator's continuing demands to put more money in the slot and before she ran out of coins. Archie had her confirm the details. The call ended and there was a penny left. With nothing more for her to do, she went to the station and, with a pound note, purchased a ticket to London.

Chapter 9

Scouting Party

In the brilliant early morning of Sunday, the fifteenth, Lady Shelling, Elizabeth, and Sophie set out in Rabbit and drove to Wiltshire. They started early in the morning because it would almost certainly be uncomfortably hot in the car by the afternoon. During Sophie's absence, the weather had continued warm and, although there had been several light drizzles, the otherwise relentless sunshine had put the land into a water deficit. While the early crops struggled, the grass, tall for silage, was still doing well, and so far the trees were untouched by the lack of moisture.

"At present, reading the weather report is worse than reading the obituary column." Aunt Bessie was sitting in Rabbit's back seat, staring at farmland. "No rain for the foreseeable future. How is a farmer to take news like that? Must be downright distressin' for them. The forecasters should add 'a chance of showers later' like they usually do. Whenever they say that, it always rains."

"They don't affect the weather, only forecast it," said Sophie, who was driving.

"Thank you for explaining that. I don't know *what* I'd do without you. Of course, they can't affect it, but they should consider their readership. Give a little hope, even if it is a chimera, to those who depend upon the weather to grow crops. No rain spells doom. A chance of rain gives the farmers a chance... I suppose it doesn't much matter in the end... Where are we now, Elizabeth?"

Sitting in the front passenger seat, Elizabeth had the map on her knees. "Thatcham is next, and Newbury right after it."

"Can you hear the bells?" asked Sophie. They were just discernible above the hum of the engine.

"Yes," replied Elizabeth. "They always sound their loveliest across open fields. May we stop a moment?"

"Are we to hold a service by the side of the road?" enquired Aunt Bessie.

"It's a delightful idea, Auntie."

Sophie stopped the car, and they listened through open windows. A warm breeze stirred the leaves of hedgerows and roadside bushes.

"Yes, quite spiritual," said Aunt Bessie. "I hope we can find an evening service at a suitable place. I hate missing church on Sunday. It makes me irritable all the week." She was quiet for a moment. "May I see the map, Elizabeth?"

She passed it back, and Aunt Bessie scanned it.

"Look at that. Havering-under-Lyme is not so very far away. If we just turned up at Henry's church unannounced, would it shock him out of his surplice and gaiters?"

"Although that sounds like an interesting experiment," said Sophie, "we unfortunately don't have the time." A little ruefully, she added, "I'm seeing much less of Father these days."

"Hardly unexpected with all the work you do. You're missing him, hmm?"

"Yes. I feel guilty about it, too. Although I'm relieved the new housekeeper takes such good care." Sophie restarted the engine, and they began moving.

"Can we go over the most recent murder once more?" she asked when the car reached its cruising speed.

"The newspapers were rather short on details," said Aunt Bessie, "either because the police know little or they prefer withholding information. Wilfred Munday was found dead in the road in the village of Wynbourne — dead from two bullet wounds in the back. For some inexplicable reason, he was already dead when conveyed to Wynbourne. The addle-brained maniac who left the body in the road fired two shots in the air. Clearly, they must be mentally deficient. Should I ever murder someone, I wouldn't dream of such absurdity as to alert the neighbours while I was still in the vicinity! However, that is what he or they did. The papers made a big fuss over it, claiming it to be a dastardly act and the greatest of mysteries, but now they've entirely dropped the story. Since the first big splash, there has been nothing. The police are pursuing their enquiries, and the press is now consumed with Emperor Hirohito's visit and commenting on Northern Ireland — as well as its latest preoccupation, of course, which is how the sun is trying to kill us all with its spots. I've never heard of anything so silly in all me life. The sun looks the same as it always has. What has sent the press mad, I wonder?"

"It is causing widespread disruption to the telegraph services," said Elizabeth.

"I can attest to that," added Sophie.

"Well, I can't see it. Because of their reckless reporting, they're making me think the sun is going to explode. We have enough to deal with without worrying about the sun incinerating us."

"Nobody is even suggesting it will do that, Auntie."

"Ah, but no one suggested the sun would destroy the telegraph system, yet it has, supposedly. When will they suggest the sun will explode? *After* it has happened? *Ha!* They'll be too late to stop the presses for *that* story."

"Do you really believe the sun is going to blow up?"

There was a long silence in the back of the car.

"No. But it starts one thinking, doesn't it? I prefer not to contemplate such a catastrophe, thank you."

"Of course, the sun won't blow up."

"I sincerely hope you are correct. Let us now talk of something else."

"Very well," agreed Sophie. "Why did the murderer — I'm assuming it was the murderer — fire two shots when he needn't? It only drew attention and, as you say, no one in his right mind would want to do that."

"As a warning?" ventured Elizabeth.

"To whom?"

"I suppose that depends upon who fired them. If it was one of the Eldred family, which would be logical, then I suppose the warning was directed to the Munday family. It is how they have always operated."

"Surely, the two bullet wounds in Wilfred Munday's back would have been ample warning. Why fire two shots in the air?"

"For the sake of the villagers, of course," said Aunt Bessie. "To keep 'em *all* cowed or to scare off someone in particular."

"Perhaps. Maybe it was done deliberately to involve the whole village."

"Only by now they'd be too frightened to say anything," said Aunt Bessie. "Having a dead body so callously dropped off in the road must have unsettled 'em no end. I'm sure I'd be outraged if it had happened in White Lyon Yard."

"Wouldn't you be frightened, Lady Shelling?" asked Elizabeth.

"Of what...? Oh, I see what you mean." She considered for a moment. "Not unduly. I know what I *would* do, though. I'd get on to the proper authorities and give 'em no rest, day or night, until they caught the wretched man. It's making me annoyed just thinking about the ineptitude of, of... *everyone!*"

"Changing to another topic," said Sophie, "We should stop in Newbury for petrol, and then lunch in Marlborough. How does that sound, Auntie?"

"Tolerable, tolerable... Provincial hotels are always risky, though. Either the meat is grey and anemic, or it looks like it fell in the fire and was forgotten. Then there is the matter of seasoning. However, today I shan't complain, I promise, as long as lunch is hot and edible."

They lunched in Marlborough, where Lady Shelling found no reason to complain and, therefore, kept her promise. Afterwards, they travelled west almost ten miles, and then turned onto a pretty country lane before reaching the drive to the house they wanted.

"Ooh, how lovely!" said Sophie, as an old three-gabled, three-storied, ashlar stone house covered in ivy came into view.

"Dot always complains about spiders, but she'll never cut back the ivy. The original vine is supposedly three centuries old... As old as the house."

"Have you stayed here before?"

"Several times, but only once since her husband died. That was in seventeen... The place hasn't changed at all."

Sophie parked the car near the double front doors, which were wide open.

"Is there anyone here?" she asked.

"She's bound to be in the gardens," said Aunt Bessie.

They got out and, leaving their luggage, mounted three semi-circular steps to enter what proved to be an exceptionally fine house. Beautiful, old paintings and rich carpets lined the dignified and well-proportioned hall.

"Hello!" called Sophie.

The house was silent, except they now heard someone in the drawing room making the unmistakable noises of waking up.

"It's only me, dear," said Aunt Bessie as she stepped to look into the room. "Oh."

In an old bent-legged and sumptuously upholstered Georgian wing-back chair that had seen better days, a huge Pyrenees Mountain dog yawned widely. The dog did not so much fit in the chair as drape himself over it.

"It's only Bernard," said Aunt Bessie.

"But wasn't that Mrs Callan's husband's name?"

"Yes, and that used to be his favourite chair. The dog claimed it after he died, so Dot started calling the dog Bernard. Originally, his name was Buccaneer."

While the dog and the people surveyed each other, a Yorkshire Terrier scampered into the hall, saw the visitors, growled, barked, and then ran off.

"I am not impressed by Dot's welcoming committee."

They followed the dog, and Bernard the Pyrenees joined them. The Yorkie, stopping occasionally, led the little party through the drawing room and out onto a wide flag-stoned patio bordered by a narrow lawn.

"What beautiful gardens," said Sophie.

The land gently sloped away from the house. In the foreground was a maze of tightly planted flowerbeds with winding paths. The beds were arranged to be viewed from the patio so that all the plants — from the smallest at the front to the tallest in the farthest beds — were visible. Many plants were in bloom but, as it was still May, the explosion of colour to come was yet a promise to be fulfilled.

"*Clear off!*" a woman shouted. She had a county accent and a strong and commanding voice, which boomed from among the shrubs to the right. A Dalmatian carrying a ball in its mouth streaked across the lawn in front of the patio, closely pursued by two cross-bred dogs. The Yorkie went after them, while the Pyrenees sat down.

"That's Dot," said Aunt Bessie. "She's in the Rose Garden."

To get there, the little party passed through an archway in a very tall privet hedge. Two scenes greeted their eyes. The first they expected: the loveliness of a well-tended garden of prize roses laid out in sinuous beds among old flagstone paths. Some plants were already blooming, but most were not. The second was that the secret garden was full of people, and they were all bending over.

"*Hello, Needle! Have you had your lunch!?*" Dot Callan, the only upright figure among the roses, shouted from the middle of the garden. The seventy-year-old lady walked towards them. Startling to both Elizabeth and Sophie, Aunt Bessie responded in like manner,

"*Hello, Dot! We had our luncheon on the way!*"

"Good!"

The woman striding towards them was sometimes more fully revealed as she passed by rose bushes which screened her. She was tall, wearing a battered straw hat that had holes in it. Her light-coloured, thin coat had been fashionable twenty years earlier, but now it was heavily stained. She wore trousers, a pair of heavy shoes, and a pair of large leather gauntlets. In one hand, she carried a lethal-looking pump sprayer.

"What are you all doing?" asked Aunt Bessie when she could attempt normal conversation.

"*Aphids.*"

"We're not on the other side of the garden now, dear."

"Sorry. I usually shout at the dogs, horses, and servants, you see. Bad form to shout at my guests." She primarily spoke to Sophie and Elizabeth. "I was out here in the morning and saw aphids on my Thisbe and Danae." She pointed to two different yellow rose bushes. "This hot weather is bringing everything out early, including aphids. I never work on a Sunday as a rule, but if a plague of biblical proportions is about to break out, then what can one do? So, I set all me staff to destroyin' the little beggars... Do any of you have aphids?" They all replied that they did not. "Then count yourselves fortunate. The earwigs are lively, too. But the slugs have gone and, touch wood," she put a hand on her head, "there's no mildew. I put that down to watering early in the morning instead of in the evening." She looked at each of her three guests. "Come on, Needle. Introduce us."

"This is my niece, Sophie Burgoyne."

Mrs Callan pulled off a gauntlet, then vigorously shook Sophie's hand while exchanging greetings.

"And this is Miss Banks. She is a researcher."

"Researcher, eh? That means libraries... What's your first name?"

"Elizabeth," she replied shyly.

"Well, Elizabeth, me library's in a shocking state. Needs cataloguing and all that business. Fancy having a go at it?"

"I, um..."

"I'll pay you, of course. Room and board thrown in and all that. What do you say?"

"Elizabeth politely declines your offer," said Aunt Bessie. "She's not here about your blasted library. There is a much more important matter for us to investigate."

"As you implied on the telephone. However, Elizabeth should speak for herself. My library is important to me, thank you."

"I'm sure it is, but..."

"Excuse me a moment," said Sophie, rather alarmed at this unexpected turn in the conversation. "Elizabeth provides me with her invaluable assistance. However, I would first like to hear her views on the subject of cataloguing your library. Then, it might be possible to come to some arrangement — *if* she is agreeable."

"Quite right," said Dot. "Do you know you're very much like your aunt? Isn't she, Needle?"

"Do you think so?" asked Aunt Bessie.

"Good heavens, yes. In looks, a little, but in manner and bearing, much. It strikes me that way even though we've only just met. And Sophie, don't mind me discussin' you like this. Take what I've said as a compliment, dear."

"Dot," said Aunt Bessie, "don't confuse the gel. She's already alarmed by our squabbling."

"Are you? Sorry about that. Ever since our schooldays, we've argued over the smallest things. It's just our way, you see."

Sophie smiled.

"Can I ask why you're wearing trousers?" asked Aunt Bessie. "They look dreadful."

"They do, but they're practical. These were Bernard's, but I altered them... The shoes were his, too, and they fit like gloves."

In drawing attention to the footwear, they all naturally stared down. Sophie and Elizabeth now discovered that Dot's feet were extraordinarily large. As if divining their thoughts, Dot said,

"I have all me shoes and boots custom made. Useless my going to a shoe shop and showing them these great plates of meat. It deranges the shop assistants, and they fuss so annoyingly. A bootmaker in Marlborough takes care of me normally but, when I found that Bernard's shoes fitted, I thought, why not? They'll do for the garden. I absolutely despise waste."

It occurred to Dot that she was the hostess, so she turned and shouted. *"Robert! Tea outside! Make sure everyone washes their hands!"*

"Yes, madam!"

As they went up to the house, a small pack of dogs joined them. Sophie counted eight. "How many dogs do you have?" she asked, as a golden retriever walked next to her.

"Eleven."

"Do they ever run off?"

"Rarely. They always come back if they do. I haven't lost one yet, and that's because they're not silly and know when they're onto a good thing."

In half an hour, Dot had changed into a frock and they were all now sitting on cushions in wrought-iron chairs at a table laid for tea on the patio. A yellow-striped umbrella shaded them from the afternoon sun.

"As we're settled, tell me now what all the secrecy is about," said Dot.

Sophie, with Elizabeth's help, explained the police interest in the recent murders in the Eldred-Munday feud. The one item she held back was that Burgoyne's Agency would be at Dumond Hall.

"Is this an official enquiry, or just you taking a keen interest?" asked Dot.

"I do work for the authorities occasionally, and it would be helpful if you could provide some information, but I am also very curious myself."

Dot looked enquiringly at Aunt Bessie, who added,

"Sophie must be sure that you won't repeat anything you hear today to anyone else. Likewise, she won't repeat anything you say unless it helps the police in their cases."

"Ahh... I understand now. I shan't repeat a word, but you're right to be cautious. I suppose this means you'll never tell me what you're up to. Is that right? It's very galling, not knowing."

"I'm sorry, but I can't. It's a standing order."

"Yes, of course, it is. But it's irritating, nevertheless. Could you, perhaps, tell me everything *after* you've finished investigating? Would you? Please?" Dot suddenly looked comically pathetic.

Sophie hesitated. "I don't see why not."

"Excellent! That's more like it. Fire away."

"What is the general opinion of the feud among the people you know?"

"Simple. Both families are barmy. They have to be, otherwise why do they kill each other? We're all used to it after a fashion, but it defies logic if you study it closely."

"Do you know any of the Eldreds or Mundays?"

"Not really. Some years ago, I was reasonably well acquainted with Lord Alan Eldred. I often saw him in church. He was very much the Victorian gentleman. After he went into a decline, I didn't see him until his funeral. Not that I saw him then, of course. Despite that, we're all certain that it was he who murdered Robert Munday in Cardiff. That was in, ah, in..."

"1881, I believe," said Elizabeth.

"Yes. That's it. 1881. Alan Eldred, he wasn't the viscount then, but he was in Wales when the shooting took place. And with Cardiff being in Wales, naturally, we all concluded that Alan killed Robert Munday. Bernard and I were not living here when this all took place, so I've got everything second hand. Having delved into it, I agree with the consensus."

"Why did he kill him?"

"Excuse me a moment." She stood up to shout at a dog. "*Stop it!*" The dog, caught in an indiscretion, slinked towards Dot and then lay down at her feet. "I have told you before that you do not do *that* on the flowerbeds. Go to prison. Go on." With head down, the dog hurried into the house. "I shall call you when I want you." She looked at the table. "We could do with some more tea, I think." Dot went to the door and shouted, "*Tea!*"

When seated again, she explained,

"You probably wonder why I shout all the time. I find it's the only way to get anything done in a timely fashion. Servants often dither, and there's nothing more irritating than when they stare at you like a fish out of water gasping for air. Do your servants dither, Elizabeth?"

"I don't have any."

"That's probably a wise choice. They're always getting the sniffles or wanting to get married or taking a day off to bury someone. I know these things happen, but my servants seem to revel in them. Combine that with the dithering or the lack of training for the younger ones, and what have you got? Poor service, and it comes at a steep price, too. First time I lost my temper with a servant it worked wonders. The household ran smoothly for several days afterwards. The change was so pronounced, I took to shouting all the time. Not in anger, I'll add, but only in the way sergeants do on the square ground. And I've never regretted it... Although, there is one drawback. Over time, the servants have lost the habit of thinking independently, so I must do all their thinking for them. In a way, that gives me an interest, and shouting is very good for the lungs. What do you do, Needle? Make caustic comments?"

"I would never shout at a servant in anger or otherwise," replied Aunt Bessie. "Nor would I describe my reprovals as caustic, but my comments are admittedly occasionally incisive."

"You make 'em wilt on the spot, no doubt."

"During the initial training period only. Once trained, my servants anticipate my needs more often than not."

"That's the *one* thing I'm missing. When you have servants, Sophie, make sure they don't get above themselves. No matter how you do it, you must be firm from the outset."

"Naturally, she will," said Aunt Bessie.

"I will bear everything you've said in mind," said Sophie, smiling diplomatically. "Returning to 1881, why did Alan Eldred shoot Robert Munday?"

"We all believe there was a woman behind it. Both men were courting the same girl from a local family and Eldred got knocked out of the running when Munday took an interest. Anyway, rumour has it that Robert Munday took the girl off to Cardiff. That doesn't strike me as particularly romantic, but it's only a theory after all. No one has actual knowledge because, even back then, no one had anything much to do with either family. Subsequently, the girl pushed off somewhere and was never heard from again. Those are facts. Of course, speculation ran rampant and, many assumed, there was a child. But as I say, that's only talk, and no one has ever investigated the matter. I doubt even the police did. Anyway,

Alan Eldred got away with murder — of that part, most are certain — although I cannot bring myself to believe he would ever do such a thing. Still, somebody did, and he's the obvious candidate, I must admit."

Sophie nodded slowly. "Would it be possible to find out the girl's name?"

"Is that important?"

"I don't really know. It might be. I suppose she would have married long ago, or she might be dead."

"But Alan Eldred is dead. He can't be brought to book."

"That's true, but it's an avenue of enquiry which might lead to something else."

"Rather you than me. I believe the Dowager Marchioness of Calne will know."

"Maggie Gaines?" said Aunt Bessie. "That's right, she's your neighbour. But she must be in her eighties."

"Eighty-three. Her mind's still sharp, though, but her attention often strays. I see the poor old gel once or twice a month to cheer her up. Actually, I'm about due for a visit... Here's an idea. Why don't Needle and I ride over there tomorrow? I know you two are busy so *we* can get that information and save you the bother. What do you say, Needle? Can you still throw a leg over a horse?"

"Better than you can, I suspect, but, if you recall, I ride side-saddle. I would enjoy seeing Maggie again. The last time I met her was all of twenty years ago."

"Don't be disappointed if she doesn't remember you. She might not. Maggie's good at remembering the distant past, and understands all points under discussion if you go slowly for her, but ask about last week and her mind's a total blank. Be warned."

"I'd be grateful if you could find out the girl's name," said Sophie. "Thank you."

"No need to thank me. I thrive on this sort of stuff, just as much as Needle does. Anyway, Maggie's me next-door neighbour, or rather the Marquess of Calne is, with his six thousand acres. That's him there." She pointed towards the back of her estate at a range of low rolling hills. "We'll have to ride all the way round to the house because he's touchy about people crossing his land. I have a few stories about *him*, let me tell you. Which reminds me. We haven't seen each other in a while, Needle. Surely you must have some new and exciting stories?"

"Dozens," said Aunt Bessie with significance, but glancing briefly at Sophie. "Why don't you come to stay at White Lyon Yard for a few days, Dot?"

"I'd like that very much. Although, it would have to be next month."

"Then why not do this? Come for Chinese Night. I always have it the third Thursday in the month."

"You're still keeping that up? What a splendid idea. It will be just like old times. Tell me, how is Cowie these days? Is she speaking again?"

"Sadly, no. If there had been any change, I would have written to you. I believe she's very content within herself. Happy, I dare venture to say. She'll be most glad to see you, though. But let's discuss all that later, dear. I believe Sophie has more questions."

"Only a few more. For the 1920 murder in Scotland, the police cannot place Pascoe Eldred near the scene. In fact, he has a solid alibi. What do your friends say?"

"Pascoe did it. We don't know *how*, but it can't be anyone but him. Now, it's possible he arranged for a thug to do the work, but he's involved, of that we're all certain."

"And what about Bartholomew Munday? Pascoe Eldred was in London when the murder occurred, and he says he was in his hotel room when it took place. Although two members of the hotel staff say they saw him, there is an interval between their sightings just sufficient for him to leave the hotel, travel, commit the murder, and return. The police were quite exhaustive in their enquiries, but nothing further has turned up to put Pascoe in the vicinity, so their hope is waning in that direction."

"If he slipped in and out of the hotel unseen, well, there you are. Pascoe murdered Bartholomew."

"Thank you. That leaves Wilfred."

"Yes, him, too. Obviously, Pascoe is a lunatic, although he looks nothing like one. It's really too bad, because he's put the whole feud out of synchronization. It should be an Eldred, then a Munday, an Eldred, and so on. Pascoe keeps killing Munday gentlemen one after another, and that's all wrong. He's not playing the game. Furthermore," Dot's manner became quite intense to the point of outrage, "the murder took place right *here*. He's broken the long-standing tradition that all the deaths must take place somewhere else. He is a shy, retirin' type and to look at you would think there's nothing wrong with him, but there has to be. I will say this in his favour. He's an excellent farmer, but he's gone too far, and something must be done."

"I understand he's the last of the line," said Aunt Bessie.

"Viscount Eldred has a young son, aged thirteen," said Elizabeth. "The title becomes extinct should he die without issue."

"Are there no distant relations?" asked Dot.

"None that I could discover, Mrs Callan. I suppose a lawyer might find someone through other means, such as advertisements. According to the public records, I can definitively state there are no more official male relations to be found."

"Then are we to infer," said Aunt Bessie, "that he intends destroying all the Mundays before they get to him?"

"Isn't it ghastly?" said Sophie. "There seems to be no other motivation for this sudden spate of killings. As far as you are able, Mrs Callan, can you say what produced the sudden change in him?"

"Call me, Dot, Sophie dear. You, too, Elizabeth. Everyone does. Eldred is bankrupt or so close to it there's no difference. Successive death duties have finished the family, and farming is barely profitable at the best of times. It can never restore fortunes. We all agree that it is only a matter of time before the crash. That's what has sent him loopy."

"Loopy? Where did you pick up such a low term?" asked Aunt Bessie.

"The young people are all saying that sort of thing these days. I find it amusin', so don't go picking on me."

"If you choose to have no respect for the English language, that is your affair, but you should at least consider your guests' sensibilities."

"Oh, utter tosh. That's slang, and a term you used at school."

"Only because it was necessary to utter something once you had finished speaking."

"Ha! There's no point in arguing with you. I always came off the worst."

"You seem to mix with a broad cross-section of society," began Sophie. "Who are your sources of information? I don't mean names, of course."

"A great deal is through horse and dog-owners. Common interests, you see. Bernard was a self-made man. Never got a title. Never even considered for one, but he did very well. When we first moved down here, we were outsiders. We got to know our neighbours through riding with them at the various events, and talking about dog-breeding. Naturally, because of rank, one soon got put in one's place. Not by all of them, mind you. Some with titles were very friendly, but others... Well, they like to look down on everyone else. I attribute it to their feeble-mindedness and you can't do anything with someone if they're dense. By accident, I discovered a secret weapon that opened the doors to all the big houses and the most reserved of families, as well as those of the policeman and the milkman."

She paused, expecting to be asked what it was.

"What secret weapon was this?" asked Sophie, obligingly.

"I'll tell you. When I was planting out the Rose Garden, I ran into several difficulties. I cast about looking for help and couldn't find any. I ended up corresponding with a few people, and one of them was the Reverend Pemberton. Helpful fellow and absolutely devoted to roses. We became friends, and I've visited his garden in Romford several times. Bernard wasn't at all keen on gardening, so it was rewarding for me to find someone so sympathetic. I got to meet Mr and Mrs Bentall, the lovely couple who assist him. The Reverend has a commercial nursery now. The Bentalls work there, and we frequently exchange letters, and have done so for years.

"During these exchanges, and without really meaning to, I became something of an expert on roses. Now, I'm considered the leading rosarian authority in these parts. Some people call me Lady Rose. How about that?" She leaned forward in her chair. "What you probably don't realize, and I certainly didn't at first, is this: having expertise in gardening throws open all doors. All doors! Everyone grows roses, and they all regard me like some kind of Delphic oracle. Literally, I can drop in to anyone's house, anytime I please, and ask, 'How are your roses doin' today?' and they'll treat me like royalty. Quite astonishin' when I consider the effect. Therefore, anyone in possession of a rosebush and who's inclined to talk becomes a source of useful information. Believe you me, nearly everyone who has a garden has roses."

"How remarkable," said Sophie.

"It's the perfect situation for anyone who enjoys scandal and gardening, which I do."

"Here's something I've been wondering about, Dot," said Aunt Bessie to her friend. "Are there Munday and Eldred party supporters?"

"You'd best believe it, and never the twain shall meet."

"Which is the bigger faction?"

"Do you know I've never really given it much thought? Amongst the upper class, I would say there is an even division, but there's a third faction, which is entirely neutral.

Doesn't want to know. With the middle-classes, it's much different. The Mundays have always been well off, and their wealth has come through trade and business ventures. Possession and the spending of money attract the middle classes like flies. Viscount Munday has strong support among them because he spends money. He's always doing something with the estate... He's quite liberal in his spending, as his forefathers were, and he gets involved in local matters. That type of behaviour carries a lot of weight with the local business and professional classes.

"Conversely, I imagine Pascoe Eldred has the best support among the other farmers who like him because he's devoted to the land. I've heard he deals fairly with those whom he employs. They're extremely loyal to him."

"Can people really support either family when they are murderers?" said Sophie. "I'm finding this all quite incomprehensible."

"One would. I know I certainly did at first. But the feud is a tradition of such long-standing, we all take a sort of pride in it. I know that may sound ridiculous, but it's true. You really need to live here and see how everyone else reacts to the ongoing saga... I suppose it's about fitting in — for me and Bernard it was, anyway. Once one attempts to accept the feud as normal, it then soon becomes just another feature of life in these parts. I even think the Eldreds and Mundays believe they're expected to murder each other, so they oblige us. Strange, isn't it? But it's what we do."

"May I ask a question?" said Elizabeth.

"Of course, dear. What is it?"

"The original grievance between the families was over the Tongue. Is that land still of any significance?"

"I don't think so. Certainly, no one ever mentions it. You may find this interesting, however. When the Mundays built the original Dumond Hall, they were desperate to buy more land. They farmed back in the eighteenth century, as everyone did. However, the Marquess of Calne owned land around

Wynbourne and was looking to buy more. Across the River Kennet, Burdett at Ramsbury Manor had his estate and wouldn't sell off any. Then there's Savernake Forest. The Brudenell-Bruces would never part with any of their forty-thousand acres. In effect, Wynbourne has always been ringed around by peers of higher rank holding large tracts of land. This hemmed in the two viscounts and prevented expansion.

"At one time, Viscount Munday, while the family was interested in farming, offered to buy the Eldred estate. Viscount Eldred refused. After that, the dispute over the Tongue began with much ill-feeling on both sides. As the acquisition of more land was out of the question, every square foot they possessed became so much more valuable. It was rather dim-witted of them but, once pride is involved, there's no tellin' how far a thing will go. This dispute produced a lot of ill-will that neither family could nor would set aside. When the duel at Kew took place and after Susanna took her revenge, well, it just all got put into one enormous ball of stupidity that's rolled along ever since."

Dot's audience was quiet for a few moments. Elizabeth wrote some notes.

"What happened to Susanna in the end?" asked Aunt Bessie.

"Despite her being a murderess, we all rather admire her. At least, the women do. She has a long and fascinating history of her own. Travelled Europe, married, and lived to be ninety. She even got caught up in the French Revolution. We know so much because she had a lifelong correspondence with a lady friend living in Marlborough. Susanna had to leave England because she was on the run, or at least she believed she would be arrested and charged. Marvellous stuff, eh? I'll tell you everything when I'm up in London."

"Did she kill anyone else?"

"Needle! You surely don't expect me to spoil a riveting story, do you? Just be patient."

Dot abruptly got up, which caused instant alertness among the lazing pack of dogs, except for the Pyrenees.

"I must see what the servants are up to in the Rose Garden. If I don't tell 'em to stop looking for aphids, they'll be out there bending over all night, and we'll get no dinner or breakfast."

She walked away with the dogs following.

Chapter 10

The Swan by the River

It rained during the night. Not the desired soaking rain bringing two gentle inches of water to start the land's regeneration, but only a relieving quarter-inch. It was most welcome, but it only prolonged the precarious situation, stretching further the already strained hopes of those who depended on the weather for their livelihood.

The morning was a glorious one — smelling and looking fresh, with the earth dark and damp, the plants rejuvenated, spider webs and leaves glistening with droplets, and the sun pleasant, warm and friendly in a clear blue sky. On the surface, spring was reaffirmed, along with the hope that growth might now continue again to fruitfulness.

Sophie and Elizabeth made an early start. The empty Sunday roads had transformed into those of a rural Monday — alive with their real purpose, wherein patience was not a virtue but a necessity. Several times Sophie had to bring Rabbit to a standstill, variously caused by a flock of sheep in a narrow lane, a reluctant bull being ineffectually cajoled to cross the road from one field to another, and the inevitable slow-moving carts and wagons — impossible to pass until they turned off or the road widened sufficiently.

Dot Callan had mentioned several things the previous evening, entailing that the search for public records would be wider than anticipated. The two researchers began in Marlborough, although they would now have to visit two other towns.

In the old cottage library on Silverless Street, Sophie was careful to preserve her anonymity, allowing Elizabeth to do all the talking. It came as a pleasant surprise to hear the normally shy Elizabeth emphatically stating what she wanted in the way of information. It was apparent that Elizabeth, now deep among the back issues of newspapers, did not need her help in the slightest. So, at a little after ten, Sophie left Marlborough for Wynbourne. She had the idea of investigating the most recent crime scene. Although risky, she believed she would look sufficiently different as a maid at Dumond to how she looked now, her hair loose and wearing a stylish sun hat. No one surely could connect the two seemingly entirely different persons. Unable to think of anything more useful to do, her logic became irrefutable.

The direct and scenic routes from Marlborough to Wynbourne are, in fact, one and the same road, which is about two miles long, unless the County Council has done some digging at Mildenhall and rendered the bridge unusable, which it had. The also scenic but indirect route proved to be five miles long. Sophie received rather sparse and dubious directions, given with great certainty from the man in charge of the burrowing operation, who added, when questioned, that they would finish the roadworks in a couple of days. She doubted that was true and set off, got lost, of course, but not too badly. Hampered by not knowing her exact location because the roads were unmarked, she began thinking she might now be trapped within the same set of country lanes for the rest of her days. She brought Rabbit to a screeching halt.

"Parrish Row." Sophie read the sign at a turn and remembered an address in the police files. This was where the Eldreds lived. "Surely, this can't be another dead end." She put Rabbit in gear and set off in this new, more promising direction. The car skimmed along between the hedgerows and her hopes grew as she neared Capel House because the lane widened. She passed the drive but could not see any building. The road ran northward down a gentle slope and, at a bend, she caught a partial glimpse of Capel House. She instantly liked the place but drove on so as not to be noticed.

Soon, she reached Wynbourne and found herself at the northern end of the village and by the church at the junction with Loxie Lane. This was the murder scene or, as she quickly corrected herself, the place where Wilfred Munday's body had been found in the road and where the shots were fired. She was reluctant to drive over the spot, not that she knew exactly where it was. She parked Rabbit and got out.

A quick search around and about revealed nothing. She had not really believed it would, but there was always a hope. What she then did was to drink in the pastoral scene. The small, squat-towered Norman church sat on a slight prominence, and Sophie stood to look out over the verdant and usually fertile country from beneath the shade of an ancient beech by the church's stone boundary wall. In every direction were fields, hedgerows, and trees. A line of exuberant growth like a green divide marked the track of the River Wynnet as it flowed north to the Kennet. A bumble bee seeking nearby blooms passed close to her face. The soft breeze barely stirred the leaves overhead. Swifts, swallows, finches flying... A noise in the village beyond the bend... A lowing cow somewhere. The beautiful scene etched itself into her memory. This was no place for a body to be discarded in the road. It was a sacrilege to both the deceased and this calm corner of creation. She shook her head, amazed that anyone could devise such a thing.

Outside The Swan public house, Ben and Fred sat in their customary places on the settle.

"Reporter, no doubt," said Fred, as Sophie's Austin Twenty pulled up some little distance away.

"How'd he get here when the Mildenhall bridge be closed?" asked Ben.

"They be a tenacious lot."

"Who'm be tenacious?"

"Reporters."

"I hope you're roight and he *is* a reporter. They're ain't been none through here for nigh on a week."

"I *know* it. So, look sharp, and we'll get pints a piece out of this'un."

"That's roight. Hold back the juicy bits until he's a-slavering for 'em."

Like a pair of hawks, they watched the car.

"Can't be a reporter," said Ben. "He's a woman."

"But they do have female reporters."

"No, they don't."

"Yes, they do. They writes them household hints, society columns, and beauty articles. That type o' thing."

"That's not real reportin'... We won't get no beer now."

"No. Our prospects be dimmed."

The old men stared unabashedly at Sophie as she looked about the village. She noticed and then approached them.

"She'll have lost her way," said Fred.

"Reckon she's a lady? Driving a car an' all."

"S'pose she might be. Here she comes."

Ben and Fred touched their caps when Sophie drew level and stopped.

"Good morning, gentlemen. I hope I'm not disturbing you?"

"Oh, no, ma'am. You not be a-disturbin' us," said Ben. "Would you be lost?"

"Fortunately, not anymore," Sophie laughingly replied. "You see, I'm very interested in that dreadful occurrence of ten days ago. Did you see anything of it?"

Sophie knew who they were and had read through the summary of their depositions in the police files.

"Well, you moight say that we saw the whole thing, from start to finish," said Fred.

"Is that so? Although dreadful, it must also have been fascinating for you. I'm very interested in the story."

"Are you, ma'am?" said Ben. "You wouldn't, by chance, be a reporter?"

"I am."

"So, you're not a lady with a title," said Fred. "Is it a Lunnun paper you work fer?"

"Yes. It's the Park Lane Herald," said Sophie, creating a newspaper on the spot. "Have you heard of it?"

Fred shook his head, while Ben said, "I think I have."

"It'll be a hot one again today," opined Fred.

"Gives one a mortal thirst," said Ben.

The two old men stared at her unblinkingly.

"Ah, I see. You want to trade information for beer. Is that what the other reporters do?"

"The better ones," said Fred.

"What is the going rate?"

"You'm be going about it all wrong," said Ben. "We don't barter loike that. A reporter fills our glasses, keeps us supplied as long as we keep swillin' and talking, then gives us a pint as a farewell gesture. That's how it be done."

"Why'd you go tellin' her that? You make it sound loike we're boozers when we're not."

"Gentlemen, let us come to terms before we go any further. I'll buy you half a pint each for the sake of the warm day. Here's a shilling." She held out the coin. "You tell me everything you know, and then I'll give you half-a-crown. Mind, you must answer all my questions to the best of your ability. What do you say?"

"Um..." Fred wanted to hold out for more.

"Agreed," said Ben, who took the shilling. "What'll you 'ave, ma'am?"

"Actually, I'm Miss Brown, and I'll have a milk stout, please. The smallest bottle possible, because I shan't drink it all." Sophie loathed beer, but she had to show willing.

"T'ain't but the one size. My name's Ben Tubb, and this be Fred Gardner. Find a seat, miss, and I'll be roight back."

A few minutes later, Sophie found herself with a pint bottle. Sipping from the inch of liquid she had poured into the glass, she was confirmed in her opinion that she really did not like beer, although the milk stout was not now quite as bad as she had remembered it to be.

Ben and Fred told the story between them. It included everything in their statements plus embellishments, emphasis, significant pauses, and minor disputes between the two tale-tellers, because while the facts remained few and rather dry, the event itself was of great significance to the old men. The narrative had expanded with each performance they had given to reporters visiting the Swan. Ben and Fred's story had begun its literary journey as a single short police statement, which they had both signed. The version Sophie received was of epic proportions, delivered as only could be told by two old country boys — ones with nowhere to go, nothing else to do, and beer in their glasses. By the end, Fred had dozed off, and Sophie, pencil and notebook in hand, nearly had, too.

"How fast was the car travelling?" asked Sophie.

"Normal, loike," said Ben. "Not fast, fast, if that's what you mean."

"Very good. Now the passenger. You say you didn't recognize him, but did he do anything? Was he talking, for example, or moving?"

"I didn't notice him doing nothing. All he done was stare straight ahead."

"So, the car crossed that bridge. Lord Eldred was driving, and you saw him clearly, but the passenger didn't turn his head or make any other movement. Was there anything in or beside the road in front of them attracting their attention?"

"No. 'Twas clear. And it's no good waking Fred to axe him, 'cause his eyes are worse than mine. He wouldn't have noticed if there wor a pig in the front seat."

"His eyes are quite bad?"

"Oh, yes."

"What about your eyesight?"

"Everythin's a blur at a distance. Middlin' distance is good, though, but I struggle now to read the printed word. I can read my bible outside in the day, but not b'candle, an' it's the evenin's when I loike to read. That's hard to do in the winter."

"I am sorry to hear that."

"No, don't you be sorry, Miss Brown. Enjoy all your gifts while you 'ave 'em, 'cause you never know when they'll go. We're all given a portion o' loife an' good health, an' then comes the hereafter. It's the same for all, whether king or pauper. There's no point a-moanin' or a-frettin' when your strength goes." He took a sip of beer. "But here's summat that bothers me. If you'd told me the day before that Lord Eldred would do down a fellow-being loike that, I'd 'ave laughed in your face, that I would. I took him for a sober, decent man, quiet, and one to be respected."

"Interesting... In the feud, which side do you support?"

"Well, Fred's for the Mundays, and I'm partial to them because they're liberal in their ways, and not stingy loike some. Not that the Eldreds were ever stingy, but now they've lost all their money. But it's loike this. I respected Lord Eldred. I thought he wor above all the feudin'. Very disappointin'. And for what do they feud? A strip o' land that neither has ever had the use of. It don't make no sense."

Sophie could see that the warmth, beer, and extended conversation was also taking its toll on Ben. Before he really started to ramble, she thought it best she should take her leave, but she still had a couple of questions.

"Have you considered why Lord Eldred should have come down Loxie Lane when he lives on Parrish Row?"

The question revived the old man. "That's roight! He wouldn't do that."

"Are the two roads connected?"

"Yes. By Chopping Knife Lane, but it's a long way round. Though if walking, there be other paths to take."

"Would it be fair to say that Lord Eldred stopped at Dumond Hall to collect Wilfred Munday?"

"Had to be that, though it don't seem roight."

"How could he collect Wilfred if he had been dead for an hour, as the police surgeon reported?"

"I just dunno how that's possible. They never do visit the other's place but once a year, turn and turn about."

"There had to be two sets of shots, Mr Tubb. The signal in the village you heard. And the fatal shots fired an hour before. Did you hear any shooting earlier?"

"No, nothin'."

"What about loud noises? Were there any that might mask the sound of pistol shots?"

"No... No... 'Cep' for Farmer Cordery's tractor — noisy contraption. He has an arrangement with Lord Munday to grow crops in his fields. That day, he wor up at Dumond a-diggin' a new drainage ditch and used his tractor, but that wor, lemme see... two hours afore I saw the car. Heard the tractor from my cottage."

"And for how long was Farmer Cordery using his tractor on the Munday estate?"

"Had to be a good hour."

"Oh."

"Does it matter?"

"No, I don't think so," said Sophie, hastily recovering. "I doubt our readers will be interested in Farmer Cordery's workday. Answer me one more question before I leave. How did you *know* it was Lord Eldred driving?"

"I just knowed... Arrh, that's it. I remember now. He always wears a straw trilby. Only man who does hereabouts. I've always admired the shape of it, but a cap suits me foine. He was wearing his trilby that day, as he always does, and I'll take my oath on that in court *if* an' when they get around to arrestin' him."

"Thank you *very* much. Say goodbye to Mr Gardner for me when he wakes up. He really should go inside to escape sunburn."

"He be 'ardened to it, but I'll allow him another quarter hour, then give him the nudge, loike." Ben stood up, removed his cap, and received a half-a-crown from Sophie. "Goodbye, Miss Brown. And on behalf of the village of Wynbourne, thank you for stoppin' and takin' such an interest."

"And I thank *you*, Mr Tubb. This most illuminating interview has been entirely my pleasure. Goodbye."

He remained standing to watch her get in the car and drive off. He mumbled to himself, "Illuminatin'... How about that?"

In two days, Sophie and Elizabeth had discovered nothing very useful. They considered three female Eldred relations as candidates for having committed the murder, but only one, a second cousin, was in any degree capable of carrying out such an undertaking. She was married with young children and, although she only lived ten miles away, was, according to Dot Callan, not on close terms with Lord Eldred. Even so, it was hard to see where she would fit in.

Elizabeth collected numerous small details, confirmed many facts, and thoroughly searched back issues of local newspapers covering several critical dates of the feud. Although there was much of interest, the papers yielded no information on the whereabouts or activities of the Eldreds or Mundays which might tie in with any of the slayings.

Lady Shelling and Mrs Callan rode over to visit Maggie Gaine, Dowager Marchioness of Calne. Aunt Bessie barely recognized the frail, bright-eyed woman. The marchioness did, however, remember Aunt Bessie. She also recalled the name of the young woman courted by the two men in 1881 — Frances Harding. Sophie held little hope that anything useful would emerge from investigating her, even if she were found and interviewed. Elizabeth was privately looking forward to the test of her skills in tracking down someone lost to sight for forty years. She could not wait to get started.

Chapter 11

Waterloo to Wynbourne

On Wednesday morning, 18th May, 1921, a train left Waterloo station. It clanked, belching steam and dark smoke as it picked up speed to begin its journey across southern England, heading for Marlborough. The passengers, elevated by the train traversing an embankment, often had unimpeded views across London. The clarity of the vistas was made possible by the brilliant, cloudless sky and because no household was burning coal, there being no need on account of the warmth of the morning.

Through the window, Sophie found herself more interested in the minutiae of the view than the sweeping panorama. Odd and unusual scenes presented her with secret knowledge of a few seconds' duration. In one, a woman hung out her washing on a clothesline in a grimy, barren back garden. Long since habituated to the passing of trains so close by and high up, she nevertheless dauntlessly displayed the family's garments and underwear for the inspection of hundreds, maybe thousands, of people every wash day. In another scene, a man at a desk in a corner office was on the same level as the train. He stood out sharply — hunched over while absorbed in his work. Sophie could see him behind a tall, narrow window while a second window formed an illuminating backdrop. He appeared to be working in the open air, almost floating, but he was gone before she could study him further. Then came a succession of yards, stables, houses, schools, shops, but all seen from an unusual angle which revealed the hidden, scruffier side — a presentation of utilitarian, decayed or prosaic glimpses wherein most people lived and worked. She found the passing, minor spectacles absorbing.

"Do you think there will be any danger?" asked Douglas Broadbent-Wicks, the only man present in the party of four. He had shaved off a recently cultivated beard so that he could serve as a footman. The group sat together at the end of a carriage, which was only a third full.

"No, I don't think there will," said Ada. "They're all busy killing *each other* off, so why would that be dangerous for *us*? Now, if they start shooting willy-nilly at the Fête… Well, that's another matter."

"Both families must have nasty minds," said Flora. "People who shoot others in the back are the lowest of the low."

"It's disgustin'," said Ada. "And they've been at it for years. How do they live with 'emselves?"

"The feud has become the tradition of both families," said Sophie, turning her gaze from the window. "Whether or not they like it or agree with it remains to be seen. I can only assume they see murder as murder, as we all do, but when a member of the rival family is the target, they certainly seem able to suspend that sensibility. Instead, their considerations are justice, revenge, and family honour… What puzzles me the most is that there seems to be no end in sight to the conflict."

"It is my firm belief they should all get into a boxing ring, have at it until there's only one left, and then the feud can be declared over. That would be an end to it," said Broadbent-Wicks, smiling. "Miss King, you said you were going to bring us up to date on the train."

"Thank you, Mr Broadbent-Wicks. I will do so now, since you ask." Sophie peered along the carriage, judged the distances of the passengers and their likelihood of hearing what she was about to say, then modulated her voice accordingly — to that just above the noise of the rattling train.

"We have been invited into Dumond Hall through the police. Both the housekeeper and butler were willing, before this most recent murder, to aid them in preventing further bloodshed. You must understand, they are loyal to the Munday family, but have concluded that the feud should stop. I'm persuaded they are for the Mundays, of course, so they hope the police will arrest Lord Eldred. We must take a broader view and not become partisan ourselves. All the adults are under suspicion to some extent because of the imminent potential of retaliation, and so we shall report on all of them. Superintendent Penrose was quite insistent on that point. As far as the butler and housekeeper are concerned, they will give us a free hand within the confines of our service. They will not aid us in any degree beyond their allowing us in the house, as they do not wish to be disloyal. I understand the butler is the prime mover in this, and the housekeeper was reluctantly persuaded."

Sophie leaned to one side to glance along the carriage again.

"A gentleman of specific interest is Todor Minkov, a Bulgarian. Without going into details, he is a spy, a free-lancer of long-standing, who typically works for governments in opposition to Britain's interests."

"Was that the chap you were following on the ship?" asked Broadbent-Wicks. "I say, that was dashed resourceful of you, Miss King."

"It was hardly resourceful, as you put it. I simply observed and recorded his activities while remaining unobserved... except for one unfortunate incident."

"Ooh," said Flora. "Do tell."

Sophie saw the expectancy in their faces and caved in, succinctly explaining the accidental meeting.

"So, you used a put-on accent?" asked Flora. "Go on, do it now."

"Absolutely not. I found the entire episode rather embarrassing and prefer to move on, thank you."

"Spoilsport. But what if Minkov recognizes you?"

"I don't think he will, because I'm dressed very differently now. My hair is tied back and my conduct, while a servant, will be vastly changed from that of a ship's passenger. Then there is my voice. I'll make sure I don't look at him directly, so I will be as unlike my shipboard persona as I can be. I think I'm safe, as long as I'm careful."

"I'd recognize you anywhere, no matter what you looked like," said Broadbent-Wicks. "I think Minkov will, too, unless there's something wrong with him."

Sophie was dumbfounded, hesitant to speak, yet alarmed where things might lead if she remained silent.

"Mr Broadbent-Wicks, I value your comments if they contribute to the success of the mission. Please first consider what you say and, if it is helpful, say it. If it is not, don't."

"But Miss King, I *was* being helpful. I think he'll recognize you. As I said, I certainly would. I mean to say, is that not helpful to the mission? Pointing out a danger, don't you know? I think it is."

"That is *your* opinion. What do you say, Nancy? Is there a danger?"

"I wouldn't have said so, miss. But we should take steps just to make sure."

"Such as?"

"A disguise. Wear a wig and a pair of those blue-tinted glasses," said Flora.

"Don't be ridiculous, Gladys. That would just draw attention, as if I'm deliberately hiding myself. He's a spy, so he would become curious and then suspicious. Anyway, a servant can't do that without setting off an explosion in the servants' quarters."

"But Mr Broadbent-Wicks is right in a way," said Ada. "Once, of a winter's evening, me Dad was standing at a barrow in the Old Kent Road eating a meat pie and minding his own business. He was at the brazier, keeping warm. There was a couple of other blokes standing there an' all with their pies. So, me Dad notices one of them but couldn't remember who he was. So, he says, 'Here, mate. Don't I know you?' They got talking, and it turns out the bloke is me Dad's younger brother, Ronnie, who he hadn't seen in nearly twenty years from when he was a nipper. Then they went down the pub. Me Dad reckons it was the shape of his younger brother's face and something about his eyes. Anyway, Uncle Ronnie, who I'd never met before, comes round regular now. We don't know how he does it, and we don't like to ask, but he gets his hands on some lovely joints of meat for Sunday, and he *never* takes a penny for them. What I'm saying, miss, is if me Dad can remember his brother twenty years later, Minkov might remember you after only a week's gone by, 'cause he must have stared at you if you was talking funny."

"Oh," said Sophie.

"You mustn't look at him, not even once," said Flora. "That's the answer."

"So, it appears. Let's continue, shall we? Mr Drysdale informed me of what happened after Minkov cleared customs. He has been under observation ever since. I'm told he is usually adroit enough to realize he's being followed, and probably has, which means he'll be on his guard at Dumond Hall.

"Now, the smaller case Minkov gave Foster, the diplomat, was returned to Minkov before they left Southampton. Foster is being watched and will be questioned in due course. Mr Drysdale suspects it's possible there may be no more collusion between them than Minkov wishing to slip something past the customs inspection. In other words, Foster only did a favour for a shipboard friend whom he had no reason to distrust. If so, Foster would assume the contents were dutiable. Looked at in another way, Foster received the case in a clandestine manner, was willing enough to defraud the government on behalf of a comparative stranger, and bore the risks for no apparent reward. That doesn't make sense. No one would do such a thing unless they were under an obligation."

"Any ideas what was in the case?" asked Flora.

"It didn't appear to have any great weight to it. When Archie and I discussed Minkov, we supposed the case might have contained tobacco, jewellery, documents or cash. If Foster brought the case through customs as a favour, then he had to believe the contents were something anyone might wish to avoid paying duty on. But if he believed it was cash or documents... Then he must be involved in a larger conspiracy against Britain. As interesting as all that is, we're not involved any further except to observe Minkov."

"Why would Basil Munday be friendly with a spy?" asked Ada.

"There are only two possibilities, really. Either he knows Minkov is a spy, and therefore Basil Munday is also up to no good, or he doesn't. In which case, their acquaintance or friendship is based on other things. That's what we must find out. My idea at present is for you, Ada, to focus your attention on Minkov. I'm sure you will, but I must add this, be *careful*. Assume he expects to be observed by the government and is on the look-out for our agents."

"Will we go through his room, miss?"

"We really must, but I doubt we'll find anything. Archie mentioned we should be cautious, because Minkov might set a trap to see if anyone searches his belongings."

"Oh, I say, Miss King!" exclaimed Broadbent-Wicks. "This is absolutely the best. A duel of wits with an international spy. How can it get any better!?"

"Mr Broadbent-Wicks, please keep your voice down to the lowest achievable level."

"A bit too loud, what, considering the circs? I've taken your point to heart and will be as silent as the grave."

"Yes, I believe that would do it," said Sophie.

"Righty-ho. Not another peep from this moment on. Please continue, Miss King. I'm now all ears instead of mouth."

"Thank you. To continue, we must *all* be careful how we conduct ourselves around Minkov. Act naturally, as though you have no special interest in him. We will treat him the same as we would any other guest. This same attitude will be applied to the members of the Munday family. As far as they are concerned, we shall each be just a well-trained servant — virtually invisible to them."

"You know," said Broadbent-Wicks, "wouldn't it be spiffing if one *really* could be invisible? At will — whenever one wanted."

"As well as being as silent as the grave, or instead of?" asked Sophie.

"Whoops. Did it again. Terribly sorry. It will be as though I'm not here, I promise."

Sophie raised her eyebrows while considering several choice remarks, but she kept them to herself.

"We must strive to be unobtrusive, and I say that as a reminder to myself as much as to any of you. Gladys, you and I shall concentrate on the Mundays. We're looking for anything that might constitute a lead in the most recent case. Wilfred Munday was chosen for death for a reason, and we must find out what it was. Everyone believes, including the police, that Pascoe Eldred killed him. If true, then he almost certainly killed Bartholomew Munday in Hyde Park, and possibly killed — or had him killed — Allan Munday in Scotland. Seeing as the police have yet to arrest Lord Eldred, it seems highly likely that the Mundays will get to him first and settle matters by shooting him in the back."

"Do you mean to tell us, miss, that we can expect another murder?"

"Not while we're at Dumond Hall, if the feud continues according to tradition. As I explained earlier, the local area is treated as off-limits, except Lord Eldred broke that tradition with this recent murder... If he did it, of course. The important question for us to answer is, what will the Mundays do? We assume they will retaliate soon. And let's face it, the police haven't been successful so far. And no matter who started the whole absurd business or what the tally is on either side — all that has been rendered immaterial — they have to act now if only for self-preservation before another Munday is assassinated. As macabre as the situation looks, there is a species of twisted logic to be found within it."

"So, a murder is coming, but probably not while we're present." Flora frowned. "I don't find that particularly reassuring. Just for a moment, let's suppose we discover something vital to the Munday plan of retaliation, but that we're found out in the process. Surely, they will broaden their horizon and bump us off, too! I mean, if it were *me* killing people, would I not want to dispose of any witnesses? I'm sure I certainly would."

"I can't answer with any certainty," replied Sophie. "We're trying to gather information and evidence against Pascoe Eldred amongst a group which must contain at least one other murderer with the potential for others being present! How cautiously shall we tread?"

"We shouldn't go, Phoebe. That's how cautious we should be... But naturally, we'll throw caution to the wind and continue on our way. I mean to say, which one of us would want to miss out on this adventure?"

"Caution should still be our watchword, though. We have our blackjacks, and I have the police whistle to give the evacuation signal. Elizabeth shall be stationed in Marlborough, which is only two miles away. That's if the Council has finished playing with the road. I can't understand why they're always digging them up."

"It's so they have somewhere to sit," said Flora.

"What can you mean?" asked Sophie.

"They dig holes, erect that canvas thingy over it, then sit inside with the flaps shut. There, they brew tea, smoke, talk, and read newspapers."

"No, they don't," said Sophie, smiling.

"Oh, yes, they do. I passed one once, and the flap was open slightly. Do you know what they were doing inside? Playing cards, right in the middle of the Strand! Traffic was backed up for miles. And you could see the cigarette smoke wafting out of their wigwam! I don't know how they escape being fired."

"I do," said Ada. They all looked at her. "It's simple, really. They take breaks as they like because the work is hard, and if the foreman or manager comes round, it don't really matter who, one of 'em stands up and says, 'Sorry, guv'nor, that you find us like this on our break. We've another ten minutes due, but if you'd like us to start at once, we will.' That's what they say or something like it."

"Do they?" asked Sophie. "How on earth can you know that?"

"One of me brothers works for the local Council. He told us."

"Very interesting. Yes, Mr Broadbent-Wicks?"

He was holding up his hand to speak.

"Um, what would you like *me* to do, once we arrive?"

"Be a footman and keep your eyes and ears open. Avoid engaging in conversation with any of the family or guests as far as humanly possible. Remember, we have discussed this before, but I will re-iterate for the sake of clarity. Speak when you are spoken to, answer questions simply and without commentary, and attend to your duties with meticulous care."

"Got it, Miss King. I shan't disappoint you."

A car sent to the station brought the secret agents to Dumond Hall. While travelling up the slight incline of the drive, Flora whispered to Sophie,

"Good Heavens. It's a butcher's job."

"I *know*," whispered back Sophie. "The original house is nice and symmetrical, but all those additions give the building the appearance of an architectural jumble sale. That Victorian part really ought to go."

"Attics," said Ada. "Look at 'em. They're bound to stick us up there, and what with this *heat* an' all, we'll melt, that we will." The car came to a halt.

"I hope you're wrong about that," said Flora.

"We'll soon find out," said Sophie. "Tally-ho!"

Sophie got out and the others followed. Together, the chauffeur and Broadbent-Wicks retrieved the luggage. When set, the chauffeur led them into the servants' quarters — the Victorian section which Sophie had so recently wanted gone.

They lined up along the wall of a corridor and waited with their things.

"It's not bad in here," whispered Flora.

Ada whispered back, "Don't get your hopes up, yet."

They heard the butler's breathing before they actually saw him. Wheezing in and softly groaning out, the sounds, if left to one's imagination alone, should only have issued from a hospital patient nearing the end of life's final lap.

The superbly turned-out butler to whom the breathing belonged came slowly around the corner. He was about fifty and of average height, comfortably proportioned and possessing a healthy pallor; in fact, the very opposite of the animated corpse they were expecting. There was something amiss with his eyes, though, because when he stopped in front of the line, he stared at them in that way one does when peering into the dark to find a way out of a room where the only bulb has blown.

"I take it you are from Burgoyne's Agency?"

He had a cultured voice, sonorous and slow.

"Yes, sir," replied Sophie, who bobbed.

"I'm glad you have arrived promptly. I am Mr Surridge, butler to Lord Gerald Munday. And you are?"

"Phoebe King, Mr Surridge. Miss Burgoyne has put me in charge."

"Good, good. And these are?"

Sophie introduced the others.

"Nancy Carmichael."

"Good morning, Mr Surridge," said Ada, who bobbed.

"Gladys Walton,"

"Good morning, Mr Surridge," said Flora, who also bobbed.

"And Mr Broadbent-Wicks."

"Good morning, Mr Surridge," said he, fortunately bowing slightly instead of bobbing.

"Welcome to Dumond Hall. Mrs Lester will be along shortly to show you to your rooms. As soon as you are settled, you shall submit to a test of your skills in the Dining Room. I know your agency comes highly recommended, but you must be proven to *my* satisfaction. Wait here and, as I said, she will be along at any moment."

With that, he began walking, instantly resuming his unusual breathing noises.

"We'll know when *he's* coming, right enough," whispered Ada.

Mrs Lester arrived moments later, and the introductions were gone through again. She was in her fifties, a small woman with severe, almost frozen features, which gave no clue as to what she was thinking. Sophie noticed that the housekeeper's dark blue, high-necked, long-sleeved woollen dress, relieved by a thin lace collar, was of the finest quality.

"Follow me." Mrs Lester's was a high-pitched yet firm voice. They set off. "You are on the floor above. There, you will discover that, despite the heat, the bedrooms are quite tolerable at night."

"That is welcome news, Mrs Lester," said Sophie.

"Are you in the habit of speaking without being spoken to first?"

"Yes, I am, but it only applies to myself, and I do so infrequently. I stand in the capacity of Miss Burgoyne's representative and, as such, I model my conduct on how she herself would behave. However, if the custom here is that staff only speak when answering questions, I shall abide by the rule."

"I see... That is unnecessary in your case."

They mounted the stairs, and it became apparent that this unadorned part of the Victorian addition was purpose-built to accommodate the servants. Consequently, it had an institutional feel, despite the corridor's high ceilings and wide, well-polished floor. It would certainly be drab and rather unfriendly in winter. Today, the brilliant sunlight lit up the walls, lit up the very air, and set the wooden floor glowing. The effect made the agents feel welcome.

"You two are in number eight," said Mrs Lester to Ada and Flora. She opened the door with the number painted on it. Revealed was a sparsely furnished room containing two single beds. "Present yourselves at my office in a quarter of an hour. *Your* rooms are this way," she continued, speaking to Sophie and Broadbent-Wicks. When passing a staircase that led both up and down, Mrs Lester spoke to Broadbent-Wicks.

"Your room is number twenty-three on the floor above. Present yourself at my office with the others. Remember this: no male person shall be found on the female floor unless accompanied by myself or Mr Surridge. We observe a strict segregation of the sexes, and it is a rule that shall never be broken by anyone."

"Yes, Mrs Lester."

Sophie was certain he was on the verge of adding a comment and breathed an inward sigh of relief when he dutifully went upstairs without delivering it.

"Are you superstitious?" asked Mrs Lester when Broadbent-Wicks had gone.

"No, I don't believe so, Mrs Lester."

"That's just as well. Your room is number thirteen."
"Oh."

Chapter 12

Dumond Hall

Burgoyne's aced the Dining Room test, unfamiliar though they were with where everything was kept and the customs of the house. They set a dinner table for twelve after receiving minimal instruction. As they worked, the butler stared in his peculiar way, while the housekeeper often consulted her watch. Quietly, efficiently, and with a minimum of communication, the bare surface of the long mahogany table was transformed and adorned. Even the napkins were folded in the Bishop's Hat style.

When they had finished and stood back, Mr Surridge began a thorough inspection of each setting. That he made no correcting comment was a good sign. Nevertheless, as butlers are often wont to do, he could not refrain from adjusting the odd piece of cutlery by the smallest fraction of an inch — although an impartial judge might have said he was only doing it to justify his presence.

He finished the inspection and, in the way of all butlers, addressed Sophie thus,

"Entirely adequate, Miss King. Do you agree, Mrs Lester?"

"I believe, I do."

"Then we shall leave the table as it is for tonight's dinner."

He gave a slight nod to Sophie before leaving the room. Mrs Lester now took over, informing the agents of what was expected of them in the coming days. They learned the event itinerary. Whereas in the past there had been competing celebratory days given by the Mundays and the Eldreds, although Mrs Lester markedly avoided naming that other family, in the long distant past it had been decided that they would take turns instead. She went on to say that, until this year, there had been a fête, a dinner, and a ball all on the same day. It had to be admitted that everyone found the festivities exhausting and there had also apparently been 'problems', although she declined to state what these were. This year, the first day, called Children's Day, was devoted to entertaining the surrounding population with a series of amusements. In the evening, there would be a family party. Dumond Hall would be thrown open, in a limited sense, to everyone. She also mentioned there would be a beer tent, and then Sophie understood what the past problems might have included.

Mrs Lester continued, saying that the second day was restricted to friends, family, and visiting guests. Dumond Hall possessed a large ballroom; the guests would eat dinner there, and then it would be restored to its proper purpose. The amusements would be more dignified, as she so pointedly remarked, and would continue into the third day, on the evening of which was the Ball. Historically, the Ball had been the highlight of the celebration. It being the first year of this new arrangement, and Lord Munday desirous of making the event memorable, the Ball would be a masquerade.

"Naturally, we shall know in advance the identities of those guests with titles or of some other distinction. Another viscount and his wife shall be present. In fact, and I must impress this upon you, he must be given exceptional treatment as though the guest of honour." She paused for a long time. "I am, of course, referring to Lord Eldred."

"Very good, Mrs Lester," said Sophie. "May I make a suggestion?"

"What is it?"

"If I could make a list of our expected duties for each day, I believe we can assist you all the more efficiently."

"Do you believe so, Miss King? Very well."

The housekeeper then explained her expectations of the Burgoyne's staff, adding that they would not be attending Lord Gerald Munday, although he would be present at dinners.

Clare Munday was not interested in the management of her servants and was content to leave the running of the house to the butler and housekeeper. Mr Surridge did not trouble her when the temporary staff from London arrived, only later informing her that they would serve dinner that evening. Therefore, it came as a shock to the dozen diners — a mixture of family and friends who regularly visited, when, instead of the aged or quirky retainers to whom they were accustomed, they found themselves served in a fast, professional, and entirely unobtrusive manner by smart, young servants. The service was too good, and induced a silence around the table as everyone, the butler included, watched every move they made. Sophie was heartily relieved Minkov was not present.

"Grandfather," said Audrey, while they were all seated and the first course was being served, "are we going up in the world? Who found these?" She was referring to the Burgoyne's staff as they served the soup.

Lord Gerald laughed. "I know nothing about them, dear." From the head of the table, his voice was faint but clear. He was bent and shrunken, and his white hair was sparse and wispy. His lips had a purple hue. When Lord Gerald picked something up, he did so with one of those fussy, hesitant motions which sometimes come with advanced years. For all that, there was a toughness to him, as though he were made of wire and determined to last as long as he could despite the depredations upon his body.

"Where do they come from, then? Daddy?" Audrey could have asked Ada, who stood only a yard from her, rather than Basil Munday.

"You'll have to ask Surridge. Do you know, Clare?"

"London, so I'm given to understand."

"Well, Surridge?" asked Basil.

"They are from Burgoyne's Agency, and came highly recommended, sir."

"I think we can see why. Excellent."

At first, it was a trial for the agents to work while being watched and discussed, although the guests started talking amongst themselves once the food was in front of them. In the end, the dinner proved to be routine, and there was little learned. No one mentioned the Eldred family or Minkov, and the conversation revolved around the coming celebration and other local topics. Of interest were the family dynamics. Basil Munday liked to dominate discussions, or at least not be excluded. The advent of Audrey and her brother Luke's party of London friends particularly pleased him. He even remarked they would 'brighten up the place.' And while Audrey conversed freely with those around her, Luke was taciturn, their sister Violet was generally quiet, while Clare Munday spoke intermittently and usually in a low voice to her guests on either side. As for Lord Gerald, he spoke only occasionally of his own accord, although Violet often spoke to him, demonstrating a granddaughter's affection in her concern for his comfort.

After the ladies had withdrawn to the drawing room and then the gentlemen had joined them, the conversation over drinks was more relaxed. Violet had accompanied Lord Gerald back to his room. As Sophie served the guests, she could detect no specific reason for this social gathering so short a time before the upcoming big event. From one of the kitchen maids, she later learned that inviting friends to dinner was a regular occurrence at Dumond Hall.

After half an hour, a guest quietly asked Basil if Viscount Eldred would be in attendance over the coming days. Basil answered in tones that everyone heard.

"Well, we invited him, of course." Basil was relaxed, an excellent example of the genial host and, being such a large man, was well-suited to the part. "I didn't expect him for Children's Day, naturally. But I rather thought he would dine here the following day, as it was always the custom for our families to dine together before the Ball. But you know all that, don't you? Since expanding the event, so that it spreads over three days," Basil became familiar and playful, "it forced him to decide whether he could stomach us for two days or not. Obviously, he *can't*." Basil roared with laughter.

His guest was hesitant, wondering if he should venture another question. Basil saw it and forestalled him.

"Your glass is almost empty. Can't have that, can we?"

Within moments, Broadbent-Wicks silently arrived with two whiskies on a tray. Sophie and the butler watched him. The conversation between Basil and his friend had faltered and was not resumed, making it apparent that among guests the feud was never openly mentioned but only ever inferred.

In female servant bedroom number eight, the agents, minus the barred Broadbent-Wicks, gathered to discuss their first impressions of the family.

"That Miss Violet seems like a nice girl," said Ada. "The way she looked after his lordship couldn't have been nicer."

The rest of the family were pleasant towards him," said Flora. "But other than that, they left him to his own devices."

"Yes, I saw that," said Sophie, sitting on the foot of Ada's bed wearing a new dressing gown. "Although Lord Gerald has all his faculties, he wasn't really engaged with those around him." She moved the notebook in her lap. "I had a very odd thought during the main course. I couldn't help but think what it would be like if Lord Gerald, Basil, and his son Luke were all murdered."

"Don't say that, miss. You'll give me nightmares."

"I trust I haven't already. But my point was not so much the devastation it would cause to the rest of the family, but more along the lines of how Lord Eldred might hope to get away with it. I'm sure Lord Gerald rarely *goes* anywhere, and Luke doesn't miss a trick."

"I saw that," said Ada. "I think he's taken a shine to you, Gladys."

"I *know*, and how tiresome of him. Phoebe, I can't watch Luke, or he'll take it the wrong way should I catch his eye."

"Very good." Sophie was writing. "I'll observe him instead. You concentrate on Audrey. She's rather an outgoing person."

"I'd say she is," said Flora. "She was name-dropping all the time and couldn't possibly be friends with all of them, as she implied. At twenty-two, she's a year younger than we are... I mean, I've met a good few famous actors, actresses, and the like. Other than those I've worked with, I wouldn't say I *know* any of them, let alone claim that they're my friends."

"I don't know any famous people." Sophie wrote a note. "If she stretches the truth, I wonder how far the habit extends?"

"Quite a few people do that, though, miss; to make 'emselves interesting."

"I suppose we're all prone to that weakness," said Sophie, "if only for the sake of the conversation. She bears watching, though. Audrey struck me as a very capable person."

"Yes. I think she could bump someone off," said Flora. "I thought her to be rather calculating... Where did you get your dressing gown from? It's rather pretty."

"I was thinking just the same, miss."

"Do you like it? I had to retire my old one from active service and bought this in Debenhams. It's a little too thin for the coldest nights."

"Note to self," said Flora. "Go to Debenhams. Anyway, the way I see it is that Audrey, Luke, and father Basil are all capable of murdering Lord Eldred, but I can't see any of them actually doing it. Do you think they might?"

"Basil Munday is so big and beefy he could just hug someone to death," said Ada.

"Do you know Lord Gerald was once the same size? There's a painting of him in the hall at about the same age."

"I saw it," said Flora. "Oh, how the mighty have fallen."

"Yes, and to think he might have murdered someone, too. Dot Callan and her cronies all believe Lord Gerald's father did. Having now seen the family, it maybe a case of like father, like son, *and* grandson. Basil may have assassinated Major Ian Eldred in France, although he wasn't in the army. Luke was, however, and also present in France at the time, according to the police files. It was Sergeant Gowers who recently discovered that tidbit of information, and *not* the original army investigators."

"So, *he* did it, then?" asked Ada uncertainly.

"Luke certainly seems the most likely, but Basil *could* have travelled to France, pretended to be an officer to get near Ian Eldred in the front line, waited until there was the cover of an artillery barrage before shooting him. That seems really far-fetched, but it is just possible. Besides Luke, there were two other Mundays — distant relations — stationed in France. Someone in the army would know the ways of the trenches and could conduct themselves accordingly. Basil Munday would not. I think he would soon get himself noticed by the soldiers as a recent and out-of-place arrival. Unless he had the right uniform, Basil would become an object of interest while hanging about. The person who killed Major Eldred had to be experienced in battle. Therefore, and until additional evidence comes to light, Luke, at twenty years-old, was the most likely to shoot the Major."

"Godfathers, and him just sitting there tonight, stuffing his face with apple crumble."

"But if he's murdered once," said Flora, "surely he's the one who will go after Lord Eldred?"

"Perhaps. I'm trying hard not to rely on assumptions or become biased. None of us must do that. As the police always say, it's evidence that counts."

"When are you meeting Sergeant Gowers next?" asked Ada.

"Tomorrow, midnight, at the Mildenhall Bridge. Do you know he's also staying at the Ailesbury Hotel in Marlborough? I can't imagine what he and Elizabeth would talk about, unless they've chosen to ignore each other on account of the mission."

"You're going to walk alone all that way in the dark?"

"I've lived in the country all my life, so it holds no terrors for me. Besides, it's only half a mile, and the bridge is now passable again, although the Council hasn't finished digging. My greatest danger in the dark is falling into the hole they've dug."

"But s'posin' someone's waiting in the *hole* to grab you?"

"Then I'll hit him with my blackjack. But what a most *extraordinary* idea."

"That's because I've always lived in London," said Ada. "At night, you have to keep a sharp eye out for dark places, 'cause you never know who's lurking in 'em. A *hole* in the road in the country is a dark place. So, I thought there'd be someone in it. Stupid, ain't it?"

"No, it's entirely understandable... Are we all finished?"

"What about Clare?" asked Flora.

"Oh. Did you notice something?"

"Only that she's like a piece of Dresden China. I doubt she's even capable of *hatching* violent plots, let alone carrying them out. But you see, if you put her on the list and then strike her off, it looks like we're getting somewhere."

155

"She's already on the list but shall remain unstricken. For all we know, Clare Munday could be an Eldred relation and *she* might be the evil genius behind all this dastardly behaviour of late."

"Wouldn't that be *tremendous* if she were? The beautiful tyrant queen with ice in her veins and malice in her heart — ooh, scrumptious."

"Now I'm thinking of apples," said Sophie. "There's scrumpy cider, and scrumping for apples."

"Don't tell me, after all these years of our friendship, that you're on the verge of confessing to the theft of apples? I simply won't believe it of you, Phoebe."

"Pfft, as they say on the Continent. Of course, I haven't. Is that everything?"

"One little thing, miss. Mr Broadbent-Wicks has been asking that we call him Duggie. Says it's friendly, and he don't have a pseudonym like what we do."

"He mentioned it to me, too," said Flora.

"As his employer, I will not call him Duggie. You already know the difficulties I'm having with his all too familiar conduct."

"I thought about a name, miss. Some people get called by their initials. Why don't we call him BW?"

Sophie thought for a moment. "That's brilliant. I'll talk to him tomorrow and get his approval... Right, I'm off to bed. Tomorrow's going to be a long day."

"It's Children's Day! That shouldn't be too difficult," said Flora.

"From the name, one wouldn't think so. According to Mrs Lester, they are setting up a beer tent. I doubt very much that's for the children, so we're bound to have our work cut out for us. Good night."

Chapter 13

The Fête

The servants at Dumond Hall were up with the lark. Within the house, and on account of the day, the resident staff moved with more alacrity than was their custom. Although quiet, so as not to disturb the viscount and his family, their efforts were largely in vain. A gang was outside hammering, hauling, clattering, and calling, gripped by the oblivious devotion to the work at hand with its total disregard for all else that only a group of workmen can attain when determined to get a job done quickly. Setting up the ropes to define the course for the three-legged and the egg and spoon races should have been a quiet affair but, at a quarter to eight, someone with a long-distance voice insisted, "To the left... No! Don't be foolish. To the *left*... That'll do." Clare Munday, a light sleeper, drowsily opened her eyes and asked herself, "What are they putting to the left of what?" Deciding she must know the answer, she got up. There was a reason for her anxiety. As the sole leading light of the Wynbourne and District Amateur Art & Dance Society, Clare was concerned that, of the two pavilions, the one which let in the rain was *not* to be used for the art exhibit as it so disastrously had been two years earlier.

In the Breakfast Room, Sophie and Ada were clearing things away after the meal.

"Mr Basil has *six* eggs every morning, so I've been told," said Ada.

"Six! That's rather excessive."

"It is an' all, miss. Although they said that during the war, he only had three."

"I should think he did!" Sophie finished loading a tray. "In our village, we often gave up our eggs to send to the wounded in France… Three eggs a day, indeed."

"Quite a few got away with that sort of thing, miss. If they had the money, they got by all right, thank you very much."

"I know, but I find such selfishness irksome. I'll be back in a minute."

She carried the heavy tray to the kitchen. On the way, she met Mrs Lester.

"After you have finished in the Breakfast Room, go and see Mr Surridge. You'll find him in his pantry. He will explain your staff's duties for this afternoon."

"Yes, Mrs Lester."

Within minutes, Sophie was standing in the Butler's Pantry, a modestly sized room, somewhat cramped by cupboards. One of them, large, heavy, and lockable, had metal grills and Sophie could see it contained spirits and wines being brought to room temperature. She also could not fail to notice the line of bottles on the butler's table — nine of gin and four of wine. He arose from behind this fence of glass.

"Good morning, Miss King."

"Good morning, Mr Surridge."

"These are for the gin punch for the ordinary guests," he said. "The Champagne for the royal punch is, of course, being chilled. I wish to impress upon you that the ordinary guests are not to partake of the royal punch." He came out from behind the table, immediately wheezing while doing so. "Although the drink for guests is without cost, it is restricted." He stared at Sophie. "There have been regrettable incidents in the past, you understand. To prevent another such incident, we have wholly gone over to a ticket system.

Mrs Lester will oversee the distribution of these tickets and the dispensation of the gin punch, both ordinary and royal. Misses Walton and Carmichael shall assist her in this. Mr Wicks," Sophie noticed he had shortened the name, "shall assist me throughout the course of the day." He raised his eyebrows.

"Yes, Mr Surridge."

"Very good. There is, however, a potential weakness in our ticket plan, which is this. The beer tent."

As soon as he mentioned it, Sophie knew what was coming next.

"I cannot attend his lordship and supervise the serving of beer and cider. Therefore, I am delegating the responsibility of the ticket collection in the beer tent to you. It may seem unusual — my putting forth such a demand — but I do so after careful consideration. It is a simple matter of expediency because you are not from the area. Therefore, you are unlikely to show partiality when excessive demands are made." He paused momentarily. "Many of the villagers are related or are neighbours or friends. Two years ago... there was a *lamentable* outbreak of oversupply. Lamentable. I attribute it to an excess of exuberance and relief over the war being so recently concluded. His lordship and Mr Basil were not unduly concerned, but they instructed me that there shall be no such further outbreak in the future." He raised his eyebrows again.

"I fully understand your position, Mr Surridge."

"I was sure that you would. Do you have any questions, Miss King?"

"Yes. What time do the festivities begin?"

"At one o'clock. The school is closed for the afternoon so that the children may attend. Indeed, some are participating in various events, therefore it is necessary they be present."

"I see. And what will be the total attendance?"

"With the weather being ideal, at least two hundred and fifty adults, with the family and intimate guests adding another forty. The number of children will be legion." This last he uttered in a hollow tone.

Sophie surmised that the butler's barely veiled aversion was probably also rooted in past experiences. Sophie envisioned quantities of excited children running rampant and that they had threatened the calm and established order of the estate.

"That is a very large number, Mr Surridge. Greater than the population of Wynbourne, I should have thought."

"It is. Many come from Marlborough and beyond." He sounded as though he wished they would stay where they were.

"May I ask one last question?" Sophie knew she must address the delicate matter — the unique reason for Burgoyne's presence.

"Please do."

"Will any other peers of the realm be present today?"

"No."

Despite the brevity of his answer, Sophie knew it was a complicated and difficult one for him. The peers in the area avoided the Mundays — the family was embroiled in a feud, and the archenemy would soon be present. Then there was Surridge's personal conflict — loyalty to the family pitted against a desire for their well-being and lawful peace in general. He was now acting in secret, without their knowledge, and most definitely against his lordship and Basil Munday's wishes. Surridge would be discharged should they find out.

"Am I correct to assume that Miss Burgoyne has entrusted you with her full confidence in the, er, the, er…"

"Other business?"

"Exactly."

"Yes, Mr Surridge. I would venture to say that Miss Burgoyne has given me a complete understanding of the situation, and expects me to conduct myself as she, herself, would act."

"Ah. Then you must appreciate the invidious nature of my position. It is not incumbent upon me to provide an explanation, but I wish you to understand that I have allowed… the *other* business to be conducted solely for the means of preserving life. It has gone on for far too long, and that *man* must be stopped. If the police have him in custody before retaliation or another outrage, I believe that would be the end of it all."

"I'm sure it would."

"Well, yes… I must add that I cannot aid you any further in the matter. Mrs Lester takes the same position. We have done all we can."

"I fully appreciate the delicate balance that must be maintained and hasten to assure you that we shall be circumspect in all we do."

"Very good. I think that is all for the present, Miss King."

Although Sophie had seen Broadbent-Wicks about the place several times, it was not until mid-morning in a quiet corridor that she had the chance to talk to him privately.

"I need your report," whispered Sophie.

"Nothing much to report. Unless you count my natter with a chap in the middle of the night."

"Middle of the night? What chap?"

"I share a room with a fellow named Benjamin, that's who."

"Yes?"

"Well, he started talking in his sleep, don't you know? Woke me up with his chat. I'd had about enough of it after a while, so I chucked my pillow at his head. It was a good shot, too, and put a stop to his row. Of course, I had to get my pillow back. As I was reaching down groping for the thing in the dark, Benjy started off again and I had a brainwave."

161

"Did you?"

"Yes. A large one. I decided to interview him. What do you think of that for an idea?"

"I don't know, yet. Go on."

"Well, I made myself comfy on the side of his bed and asked him if he had killed Wilfred Munday."

"You didn't!?"

"Oh, I did. You see, I hadn't put my slippers on and my feet, which had been as *warm* as toast, but they were getting cold and so, I thought, why muck about?"

"What was his answer?"

"As near as I can remember, it was, 'Shung burff wee ut,' or something like that. He has an accent."

"What? He was just mumbling then?"

"I suppose he was, really, but *he* obviously meant something by it, only I couldn't make it out. Do you think we speak foreign languages in our sleep, Miss King?"

"No. Was that all you asked him?"

"No. I thought he might need encouragement to become intelligible, so I had him recite Baa, Baa, Black Sheep."

"And?"

"He said, 'Uh, uh, fa'ship, a ooo nenny uulll,' but had me completely flummoxed after that; he made no sense whatsoever. Then I asked him if he had gone to London to kill Bartholomew Munday. And guess what he said?" Broadbent-Wicks grinned.

"Just tell me."

"Nothing. Absolutely nothing. That's important, because it can only mean he was hiding his guilt. It means he murdered old Barty Munday."

"It means no such thing. And Mr Munday was not *old* and, may I remind you, he was the tragic victim of a vicious attack."

"Yes, poor blighter, and I meant no disrespect. But, Miss King, I believe Benjy killed Barty."

"I'm far from convinced, Mr Broadbent-Wicks. In fact, I find..." She was about to use the word idiotic, but checked herself in time. "... I don't think such evidence would be admissible in court."

"No, of course, it wouldn't. You're *absolutely* right. But what if they could get Benjy to fall asleep in the dock and *then they* questioned him?" He considered what he had said. "I doubt they'd do that, though."

"Highly doubtful. This afternoon, you are to assist Mr Surridge in attending the family and their guests. Remember to be quiet and on the alert for Minkov. It is possible he will arrive this afternoon."

"Righty-ho. All ears and no mouth bags the spy."

"Let us hope it does. I must go, but there is another matter. A rather personal one."

"Oh, I say. Whatever is it?" His look became indescribable — a mixture of equal parts joy, alarm, and vacancy.

"It is your name..."

"You're going to call me Duggie?"

"I shall *not* and don't interrupt again. The suggestion has been made that we call you BW instead of Mr Broadbent-Wicks."

"Now, that's *very* interesting, Miss King. Please, allow me to think it over." He thought out loud. "Hello, my name is Broadbent-Wicks... But you can call me BW... B... W. BW. It has a certain ring to it, a sort of importance... Rather *special*, I would say. Yes, BW gets my approval and has jolly well bucked me up no end. Miss King, I hate to say this, because I would dearly love to stay, but I really should shove off. There's a pile of work to do, and I don't want old Surridge coming down on me like a ton of bricks. Can't have my slacking off pitching the lovely agency into the soup, what?" He laughed.

"Yes, please shove off. I also have work to do."

They parted and walked away in different directions, BW smiling broadly, while Sophie was shaking her head.

They came in droves and, in the twinkling of an eye, generated that hundred-headed organism which possesses the single thought — Come on! — commonly known as The Queue. There, on the grass next to the gravel drive, the people waited under the bright May sky, brought to a standstill by a single, auburn-haired woman. She was seated on a chair behind a rickety deal table bearing rolls of tickets, protecting herself from sunburn by means of a large umbrella. This was Daisy, the formidable laundress of Dumond Hall. A living legend, her reputation rested upon that of someone never, ever, to be crossed. To an initial polite enquiry, she had answered,

"I'll give the tickets out at one o'clock, loike I'm s'posed to. So, don't no one go axing me again or you'll get none!"

To the mother of a straying child who had wandered close to her table, the laundress imparted the following advice,

"That child wants a good wallop."

To the time-saving suggestion of the tickets being handed out first so that everyone could go up to the house upon the stroke of one, she replied,

"Don't tell me my job. Who d'ya reckon you are? Get to the back of the queue."

Seeing as she was in one of her better moods, those at the front deemed it best not to engage her in further conversation. Otherwise, when the inevitable argument broke out, the laundress's opponent would feel as though he or she had placed his or her head in Daisy's mangle while she leisurely cranked away. Many knew her and, as she was impervious to reason, ignored her, which was just how Daisy liked it.

The line grew longer. One o'clock came and the church bell remained silent.

"Here, Daisy," said a man near the front of the queue. "It's one o'clock. You can gi'us our tickets now."

"I didn't hear no bell."

"But my watch says…"

"I didn't hear no bell, so it's *not* one o'clock."

From willing mouth to expectant ear, a whispered summary of the exchange sibilantly fizzed down the line. Moments later, a small old man known to all as Flying Billy, because he was the church's bell-ringer and the great bell, Gethsemane, always lifted him off the ground, stepped out from the queue and trotted to the front.

"Billy? What are you here fer?" asked Daisy, incredulously. "Go ring that dratted bell. You've set a-holt on the doings."

"Er, it's better'n half mile away, and I want to go in," replied Billy plaintively. He hopelessly looked to the laundress who glared him into submission. "I reckon I'll be off then."

Fortunately for everyone, Mrs Lester exited the house at that moment, and headed towards the table. The queue breathed a collective sigh of relief and was heartened in a manner similar to that of the wounded in Crimea upon Florence Nightingale's entering the dark tent with her lamp. Daisy, who was in her way enjoying herself, was the only person unaffected, and stolidly waited to hear first what Mrs Lester would say before handing out a single ticket.

With the distribution begun, and while the first eager celebrants rushed forward into paradise, their recent thralldom forgotten, a car proceeded slowly up the drive. In the back, Todor Minkov surveyed the oddity of a large queue in the middle of a park, musing over the quaint habits of English country life.

So far, the agents had learned nothing. They were in a house on a busy day and worked hard accordingly, having no opportunity to get near anyone who might yield information.

Even then, Sophie believed, the chances of someone blurting out something useful were slim to none. Her only genuine hopes were when Minkov arrived, and then again on Saturday, when Lord Eldred attended the ball. Until these events occurred, she could not expect much. In fact, she expected even less now, because she was stuck in the beer tent — again. *Why is it always me?* she wondered. Elements of her life seemed to be awash with beer even though she positively disliked the drink.

Carts and lorries had come from Marlborough over the preceding days, bringing food and items necessary for the success of the Fête. This being the first year of the event, it was called a Fête to distinguish it from the summer Wynbourne Fair, which was a name that made it sound grander than the ancient holiday had ever been. However, the affair at Dumond Hall lacked some of the true distinguishing features of the now popular fêtes that had arisen around the country — a result of efforts to raise money for good causes during the war. At this one, though, no money would change hands for anything, because Lord Gerald was underwriting the day. But there were tickets, though. A ticket for a heaped plate of good food, a ticket for Tombola (that raffle for prizes of a puzzling nature), a ticket for a try at Lob the Boot — mercifully only a local game involving a boot, a small wooden trigger, a string, a chamber pot filled with water, and a willing victim. There were also three tickets for alcoholic beverages.

In the beer tent, the barrels were set up, crates of bottles stacked, and the counter, a wide plank of wood on trestles, was cleared for action. The flaps of the tent were tied back. From behind the makeshift counter, Sophie surveyed the empty south lawn as a commander does the battlefield before a coming contest. The troops, all two of them, were ready — if a sixty-year-old man who moved at a snail's pace and a lad of sixteen who had to be told to do everything could ever be considered ready. Sophie had been given to understand she was only to collect the tickets. Now, she quickly realized, she would also have to serve, because — they were coming.

They marched quickly across the lawn. With no warning trickle to prove the beer tent's readiness, men, nearly every ticket-holding man, came on as a deluge, a river in full spate, and the tent was suddenly filled with noise and bodies, waving tickets, and impertinent demands. It was a nightmare. The throng pressed forward, threatening the overturn of the counter because the beer servers were too slow. Demands increased, the beer servers fumbled, and the mood of the men soured over the delay. Instead of pitching in to help in what was obviously a losing fight, Sophie took a step back even while a man waved a ticket in her face. She bawled,

"*Silence, Gentlemen!*" They obeyed her command. "There will be no more beer served until order is restored in my tent!" The beer-servers stared at her.

"That's roight, lads," said a voice from the middle of the pack.

As if by magic, the men hurried to form an orderly queue which snaked out onto the lawn. After that, things ran more smoothly. Later, Sophie had to refuse service to several people. One was trying to negotiate his tombola ticket for an extra pint, declaring that he never had any luck, so it was of no use to him. Another was a boy, tall for his age, about thirteen.

However, it was within the first twenty minutes that something interesting occurred.

"What do you think?" said one man to another. "Will Lord Eldred come today?"

Sophie's ears pricked up, and she avoided looking in the speaker's direction.

"No," loudly drawled the second man. "He'll not be coming today. To the Ball, yes. Today, no. Won't show his face."

"Arrh. They always have gone to the Ball, but it's a different business now. Three-day affair. But what if he came, though? Reckon they'd do for him?"

"Up until this year. I'd 'ave said no." A third man had joined the conversation. "That's all changed, what with this here last killing. *Roight* in the village it wor'. It means anything can happen now, and probably will. You mark my words."

"That's how I see it," agreed the first man. "Anyone seen Lord Eldred, then?"

Several shook their heads, saying they had not.

"Best drop it," said someone further back. "A couple of his men are outside, an' they told me t'other day that he had no hand in it."

"Did they, now?"

The conversation dropped.

The Munday family and friends, dressed in light summer clothes, occupied seats at linen-covered tables set beneath a pair of ancient oaks. The spot was close to the house and overlooked the south lawn, with a panoramic view of the hills beyond.

"Marvellous to see the villagers enjoying themselves," said a middle-aged doctor named Hurst. "They derive such great pleasure from the simplest of pursuits."

"You sound like you envy them," said Basil Munday.

"The truth is, I *do*." The doctor laughed. "I wouldn't exchange places with any of them. Nevertheless, they have something I've lost... or never had. I suppose it's because they don't understand so very much of the world, therefore it remains a mystery to them. We, on the other hand, constantly strive to know more, and in the process we shed the attitude of childish innocence we see at play before us."

"You could always enter the egg-and-spoon race."

"Do you know, Munday, I think I shall. That will tickle them no end."

"It is my belief that they're constantly on your mind, as well as in your heart."

"Yes... They're like my children, really, the ones I never had. And there's *always* something the matter with them."

"Perhaps it is you who has the enviable position."

"Not when I'm called to an emergency at three in the morning when it's raining. But there, I shan't bore you with my trials and tribulations."

"I think you glory in them, Dr Hurst," said Clare Munday, who liked the man.

"I wouldn't go as far as saying that, Mrs Munday, but to see a patient recover after challenging difficulties is immensely rewarding."

Clare smiled. "Some punch, Doctor?"

Ada approached the table with a tray of fresh drinks.

"Yes, I believe I will, thank you." He took a sip. "Hmm. If all medicine tasted as good as this, I'd never hear a patient complain again. Although they might be sorely tempted to go beyond the recommended dose." He laughed once more.

At a serving table near to the group under the oaks, Flora was ladling punch from an immense glass bowl to fill a tall glass.

"Go a bit faster," said Ada. "They're all gasping."

"They shouldn't drink like fish," said Flora. "I'll try, but there's so much fruit *and* they've left the pips in. Makes it very fiddly keeping the bits out." She put another glass on the tray. "Are they talking yet?"

"The usual twaddle. There's a doctor who seems like a nice bloke. I don't think Minkov's arrived yet — none of 'em look foreign. No one's got an accent."

"His English might be perfect."

"I *hope* not. If it's too good, I won't know it's him speaking, and will have to look to make sure. Mind you, if he's got a thick accent, I'll have trouble understanding him. He needs to be right in the middle, he does. That'd be perfect."

"Supposing he requires an interpreter?"

"Oh, don't say that, Glad. That'd be the worst of the lot. Anyway, Miss King would have told us if he had trouble speaking English. We'll make that do for this trip. Keep ladling while I'm gone."

169

"Tyrant," said Flora.

They both smiled.

At about two, Minkov joined the group under the oaks, and Ada and Flora were on hand to witness the meeting.

"Todor! My dear friend." Basil Munday was out of his chair and soon heartily shaking the visitor's hand.

"Basil. It is good to see you again." Minkov spoke English well but with a definite accent, which Ada found most satisfactory for the purposes of eavesdropping.

The immediate Munday family rose from their seats to greet the newly arrived guest.

"This is my wife, Clare..."

Basil went through the introductions, and Minkov was punctiliously delighted to meet everyone.

"A chair," said Basil to Broadbent-Wicks, who had one ready and now placed it at Basil's table.

Over a short distance, Flora took note of the fact that Basil had evidently met Minkov before, probably several times and, although Minkov had never met the Munday family, they all knew of him by the way they reacted.

After the rush, the beer tent emptied because Sophie insisted the men smoke outside. She found the atmosphere under the musty canvas with the smell of stale beer was bad enough but, once the tobacco pouches came out, she laid down another of several rules. As the beer was free and Sophie had the power to revoke tickets, they meekly did whatever she cared to command.

Two old boys doddered in. They were Ben Tubb and Fred Gardner, and Sophie nearly had a fit as soon as she recognized them. The meeting was unavoidable. As the young lad was washing glasses, and the slow fellow was fiddling with the tap on a barrel, that left only her free to serve.

"Good afternoon, gentlemen," said Sophie, in her best Scottish accent, modeled on the lyrical tones of her aunt Fiona. Sophie thought it a rather good impersonation, but any Scot would detect deficiencies. "Only drink tickets are accepted for beer. You canna buy a pint, so don't try; do not trade with others for extra tickets; there's no smoking in the tent; and you shall not blaspheme or use coarse language. Break any rule and it's no more beer for the likes of *you*."

The two men gaped at her.

"What did she say?" asked Fred.

"We must behave," said Ben. "We'd loike two pints of best bitter, please. Here's my ticket. Go on, Fred, give her one of your'n... No, the other type... That's it."

Sophie averted her gaze, busied herself, and listened while the two men sipped their beer and talked.

"That's a good drop," said Ben.

"I've had better," said Fred.

They were silent for some time.

"Do you think any reporters will come?" asked Fred.

"I dunno... Why?"

"He could buy us a pint for our story."

"Can't be done. The Scottish lady just said so."

"You mean you can't buy a pint? It's just them tickets? T'ain't roight."

"You'll have to bear it like a man." Fred found his comment immensely funny.

"Well, let me tell you summat *I've* remembered an' a reporter will pay fer. I get to tell it, so don't you go sayin' nothin' when the time comes."

"I won't. Go on."

Some men came in, and Sophie had the lad serve them so she could continue listening.

Fred sipped his beer. "You know my eyes are bad over a distance? Well, I've never told anyone this afore. My ears are so much the better. And not just my hearing, loike, but the *remembering* of what I heard. I notice more nowadays in what goes on around me."

"You mean your ears have growed?" Fred looked puzzled.

"Don't be daft or I shan't tell. 'Course my ears ain't growed. I'm remembering noises better than I used to, that's all it is."

"So, what did you hear and remember with your great lugholes?"

"Reckon you always did play the fool, Ben Tubb."

"And I reckon you always made a meal o' the simplest thing, Fred Gardner."

"Do you want me to tell you or not?"

"I wouldn't be standin' here a-listenin' if I didn't. Get on with it."

"Very well, then. That car had a bad tyre."

Fred considered the statement for a moment. "So what?"

"I know'd I'd have to do your thinkin'. That there is a clue, roight enough. We didn't seed the number plate 'cause we don't have a good eye between us..."

"Speak for yoursel' but go on."

"The police can't find the car, but if'n they did, they can identify it for certain by the tyre, see."

"So, they could... You must tell them."

"I will, arter I get extra from the next reporter."

"No. You must go to the police first."

"I will go to 'em, but arter the reporter."

"Suit yoursel'... What type o' sound did it make?"

"Like a quiet slap, reg'lar, as the wheel went round. That's a patch, that is."

"Sounds loike... Come on, let's push off. I want to smoke my pipe."

They left, and just in time. The next person through the flaps was Daisy, the laundress.

"I want a pint o' bitter," she said to Sophie. "Out all day in the sun, I've earned it. Here's the ticket," she smacked it on the counter, "an' I didn't steal it, so don't you go thinking I did."

"My name is Miss King." Sophie's voice had returned to normal. "If you wish to be served, you shall address me properly or you'll get no beer. Now, having said that, you may try again."

Assuming she was dealing with a social equal, Daisy now perceived her blunder. The cut of Sophie's dress and the way she carried herself became apparent and Daisy's confusion deepened. Really, there should have been an audience present to bear witness to the change that overcame the laundress.

"I'm ever so sorry, Miss King. Here's my ticket, and I'd like a pint, please, if it ain't too much trouble."

Sophie said nothing and served the beer without spillage.

"Thank you," said Daisy, who managed a subtle curtsy before leaving the tent with her glass.

The young lad came up with an open mouth while staring at the departing laundress. "That was Daisy!"

"Was it? Have you finished the glasses?"

"Yes, Miss King... May I ask a question?"

"Of course."

"Are you Scottish?"

She smiled at him. "Sometimes. Let's get back to work, shall we? Clear away the bottles next. We'll do them together."

Chapter 14

Tripping the Light Fantastic

It was universally agreed that if Dr Hurst had not dropped his egg only steps from the finishing line, Basil Munday would have had no chance of winning. However, the sight of a viscount-in-waiting and the local doctor lumbering along the beaten grass track, once the children had finished their races, gave such merriment to all that it was easily the day's highlight. The two men enjoyed the exercise as much as the onlookers did.

"Thank goodness we got the race in before father came out," said Basil, recovering from his exertions in the shade of an oak. He was alone with his wife. "He would never approve of such antics."

"I'm not sure I don't agree with him," said Clare. "Promise me you won't repeat the exhibition when you are viscount."

He put his hand on his heart. "I assure you, I shall not. Dignity shall be restored and maintained... What do you make of Minkov?"

"I find him well-mannered and pleasant. There is a formality about him that many continentals possess, which I find rather engaging."

"He's trustworthy, you know. Has a good head on his shoulders."

"When did you first meet him?"

"Oh, a few years ago. Remember when I went to Marseille during the war? I met him in an hôtel, and we got along famously from the start. Although young, he was representing, and expanding I might add, his father's business."

"That was when you were trying to find a supply of sardines or something, wasn't it?" asked Clare.

"That's it. There were other commodities besides, but I was having no luck finding a source of fish at the right price anywhere. Then Minkov gave me a tip — completely gratis, mind you. Told me to see a chap in Algiers, and that worked out for a while, if you recall. After that, the German submarines began taking too high of a toll on merchant shipping, so around the Med they were reluctant to risk ships in voyages to Britain. Can't blame them, really."

"And you've kept in touch ever since?"

"Oh, we've met a few times, and corresponded often. Occasionally, we put business each other's way when we can't use the opportunity ourselves."

"Now I understand why you trust him. What you do in business is all beyond me, but if you are satisfied, so am I."

"Ever cautious, eh, Clare?"

"One of us needs to be."

"True. Shall we go for a stroll?"

"Yes, we should. I must visit the art exhibit and the Greek Dance is in an hour. Your father is intent upon watching it."

They got up from the table. Flora silently, quickly, and as naturally as she could, moved away from the other side of the tree.

Lord Gerald, using two canes, was determined to leave his wheelchair in the house and appear before the people on his own two feet. Mr Surridge accompanied his lordship. In close attendance were a nurse and a footman, in case the effort taxed the viscount's strength. The path was an easy one, and he was soon among the villagers and visitors. When he drew close, men removed their hats and became suddenly awkward; women bobbed, although the local tradition had it more in the way of a duck of the head. Every so often, Lord Gerald espied someone he knew and conversed — about the weather, crops, or inquiring into the well-being of the family. Slowly, the little procession arrived at a corner of the lawn, where a row of chairs had been set up in front of a flat open space, bordered by trees and bushes on two sides. On a nearby platform, a small band was playing pleasantly, demonstrating its classical training. The band stopped as Lord Gerald took his seat.

"As promised, dear, I'm here to see your dance," said Lord Gerald to Clare.

"Thank you," she said with a simple smile. Clare was dressed in a pale blue, filmy dress in a style of ancient Grecian garb strongly subjected to English twentieth century tastes. A critic might have thought that Clare had taken an old summer frock and cut it down, but that was not the case, because the garment flowed and gracefully fluttered during movement far too well for that.

To ensure that Clare Munday received her proper acknowledgment for the exertion she was about to put forth, as much of the household staff as could be spared was assembled close behind the Munday family. Mr Surridge, a wilier bird than appearances would lead one to believe, demanded decorous yet enthusiastic applause from the body of servants he had strategically stationed. While the exhibition dance was in progress, all other diversions were closed, including the beer tent.

"Do you know," Sophie quietly said to Flora, "since school, I had completely forgotten about the existence of Classical Greek Dancing? Yet in the last few days, I've run up against it twice — was *in* it on the Rangoon, for goodness' sake."

"Coincidence," said Flora. "It's a strange phenomenon. Several times recently, I've thought of people I haven't seen for ages, then I meet them within the next day or two. I haven't minded so far, because they were all people I liked. What do you think I should do if, out of the blue, I think of someone I detested?"

"Stay in bed until the danger has passed."

"That might do it." Flora lowered her voice. "Have you had a chance to think over my report?"

"That was good work of yours. What I found interesting was that you-know-who was in France. What a pity he didn't mention the year."

Flora looked behind her. "Major Eldred was killed in seventeen. Surely, the police examined Basil Munday's passport to see if he was there that year."

"Perhaps they didn't because he's the son of a peer and they've never considered him as a possible suspect. Anyway, everyone seems to have a laissez-faire attitude towards the feud."

"Don't they just? No mention was made of it while they were swilling gin punch. And a maid I spoke to earlier was barely interested in the subject beyond saying, 'It wasn't very nice.'"

"In the beer tent, they spoke of it openly. But it being a contentious issue, like religion or politics, they dropped it to preserve the peace. They all have opinions, though. Look, there's Nancy and BW."

Sophie waved to them, and they came over — just in time — because the band had struck up again, playing an introductory piece. The crowd drew in closer.

The first of three dances began, and the music matched the theme. First, a placard was placed on an easel, entitling the coming spectacle: A Woodland Scene. Clare, leading a small troupe of young girls, burst through the bushes at the back and the audience went 'Aah!' because in their simple fawn dresses and green muslin caps, the six girls looked like delightful pixies. Around and around they danced, hopping and skipping, led by the exuberant and graceful Clare. If the audience were to have uttered a single phrase, it would have been, 'How *sweet* they all look.' The dance was quite complicated, with many weavings in and out, and a great deal of travelling across the space. The agency had to change its assessment of Clare Munday at the age of forty-three. She was more than decorative in the drawing room — now she was also vital and strong, tireless and accurate in her steps, sinuous and inventive in her interpretation — qualities both physical and mental that they could not have deduced when observing her in the house.

Sophie noticed Audrey sitting in the front row, leaning very close to Minkov and whispering. Minkov nodded his head in response, and Sophie looked away. The dance then ended to strong applause, much strengthened by the servant party.

The next dance began. Entitled, The Child, the audience sighed sentimentally upon seeing a girl of about four, dressed all in frilly white, and sitting on a toadstool. She was the centerpiece of the dance. The troupe of young dancers weaved and bobbed about but always their attention came back to the small child, while Clare, similarly devoted, gave a more spinning and acrobatic performance which drew the admiration of all.

"She's very good, and at her age, too," whispered Sophie. "Obviously, she's studied ballet."

"Yes, and she must be hot on exercising," said Flora. "Any idea what the dance is about?"

"Not in the slightest. Have you seen Audrey and Minkov?"

"Oh, yes. *Very* friendly. I think we can expect developments there."

"So soon, as well... Quite fascinating."

Before the placard for the final dance was displayed, they observed Clare carrying a bow and arrow.

"Oh, it's going to be Artemis and Orion," said Flora.

"Bound to be. Remember us doing that?"

"How can one forget? I particularly recall Miss Robertson shouting at you."

"I explained to her it was an accident, but she insisted — oh, never mind. It was just very unfair of her."

The placard, when revealed, read: Diana's Tragedy.

"We always called her Artemis," said Flora, believing she used the more correct name.

Clare was excellent, but one or two things detracted from the overall performance. The tallest of the pixies, who now played Apollo, was less convincing in her part. Also, the size of the diminutive bow suggested that this particular iteration of Diana might be a virtually useless huntress. When the giant scorpion appeared, the audience had to make allowances, and held to the view that the children were trying their best.

The climax came, and Diana dramatically loosed the shaft, which travelled about fifteen feet before disappearing in the short grass of the lawn. Everyone had to imagine as hard as they could that the little arrow had struck the distant Orion as he swam in the sea. Among the spell-bound audience, only a single person was moved sufficiently to gasp out loud — Sophie.

Discovering that Apollo has deceived her into killing the only god she had ever truly loved, 'Diana' then 'swam' across the 'sea' and retrieved an 'Orion' who happened to look very much like a sack stuffed with straw, having appurtenances attached purporting to be his head and limbs. She tried to revive 'him' but he was 'gone'. That Diana could ever bring herself to love such an object was too much for several in the crowd. However, the compelling display of tragic emotional distress that Clare achieved next through her art reestablished the wondrous nature of the spectacle.

The clapping and cheering were immense as the participants took their bow. When the noise died down, two pixies unfurled a banner between them. It read, Three cheers for Lord Munday! At the appropriate moment, a breathless Clare called the first, "Hip, hip!" and the audience hoorayed magnificently, giving thanks to the peer for the day's entertainment.

As they walked away, Flora asked,

"Why did you gasp?"

"It struck me that Clare was enacting a scene similar to that in which Susanna killed James Munday. I know it's different in some ways. Artemis unwittingly killed the person she loved, whereas Susanna deliberately killed the man she *once* had loved, but many of the same elements are there."

"So, you're thinking Clare is in on it, then? Hold on, though. She's a Munday!"

"Yes, but she *married* into the family. I knew it was far-fetched when I mentioned it before, but just suppose she really *is* a distant relation of the Eldred family. What then?"

"That's too much to be believable... But wouldn't it be lovely if it *were* true? Clare married into the Munday family with the object of finishing the feud by destroying her own household. That would give old Apollo a run for his money in the Subterfuge Stakes."

Sophie laughed. "I'll get Elizabeth to investigate, if she has time. Should she find Clare has a connection to the Eldred family, it might prove *very* interesting."

Mr Surridge walked towards them across the lawn, so they turned to meet him.

"You may resume your duties, Walton."

"Yes, Mr Surridge," said Flora, who continued on.

"Miss King, Mr Basil has ordered the beer tent be reopened once the tug-of-war contest has concluded. He will announce that anyone desirous of an extra ticket for drink shall receive one."

"Yes, Mr Surridge."

"There will be a rush, of course. Will you require additional assistance?"

"No, Mr Surridge."

"I thought not... Earlier, I took occasion to pass by the tent, and was satisfied to find everything conducted in an orderly fashion. You are to be commended, Miss King."

"Thank you, Mr Surridge."

"That is all for the present."

The butler, wheezing as he went, returned to the house. Sophie trudged over to the beer tent.

By five, the Fête was finishing up, and many had already departed for their homes. The tombola prizes had been distributed at four and that was the watershed moment for people to leave. First prize had been a brand new, latest model, and most advanced electric vacuum cleaner. The lady who won the opulent prize lived in a tiny cottage without electricity and with little in the way of carpeting. Still, her win was the envy of the village, and the vacuum cleaner could be sold for ready money in Marlborough, which it was the following week.

"Miss King?" asked the older servant. The lad was hovering in the background. "Are we done fer the day?"

Sophie looked at her watch and then around the tent. "I believe so. There's no sense in our all being here. Both of you report to Mr Surridge. I'll stay, because there might be a laggard or two who still have tickets."

Nearby, Minkov walked among a group of the younger set within the Munday party. He was one of the oldest present and not quite of their generation.

"I say, Minkov," said Luke Munday. "I insist you call me Luke. Mind if I call you by your first name? We're determined to throw off tiresome formality these days."

"Times have changed; indeed, are still changing. No, I do not mind."

"Well, Todor, they can't change fast enough for me."

"Is that so? Do you mean politically?"

"Good heavens, no! Who has time for all that rot? I mean socially. We're still in the grip of the Victorian age, and it needs to go."

"I would state it already has. Naturally, in my country, it is rather different — we had no Queen Victoria, for example, but similar trends are playing to eventual conclusions, only much slower than here. Most noticeably, the control of the church declines, while the power of the ordinary worker increases… A changing of the guard, merely. The by-product of those changes is felt in society, which changes, too. Here is a question I put to you. Do changes in society precede or follow the changes in political control?"

"A bit on the deep side for me… I'd say precede."

"And I say they follow. But let us leave that. I notice the land needs rain, and it is only May. Are these the usual conditions for the area?"

"Absolutely not. Everyone's complainin' about the weather, don't you know? Such a dreadful bore, but what can anyone do when Mother Nature won't co-operate?"

"Take precautions?"

"Yes, I suppose so… Now, listen Todor, dear chap, we've got some very interestin' friends coming down from London for the party. And there'll be a red-hot band, dancing, and," Luke gave Todor a gentle nudge with his elbow while lowering his voice, "*anything* goes, and probably will."

"Indeed?" said Minkov.

"My advice is for you to *prepare* yourself. Excuse me for a moment, old boy. Darling sister Audrey wants me for something."

Left alone, and with no one in his immediate vicinity with whom to converse, Minkov came to a stop. Then he noticed the beer tent a few paces away, so he went inside.

Earlier, Sophie nearly had a fit, fearing she might be recognized. Now she had a full-blown panic attack. To buy time and, instinctively, to hide, she turned her back towards

Minkov before he entered, bent down, and pretended to be busy with a crate of bottles.

"Excuse me," said Minkov upon reaching the counter.

Sophie shot up and turned around. Wearing an overly bright smile, she said,

"'Allo, sir. Do you 'ave a beer ticket?" She spoke in a cheery East London accent.

"Beer ticket?" Minkov asked uncertainly.

"Yes, sir. No beer may be served without a ticket. Them's the orders. 'Pon my life, I'm not 'lowed to take no money, even if I wanted to."

"Oh... I believe I follow."

"I'll tell you wot," Sophie looked to see if anyone was watching, "seein' as it's just you an' me an' the doorpost, I'll let you 'ave a pint, I will an' all. Because you must be from his lordship's party, an' there's only been a mistake made. But, if anyone asks, can you say you gave me a tickct?"

"Shall it be our little secret?" asked Minkov, obviously amused.

"That's right, sir. What'll you 'ave?"

"Now that I have given you a ticket, can I please have a bitter? Is that right?"

"Yes, sir, and a pint of best bitter is comin' right up."

After he had gone, and Sophie had pocketed the sixpenny tip he left, she breathed a massive sigh of relief, then closed the tent for the day. Had he recognized her? Despite a niggling doubt, she was almost sure he had not.

Chapter 15

The Breaking of Silence

The elegant dining room could accommodate thirty in relative comfort. Tonight, it accommodated thirty-six in relative discomfort. Not at all pleased with the overcrowding were Clare Munday, Mr Surridge, the Agency, and Mrs Gosling, wife of John Gosling, Mayor of Marlborough. Whereas her husband, seated next to Lord Munday, had the luxury of putting his elbows on the table, if he had the bad manners to be so inclined, she had to keep hers tightly pinioned to avoid the embarrassment of contact with those on either side.

"I'm sure to spill the gravy over someone," said Flora, as she carried a tureen of the stuff from the kitchen.

"They're packed in like them sardines Mr Basil was talking about," said Ada.

"Sardines who are forced to be contortionists when we put food on their plates. It makes it so awkward for us."

"Really, no dinner comes off perfect, but this one's set up wrong from the start."

"And poor Mr Surridge isn't at all happy."

They met Sophie coming the other way.

"It's ridiculous!" she said, quickly stomping past them on her way to the kitchen.

"We'll get through it somehow, miss," said Ada, philosophically.

For the entirety of the dinner, the agents needed to pay greater attention to how they served and less to what they might overhear. It did not matter so much in the end, because the conversations they witnessed were mostly on local topics and quite ordinary. Throughout the dinner, the most notable item was that Audrey Munday sat next to Todor Minkov and that she paid him much attention.

After the meal, the men remained in the dining room, which was hurriedly cleared for the enjoyment of their post-prandial port. The women removed to the drawing room.

"You'll *never* guess what Audrey said to Minkov," said Flora in the kitchen, after giving the dishwashers the last of the serving bowls.

"I dread to think," said Sophie, her sleeves pulled up while she shattered ice to fill a silver ice bucket.

"She said, 'I'll see you later, Minky, darling.'"

"Minky, darling? How positively atrocious."

"Isn't it? Our Audrey's a quick worker, though."

"So, it appears. How did Minkov receive the appellation?"

"With a mild and rather charming confusion — not exactly a flushing up to the roots of his rather remarkable hair." Flora looked thoughtful. "I think his hair has her bewitched. That must be it. He has quite the fine head — just like Mozart's."

"You mean Beethoven's," said Sophie.

"No, Mozart. I remember him from the plaster bust in the school's music room."

"There were two busts in that room. Beethoven had the shock of hair, and Mozart used curling tongs."

"Do you mean I've had it the wrong way round all this time? How will I ever live with myself after this?"

"I'm sure you'll manage somehow," Sophie smiled. "Seeing as we're on the subject, here's a snippet of singularly useless information." She continued smashing the ice. "Beethoven is Dutch for beetroot garden. What I've always wondered is that, if his symphony had been announced as 'Beetroot-Garden's Fifth', would it have been so well received?"

"Definitely not. It gives entirely the wrong idea of what to expect."

"But the Dutch have known the truth all along."

"Then they've deliberately kept their ghastly secret to themselves for fear of embarrassment. Let me take the ice bucket to the drawing room." Flora picked it up.

"Thank you. I'll be along in a minute."

By nine-thirty, old Lord Gerald's confirmed opinion of the surrounding conversation was that it was boring, and he had heard it all before. The old peer was tired, and he wished to go to bed. He was now of an age and disposition where he no longer cared what happened to his guests. As far as he was concerned, they had been fed and now they could go away. Lord Gerald also expected the imminent arrival of a party of young idiots from London, and these he wished to avoid as if they were plague-bringers. He looked around for Surridge, but the butler was temporarily absent from the dining room.

"You, there. Where's me nurse gone?" said Lord Gerald to Broadbent-Wicks.

BW stepped closer to answer. "My Lord, she left the room because the gentlemen were about to drink port."

"Oh. Know how to push a wheelchair?"

"I doubt it's difficult, my Lord. The stairs might be a bit of a puzzler, though."

"I can manage the stairs. Get me out of here… Good night, everyone! So glad you could all find the time to come."

The gentlemen arose and in heartfelt formality gave him thanks for the dinner and returned him a good night.

"Basil, come here."

His son quickly approached.

"Give my apologies to the ladies. Tell them I'm feeling tired."

"They will be most understanding," said Basil.

Lord Gerald waved a finger, indicating his wish to depart. BW pushed the creaking wheelchair the length of the silent room. The men remained standing, obsequious and patiently smiling until his lordship's exit. As they crossed the carpeted hall to the stairs, BW heard Lord Gerald mutter to himself, "*Most* understanding," followed by a faintly derisive noise. They reached the foot of the staircase.

"Help me up," said Lord Gerald.

After BW had got him out of the wheelchair, the peer slowly began climbing the stairs.

"My Lord, how may I assist you?"

"By not speaking."

"People often say that to me, my Lord."

The viscount stopped and stared at him. "What's your name?"

"Broadbent-Wicks, my Lord."

"What are you doing with a name like that?"

"I was born with it, my Lord."

"Are you being deliberately stupid?"

"Oh, no. It's not deliberate, my Lord."

"But where'd you spring from? Do I employ you?"

"Technically speaking, you *might*. You see, my Lord, Mr Basil Munday, on your behalf, asked Mr Surridge to find extra staff for the Fête, Ball, and all the other palaver. So, he called in Burgoyne's Agency of London. Miss Burgoyne sent Miss King here, and I report to her. Can you see, my Lord, my difficulty in saying exactly who it is I work for?"

"But I'm the one paying, which means you work for me."

"My Lord, you have made the whole situation abundantly clear. Thank you." He bowed.

"Now, be quiet."

"Yes, my Lord."

"I'll speak to Surridge about you." The viscount began moving again.

"Am I in trouble, my Lord?"

He stopped again. "Don't speak unless spoken to."

"But you keep speaking to me, my Lord. Surely it would be extremely rude of me if I didn't answer?"

"Are you suggesting that I must stop speaking in order for *you* to be quiet?"

"Putting it like that, I suppose I am, in a way, my Lord. But that is certainly not my intention."

"What is your intention?"

"Your absolute comfort and peace of mind, my Lord."

"If that's true, then clear all these people off my property so I can go swimming."

"Do you mean to say, my Lord, that you have a swimming pool? How splendid."

"You haven't seen it? Although it's not finished yet, it looks rather good — like a Roman pool."

"Then I'll make sure I see it, if you have no objection, my Lord."

"No, I don't mind."

"A bit difficult, what, my Lord? — having guests when you just want to splash about."

"You can blame Basil for all that. It was his idea to turn a day's simple dinner and dance into a three-day fiasco. I told him not to, and he completely ignored my wishes."

"I don't think he should have done that. Of course, it's not my place to say anything, my Lord."

"But I'm glad you did. Do you know how isolated and powerless one can feel in one's own home?"

"Not exactly, my Lord, but you have my complete sympathy. Why shouldn't you swim in your own pool when you want to?"

"Precisely my point. But it's much worse than that. Oh, yes. Do you know they're all having a day in *my* pool tomorrow? I haven't even put a toe in it yet, because they've only just filled it."

"I'm so sorry, my Lord, but I find that to be absolutely disgusting of them. It's obvious you should take the plunge first. You paid for it, it's yours, and you're a viscount. I mean to say, it's jolly unfair."

"You're the first person I've met in a long while with exactly the right attitude. Most heartening."

"Well, far be it from me, my Lord, to offer you any advice, but why don't you join them tomorrow?"

"Because, and I tell you this in the strictest confidence..."

"Oh, absolutely, my Lord."

"...I'm *fed-up* with always being on display... And bullied. I'm forever bullied. All I want is to be the first to swim in the pool *in private* to make sure I still can. I used to be a good swimmer, and I'm sure it will all come back to me given half a chance. But if I go in for a dip tomorrow and start struggling in front of them, they'll make such a ridiculous fuss. I'll be forbidden me own pool, and it's Basil who'll do it... *Most understanding*, indeed. He struts around as though he has the title already."

"My Lord, I am most surprised. I wouldn't have said he was at all like that."

"Aha! Stay here long enough and you'll soon find out."

There was a noise of someone approaching on the floor below.

"Who's that?" asked the viscount.

"It is I, Surridge, my Lord."

"Good. Send me nurse up. I'm off to bed. Tell her not to forget my cocoa."

"Very good, my Lord."

Lord Gerald continued up the stairs, talking with Broadbent-Wicks.

"I must have cocoa, because the woman insists upon pouring *vile* medicine down my throat. Does it all the time."

"I don't know how you stand for it, my Lord."

"Have to. Doctor Hurst's orders, so I've got no choice."

They reached the first floor.

"You can go now. I'm fine on the flat."

"Are you certain, my Lord?"

"Now don't *you* start fussing. I was beginning to like you."

"I promise you, my Lord, I shall never be annoying again."

"Hmm. See that you don't. Good night."

"Good night, my Lord." BW bowed towards the bent back of the old viscount as he set off along the corridor.

Under a waxing gibbous moon, Loxie Lane between the hedgerows was partly in shadow and partly light enough for Sophie to walk without resorting to her torch. Although warmed by the exercise, she wore a light coat against the damp night air. She was glad of the peace and pleasant stillness after what had been going on at Dumond Hall. Having finally extricated herself from the party, it was now nearly midnight and, for the last two hours, the place had been in an uproar. She stopped to listen and could just hear the band playing in the house, even though she was two hundred yards away.

It had started at ten when a small coach and three cars rolled up the drive. From the vehicles there poured forth a four-piece band and twenty or more young men and women intent upon having a party. Discordant laughter, shrieks, calls, and loud jocular remarks shredded the habitual quiet of Dumond Hall. Mr Surridge was scandalized; Mrs Lester, too. Clare retired to her bedroom, and the party took over the ground-floor of the house, one lounge in particular. This was where the band had set up and the windows were flung open. The drums were maniacal and the bass hypnotic. A scirocco blast issued from the trumpet, while the piano weaved a spell. Together, they commanded all to dance. The place jumped and, to Sophie's utter astonishment, Basil Munday jumped, too. A bear among half-grown cubs, he insisted upon learning the steps of the latest dances, and the girls in the party laughed, vying for turns at being his teacher. He lasted an hour and then retired for the night after having a private word with Minkov. The light-hearted atmosphere of the party changed once Basil left, becoming harder and more abandoned.

Surprisingly, the noise did not travel within the house, and so the rest of the family and the servants managed to sleep through it all. Sophie, to avoid any potential problems, sent Ada and Flora to bed after eleven, leaving BW and a Dumond Hall footman on duty. Similarly, Mr Surridge made himself scarce, taking the keys to the cellar with him to his room. He had left plenty of drink for the partiers, and they, helping themselves, were working through it at a great rate.

As she walked, Sophie put her thoughts in order. Although she had her report ready for Sergeant Gowers, she mentally skimmed through the day's events. Of all the things she had seen, heard, and done, it was the memory of two people at the party that came to mind the most frequently. The first person was Minkov. He was at first bemused by the antics he witnessed. Audrey flung herself at him — Sophie could find no other word for it — while he, after a single dance with her, politely distanced himself afterwards. She did not know what to make of either's behaviour. The second person she remembered even more vividly, and this was Violet Munday — quiet, glittering-eyed Violet who did not dance, drank no alcohol, took no drug when it was passed to her. She rarely spoke to anyone. Yet she watched, not in a corner but in the forefront of things, avidly, and with an exultant look, as if wanting the music louder, the dancing more boisterous, and as if willing all inhibition be cast off. She looked a little crazed but only in as much as her gaze was so intense, as though the excitement and recklessness of the party was filling up a void within, and she was driven to look on, greedy for more. Sophie had seen the girl staring and, of all the people at Dumond Hall, it was only Violet who gave the impression that she could indeed murder someone.

Dreading what would happen when Lord Eldred arrived, Sophie quickened her step. She passed the road works, which comprised a roped-off hole and a pile of what was presumably dirt covered with a tarpaulin. Right at the bridge, she felt the soft soil underfoot of a hastily in-filled trench that spanned the road. The bridge itself was in moonlight, but under the trees arching over the road on the far side, everything was solid darkness. Although Gower's car was invisible, she gave the signal with her torch and was rewarded when a pair of headlamps responded. Sophie crossed the bridge to the rendezvous.

"Hello, Miss King," said Sergeant Gowers. He held open the door to the back seat.

"Hello, Sergeant Gowers. I hope I haven't kept you waiting."

"Not at all. Miss Elizabeth has been keeping me company."

As she got in, Sophie and Elizabeth greeted each other.

"Here's my written report. We have discovered that Basil Munday has known Minkov for years, and they sometimes help each other in business. That means that Minkov is here representing his family's interests, so they're probably working on a venture together. The most interesting part is that Basil met Minkov in Marseille during the war. At the least, it demonstrates that Basil occasionally travels to France. If that Marseille meeting occurred in 1917, he may have had an opportunity to kill Ian Eldred."

"I'll look into that," said Gowers.

"Between Lord Gerald and Basil, there exists some tension. We don't know the basis for it, but have learned that Basil extended the one day celebration to three days against Lord Gerald's wishes. Hopefully, there's more to come on that score. I must confess to feeling quite anxious about Lord Eldred's arrival. It's possible an attempt on his life will be made during the ball."

"Do you really think so?" asked Gowers.

"Yes. Having heard the attitudes towards the feud, you would be shocked to find how conditioned everyone has become into accepting it as a... as a matter of fact. Something that just happens and is unavoidable. I heard people speculating publicly on the possibility of an attempt being made on Lord Eldred with the same detachment as though they discussed a newspaper report or an upcoming boxing match. If the locals can entertain the possibility of an attempted murder, we should, too."

"Well, I'll pass that along. Maybe the Wiltshire police can do something, but not unless they're called in."

"I doubt they'll do that, and precautions really should be taken."

"Say it plainly, Miss King. Will an attempt be made on Lord Eldred? Yes or no?"

"Yes. Or rather, it is a strong possibility."

Gowers scratched his head. "I'll mention that, as I said. That's all I can do."

"To whom do you report?"

"Inspector Haddock. He's a nice chap, but the Chief Constable has a hand in this and, um, he's what you might call a *decided* person. Likes rules so much, he makes them up himself."

"I think I know the type. Talking of types, Basil Munday is rather difficult to pin down. He seems very outgoing. For example, he ran in an egg-and-spoon race and was dancing at the party that's going on. By the way, if you were to raid that party, you would find a lot of drugs."

"Interesting. Does Basil partake of them?"

"No. The young set waited until after he and Minkov had left."

"No doubt the guests from London brought the stuff with them."

"Precisely."

"That doesn't help but just complicates the matter. I'm surprised he lets it go on in the house."

"I'm not at all sure he knows."

"Maybe turns a blind eye. If, er, if someone was to have a go at Lord Eldred, who would be your choice?"

"That is *such* a hard question. Basil and Luke, of course. There were an uncle and three cousins present today, so they're all possibilities. However, they all live out of the area. They might not see the feud as *their* business. Clare Munday certainly has the physical capability. She's surprisingly strong and energetic. This afternoon, she performed several exacting dances without showing any signs of fatigue. For her age and considering how she seems normally, you would not have believed it possible. So, it makes me wonder if she could commit murder. Physically, yes, but otherwise, I really don't know. I know this is all speculative, and you may think it foolish..."

"Can I just point something out, Miss King?"

"Of course."

"It takes very little strength to pull a trigger. Anyone can. The question is not could they, but *would* they murder another? Most never will. A few would if they felt threatened. We want the type who'll plan such a thing in advance, and there's very few of those about, I'm happy to say."

"I take your point. I suppose that her dynamic dancing came as a surprise and made me think of what else she might be capable. The same could be said of the youngest daughter, Violet, who is usually quiet, and most attentive to her grandfather. She behaved oddly at the party. With Audrey, it is different. She seems much more calculating than the rest, including her father, and, let me tell you, she also has an unpredictable side. Audrey has been pursuing Minkov almost from the moment he arrived."

"Oh, I see... Did she catch him? I find that type of a thing fascinating, although I s'pose I shouldn't."

"Not yet, she hasn't. She met with a rebuff, so we're all watching for her to make a second attempt, because she didn't go into a sulk afterwards. In fact, she did the opposite and was laughing. We now believe she might try again but won't hold a grudge even if she fails a second time."

"Could you let me know how that works out?" asked Gowers.

"Most certainly."

"Why would Audrey set her cap at Minkov, a visitor, and a complete stranger to her?" asked Elizabeth.

"I can't say," said Sophie. "At present, we can only think she's besotted with his untamed hair. Minkov looks like Beethoven, moody, strong, and with dark eyes. Also, his family is well off."

"That often helps," said Gowers.

"I should go soon. Here's a question, though. What are the Wiltshire police doing about Lord Eldred? If they believe he's the murderer, why is he still at large?"

"Well... I passed along that information about the fatal shots being fired while Cordery was running his tractor, but they're taking their own sweet time over everything. Inspector Haddock spoke to the farmer and the man who was with him, but they claimed they heard nothing. That's fair enough, but instead of canvassing over a wider area for witnesses, they've just left it. They ought to be knocking on doors, but they haven't even started."

"Is that because they think Lord Eldred is their man?"

"Has to be. They don't see anyone else with a motive, so they think Lord Eldred killed Wilfred Munday somewhere else. Now, to be fair, Inspector Haddock has an open mind, but he's waiting until this shindig is over. They're reluctant to spoil the event, which makes no sense to me."

"It does to me," said Sophie. "You live in London, where there are many attractions. In the country, there are few, and people look forward to a fair or a celebration for months on end. If the Fête had been cancelled, it would have been a devastating blow against the community and for each individual. There's nothing that can be done to replace such an annual event, and they wouldn't want a substitute, anyway. Many would make a fuss, too, holding the chief constable responsible, even if he made an arrest with a subsequent conviction. Countryside traditions cannot be overthrown without there being consequences."

"Ah, now I see why they're going slow. From an operational viewpoint, it's bad, but if you make trouble for the people you live amongst, they'll not forget or forgive."

"That's right. I'll go now. Elizabeth? May I see you outside? We don't want to bore you, Sergeant Gowers, with all our tiresome inner workings of the office." Sophie laughed.

"That's all right, Miss King. Good night."

"Good night," said Sophie, and got out of the car.

She and Elizabeth walked onto the moonlit bridge. In the quiet night, the dark stream below reflected occasional glints. Sophie looked up at the stars and the dark form of a bat flew past.

"Are there any messages from the office?"

"Miss Jones says it was quiet today, but that everything is running smoothly. There were two more bookings for small dinner parties."

"That's good news. And how are your cats?"

"Thank you for asking. Nicholas informed Miss Jones that Desdemona was no trouble, and Mr Falstaff is as right as rain after eating all his food last night. I'm sorry to mention it, but he's been very finicky of late, and I'm much relieved."

"That's excellent. May I ask where it is you're keeping the pistol?"

"I have it in my pocket. Do you wish to take it with you?"

"No, I don't think so. I'm concerned about Saturday, but not unduly so. I just wondered if you had left it in your hotel room."

"I would never do that, Miss King. One cannot be sure who might find it."

"Does Sergeant Gowers know you have a pistol?"

"No, he doesn't, and I will ensure it remains that way."

"That's good. I really must get a licence one day, but never mind. How do you find your room?"

"Splendid, Miss King. It's been such a long time since I've stayed in a proper hotel, I'm afraid to say that I'm feeling rather spoiled. You have shown me much kindness, for which I am very grateful."

"Oh, don't mention it, Elizabeth. I'm pleased you are content. Is that everything?"

"I've parked Rabbit in a very safe place. Concerning Frances Harding, I fear that to discover anything locally is impossible because she left the area forty years ago. I made a few unsuccessful enquiries today, and I don't know where else to look until we're back in London."

"I see. That will have to wait until we return, then. However, there's another name for your research, and it seems outlandish now that I'm making the request. Clare Munday. Is she connected to the Eldred family?"

"Her connection would be very ancient if she were. She is from Cheshire and her family's name is Booth-Griffin. I can go back further than her grandparents if you wish it, Miss King."

"What you have seems sufficient, so I don't think it's necessary for you to look. Despite the lack of evidence, everyone believes Lord Eldred has murdered several people, but I'm casting about to see who else it might be. What is your opinion?"

"I don't know that I have one yet. I can't help thinking Lord Eldred must be involved somehow."

"I know... It seems he must be, really... But we know he's in financial trouble, and yet, instead of trying to safeguard his family's fortunes, he's prosecuting the vendetta? I should imagine he is a very arrogant man... But there, I'm judging him before even seeing him, a thing I vowed not to do."

"But, Miss King, it's often like that with the newspaper accounts of a trial," said Elizabeth. "While one really shouldn't, one condemns before the verdict is given."

"How true. Good night, Elizabeth."

Chapter 16

The Morning After The Night Before

The Roman Pool at Dumond Hall turned a tempting blue when the sun rose above the low wooded hills to the east. The carefully chosen sapphire and cerulean tiles below the water, together with the clear sky, might have prompted wistful memories of the Mediterranean. And if onlookers had never visited Greece, Italy, Egypt, or the South of France, then the alluring depth of the unruffled water made them wish that they had. Yet it was early, and no one was about. The day would be hot, making proximity to the pool all the more desirable.

Broadbent-Wicks, one of several servants, walked along the newly laid flagstone path across the still scarred lawn. It was evident the builders had finished in a hurry and the pool complex sat awkwardly on the landscape and had yet to settle in. BW carried two wicker chairs to the open area between the pool and the changing rooms. Built of stone, these rooms opened onto a portico of sorts — open-sided with fluted columns supporting a gently sloping tiled roof. He passed by the low perimeter wall of smooth stone, which had plinths and benches incorporated at intervals. On each plinth was a statue. He put down the chairs, then inspected the nearest and largest statue — a bearded Neptune seated, holding a trident. Returning to the house, BW found it warm and so, as the family was yet to arise, he removed his swallow-tailed coat and carried it over his arm.

In the Breakfast Room at nine, Ada was on hand to serve, and Clare was already present, with Lord Gerald just arriving.

"You can go," said Lord Gerald to his nurse after she had pushed his wheelchair up to the table. "Leave me my sticks."

The nurse hesitated, for her job was to accompany his lordship wherever he went, but when he took the walking sticks from her, she knew it was useless to protest.

"Did you sleep well?" asked Clare.

"I did, thank you. And how about you, after your marvellous exertions of yesterday?"

"I had a good night, but I confess to a little soreness this morning." She smiled briefly.

"I'm sure it will pass."

"Swimming shall see to that. Will you be joining the party at the pool today?"

"No, I'd rather not. I'll swim after they've all gone. As I've said before, I don't want all these strangers in my pool. Turns it into a public bath."

"It's a shame the builders couldn't have finished earlier." Clare knew it was unwise to contradict him.

"They took long enough... I haven't even seen the pool filled yet."

They ate in silence for some moments. Lord Gerald spoke again.

"Where's Basil? Why can't he come to breakfast at a decent time?"

"I know he's up, so he must be busy with something."

"And the children?"

"They were up late last night."

"Hmm."

The children were long past their childhood. Over the years, Clare and Lord Gerald had not always seen eye to eye over the children's behaviour or the way they had been brought up. To preserve the peace between father-in-law and daughter-in-law, Lord Gerald refrained from commenting on the conduct of his grandchildren. Early on, Clare had threatened to leave Dumond Hall, and that ultimatum sufficed to institute a peace which had endured up to the present time.

"What do you make of this coalman from Bulgaria, eh?"

"He's not a coalman, father." She often used this term when Lord Gerald was unsettled over something.

"Well, whatever he is, Basil's fawning over him."

"He's making Mr Minkov welcome because he is a close business associate, and they have a very important scheme that is doing rather well." Clare glanced at Ada, who was at that moment by the sideboard staring across the room.

"Yes, yes, that's all very good. But who is he? How can he be trusted? That's what I want to know."

"Basil and Mr Minkov have been acquainted for many years..."

"So, I've been told."

"Basil is clever at business. You should really trust *his* judgment of people. There's nothing to be alarmed about."

"Who says I'm alarmed? Listen, Clarry, when a fella is invited to *my* house as the guest of honour, it would be the done thing if I were the one to invite him. Basil doesn't have the title yet, you know. He didn't ask me about Minkov, he *announced*... And after that recent business, when Basil asked for..."

Clare deliberately cleared her throat.

"Quite right," said Lord Gerald, now made aware that a servant was present. "But you know full well what I'm talking about."

"It was just an idea," said Clare, "and it all came to nothing as far as you were concerned. Basil made arrangements elsewhere."

"Hmm."

When he had finished eating, Lord Gerald addressed Ada,

"There's a footman with a preposterous name. Send him to me, will you."

"Would that be Broadbent-Wicks, my Lord?"

"That's the one."

Ada left to find him.

"We've got away with it, my Lord," said BW, while pushing the wheelchair towards the pool.

"Are you sure she's not looking out of the window?"

They stopped, and BW scanned the house.

"I can't see her, my Lord. But if we don't move along sharpish, she might spot us."

"Then stop blathering and *push*," said Lord Gerald, pointing ahead with one of his walking sticks.

As they continued, he said,

"It's bumpy. They'll have to lay the stones again or I shan't pay 'em the balance."

"This all must have cost you a packet, my Lord."

"A big packet, let me tell you. We'll soon see if it's worth it... Over there will go Diana's Templet... Know why I'm building it?"

"I don't, my Lord."

"For Clare... My daughter-in-law is a lovely woman. You should have seen her face when I said it was a little memento for her... I can't see what she ever saw in Basil... Great lump. Still, he's my son, I suppose."

"What has he done to you, my Lord?"

"Not saying. You're a servant, so mind your place."

"Righty-ho, my Lord."

"Be careful, there's a steep part coming up."

"You're in safe hands, my Lord. We'll go nowhere near top speed."

"I suppose you were born like it," said the viscount.

"Like what, my Lord?"

"Compelled to utter every thought that comes into your head, no matter what it is."

"That's always been the case, my Lord. My parents used to get annoyed, but then they became resigned."

"How they must have suffered... Stop here. What do you think? Does that not look fabulous?"

"I'd say it's superb, my Lord. Monumental. I don't think there can be a finer Roman pool in all of Wiltshire."

Lord Gerald looked up at him sharply.

"It's the only one in Wiltshire."

"What about all that ancient stuff in Bath, my Lord?"

"That's in Somerset... Of course, this is not anything like those."

"It's much better, my Lord."

"You think so?"

"Although I've never visited Bath, my Lord, I shan't even bother now — not after seeing this lovely lot."

"For goodness' sake, let's push on."

Within the ring of statues, Lord Gerald got out of his wheelchair to walk with the help of his canes.

"I think they've done a tolerable job."

"I must say, my Lord, the water looks beautiful."

"Yes. It's a pleasure just to gaze into the depths... Next week, you'll bring me down here so that I can go swimming. No nurse, no visitors, and no family, you understand. I'll stay in the shallow end near the steps... I have it all planned. Now, let's go back before any of those visiting creatures finds us here."

"Don't you like visitors, my Lord."

"Not if there are too many of them. If they're young, they take over. Then they drink, the women shriek, and the men become stupefied fops... All at my expense. In my day, it was different. Everyone knew their place and acted with dignity. This is all Basil's fault. He over-indulges his children, and their friends disgust me."

"I can see how it must be very trying, my Lord. If I were you, I wouldn't put up with it."

"That's easy for *you* to say. When you can no longer get about through illness, everyone writes you off as a dotard; they consider you a wreck who must be pandered to and fussed over. It's perfectly sickening."

"I cannot answer knowledgeably, my Lord, because no one has ever pandered to me. But thinking a bit further, the experience might be novel."

"Break both your legs and then you'll find out."

"I couldn't do that, my Lord. I must work for a living. Besides, I don't think I'm the sort of person people naturally pander to."

"You talk such rubbish. Let's go back, before anyone comes. Now, don't mention my going swimming alone to anyone, understood?"

"They won't get a word out of me, my Lord. I'm supposed to go back to London on Monday, but I'll hang on here until you've had your dunk."

"Decent of you."

On the return journey, BW asked,

"What is this I hear about a feud with the Eldred family, my Lord?"

"What do you know?"

"Very little, my Lord."

"Keep it that way."

"I will, my Lord. I just wondered if you had done any of the killings."

"Don't be ridiculous. I wouldn't kill anyone."

"So, you're not involved, my Lord? I'm very much relieved to hear that."

203

"I'll tell you something, though. Not all we Mundays are at war with the Eldreds... And vice versa, I suppose. The whole business is the height of stupidity, if you ask me!"

"Then I can't quite grasp how the murders come about, my Lord."

"It's simple, really. We're not actively plotting the other family's downfall. We are neighbours and, as such, we naturally have the occasional dispute over minor matters. The way some have settled their differences is through this wretched tradition of murder and duelling which has been allowed to continue."

"Then it's not really a feud, my Lord?"

"It is and it isn't. Some are ardent supporters of the feud and, I suppose, are willing to commit murder. My father was one of those. Others, myself included, wish it would end. Now Eldred has gone mad with the idea. He's taken it further than anyone has before, and he knows what to expect. Considered calmly, such derangement had to happen eventually, yet he was always such a modest, likeable chap. You can never tell, though, can you?"

"No, you can't, my Lord. I find it strange that Lord Eldred is coming to Dumond Hall tomorrow, considering he's so recently knocked off several of your relatives."

"Tradition — strange to say, that's all it is. A truce in the middle of a war, like when British and German troops played football in no-man's-land on Christmas day. Here's another surprise for you. For the first dance, Lady Eldred will be my partner. Eldred and Clare will also dance together. The duty falls to her because my wife is no longer with us."

"Now that *is* a rum go, my Lord. Does she mind hoofing it with the enemy?"

"She hasn't said she does, but she must do it, whether she likes it or not."

"Do *you* mind, my Lord?"

"That is curious. I hadn't considered what I feel. In a way, I'm rather looking forward to it. I know Lady Shelagh dances well and I hope I can keep up. They'll play a slow waltz, so I have a chance of staying upright... After that, I'll be stuck with me nurse all night. I detest her hovering all the time, but I'm definitely going to be saddled with her presence tomorrow night... It's enough to drive me to drink. There must be some way of getting rid of her... Look, here she comes. Don't say a word."

As far as she was able, Flora followed Minkov about the house. He managed to occupy himself by doing very little, although he did write two letters. When she examined the desk and blotter afterwards, Flora could find no clues. When he spoke to Basil Munday, she could not get close enough to overhear what they said. Most of the time she worked at something or other while in his vicinity, but when he went outside to sit on the terrace, there was no pretext she could think of for her to be out there, too.

Through hurried discussions in secluded spots about the house, Sophie learned that Lord Gerald had a few things against his son Basil. There had been a recent contentious incident when Basil asked for... what? She assumed it had to be money. But money for what purpose? Clare had said Basil found what he needed from another source. Sophie already knew the Munday family was rich, but had not been informed of Basil's personal income or wealth. All she knew was that he was 'in business' but no one had mentioned what type it was.

Lord Gerald had called Minkov a coalman. Was his actual social standing that of a tradesman, or was the implication referring to something like the ownership of a mine? Historically, the Minkovs had been civil servants or otherwise involved in Bulgarian affairs of state. More recently, they had established themselves in a few different industries, most notably railways, road building, and the electrical grid. Two of those industries required coal, but she could not trace the connection to Basil Munday. Other than that, she really knew very little about the family.

Sophie had the luxury of time to contemplate these matters while serving late breakfasts to the living dead. Those who had overindulged were in the process of recovery from the previous night's excesses. Most requested coffee, aspirin, and toast, while claiming they were incapable of facing anything more solid. Violet was the least afflicted. The members of the band, hardened to late nights and alcohol, ate full breakfasts. Besides coffee, Audrey managed a glass of milk, and looked almost as pale as the liquid. Luke ate something, but the light hurt his eyes. Twenty souls entered the room at various times, several were too tired to speak. It was said in the kitchen that a man had passed out behind the piano only to be discovered at first light by the maids when they arrived to clean up the room. The room, it was reported, was in such a dreadful state it had the scandalized staff muttering things like 'such goings on' throughout the early part of the morning.

After breakfast had been officially cut off from last night's survivors, and as lunchtime was rapidly approaching, someone amongst them remembered there was a pool, and vigorous life returned instantly. Moribund one moment, and charging off to retrieve bathing costumes the next, the Breakfast Room emptied of its clientele. Sophie began clearing up the mess they had left. She found a woman's expensive watch left carelessly under a napkin. It was a Patek Phillipe with a gold mesh strap. After giving it a cursory yet admiring glance, Sophie took it at once to Mr Surridge for safekeeping. She had to because, if she left it where it was, the watch might disappear. Then again, should the owner return and the article was still safely in Sophie's pocket, she might be accused and would certainly come under suspicion. While on her way to the butler, she wondered how often servants had been falsely accused of theft under similar circumstances.

Chapter 17

Around the Pool

The afternoon was hot and, while the land became more parched, the guests around the pool found welcome relief and much more. They splashed and sported like carefree children.

"What costume are you wearing tomorrow!?" called a woman of twenty, sunning herself in a deckchair.

"Just you wait and see!" replied the man in the water. "I had it all planned, and with this place, it's perfect."

"A toga! You're going to wear a toga!"

The man laughed. "Not even close!"

"You're playing with me! Give me a proper clue."

"Darling, you look lovely when you're cross." He dived under the water and swam away.

Slightly mollified by the compliment, she sipped her iced drink before leaning back to soak up more sun.

Ada and Flora had been told to serve cold drinks by the pool. Left to their own devices, Flora had the idea of setting up a refreshment stand in the shade under the portico, and Ada enthusiastically agreed. They did such a good job that, when finished, their little establishment looked like a stall in the street minus only the signs. Occasionally, one or other of them would take a tray of drinks around the poolside for the family, but often the guests came to the stall themselves. It was hot, and the maids were busy.

"They'll all be red and burnt by tonight," whispered Ada in a spare moment, when they were not manufacturing drinks from the piles of fruit, bucket of ice, and bottles.

"And they'll all want the calamine at the same time, you wait and see," said Flora. "I hope they've got some in the house."

"Even if they do, we'll have to ration it. That one in the deckchair, who was just calling out. She's really asking for trouble."

"You mean Miss Lobster?"

"I'll give her the chance to save herself next time I take the jug round. Blimey, here comes what's-his-face."

"Don't go *anywhere*," hissed Flora.

Luke Munday, dressed in trunks and a singlet, approached the table.

"Hello," he said, addressing Flora in a bright, over-friendly drawl. "It's *dashed* hot today."

"Yes, sir. It is very hot," answered Flora, while Ada stared at a distant tree.

"Um, now what is it I *want*?" He looked over the table. "I really can't decide… So, why don't you *suggest* something, and we'll see if it takes my fancy? How about that?"

"Yes, sir," replied Flora, who then, in a sing-song voice, daintily pointed out the items. "We have lemon squash and lemonade, lime juice and orange juice, Kaola, soda, and seltzer. Hop ale and ginger beer, Apollinaris and Vichy, and we mustn't forget dandelion and burdock. All with or without ice. Shall I run through the cordials, sir? They are *right* in front of you and can be had with plain water or a squirt from the soda-siphon, whichever you prefer."

He looked bemused. "*Actually*, I was hoping for something a little stronger." Luke then smiled in a meaningful way.

"I am sorry to hear that, sir, because all we have here is hock and light beer, but both are only suitable quality for mixing."

"Hmm, I see... What do you... what do *you* like out of this lot?"

"Plain water, sir. I'm habituated to it because I'm a strict teetotaller and a pillar in my local church."

"Oh, *are* you?" His eyes bulged. "Um, then, just a ginger beer, I think."

She served the drink, and he left.

"I don't know *how* you kept a straight face," said Ada.

It proved too much for her. She dashed off to the back of the changing rooms to explode with laughter in private. When she returned, Minkov, wearing a white linen jacket and a Panama hat, was talking to Flora.

"Dandelion and Burdock," he said. "I have never heard of this drink. Eh... yes, I think I will try a glass."

"Would you like it with ice, sir?"

"Yes, if you please."

"You're not swimming today, sir?"

"No, perhaps tomorrow. I am fond of swimming, but do so for the exercise... Eh, how can I say it in English? To splash like a child is not something I care for. In my country, we have very few swimming pools. Happily, I live on the coast and take the advantage of the sea."

"It must be lovely living by the seaside, sir. That's always been a dream of mine."

"Has it? Then how will you fulfill your dream?"

"I don't really know, sir. I hope something will turn up one day."

"Turn up?"

"You know, sir. Fate."

"Oh, *fate*. Yes, yes. Very unreliable. To fulfill your dreams, you must make plans."

"I don't think I can do that sort of thing, sir."

"Servant, yes? That makes it very difficult... You do not speak like the other servants here. Your voice is different."

"I'm from London, sir."

"Are you here permanently?"

"No, sir. I'm here temporarily."

"Ah... Then find permanent place at seaside. Help fate a little." He smiled.

"That's a *very* good idea. Here's your drink, sir."

"Thank you." He took a sip. "Oh, that's rather pleasant."

He lifted his hat and smiled, then went back to his chair.

"Is he on to us?" asked Ada.

"I don't think so. If that was an act, it was *very* natural."

"But Minkov's a spy, and we should always think the worst of him, we should an' all."

"I know I prompted him, but I suppose he did ask some fairly searching questions."

"He's not to be trusted," said Ada. "I don't know what to do. I was goin' to *h*ang about near his chair. Now I'd better not."

"No. Leave it for a while."

"We're not doing very well, are we?"

"No. I don't see how we can. I suppose we're waiting for something out of the ordinary to happen."

"That's leaving it to fate, that is. He said so." Ada smiled.

"Ah, but we have a plan. You're searching his room tomorrow during the Ball."

"But if he's as good as they reckon, I won't find nothing."

"You might. Anyway, it's worth a try."

"Hope so...Have you noticed how Minkov only talks to those older than him?"

"Yes, I had, or rather, I'd noticed he avoids anyone younger than himself."

"He's got something serious on his mind, then. You see, if a bloke likes swimming, wouldn't he want to 'ave a go today when it's so hot? I know I would."

"He thinks it's beneath his dignity. That means he holds the younger Mundays and their friends in contempt. Minkov comes from a different culture, and he's unused to their behaviour, so he sees it as unacceptable."

"Oh... That's obvious now you've said it."

While tending their stall, Flora and Ada surreptitiously monitored everyone, but particularly Basil Munday and Minkov. They therefore noticed straightaway when they left their chairs to walk to a shady tree to talk.

"Have you received word on the miners' strike negotiations?" asked Minkov.

"They're not even talking," said Basil. "Technically, it's a lockout, because the miners are still refusing to accept the wage reductions that were necessary when the Government returned the mines to private ownership. They don't seem to realize the special war measures cannot continue."

"It is imprudent of your government not to intervene. I am surprised it has not done so already."

"Had the other unions supported the miners, then it would have forced them to act. At present, they are prepared just to wait it out."

"Before the winter, there shall be a resolution. Munday, you must talk to the Government and go to the Mediterranean to extend our coal contracts at this opportune time, before the owners and miners settle."

"I've been thinking about that. Let's get this weekend out of the way first, shall we? Next week, I'll meet with a few people in the Admiralty and get them to agree to an extension. They'll raise no objections, and I'll spur them on by saying the demand for coal is hotting up, and they need to lock in the price immediately or be faced with an increase. However, I don't think they'll go beyond the end of this year. When that's in place, I'll travel around the Med, urging the local chaps to get their orders in while they still can."

"Yes, I agree with this proposal... Also, I should speak to my father."

Munday glanced at him sharply. "Yes, I think it's time that you did... And about what we were discussing, once the contract has been extended, I'll inform our Greek friend. We can't have him tying up his ships with other cargoes."

From their vantage point, Flora and Ada wondered what it could be that the two men were discussing. Then Sophie arrived.

"How is it going in the Ballroom?" asked Flora.

"It's practically ready for tonight. It's taken a lot of work because the room is as big as a barn. BW is still there and Mrs Lester is overseeing the operation. No one is supposed to know this, but everyone does, of course — Mr Surridge has gone for a nap. What's been going on here?"

They told her what had happened so far.

"They're up to something," said Ada.

Sophie risked a glance towards the trees.

"They're discussing business," said Sophie. "Men always look like that when they do." She tapped her chin with a finger. "I wish I knew what it was about."

"Don't we all, miss?" said Ada in a flat, wry tone.

At that moment, Clare Munday, attired in a coral chiffon summer dress, walked towards Minkov and her husband.

"She has that dancer's walk," said Flora, "and simply floats across the landscape."

"How does one do that?" asked Sophie.

"By having strong leg muscles and good posture. Then one must always remember to tread as lightly as a fairy."

"But does that mean she always expects to be watched?"

"Look around the pool."

They saw that numerous others were also following Clare Munday's progress as she glided across the lawn.

"Good grief," said Sophie. "It's because she gives the impression she's about to leap into dance at any moment."

"My pound to your penny — she will be the star attraction tomorrow night."

Under the tree, Clare said to Minkov,

"Please excuse my disturbing your important conversation."

"Not at all, Madame," replied Minkov, who inclined his head.

"I have to remind Basil…"

"Julia! Good heavens, I'm supposed to collect her from school!"

"You have plenty of time, if you go now. The chauffeur can't. He's out purchasing a few last-minute things."

"I'm terribly sorry, Minkov."

"Naturally, you must go."

"I'll be more than an hour. We'll continue our discussion later."

Basil went to the house.

"I apologize for the intrusion, but…"

"Needs must," said Minkov, smiling.

He gestured to walk her back to the pool.

"And how are you finding your stay in England?"

"It is delightful, Madame. There is such a sense of peace here… A slowness of time, as it were. I find a similar rhythm on our rural estate in Bulgaria, but here it is more cultivated, more like an art form. It is as if a moment could last forever, and yet one welcomes the prospect without fear of ennui."

"Thank goodness for that," said Clare. "I should be horrified to think you found us boring." She laughed.

"Never could it be said that you are boring, Madame. Very much the reverse is the truth."

"How kind of you."

Watching them from a distance, Ada said,

"He's chatting her up."

"That's what it looks like to me," said Flora.

"How can you tell?" asked Sophie.

"Similar repartee happens all the time in the theatre. It's all in the mannerisms. You watch. She's staring at the ground now because she's reflecting upon his last comment. Any moment, she'll deliver a reply while staring into his eyes with great, innocent frankness."

The three maids studied the pair intently. Two steps more, and Clare turned to speak to Minkov, bringing him to a halt with her intent gaze.

"Well known is the gallantry of the French and the passion of the Italians, but now I shall add the delightful charm of young Bulgarian gentlemen to my list."

"Madame…"

"Call me Clare, Todor."

"As you wish, Clare. But not Todor, if you please. At home, they call me Toshko."

"Toshko… Very well." She turned gracefully away.

They resumed their walk. Minkov returned Clare to her seat and gave her an informal bow.

"He should have kissed her hand, really," said Ada.

"No. He won't do that," said Flora. "She's married, and they're in public."

"Good grief," said Sophie.

"It's his hair that's doing it," said Flora.

"So, you say… Where's he going now?" Minkov had set off for the house. "I think he's going to make a telephone call." She hesitated a moment. "Gladys, you stay here. Nancy, come with me. I need a lookout." Sophie marched off.

"Blimey… I must 'ave a reason to leave my post."

"Um, um, um… A fresh bucket of ice!" exclaimed Flora.

She threw all the ice they had onto the lawn, then handed the bucket to Ada, who hurried off. A man on his way to the stall noticed what Flora had done.

"Is there no more ice?" he asked.

"We've gone for a fresh supply, sir." She smiled. "There was a dead fly in the last lot."

For the middle of the afternoon, the house was extraordinarily quiet. Surridge was hopefully still asleep, and Mrs Lester was busy in the ballroom which, in this sprawling house, was some distance and several corners and corridors away. The telephone was in a study with a south-facing window. This room was reached by a short corridor leading off the entrance hall. Danger could come from two directions — the staircase, and Sophie knew Mr Basil had just gone upstairs, and the front door. She bent an ear to the keyhole with her notebook at the ready, while Ada, in full view of the front door and the stairs, waited with the bucket in hand, worrying that the guests at the pool might become annoyed about the lack of ice for their drinks.

Through the keyhole, Sophie heard Minkov's voice.

"Hello, operator. This is Marlborough 273... Dumond Hall...I wish to place a call to the Great Western Hotel, Swindon... Yes, Swindon... I have the number... You have it? Most efficient... Yes, person to person. The name of the guest to whom I wish to speak is Graham Nye... N. Y. E... E as in egg... Yes, I shall await your call. Thank you."

Sophie quietly stepped away from the door.

"Has something happened?" whispered Ada.

"The operator is to ring back."

"Oh. What about the ice, miss?"

"Find someone to take it to the pool before anyone complains. Come back, though."

"Yes, miss."

Upon hearing footsteps on the flight above, they both vanished.

When Sophie cautiously returned to the study door several minutes later, the only thing of which she could be certain was that Basil Munday had left through the front door. Upon hearing a motor car, she was sure he was also leaving the estate. Listening intently, but detecting nothing except a clock inside the room, she considered the possibility that Minkov was no longer inside. As the seconds dragged by, she fell prey to the absurd notion that Minkov was on the other side of the door, listening exactly as she was. She knew it was a stupid idea, yet it was nevertheless alarming. It was getting to the point that she felt she must either move at once, or be discovered, when two things happened, virtually in the same moment. There was a furtive noise in the hall, and the telephone rang in the study. As she moved to investigate, she heard Minkov pick up the receiver so quickly that he could only have been next to the telephone. Ada had made the furtive noise. She was back in position and holding a bunch of mint for an excuse — in case someone asked, she would say she was taking it to the pool.

Sophie breathed a sigh of relief. Ada waved the mint and mouthed, 'For the drinks.' Sophie nodded and returned to her position.

"Hello, Nye...? Yes, this is Tanner. Any trouble...? Good. It's all on. I will meet you later, as we agreed. Goodbye." He replaced the receiver.

Sophie left. She grabbed Ada by the arm, and they fairly ran away along the corridor.

Chapter 18

Conspiracy

At thirteen and three-quarters, Julia was her mother at that age. Obsessed with ballet, she even emulated Clare's distinctive walk, sometimes adding a glissade or an arabesque. When her father spoke to her in the study, she stood in the finish position.

"I must practise, Daddy, and the teachers simply crush one at school."

"Yes, I know, but don't do it while I'm speaking to you."

"Sorry." She stood normally, but her father could see that ballet was still uppermost in her mind.

"We have guests, so there is to be no showing off in front of them. Understood?"

"Yes, Daddy."

"There is one gentleman to whom you shall give the utmost respect. His name is Mr Todor Minkov. He's a very important man of business."

"I thought you were going to say Lord Eldred."

"Him, too, but he'll only be present tomorrow night."

"I know, Daddy, I know. Treat Lord Eldred as though he's my favourite uncle, despite what anyone says about him. Shall I treat Mr Minkov the same way?"

"Yes. Many of the guests, the younger ones, are friends of Audrey and Luke. I will have it that you shall be polite when you meet them, but otherwise you are to keep out of their way." He raised his eyebrows. "Don't try making friends with them."

"Do they have bad habits?" she asked, her eyes wide.

"Some do and, for the sake of your dancing, you shall avoid their company. They keep late hours, among other things."

"Do you mean I have to go to bed early tomorrow!? But it's the Ball, Daddy!"

"If you behave, you may stay up until midnight... Don't jump about... But not a second later. And you shall remain where I can see you at all times. Is that understood?"

"Yes, oh, yes! Thank you, thank you." She hugged him, then jumped to kiss him on the cheek.

"Now, get along."

When outside, she saw a maid walking quickly in the hall whom she did not recognize. Julia caught up with her.

"Hello. You're new here, aren't you?"

"Yes, Miss Julia, I am," said Ada.

"You're from London. What's your name?"

"Nancy Carmichael, miss."

"Nancy... I believe I like that. I won't change it as I do with some of the others."

"Do you make up funny names then, miss?"

"*Oh*, I did when I was a *child*. Now, I invent beautiful names for the servants." She suddenly looked very mischievous. "Guess what I used to call Mr Surridge?"

"I don't know, miss, I'm sure."

"Surry-wurry Wheeze-bottom."

They both laughed.

"I hope he didn't *hear* you say that!" said Ada.

"I would *never* hurt old Surry's feelings. He's been here since the year dot."

"That's very good to think of another's feelings. I'll keep your secret, then, miss. Cross my 'eart, I will. I'm busy right now and I must get on, but if you ever want to have a natter, Miss Julia, just you come and find me."

"I might do that... Nancy, Nancy, takes my fancy... I like you. Goodbye." She danced away.

Clive Munday raced his two-seater car along the drive. He was twenty, at Oxford, and seriously attempting to grow a superb moustache but, despite his daily ministrations, the downy thing was still far from perfect. He braked. Accompanied by squeals, the vehicle skidded across the gravel to a well-positioned halt between two other cars. Clive often struggled with his classical studies, but had his degree been in British and Foreign Motor Racing, he would already have a diploma bearing the phrase Summa Cum Laude.

"Oh, a new face," he said in a supercilious tone to Broadbent-Wicks, who was a couple of years his senior.

BW answered, "Yes, sir," while retrieving Clive's luggage from the back.

"And?" asked Clive, leaning against the car.

"And what, sir?"

"Are you from an agency or hired permanently?"

"Temporary, sir, from Burgoyne's Agency."

"Never heard of them." He watched closely for a moment before saying, "Take the luggage in."

BW went ahead with the bag and cases while Clive sauntered. The young man found the footman waiting in the hall for him.

"What are you doing here? Take my bags to my room."

"I would, if I knew which one it was, sir."

"Are you not properly trained?"

"I am properly trained, sir, but I don't know the way to your room. If..."

"Don't answer back. You're a servant."

"That's true, sir, and a very puzzled one."

"What did you say?"

"If you would be so kind as to direct me to your room..."

"No, no, you're not getting away with that. You passed an unnecessary comment."

"My profuse apologies, sir."

"Don't do it again."

"I shan't, sir. Your room is which way?"

"Upstairs, turn left, fourth on the right."

"Thank you, sir."

BW led the way, his neck red with irritation. Clive walked behind, smiling. They reached the room and BW opened the door.

"Hang up my things." Clive entered, then hurled himself onto the bed and lit a cigarette. He did not take his eyes off BW. "Get a move on." He was enjoying the uncomfortable silence in which the footman dealt with the contents of the luggage. "You're not very good."

"I'm not trained as a valet, sir."

"You're not really trained for anything, are you? What's your name?"

"Broadbent-Wicks, sir."

Clive laughed. "Family penniless, is it?"

"No, sir."

"Then what are you doing as a servant?"

"Earning my keep."

"Barely, I should think… I really ought to mention your fumbling ways to Surridge… Perhaps I won't, though. If you were to do me a small service or two, I might overlook such incompetence and your growing list of transgressions."

"What services might they be, sir?"

"I'll tell you when necessary. But here's a little one for you now. Get a bottle of brandy from the cellar without asking Surridge. Do I need to give you directions?"

"I know where the cellars are, sir. However, I must refuse your request."

"You'll get me that brandy if you want to keep your position."

"The cellar is the responsibility of Mr Surridge. I can speak to him on your behalf."

"Your hearing is defective. He is to be kept out of it."

"Then I cannot do as you wish, sir."

"Perhaps you don't know... That must be it. I'm Clive Munday — *Munday*. People who cross us come to regret it."

"Would you be referring to the feud, sir?"

"So, you have heard... Last chance, friend, or out you go. I'll get you fired from that seedy agency you work for. I suppose the owner is some little money-grubbing ass who'll soon kick you out to save his wretched business."

Broadbent-Wicks stopped what he was doing and stood up straight, then he quickly removed his coat.

"What are you doing?"

BW removed his gloves.

"I say..."

"Stand up, because I'm going to give you a sound thrashing."

"You can't do that!"

"Do you box at Cambridge?" BW had raised his fists.

"It's Oxford, and no."

"That's a pity, because I'm rather good."

"No. Listen, I'm tired. I didn't mean what I said."

"Get off the bed. I can put up with petty tyranny and meaningless insults, but when you besmirch others whom I hold in the highest esteem, then you've gone too far. Also, someone must put a stop to your vile behaviour before you inflict yourself upon too many others. So, get up."

"No, I shan't. I'm sorry. Here. Take some money... Forget the whole thing."

After giving a long, disdainful look, BW ignored the pound note and turned to put on his coat and gloves. When he was ready to leave, he said,

"Behave like that again, and you know what to expect." He had almost gone when he popped his head back in. "Your moustache looks like a dead caterpillar." Then he firmly shut the door.

Sophie was anxious to use the telephone to relay the latest information on Minkov, but work and the movements of the family and guests had so far prevented her from doing so. Despite several attempts, she could not get into the study because it was in use. Now Mr Surridge had just gone to sound the dinner gong. In the kitchen, the cooks were in that final frantic state between finishing the cooking, keeping dishes hot, and serving into bowls. A crowd of servants busied themselves and were ready to carry in the first course once they received the signal. The agents were ready in the Ballroom.

"If only there were a way I could telephone while they're eating," said Sophie.

"There won't be, miss," said Ada. "Mr Surridge will notice. The only way you could do it is if you said you was about to throw-up. Then he'd get you out of the room fast enough."

"I couldn't bring myself to utter such words."

"I know, miss. That's the disadvantage with you being educated, if you don't mind my saying."

"What if I said I *felt* sick?"

"That's more polite, like, but he'd think you'd only want to have a sit-down for a minute. You must make Mr Surridge believe you're about to ruin the dinner. The first house I worked in where I served at table, there was this lady at dinner who was lookin' a bit queasy. She 'ung on as best she could but had to excuse herself in the end. When she bolted for the door, the poor old soul didn't make it. And guess who had to clean up after her? The others couldn't ignore what happened, 'specially with all the noises, so they left early. Mr Surridge won't want that. No one does."

"Can we talk of something else, please? It sounds much too risky, and I can't be caught using the telephone… I'll just have to be patient until midnight, when I'll be able to tell Sergeant Gowers about Minkov and Graham Nye."

The gong had sounded the last call, and the agents waited quietly while guests filed in. The dinner began.

The Dumond Hall ballroom was far too large for the size of the house. It was originally built to accommodate the biennial dance, which it did amply, and was the preferred venue for that reason. The ballroom at Capel House was diminutive by comparison and was really too small for the event. The Eldreds' ballroom was, however, of perfect proportions, exquisitely decorated in the Regency style and was by far the prettier of the two.

The Munday ballroom was rectangular, high-ceilinged, and brightly lit with electric light. The one truly attractive feature it possessed was next to the longest side of the dance floor. There, behind a colonnade of white painted wooden pillars, was a comfortable, low-ceilinged area suitable for sitting and talking while viewing the dance. Tonight, servants had rolled out a large carpet over the centre of the parquet dance floor. Upon this stood three equally long tables arranged in rows, which suggested a boarding school's refectory. They switched off many of the overhead lights once the guests were seated and, with candelabra on the tables, the ambience was greatly improved.

There were ninety-one at the tables, yet there remained a wide border of dance floor surrounding them. Across this space, like marching ants, a seemingly continuous stream of dark clad servants bearing food in one direction kept a serving table supplied, while going the other way a similar stream took away used dinnerware. Stalking up and down in front of this commissariat, Mr Surridge, doing his best not to wheeze, surveyed each dining table, sending in a servant wherever needed. By hand movements alone, he conducted the serving of courses, their subsequent removal, and also, through his proxies, attended to any minor difficulty which arose.

There were others serving besides the four agents, but together they were too few for the number of guests present. Everyone rushed just to keep up, which meant the agents had no time to linger or listen.

Another factor played against the agents — the placement of the guests. Although the total was one part extended Munday family, one part local persons of distinction, with the third part being the London friends of Audrey and Luke, they were all haphazardly mixed. For example, at one table, the energetic London drummer sat next to the vicar, and they were often deep in conversation. At another table, Lord Gerald sat next to Pruney, short for Prunella, whom the agents referred to as Miss Lobster. She had gone as pink as biology permits and regaled Lord Gerald with a full account of her sunburn, and fifty other disassociated things, to the accompaniment of loud laughing, dramatic gestures, and an inability to sit still for three seconds — a usual habit augmented by her current discomfort. At a third table, Basil Munday and Minkov were systematically being bored into oblivion by the Mayor of Marlborough, who recounted all the ins and outs of a recent town hall vote. The Munday aunts, uncles, cousins, etc., were scattered in small groups throughout the whole. Many of the family were aloof towards other guests to the point of being stand-offish.

These latter gave Sophie the impression that had Lord Eldred entered just then, the assorted Mundays would coalesce into a single body intent upon seizing and hanging him there and then. Often, there is a malcontent at a dinner, but for there to be so many and all related, there had to be a common cause, and to Sophie's mind that could only be Lord Eldred. She believed their attitude did not bode well for tomorrow's masquerade and wondered why they felt so ill at ease.

At a certain moment during the main course, Sophie noticed Basil Munday beckoning Surridge to him. He discreetly whispered to the butler, who nodded and returned to his station. Immediately, a footman, a wine-waiter with a bottle

225

in a silver basket, approached Basil's section of the table. The standing procedure was to offer more wine to the guest only when the glass reached a quarter full. The footman inspected several glasses, but only refilled the mayor's glass — almost to the brim. After this was done, Sophie had moved close enough to hear Basil, while holding up his glass, say to the mayor, "What do you think of the wine?"

In answer to this direct question, and seeing Basil holding his glass, the mayor picked up his own. "A most excellent vintage." He then drank. As soon as he set his glass down, the footman refilled it without asking.

It was a deliberate ploy, and Sophie supposed it was to induce the mayor to forget town hall business through the medium of an extra glass or two of wine. She risked glancing at Minkov, whom she had been carefully avoiding. By his faint smile, she believed him to be fully aware of what had just occurred.

After dinner, something approaching a cocktail party ensued. Rather than an adjournment to other rooms, there being no single room that could accommodate the company, the guests were served from a temporary bar set up in the lounge area within the colonnade. While everyone was convivially occupied, the servants removed the tables and chairs from the room. While the carpet was being rolled up, an orchestra began to play. Their music was smooth and rather bland, yet danceable — but not at all what the Londoners wanted. The locals loved it, though, and couples of all ages drifted pleasantly across the gleaming wooden expanse without fear of collision. Later, the London band joined the orchestra and, although they stuck to an agreed-upon set, the tea-time waltz music achieved an unaccustomed level of syncopation and urgency which some of the older couples found challenging.

Before that occurred, there was an intermission. The Roman Pool was about to be illuminated. To this purpose, a special switch had been rigged so that Lord Gerald could do the honours from a table on the eastern terrace. At ten o'clock, with everyone assembled outside in the mild night air, he threw the switch. A great 'Ahh!' arose from the spectators. The entire complex, invisible the moment before, was suddenly revealed, as if contained within a dome of brilliance, with every detail apparent inside the floodlit cocoon — a vision of ancient Rome floating at the end of the dark lawn.

"Bloody marvellous," said someone within the anonymity of the crowd of onlookers. They applauded Lord Gerald's accomplishment.

In a few moments, people wandered down to the pool for a closer inspection. Within a quarter hour, they had seen enough and returned to the house, except for one gentleman, content to stay a little longer. He sat on a bench smoking a cigar while appreciating his surroundings.

At eleven, the orchestra stopped for the night. Those who were staying found their way to their rooms, while visiting guests departed. In the lounge that the Londoners had taken for themselves, a small clique had gathered to talk and drink while a gramophone played in the background. Ada and a footman served drinks to the young crowd.

"Luke!" called Kit, a tall man, handsome, well-dressed, and slightly dissipated. "What's this I hear about a feud? I mean, surely, it's a gag?"

"No gag, but we don't speak of it, old man. Not the done thing."

"Maybe for you, it isn't. But I want to hear all about it. We all do. Come on, spill the beans. Be the perfect host, and all that."

"Yes!" cried Pruney. "Tell us the *gory* details lurking in your family's past."

"It's not an old story, Pruney," called Kit. "It's up to date, modern, and the latest thing. Luke's uncle was murdered in the village a few days ago."

"*Really!?*" Pruney was wriggling and wanted to hear everything.

Audrey came into the room and got a drink from Ada.

"Not much to tell," said Luke. "Great, great, great, etc. Uncle James fought a duel with Martin Eldred. Eldred lost. Actually, he died from injuries sustained. Then his demented sister murdered Uncle James a year or two later. Ever since then, our families have settled matters out of court by shooting one another. That's all there is to it, really."

"But what about your Uncle Wilfred?" asked Kit.

"Luke, bless his heart, is trying to pass everything off as of little consequence," said Audrey. "But it *isn't.*" She spoke to Luke as she casually took a cigarette from a box. "Allow me." Audrey approached a long settee. Those on it made room for her. She had her audience, and she sat down on the edge of the seat cushion. The man next to her lit her cigarette. Others moved their chairs closer. It was apparent they looked up to her.

Everyone waited. Audrey blew a jet of smoke into the air. "There has always been a streak of madness in the Eldred family. One wouldn't notice under ordinary circumstances, but it's there all right. More pronounced sometimes than at others, but it's true that every generation of the Eldred family produces a killer. They're a subtle and cunning lot, and I believe it is their main purpose in life to destroy us. They transmit this idea from father to son. Indoctrination obviously begins at an early age; it's positively a mania with them."

"Oh, I say, sounds like a cult or a league of assassins," said Kit. "How have you all escaped, then?"

"By simple expediency. In each generation, when an Eldred has killed one of ours, we put down one of theirs much like one would a mad dog."

"Ooh! Gives me goosebumps," said Pruney. "And how *petrifying* for you, darling, but why don't you go to the police?"

"I told you they were clever, Pruney. We're *never* able to prove anything against them, so there's no point bringing in the police. This forces us to act outside the law simply to protect ourselves. Naturally, we only want peace as anyone would."

"How *positively* Italian," said Kit.

"To tell the complete story would take hours. I'll relate a few of the juicier parts in a moment."

"Oh, yes, *do*," said Pruney.

"Perhaps you don't realize this, but the current Eldred madman of this generation will be our guest of honour here tomorrow. He killed Uncle Wilfred."

The guests were shocked and showed it in their gasps of surprise and by their exclamations. Audrey waited until they had settled.

"Before we go further, I feel Lord Eldred ought to receive a very *special* reception when he arrives."

"I'm not sure that's a good idea," said Luke.

"Hold on just a sec," said Kit. "Let me get this straight. The fellow who killed Uncle Wilfred will be the guest of honour? That's outrageous. How can you possibly allow it?"

"Darlings," called Pruney, "should we be discussing this with servants in the room?"

"No," said Luke. "You may both go." He waved away Ada and the footman.

As they opened the door, Clive Munday was entering.

"Sorry, I'm late. I was talking to Mother."

"Where's Violet?" asked Luke.

"She went up to see Grandfather. By now, she's probably gone to bed."

Luke stood up and put an arm around Clive's shoulders. "Everyone! If you haven't met him before, this is our youngest brother, Clive. He's a good sort, so be gentle with him."

"What's your poison!?" shouted a man who had elected himself the bartender.

"I'll have a look, if I may," said Clive.

"Sit next to *me* when you return." Pruney smiled at the young man.

"Be careful she doesn't devour you," said Luke with a laugh.

Real or feigned, Pruney was annoyed. "Take no notice of your *beastly* brother!"

"Clive, you're just in time to help," said Kit. "We're going to put something over on Lord Eldred."

"Not *yet*!" cried Pruney. "Audrey hasn't told us the stories. We want to hear them first. There's all night to plot revenge."

Hearing this, Ada pulled her ear from the door and left. She was quite certain someone would eventually catch her listening, and it was not worth the risk.

At midnight, as Sophie was reaching an open part of Loxie Lane, a finger of cloud obscured the full moon, and she retrieved her torch from a pocket. Before switching it on, she noticed many points of pale green light dotting the road and among the short growth on either side. Glow-worms — she smiled to herself as magical childhood memories rushed back. She bent down to examine one. "Hello, Glowie. Where are you off to?" Sophie stayed to watch for a few moments, but her business was urgent, so she pressed on. The trees closed in again and here the glow-worms disappeared, so she now switched on her torch.

At the bridge, she exchanged signals with the car. It was her own vehicle, Rabbit, which meant Elizabeth had driven. Sophie got in the back and they all said hello.

"Everything all right, Miss King?" asked Sergeant Gowers.

"Yes, thank you. It's a lovely night, and I saw lots of glow-worms on the way."

"Did you, Miss King?" said Elizabeth. "I haven't seen glow-worms in years. They're so charming."

"Then you should go up the lane about three hundred yards. They're all over the place."

"Very nice," said Gowers. "Would there be anything to report, Miss King?"

"Sorry, and yes, there is." She handed him her reports. "In the feud report, it's mostly minor observations which you can read at your leisure, but the big urgent thing is in the Minkov report. He contacted an accomplice named Graham Nye, who is staying at the Great Western Hotel, Swindon. I tried to call you as soon as we found out this afternoon, but I couldn't get near the telephone."

"Pity that. What is he up to, do you think?"

"We don't know. Minkov, who identified himself as Tanner during the brief call, said it was '*all on*' and that he and Nye would meet later '*as agreed.*' It's obvious they have a plan worked out between them, but it's positively infuriating that he gave no specifics."

"He gave the one about Swindon, right enough, Miss King. I'll pass along the information to Penrose as soon as we get back to the hotel."

"Surely, he's at home asleep?"

"If he is, this'll wake him up fast enough. Anything for Inspector Haddock in the report? We have to keep him sweet and, by that, I really mean the Chief Constable."

"As I mentioned, there are lots of little things. Something you should know about that has yet to develop into anything is the widespread antipathy for Lord Eldred. I hate to think what will happen tomorrow, because there are undercurrents. The wider Munday family, none of whom are living at Dumond Hall, gave me the impression that they're waiting for a grim event, such as an execution. I'm probably making more of it than I should but, unless they are just *grim* people, they look like they're at a hanging. Just an impression, as I say, but it was quite pronounced."

"I don't know what to make of that," said Gowers. "As you know, I can't really do anything unless someone utters threats. You might be mistaken, Miss King, but under the circumstances, I can see how such an impression carries weight. Although, I reckon it won't mean a thing to the Chief Constable."

"There's more. As previously mentioned in my report, Audrey and Luke Munday have a large group of their London friends staying. Tonight — in fact, it may still be ongoing — they are openly discussing the feud amongst themselves *and* plotting some type of action against Lord Eldred. We don't know what it is, because we could not listen any longer — there was a real danger of being discovered. *But*, whether a prank or a felonious assault, they are plotting something."

"Oh, that's different... I can see I'll have to move that up the chain of command right away."

"Then you should know that Luke only spoke lightly of the feud in response to a direct question, but it was *Audrey* who took over and made it so serious... I suppose they were conspiring, really. All that was underway when Clive Munday joined the group. The people there were all of an age or disposition to actually pull off a stunt. Now, how far it goes is anyone's guess. However, Audrey is very much a prime mover within the group, and she bears a deep grudge against the Eldred family, and especially against Lord Eldred. She announced to the room he was a murderer, mad, and that something must be done about him when he visits."

"Blimey," said Gowers. "Mind if I borrow your torch so I can write all that down?"

"Not at all… Elizabeth, let us speak outside so as not to disturb Sergeant Gowers."

They got out.

"It all sounds quite dreadful," said Elizabeth.

"Yet it may come to nothing because they are not criminals, but only irresponsible. They *can't* be openly planning a murder, yet, by whatever they are planning to do, they will increase the chances of something awful happening."

"I quite take your point, Miss King."

"How are your cats, and Miss Jones, of course?"

"The cats are doing well under Nicholas's care. Miss Jones says everything is running as it should. Mr Dexter has complained about his invoice."

"That man is nothing but a troublemaker. If I doubled the amount, it wouldn't be *half* enough for what we endure from him! I'll deal with Mr Dexter next week. Shout all he likes, I shan't knock a penny off the bill."

"Yes, Miss King. There is something else. I have the pistol in my pocket again. With everything that's going on, do you wish to take it?"

"No, I still don't need it. Is something the matter?"

"I must confess to feeling very naughty while sitting next to a policeman with an unregistered firearm concealed about my person."

"Yes. We can't have that… Um, next week. I will *definitely* register it next week. Does that help?"

"Immensely, Miss King. Thank you. I have discovered that you need only go to a local police station, fill out a form, and pay the five-shilling fee."

"*Oh!* Is that all one does? I thought it was some horrendous and expensive process deep inside Scotland Yard. However, five shillings is still far too much, but it's what they demand, so what can be done? Next week, Elizabeth, I promise."

"Very good, Miss King."

"I should get back, and I believe Sergeant Gowers has finished."

Gowers got out. "Thank you, Miss King." He handed the torch back. "A word of advice. A lot might happen between now and when we next meet, so think of your safety first. You might have difficulty in contacting *me*, but there's always the local police. Call them in if things look bad. I'm an advisor, so to speak, and there's nothing I can do officially without a nod from the Chief Constable."

"I understand."

"Hopefully, when Haddock hears of this plot, he'll get active and station a few officers outside Dumond Hall. That will make them think twice, and he doesn't have to ask for his lordship's permission to do that."

"The sight of police uniforms should make Audrey pause for thought. Good night."

When Sophie returned to the house, the glow behind it from the pool lights on the eastern side was visible. As it was quiet now, and the house was mostly in darkness, she thought to take a quick look. She quietly passed the now empty ballroom on the north side, and then a row of bushes. In turning at the corner, she discovered she had an excellent view of the pool. There was someone moving about between the house and the lights. Noticing this immediately, she drew back among the bushes. The figure was moving closer to the lights, occasionally stopping to look around. Curious, Sophie studied the oddly behaving person. Whoever it was moved slowly with a slight furtiveness. The figure proved to be a man once he became properly silhouetted against the glow. He was tall and wearing a trilby hat. He stepped onto the low wall and stood as still as the statues on either side of him.

"Hey! You, there!" A man shouted from the terrace.

The shadowy figure jumped down and fled into the darkness. Sophie lost sight of him. Several men hurried towards the pool in pursuit. She thought it prudent that she left and, avoiding the terrace, went to the side door where Flora was awaiting her return.

"I'm glad you're back," said Flora. "I want to go to bed."

"Never mind that, there's a prowler in the grounds, and they've gone after him."

"No! A poacher, perhaps? They rarely get caught; not the good ones, anyway."

"This one was hanging about the pool playing at statues. Perfectly visible, but I don't understand what he was doing."

"He wasn't a poacher, then. Did he do anything else?"

"Nothing really, other than creep about... Do you know I'm inclined to believe it was Lord Eldred? I've been told he wears a distinctive trilby, and that was the style of hat the prowler wore."

"Gosh, why would he come here at this time of night? Is he off his chump?"

"Plenty think so... Let's go to sleep. We have so much to do tomorrow."

Chapter 19

Telling conversations

It was Saturday morning and the servants were in a frantic whirl long before the family and guests were awake. Mr Surridge was not in the best of moods. The coming day was trying enough for his nerves. The fact that breakfast, thanks to the contingent of London guests, now sprawled across the entire morning, had put him into a continuous state of annoyance. By their very existence, they threatened his carefully crafted order of the well-run household. He did not go as far as to confide his extreme displeasure to Mrs Lester, because, if anything, she was in an even greater state of annoyance. There had been breakages and damages in the last few days equal in volume to all other dilapidations over the past decade. One in particular of the many had incensed the meticulous woman. It was a cigarette burn on a curtain in the lounge where the Londoners congregated, but it was at such a great height, almost at the top, that she believed it only could have been done deliberately. She had concealed the offensive mark by safety-pinning a fold in the curtain.

When she told Mr Surridge of this enormity, although he did not answer beyond a simple, resigned acknowledgment, she was certain he had ground his teeth. What they both agreed upon was that, together, they would report this wholesale ruination to Lord Gerald. It was his house, after all.

They knew, but tacitly avoided uttering, that Mr Basil would laugh it off, while Mrs Clare was disinterested, because she had yet to be elevated to 'Lady of the House' — usually a vital implicit honour, rendered nebulous under the circumstances. De facto yet absent, that's what she was, because Lord Gerald had never officially sanctioned her to replace his wife in the role. One day, she would fully take over but, until then, the old Lord and the young Master settled everything haphazardly between them.

The mood of the butler and housekeeper filtered down, making itself felt throughout the lower echelons of the servant hierarchy until it reached the laundry. Sudden, curt demands put Daisy in a flaring temper, and no one of equal standing dared go near her, except the two maids who had no choice because they assisted with the washing. These two unfortunates, keeping silent themselves, heard all about it from Daisy.

Only the agents were unaffected by the tensions in the house, because they were there for a specific purpose, an intense project and a mission, from the extra effort of which they would quickly recover as soon as they returned to London. For the rest, serving in the house was a routine and continual process. The difference, therefore, between the servants of Dumond Hall and those from Burgoyne's was noticeable. For Mr Surridge and Mrs Lester, the agency became a harbour in the storm. This meant that, despite the agents' efficiency, they, too, were up to their eyeballs in it.

The one saving grace for the agents in the situation was that their professionalism was relied upon to fill in any gaps in service to the household rather than attending to the family and guests all the time. Thus it was that, after Basil Munday had eaten breakfast with Lord Gerald and the Breakfast Room was empty, Clare came down alone, looking radiant and quite lovely, and Minkov arrived by happenstance within two minutes. With his sixth sense, Surridge knew that service was required immediately and, as Sophie was passing his pantry on her way to the Ballroom, he sent her in to plug the gap, and she arrived just in time to be astonished.

"Toshko," said Clare, in a low, vibrant tone. "How *lovely* to see you. I trust you slept well."

"Good morning, Clare. Yes, I slept well, thank you." He brightened upon seeing her, then sat down opposite. "Eh, would it be forward of me," he said slowly, "to utter a truth?"

Clare, always graceful in her movement, put her head slightly on one side, but kept her eyes on him. "That depends upon what it is."

"A simple fact... You are the most beautiful woman I have ever met."

While they stared at each other, Sophie did not know where to look, so she busied herself unnecessarily with some dishes. With Sophie's movement, Clare remembered where she was, and sought to recover from her confusion.

"That's a very charming thing to say... Um, what are your plans for today?"

"I am, of course, at your disposal."

"How thoughtful... Are you eating breakfast?"

"Yes, I will, but it is unimportant."

"I suggest you have breakfast before you go any further."

Sophie noticed Clare was colouring at Minkov's unexpected intensity.

"May I get you something, sir?" asked Sophie, as if nothing at all embarrassing had been said.

"Yes, why not?" said Minkov. "A coffee first, then, I think..."

Minkov must have taken the hint, because the conversation returned to the usual themes.

Broadbent-Wicks was minding his own business in as much as he was in the Ballroom, moving around a large potted palm to Mrs Lester's satisfaction.

"No, no. I think it's better off in the original corner, after all."

"Yes, Mrs Lester," he replied, unperturbed that she seemed to imply that it was his fault that the palm looked out of place everywhere else.

A lad came in with a message.

"'Scuse me, Mrs Lester."

"What is it, Michael?"

"I've been told to say as 'ow Mr Broadbean-Wicks is to go an' see his lordship at once, if'n it pleases you, Mrs Lester."

"It's Broad*bent*, not Broadbean."

"Ow, sorry, Mrs Lester. Oh, yes, I near forgot. His lordship is in his private sittin' room."

"You may go." Michael disappeared. Mrs Lester fixed her gaze upon BW. "Why does his lordship wish to see you?"

"I really don't have a clue, Mrs Lester."

"You had better go at once, but come straight back here afterwards."

BW made his way to that part of the house reserved for Lord Gerald's use. He knocked on a door. The next door along opened. Lord Gerald, a cane in hand, called out.

"That one's me bathroom. This one's me study."

"Good morning, my Lord. Sorry for the blunder."

"It happens. That door's always locked now. Had a maid waltz in once while I was in the tub. Don't know which of us was the more embarrassed... Shut the door."

"Yes, my Lord. Oh, I say. Your apartment's rather spiffing."

"Never mind all that nonsense. Me nurse has gone off to Marlborough, so we won't be disturbed. Listen to me, Broadbent-Wicks. Tonight, you're going to push the wheelchair down to the pool. While everyone's capering about, we shall slip away on the quiet. No one must know. Think you can manage it?"

"Oh, *ra-ther*, my Lord."

"Good man. I might swim, I might not — probably won't, even if no one's about. Too difficult to manage for one thing. Can't go back into the Ballroom soaking wet, you see. That's about it. I'll give you the signal at a propitious moment and off we'll go."

"What about your nurse, my Lord?"

"Don't worry about her. She sticks to me like a limpet, but I'll get her out of the way all right. You can go now. If there are any changes, I'll tell you tonight."

"One more thing, my Lord. What will be the signal?"

"Signal?" He sounded puzzled. "I'll call you when I want you."

"Yes, I believe that will do it, my Lord. I'll be off, then."

"Miss Carmichael, someone else will take those," began Surridge. Ada set down the punch bowl and glasses on the table in the China Room. "A pot of tea has been requested in the garage. They are getting the tray ready in the kitchen."

"Yes, Mr Surridge."

"After you have poured the tea into the *mugs*," the butler had difficulty with the word, "come away at once to resume your duties."

"Yes, Mr Surridge."

When Ada entered the garage, there were four men gathered around the engine of a car. One was a chauffeur in overalls, the other three were gentlemen who were watching him tinker. Among them was Luke. A fifth, with his head back and eyes closed, and sitting uncomfortably in a wooden chair with his feet resting on another, was Clive, and he looked awful.

"Ah, very timely," said Luke, detaching himself from the group upon seeing Ada. "Tea's here, Clive... You look in a bad way. Come on, take your medicine, hot and sweet."

"Go away," groaned Clive. He sat up. "I want the tea, though... Come here, O ministering angel."

Ada had put down the tray on a nearby and rather dirty table. She set out the mugs. "How many sugars would you like, sir?"

"Two."

"And milk, sir?"

"A little... not too much."

"You should have eaten breakfast," said Luke, coming over to get his tea.

"Don't."

"A hair of the dog, that's my motto," said Luke's friend, Kit.

"That's never worked for me," said Luke. "Believe it or not, moderation during a binge followed by aspirin and plenty of water afterwards is the only way to go."

"Moderation while on a binge? That goes against the spirit of the thing," said Kit.

"Yes, it does," agreed Luke, "but look at what we have before us. Clive's a proper caution to all who see him."

"Shut up."

"Yes, he's a difficult case," said Kit. "Perhaps this young lady has a cure?"

"Some people swear by raw eggs, sir."

"No," said Clive.

"You should try something," said the fourth gentleman, "because you're needed for tonight. I distinctly remember you swearing the blood oath."

"Oath...? What oath?"

"A private matter we'll discuss later," said Luke.

"What *are* you talking about?"

"No getting out of it, old man," said Kit. "You took it when we all did. There are plenty of witnesses to testify against you."

Ada left before they told her to leave.

The nurse returned from Marlborough and gave a bottle of calamine lotion to Mrs Lester before resuming her duties. The sunburn-suffering Pruney had to wait until Mrs Lester found Flora, into whose hands she thrust the bottle and some cotton wool, before sending her upstairs.

"Come in," responded Pruney to Flora's knock. The young woman was quite low on the social list, and the boxy little bedroom with its sloping ceiling reflected that fact. She was lying face down on the bed in her nightdress. Her pink shoulders glowed.

"Good morning, miss. I've brought the calamine."

"Where were you last night?"

"In bed, miss. Where were you?"

"No... That's not what I meant... Oh, it doesn't matter. Can you put some on for me? I can't reach the part below my shoulders."

"Yes, miss."

"Try not to get any on my nightdress. That stuff is messy and it stinks."

"Did you sleep all right, miss?" Flora sat down on the bed and put the bottle and cotton wool on the table.

"Barely slept at all. It was impossible to get comfortable."

"I'm sure it was a trial for you, miss. Do you know you've gone just like a lobster?" Flora moved the straps out of the way.

"I know I have."

Flora poured on the calamine.

"Ah, that's cold!"

"You'll soon get the benefit of it." Flora gently rubbed in the lotion. "What are you going as tonight?"

"I was supposed to be a Saxon queen wearing this harness contraption with a sword hanging off it..."

"A real one, miss?"

"No, a toy wooden one. But I can't wear it now because of my sunburn. A maid warned me yesterday about it, but silly me didn't listen. Anyway, I must go as something, but I can't think what."

"How about Joan of Arc?"

"Me, as Joan of Arc?" She sighed. "No, I don't think so."

"I suggested Joan because a simple, thin dress would go easy on your sunburn."

"I see what you mean... I'll bear your suggestion in mind. That does feel good, and I think it's working... Don't stop, though."

"No, I have plenty of time," said Flora. "Is it true there was a prowler in the grounds last night?"

"*Yes*, there was. None of us saw him, though, but they say it was Lord Eldred."

"How can they know that if they didn't catch him?"

"Well, they do, darling. The Mayor of Marlborough got a little squiffy last night, and they were just getting some coffee down him before sending him off, when the Mad Eldred came out of nowhere and started dancing around the statues. I wish I'd been there. Apparently, the Mayor recognized him, as did several others, so there you are."

"And he a murderer, as well. We shan't be safe in our beds."

"No... We've got something planned for him, but I'm not sure it's wise now."

"What could it possibly be?"

"Can't tell. It's a secret. To the left and a bit lower... Yes, that's perfect."

"So, will you go through with it?"

"Yes, we always do. One of our crowd is going as a policeman, and he gave his word he'd steal a helmet from a bobby so he'd look authentic. He did it, too! Nearly got caught, though."

"That must have been a sight," said Flora.

"Oh, it was. They ran all the way down Piccadilly... Answer me this. How is it you speak so well?"

"I was orphaned in South Africa, and a governess who was returning to England took charge of me. She was a spinster of modest means who had just inherited a house. Once we arrived in England, she treated me like a *slave*, an absolute *slave*. She used to beat me with a cane over the smallest of infractions, and I still have the scars to prove it. Of course, she always insisted on the usage of correct English, so that's how I came to retain it."

"How *utterly* appalling? You poor thing."

"I'm over it now."

"Well, good for you. Somebody said you were a teetotaller. Don't you get bored? I know I would."

"As a servant, I have no time to get bored. Should I apply a second coat? They say it's much, much better if you do."

"Go right ahead, I haven't felt this relaxed in ages... I must say something to you, woman to woman. With your looks and voice, you *really* could do a lot better in life than as a servant. Only not in my set, sweetie. I couldn't stand the competition."

"Do you really think I could?"

"It's totally possible. Get someone wealthy to fall in love with you and then you're set... Trouble is, all the handsome men who are lots of fun that I know don't have a penny."

"Does that include Mr Luke Munday? I saw you talking to him yesterday."

"Oh, so you noticed. We were an item for a while. He lives off his allowance, which isn't that bad, but I don't think his father is very free with money where his children are concerned. Supposedly, Luke's father is good at business, and that type of father is always on his high horse about knowing the value of money. That's what my father's like... I think I've had enough now."

"There's one more part I must rub in. Supposing Luke was about to inherit the title. Would that make a difference to you?"

"All the difference. Lord Gerald is worth hundreds of thousands. If Luke inherited all that loot within a year, I'd make him marry me. Lord Gerald's still alive and Basil looks set for another thirty years at least. How could I pin my hopes on such a distant prospect? It's such a shame, really, because I liked Luke. Since I let him go, he's been nasty to me sometimes."

"I've finished. Is there anything else I may do?"

"No, thanks. I'll give you something for your trouble later. Remind me if I forget. Right now, I just want to lie here in relative comfort and *drift*."

Chapter 20

Getting ready

It rained at noon — a steady drizzle which temporarily mitigated the heat. By two it had finished and so had lunch. Now came the long, wearing afternoon for the staff. The guests were no trouble, but finishing off the Ballroom and other reception areas was at that stage where everyone in authority wanted something changed. Concerning the potted palm Mrs Lester had agonized over earlier, Mr Surridge had it put in another corner, Basil Munday directed it to a third, and Clare Munday moved the palm back to its starting point. The kitchens were in that most diabolical of states wherein everything was going wrong, and nothing had yet gone right. It was enough to try the patience of a saint; and there were certainly no saints present in the kitchen. However, there were many, many martyrs, as those in culinary authority roared or banged about while venting their spleens.

The agents, for once, had little to do, and so they held a meeting in the now disused nursery.

"Please get off the rocking-horse," said Sophie. "You might break it."

"Sorry, Miss King. I hadn't considered that." BW stood up.

"We've been given our posts for the night. Nancy will supervise the buffet, therefore she cannot mingle like the rest of us who will be serving the company. However, with such a large crowd present, we can turn this to our advantage. Instead of our constantly seeking each other, we can send messages via Nancy, and she can redirect them. We will also use the standard system of signals so as not to bother Nancy too much while she works. We must be unobtrusive. Remember, Minkov will be present, and he mustn't notice what we're doing. I think if we check in with Nancy every quarter hour, that will be sufficient. Does anyone have a question so far?"

"I have one," said BW. "What if old Minkov is piling his plate with vol-au-vents right in front of Nancy?"

"Come back when he's finished."

"Ah, but he might stand about by the table talking to other chaps while shovelling it in. Then what?"

"Use your initiative."

"I'll do that."

"We have all learned a few things this morning, and we should review the important parts, and each express an opinion on them. I'll go first. It was a highly embarrassing situation, but Minkov, and this was over breakfast mind you, was overtly wooing Clare Munday. He said she was the most beautiful woman he had ever met. I think she wanted him to flirt with her, but then he bowled her over by his open and embarrassing declaration. What do you think of *that*?"

"She is beautiful," said Flora, "in that timeless and graceful sort of way. Isn't she ten years older than he?"

"I believe so," said Sophie.

"What I don't get," said Ada, "is that Audrey was chucking herself at Minkov, and he weren't interested, and now he's after Clare Munday, Audrey's bloomin' mother, and the wife of Basil, his friend. What's the matter with him?"

"Impossible to say," said Flora. "Is Audrey still chucking herself at him?"

"No, she's stopped that," said Ada. "She's forgotten all about him. Now she's all for doing down Lord Eldred. What do *you* think of Minkov's behaviour, miss?"

"I'm baffled. He is a spy, and we mustn't lose sight of that. If he has a hidden aim, I cannot say what it is. BW?"

"Do you mean to tell me, daughter Audrey has fallen for Minkov, but he's fallen for mother Clare, the wife of his host? The man's an absolute bounder."

"None of us disputes the fact. What we're trying to get at is whether he has a specific reason for paying such attention to Clare."

"Seems obvious to me," said BW.

"No, not *that*," Sophie turned slightly red. "A specific *spying* reason."

"Oh, I see... Um, no idea."

"Nancy, you go next."

"Clive got drunk last night, and now he's sufferin'. Serves him right. I told him raw eggs was the cure, but he took no notice, so that's up to him. It turns out they've got a blood oath on the go, and they're going to do something against Lord Eldred, but I don't know what it is. They went quiet with me an' the chauffeur present. I don't really have any more than that."

"Did they cut themselves?" asked BW.

"Not while I was there, they didn't." said Ada. "Why would they cut themselves?"

"Perhaps they did it last night. It's just that with a blood oath," said BW, "there must be a shedding of blood. I read up on it once..."

"Thank you, BW," said Sophie. "I'm sure what you read was informative, but we cannot stay in the nursery all afternoon. They're planning something, and we must find out what it is."

"In my opinion," said Flora, "they're intent upon some foolish prank and are merely being dramatic about it."

"That seems sensible to me. Ada?"

"I reckon that sounds about right. I don't like it, though. They all think Lord Eldred's a murderer, 'specially after the way Audrey was gettin' on at them. If it's just a trick, and the

247

bloke *is* a murderer, well, it'll turn into something 'orrible, that it will — even if they don't mean it that way."

"That's also my fear," said Sophie. "Your turn, Gladys."

"It's a shame you weren't present to appreciate the amount of total control I had over Pruney. I sincerely believe that for gathering information, a light massage with calamine lotion works better than any torture ever devised. The one point where she balked was in telling me what it is they have planned. What she revealed was that Lord Gerald has pots of money — in the hundreds of thousands. Luke has an adequate allowance but spends it all. He and she were an item…"

"An *item*? The language is becoming utterly impoverished."

"That was her word, not mine. Pruney confessed to liking him but thought a thirty-year wait for Lord Gerald and then Basil to pop off before Luke might be elevated was a little too long. She also hinted that Luke is now rather spiteful towards her."

"I saw some of that last night," said Ada.

"Did you? I've grown quite attached to Pruney. She's a dear soul in a brainless way, and so, on her behalf, I loathe Luke. There's one last thing to report. The sodden Mayor of Marlborough confirms your impression that it was Lord Eldred swinging from the statues last night."

"He wasn't swinging, he was standing still."

"Pruney said he was dancing, but I thought to improve upon her version. That's the lot. If you want any more, I can offer her another massage."

"Do you think she would accept?" asked Sophie.

"I honestly believe she would. I'd have to couch it in the right terms, though, otherwise she might become suspicious."

"BW, it's your turn."

"Thank you, Miss King. Unlike everyone else, I'm not sure I've heard anything useful. However, as you know, I'm quite matey with Lord Gerald. Today, he asked me to trundle him down to the Roman Pool during the Ball, while his nurse isn't looking. I must say he's pretty chipper about it, and it is game of the old boy to want to have a go."

"Why during the Ball?" asked Sophie.

"The old boy doesn't like a lot of people milling about. Wants to see the illuminations in peace and by himself. Actually, what he *really* wants to do is go swimming without anyone fussing over him. He's positively champing at the bit to have a good old plunge in the deep end. I wouldn't mind if he did but, although I can swim, I wouldn't rank myself as a lifesaver. So, if he gets the cramps, I'd jump in to save him, and then we'd both drown. I examined the pool yesterday. There's a deep part, a lovely blue, and just the sort of place he'd seize up and go down for the third time. Miss King, you know so much about etiquette. What is the right form of address to make a viscount stay in the shallow end?"

"I'm not sure... My Lord, you are out of your depth?"

"That sounds like both a suggestion and a rude comment," said Flora.

Ada said, "How about, My Lord, one step further and you'll drown?"

"No, too peremptory and mildly threatening," said Sophie. "We can't order him about."

"There is a shark in the pool, my Lord," said Flora.

"They're saltwater, and that's an outright lie."

"What about leeches, miss?"

"Oh, that's a good one. My Lord, I believe there are leeches in the pool. There, that's what you can say."

"But what if there aren't any?" asked BW.

"You *believe* there are, and that will suffice to get him out of the pool and avoid drowning."

"I shall use it in a case of necessity," said BW.

"Is there anything else?"

"The fact is, and I'm reluctant to mention it, I offered Clive Munday a thrashing for being an absolute tick but, like the coward he proved to be, he declined."

"You did *what!*?" Sophie's jaw dropped.

"I wanted to punch him on the nose, but he wouldn't get off the bed. I had a stern word with him, though."

"You can't do that!"

"He made comments that no gentleman of breeding should make. I did not mind his insults while he was trying to coerce me into pinching a bottle of brandy from Mr Surridge's cellar, but then he said something unforgiveable that I shall not repeat."

"What was it?"

"I apologize, Miss King, but I decline to answer. What he said is unrepeatable, and I believe he's still owed a hiding. Should he step out of line again, he'll get it."

"No matter *how* trying you found Clive Munday, you shall do *no* such thing. Don't you realize you jeopardize the mission with such behaviour? Now, listen carefully. I'm fully aware that gentlemen, particularly young gentlemen, settle matters between themselves with their fists. But it shall not, shall *never*, be said that one of my staff has pummeled a customer's son. Good grief! Who has ever heard of such a thing!?"

"But Miss King…"

"No, I haven't finished. I still have the floor. I understand this situation is trying. All I can say is, endure it. We three often must. However, on the rare occasion when action was necessary because danger threatened, then it was a different matter. I say to you now, Mr Broadbent-Wicks, avoid Clive Munday. Have nothing to do with him. I must have your word on this."

"Yes, Miss King. I shall avoid him. But what if…"

"You shall avoid him at all costs. It is as simple as that. If your duties place you in his vicinity, then do your work and nothing more. I trust I shall not hear of this matter again."

At four, the sun emerged, and the wind dropped. The humidity promised a sultry evening. Within Capel House, the high ceilings kept the rooms cool. The Eldreds were getting themselves ready for the Ball.

The two young daughters were not yet of an age to attend. They wanted to go, certainly, but as nothing had been told them of feuds and murders, they only knew that life was hard when one was young and denied the opportunity to attend the greatest social event of the year. They had seen the Ball last year — watching through bannisters from the stairs, while a flustered nurse hovered, hoping no trouble would arise in allowing the girls a glimpse of the brilliant gathering. That glimpse only created for the girls a greater desire to take part.

Edward, the son of Lord Eldred, sat in a chair and studied his shoes. Then he passed the cloth over his toecaps again. The shoes could not be shinier. Satisfied, he stood to look in the mirror. His evening clothes fitted him well. Indeed, he was pleased by what he saw. He adjusted his cuffs in the way the best-dressed gentlemen did. His costume was packed. If anyone asked if he were the sheik of a desert tribe, he would immediately correct them by stating he was Lawrence of Arabia.

His parents considered him young for his age, but he was not as immature as they believed. Last year, he had seen Julia Munday at the Ball, and believed her to be an unobtainable, magical being. He had found out afterwards that he was two days older than she. Edward had nervously avoided her, as well as others, because he could not dance. But that was then, and twelve months is a long time in the life of a growing child. At school, and unbeknownst to parents, teachers, and school friends, he had given his pennies to a nineteen-year-old maid who worked there, and she had taught him how to dance in the silence of a dusty and half-forgotten biology specimen room. She was of average skill, not the best of teachers, but very willing. By saving his sixpences, he advanced, and could enter the portals of Mrs Henry's Dancing Studio, located close to the busiest fish and chip shop in the town by the school. There he excelled, mainly because of Mrs Henry's gramophone, although she repeatedly had to tell him to relax his manner and to *flow* — concepts he found difficult. Nevertheless, his confidence was now sky high. Edward was going to ask Julia to dance. Studying the mirror, he adopted a position as if holding her who ruled his heart and, to music that only he could hear, waltzed the imaginary girl around the confined space of his bedroom.

In her dressing room, Lady Shelagh Eldred spoke to her lady's maid, Elsie, as if she were a lifelong friend, which, in fact, she was. They had grown up together. When leaving the family farm, Elsie, in service there, had gone with Shelagh to Capel House. While the maid was out of the room fetching something, Shelagh reviewed the evening's itinerary once more. Leave at five to five, arrive at Dumond Hall on the hour, and go to the rooms provided. A light dinner at a quarter to six, followed by the 'Chin-wag' with only the most senior of the Munday and Eldred families present. Retire to rooms about seven to change into costume. Shelagh cast a glance through the doorway at the Madame de Pompadour dress and curled, close-fitting wig laid out on the bed. She thought the outfit was beautiful, but that she would feel silly wearing it. Fancy dress was another of the trials of being Lady Eldred that she would never get used to, and that was of no use to complain about. Being practical, she decided it was best she just get on with it when the time came.

At eight sharp would be the First Dance — when she would go slowly around the floor with Lord Gerald. But she knew, she *knew*, that everyone watching, and they *all* would watch, would compare the way she danced to those lithe, perfect movements of Clare Munday who would simultaneously dance with her husband, Lord Eldred. It was not a contest, but Lady Shelagh knew she had already lost. Rather than dwell on such an uncomfortable matter, she moved on, in her mind, to the rest of the evening. She would meet everyone, dance a few times, eat from the buffet, drink very little, say goodbye at midnight, and then go home. Home — if only they could stay put. The Ball, itself a trial, was made far worse by being at Dumond Hall. She refused to step further along the feud's dark tunnel and started looking through the things in her case. Elsie returned, and Shelagh brightened up as if nothing were the matter.

Lord Eldred dressed himself, because there was no money for a valet — nor footman, nor butler, for that matter. He was ready to leave and was now standing in the middle of the room, staring and trying to recall something important, but could not. Often taken this way of late when he had nothing to do, his mind paused and refused to be directed towards anything. By contrast, when working outside, he could concentrate on the task in hand but, at some point, without willing it, a thought would occur, be it about the weather, or money, or recent murders, and, while busy, depression or fear or anger would eventually manifest itself, affecting what he was doing, and forcing him to stop. At other times, a hundred fragmented thoughts crowded in demanding attention — the ordinary mixing with the vital. Not a man given to tears, he had recently found his face wet while studying the diminishing water level in the stream. Pascoe had unconsciously touched his face, discovered dampness on his fingers, and was surprised to find he had cried without knowing it.

At night, he either slept heavily, or was often awake, and his dreams were rubbishy, absurd and aimless, yet always dimly lit and haunted by some forgotten yet urgent nagging thing he must do but never did.

The only times he found relief were when talking to others or writing a letter. Then, he was untroubled. But for the rest of the day, a rhythm of confusion affected his mind — a cycling through of endless peaks of forgetfulness and troughs of bewilderment from which malaise he could not shake himself free. It irked him to know clarity lay somewhere nearby, was only minutes or days away, or was discoverable within another set of circumstances. It would come all the sooner if only he could do something... And it was that very thing which eluded him. What crystal clear thought, what single revelatory idea was it that was needed for his entire existence to be restored to order? He stared, but the phantom thought did not emerge from the racket in his mind. There was a knock on the door and Pascoe remembered there were other people in the world.

"Enter."

A farm labourer acting as temporary chauffeur opened the door. "Car's ready, my Lord."

"Thank you, Harry. We'll be down in a moment."

Chapter 21

Enemies in the House

Inspector Haddock waited in the entrance hall and slowly twirled his hat while examining a George Stubbs painting. It was of an eighteenth-century English groom leading a black Arabian racehorse, with the exquisitely detailed animal commanding the eye of the viewer. Surridge approached, and Haddock turned to meet him.

"Good afternoon, Inspector."

"Good afternoon, Mr Surridge."

"Do you wish to see his lordship?"

"No, no, I needn't trouble him, or Mr Basil Munday, for that matter. But I'd be thankful if you could pass a message along, loike. We're posting two constables outside the gate. They're there to control traffic and help drivers with directions — that type o' thing. We just wanted to inform the house in case the soight of a couple o' uniforms caused any alarm, as you moight say."

"I see. Do you believe such a disposition is necessary?"

"Well, we do, yes. The Chief Constable said it's also a pro-*active* measure to discourage motorists inclined to travel at excessive speed, and I can see his point."

"Ah, the Chief Constable is behind this course of action. I shall convey your message at once."

"I appreciate that, Mr Surridge, and I'm sorry to have bothered you when you're so busy."

"Thank you for your consideration. Good afternoon, Inspector."

It was exactly five o'clock when the ancient limousine arrived. Broadbent-Wicks was one of the two footmen who opened wide the double doors for the entrance of the Eldred family. Alone on the red carpet stood Lord Gerald, waiting, supporting himself with a single cane.

Lord Pascoe ascended the front stairs and halted at the threshold.

"What is your intention, sir?" called Lord Gerald.

"Only peace, sir."

"I take you at your word. You may enter."

"Is it safe for me so to do?"

"Upon my soul, no harm shall befall you under this roof."

"What of the past?"

"It is forgotten."

"And of the future?"

"As yet unwritten. Of the present, there is only the peace you seek. Enter."

"I hesitate."

"Friend, you are most welcome here. Now enter."

Eldred crossed the threshold. He and Lord Gerald bowed and shook hands.

"My family is without," said Eldred. Lady Shelagh and Edward had paused at the threshold.

"I pledge my life for theirs this day."

"Come," said Eldred to his family.

With the annual ceremony concluded, they met Lord Gerald, who now gave a less formal greeting.

"Good to see you, Eldred."

"My pleasure, entirely."

"This dry weather's a cause for concern," said Lord Gerald. "Are you managing all right?"

"It's a tough go. I'm finding that hoping for rain and getting it are two very different and trying things!"

"Yes, I'm sure. I can't recall a spring like it."

"It is exceptional, and widespread. Although it's little consolation, Munday, we are all in the same boat together... This is my wife, Lady Shelagh."

"Don't be so formal, Eldred. Lady Shelagh and I are old friends, aren't we, dear?"

"Very much so, my Lord."

"Now, as I recall, we agreed you would call me Gerald, and I'd call you Shelagh."

"So, we did, Gerald."

The old lord smiled. "I'm very much looking forward to our dance together. My only hope is that you can put up with me. I warn you; I'm not getting any younger."

"I'm sure you'll do foine. You did very well last year." She gave him a dimpled smile as her apprehension melted.

"We'll see... Bless me. Who is this fine gentleman? Don't anyone tell me it's Edward, because I shan't believe them."

"Good evening, Lord Munday."

"Good evening, Mr Eldred. See here, shake me hand like a splendid fellow. There'll be no standing on ceremony between us from now on, eh?"

"I understand, sir."

"That's it, that's it." He turned away slightly, and Surridge was instantly by his side.

"I'll see you all at dinner." He then spoke to Surridge. "Show Lord Eldred and his family to their rooms."

"Yes, my Lord." He beckoned the footmen, and they approached carrying the trappings. Elsie, Shelagh's maid, came with them.

"If you would be so kind as to follow me, Lord Eldred. Your rooms are this way."

Led by the butler, hardly wheezing at all, the procession set off upstairs. Lord Gerald left the entrance hall by a corridor where his nurse waited with the wheelchair.

In far away London, at Scotland Yard, Superintendent Penrose was awaiting a telephone call from Archie Drysdale, who was in Swindon. The call came through from the Great Western Hotel.

"He's gone," said Archie.

"Just our luck. Did you catch sight of him?"

"No. He left first thing this morning. The staff at the hotel didn't know if he had a car — Nye hadn't mentioned how he travelled — so they assumed he came by train. The station is right across the street. I tried there but, without a proper description, asking about a single man in his late thirties with a dark brown suitcase proved useless. This is all I could get from the witnesses in the hotel. Nye kept to himself and dined out. He is of average height and build, dark-haired, and they never saw him without a hat, so he might be thin on top, but we don't know. Brown eyes, no facial hair, pale complexion, and no distinguishing features. Dressed ordinarily in a nondescript tweed jacket and the kind of grey trousers which are ubiquitous. No one noticed his shoes, the way he walked, etc."

"In other words, he doesn't stand out because he's like thousands of other chaps knocking about the country."

"I'm afraid so. I tried the nearest tobacconists, newspaper stands, the coach line, and local bus conductors, all to no avail. Any suggestions?"

"Not offhand. Trail's cold, I reckon. What will you do now?"

"Nothing, because I'm poaching on Home Office territory as it is. We missed Gavin Nuttall because he used an accommodation address to receive that telegram from Minkov. If you recall, the man at the newsagents also described Nuttall in similar bland terms. From Gavin Nuttall to Graham Nye, the same initials you may notice, it's not a great stretch of the imagination to assume they are one and the same. The modus operandi is Minkov contacts his agent, the next step in the mission starts, and Nuttall, or Nye, knows what he must do, but also moves on to cover his tracks. Whatever Minkov is up to, Penrose, it's serious business."

"Certainly looks that way. And we have no clue what it is."

"None. I'll hire a car, though. I have a silly idea I wish to pursue and, since my weekend has already gone to blazes, I may as well see where it leads."

"Then good luck. And as no one else will ever say it, thank you for trying."

"And cheers to you, too, my good man. Going home to the wife now?"

"I should, and before summat lands on my desk that keeps me here all night. Goodbye."

"Goodbye."

Dinner was really a light supper and was served in three different rooms. Someone — Sophie believed it was the butler's doing — put all the Londoners in one room, and all the other guests in another. Flora served in the former, and Ada in the latter. The immediate members of the two feuding families gathered in a small, informal room with pale blue walls and paintings chosen for their delightfulness above all other considerations. The late afternoon sun shone obliquely through the tall French doors and made the lace curtains glow pale yellow. This effect backlit Lord Gerald, crisply defining his outline while making his facial features uncertain. Lord Gerald, often taciturn and sometimes difficult, was enjoying himself immensely. This was just as well, because the conversation around the table was otherwise quite stilted. Present for the Mundays were Lord Gerald, of course, Basil and Clare, and, in descending age order, Luke, Audrey, Clive, Violet, and Julia. For the Eldreds, there were Lord Pascoe, Lady Shelagh, and Edward. Eight to three. With this imbalance, as well as the gulf between the families, it all would have become intolerable had not Lord Gerald made the effort he did.

Surridge was in the room, and Sophie acknowledged the probability that there had never been a butler born who could surpass the impartiality and correctness of behaviour that he achieved during that dinner while officiating between two warring parties. It also reassured her — in fact, she marvelled — that Broadbent-Wicks, despite his failings, was, this evening, the equal of Surridge. The young man was immune, perhaps oblivious, to the atmosphere. With trepidation, she watched him serve Clive Munday, whom BW had so recently threatened. He served with such detachment that, although Clive glowered at the footman, BW went through the motions as if the young man were a most charming person of high honour who happened to have a squint which must not be noticed. BW, when put to it, really was unflappable.

Lord Gerald set the light conversational tone for the gathering, and the rest dutifully followed his lead. Lord Eldred did well, too, and showed no reticence. Basil was quieter than usual, while Lady Shelagh, a little subdued, spoke mainly to Clare and, most surprisingly, Violet. It was as if Violet had emerged with much to say after a long stay in a cloister of quiet contemplation. She had a light and pleasant word for everyone, especially for the Eldreds, and for Edward in particular. To the slight confusion of the young man, and to the eyebrow-raising of everyone else, she boldly claimed a dance from him later. Those of the table disposed to smiling did so, but there were several who were indisposed just then. The table's expectation in the instant of Violet's request while it hung in the air was that Edward would reply with a monosyllabic answer supported by an understandably red adolescent face. Astonishingly, and far more so for his parents, he unexpectedly uttered the following words with great aplomb.

"Miss Violet, I would consider it the greatest of honours to accede to your request and I hope to prove myself an adequate partner. Truly, I anticipate our dance with great pleasure."

A fork clattered on a plate in the silence that followed. Edward had planned there would be no audience when he later delivered to Julia the original of this hastily modified speech. He had been practising its delivery for several days, but as to the crafting — it should be noted that a chum at school had helped him quite considerably.

"Oh, dear," said Violet. "I hope I'm adequate, too."

And, for the first time, there was genuine laughter around the table.

From Sophie's perspective, she heard nothing useful. What she noticed were the hidden dynamics lying beneath the veneer of polite conversation. Those who conversed as if it were an ordinary dinner and behaved within the ranges of acceptable or expected attitudes and responses were Lord Gerald, Lady Shelagh, Clare, Violet, Edward, and Julia — who was polite, and content or resigned to watch or listen as children do when adults converse.

Basil Munday was not as effusive as usual. Sophie surmised that, although he was untroubled as such, he was reserved, as if he had something on his mind. While it might be anything, Sophie thought to herself, the success of the Ball, a business matter, or something else, it was most likely because his arch-enemy, an assumed murderer, was sitting across the table.

Audrey was more urbane, less opinionated, and frankly more condescending than usual. It was fortunate she only said what did, because she might have disrupted the dinner. *How* she spoke, rather than what she said, revealed that she despised the Eldred family. As her comments were intermittent, the implicit arrogance was not noticeable to the others. However, Sophie knew, because she was paying attention specifically to the attitudes of everyone present. Even as she put food on plates, and asked a diner a necessary question in her deferential manner, she could glance and take in much, or detect nuances in statements. Sophie could hear most of what everyone said, although that was occasionally difficult when there were competing conversations. But her swift looks compiled in her mind a series of photographic portraits, as it were. Many of the snapshots in Audrey's case could have been entitled 'Contempt' or 'Disdain.'

Luke was brittle, and his politeness forced. Sophie never had warmed to him in any sense. She found the young man was that type of person who, for no apparent reason, one instantly wishes to avoid. From her observations, he had done nothing bad, but neither had he done anything good. Unsuccessfully, she tried remembering if he had ever been pleasant or light-hearted. No, he was always cold or off-hand, or talking superficially and suppressing his true motives, whatever they may have been. She guessed at a motive, more informed by her accumulated knowledge of his behaviour rather than by what she now witnessed — he was only holding the feud in abeyance for this day. She remembered other facts and possibilities. Had Luke killed Major Eldred in France? She found it entirely believable.

The person who affected Sophie the most was Lord Eldred. She found herself temporarily stunned that he was so ordinary after all. Never having seen him before, she had built up a mental picture, not an image as such, but a blending of components and characteristics she expected to see. He should have been taller, more sinister, more obviously malevolent. Where, on his tanned face, were the marks of degradation and obvious criminality? They were totally absent, and she found it difficult not to stare at him simply because he was nothing like how she had imagined. She quickly realized that, despite her efforts to remain objective, the broad-based opinion that Eldred was a killer had, by stealth, caused *her* to assume that he was. It was a revelation now to find how deeply the assumption had rooted itself before she had ever set eyes upon him.

It was only a three-course dinner. The portions were small, the food light, and therefore the meal proceeded quickly. Yet Sophie had time enough to reconsider, although the process came in stages. Having her preconceived idea of him overturned, who, then, was Lord Pascoe Eldred?

The man was polite, as they all were. However, Sophie noticed he worked at it. Eldred was struggling to be polite, but not in the ordinary ways because of shyness, indifference, or not being a conversationalist. He asked leading questions of almost everyone — enquired into their lives with interest, asked after the health of people not present, and commented agreeably on replies. He was engaged, but it was as though it cost him something each time he spoke and, if the dinner were longer, he might have fallen silent before the end.

Sophie was under the impression, for much of the time she was in the room, that Eldred was acting and feeling the heaviness of doing so. It was an act, she surmised, based upon the unique awkwardness of the meeting. There had to be at least two murderers sitting at the table, and what she found most strange was that the concept of feuding no longer troubled her — she was more troubled over not being troubled! If there were two with blood on their hands, then, logically, Lord Eldred was one of them. He had to be. As if a curtain drew back, a thought presented itself. One assassin was talking to another. If true, and it likely was, then while understanding everyone else's conduct around the table, why was she failing to comprehend Lord Eldred labouring to be polite? If he were the *only* murderer in this bizarre setting, and trying to conceal his guilt, then his behaviour would be understandable — appear at ease, be as friendly as possible, and get the trial over before anyone started an argument. But there must be another murderer present, but who was it? Obviously, he must be Basil or Luke. Eldred certainly had to know he was in the presence of someone who had killed his brother. All the Mundays believed Eldred had killed their relatives, and he must know that, too. So why was he making such an effort to be polite? And why did she not consider the Mundays in the same searching way? Her thoughts were interrupted. A maid and a footman brought in the dessert, and she needed to serve it.

By the time Sophie returned to her station, she knew the answer. Lord Eldred was worried, but not about murders. Lord Eldred farmed, and he had twice mentioned the dry weather while at the table. She also remembered he was on the point of ruin through death duties. So that must be it.

Sophie turned her attention to his wife. Lady Shelagh did not carry the title of viscountess with ease — among other things, she had stumbled in several small matters of etiquette. She was of a different class and her rural manner of speech was at odds with how every other person at the table spoke, including her husband and son. Lord Eldred was a farmer, and Shelagh, a farmer's wife from a family with a farming tradition. Sophie remembered several women from Havering-under-Lyme and one friend in particular, also a farmer's wife, who was not unlike Shelagh. So, in a way, Sophie understood and could sympathize with her. If Lord Eldred was under strain from the threat of crop failure, then Lady Shelagh would be, too. With no money and a poor harvest, looming would be the sorry conversation about which animals to sell, perhaps all of them, but it would not save them from bankruptcy. Then the estate would go.

There they were — the impoverished, worried Eldreds, attempting to do their best at dinner conversation with the wealthy Mundays, at an event only made possible because a vicious, senseless feud was suspended for the day. Her heart suddenly went out to the beleaguered family. They were the underdogs, and they were hurting. It seemed young Edward was likely to be unaware of the family's problems. Worries over money — Sophie had known them often in her life. Was

Lord Eldred a murderer, though? Looking at him, she could not say he was. The dinner ended just as another inexplicable thing had begun to bother her — why had Lord Eldred been prowling about the pool late last night?

Chapter 22

The Masquerade

It was the annual custom for one or two members of the rival families to speak together privately for a few minutes. One purpose was for the mending of fences, but only in the most literal of senses. Their lands adjoined, and they could discuss or settle such things as issues over boundaries or straying animals. It was also the time when the feud might be mentioned. Most years, it was a peaceful encounter but, in a now distant year, there had been an exchange of blows. Whenever the feud was in a hot phase, the subject was usually avoided. Whatever was said on sensitive subjects stayed within the room. Present in the study this year were Pascoe Eldred and Basil Munday — he being more involved in the estate's running than Lord Gerald.

Across the desk they talked for a while and, having thus far avoided contentious issues, were almost ready to leave.

"I wish to say something more," said Lord Eldred abruptly.

"Yes?" Basil was smoking a cigar.

"I don't know what is going on, but I swear to you, I have never thought or acted maliciously against any of your family. The last three killings... It wasn't me. I had nothing to do with them, and that's the absolute truth. I give you my word."

"Well, now... How should I respond?" He drew on his cigar. "Look at it from our viewpoint. Three of our loved ones have been brutally slain, torn from us before their time, and in ways that only an Eldred would employ. You do see my difficulty, dear fellow? Even if I wanted to believe you, I simply can't. Three deaths in nine months... It's too much. And now, with my brother Wilfred being miserably and ignominiously cast into the road in Wynbourne, we must have satisfaction."

"It was not I, Munday. That is all I can say... I don't know how to make you believe me. You've known me long enough. You know I'm not a violent man."

"Then, if not you, who?"

"I wish I could say... Whoever is behind all of this it is not anyone I know. I've thought and thought, but..." Eldred shrugged helplessly.

Basil looked at him, then put out his cigar. "Three in a row, Eldred. The price must be paid. We are now nine to your seven."

"It is not nine. You know full well that Ian was under orders to send David's unit into the attack. Men from his and other units were killed in action that day."

"It is a moot point, anyway, but I strongly disagree. The late major should have been more prudent by keeping David's unit back. But even granting you the point, we still have an imbalance, don't we?"

"I acknowledge it."

"Then what is it you're driving at?"

"To end the feud."

"No."

"With the taking of my life, let the feud finish with me."

"Ah, I see, I see." Basil stood up and took a few steps, turning to wag a finger. "That's an interesting proposition. If I alone were involved, I might consider it... but there are others."

"Can't you advise them or call a meeting to discuss the matter? I could be present, if you wish it."

"I see that you're in earnest, and it troubles me. Surely you can see our difficulties. Just put yourself in our position. What would you think?"

"That I had killed three men in your family. I have thought of nothing else."

"You are concerned for your own family, of course... I'll tell you what I'll do. I'll speak to Lord Munday and see what he says. That is *all* I can promise. He may fall in with your suggestion... your offer, even. Ultimately, it is his decision to make after consultation with the family, while *my* opinion is merely one among many."

"I had no concept of how you arrange things amongst yourselves... Thank you for your openness to my suggestion."

"I'm always willing to listen. It's getting late and we really should be..."

"Yes, of course. The Ball."

Those guests invited RSVP arrived by car, and they parked their vehicles up and down the drive. A week before the event, the Munday family could gauge by the number of replies that the masquerade would be well attended. They had hoped for an even larger number, and so they took action. Suddenly, select Wynbourne villagers and others further afield, found themselves more highly placed on the social register. These were asked to attend and, almost unanimously, happily replied that they would. They came by wagonette or a hastily washed farmer's cart. What would have happened to their costumes had it rained fortunately remained untested. That it was a warm, dry evening was most fortuitous for the woman dressed as a three-tiered wedding cake. Her headpiece terminated in a wobbling, flimsy vase of flowers which was so precariously attached, she had to beseech her pirate husband several times to slow the brisk pony.

The Ballroom was ablaze with light and full of eager, chattering, costumed people holding drinks. The orchestra was on its dais, tuning instruments. Food was laid out on the buffet tables, and the guests were eyeing the tantalizing victuals, although temporarily thwarted, because the plates and cutlery were at the back next to where Mrs Lester stood. Mr Surridge similarly controlled the drinks table. Until the dancing began, all guests were supplied by tray service only. The servants, nervously balancing glasses, threaded through the loose throng. At present, it was easy to avoid a collision, but Sophie knew it would only get worse. When the floor cleared for dancing, the press around the edges would be dense and fraught with danger.

At two minutes before the hour, Basil Munday took up a position in front of the orchestra. Dressed in a hussar's blue uniform with a pelisse over his shoulder and wearing an ornamented shako, he called for the room's attention, then gave a short speech of welcome.

With seconds to go, Lord Gerald, dressed as a Roman patrician and without using his canes, accompanied Madame de Pompadour, which was Lady Shelagh, who looked very dignified despite her misgivings, into the open space the crowd had created. Another couple joined them — Eldred dressed as Nelson, with a hat, wig, and eye patch, accompanied a gypsy, possibly meant to be Carmen, in a red velvet bolero over a white blouse, and a layered pink tulle skirt. To disguise she was fair, Clare wore a black lace scarf banded across her forehead with an edge pulled back over her hair, and the knotted end draped over a shoulder at the front.

The orchestra played a slow waltz, which set the dancers in motion. The crowd watched with avid attention until the end. Then they applauded. The orchestra played a livelier piece and couples, young and old, moved onto the floor. The Ball had begun.

Sophie was putting filled glasses on her tray when Flora approached.

"Have you seen him?" she whispered.

"Who?"

"Minkov, of course. He has *become* Beethoven. Winged collar, coat, scarf, and scowling, broody look, everything."

"Where? I must see."

"He's dancing with the Mayoress. You can't miss her. She's a very lively Queen Elizabeth."

Sophie took her tray and, after offloading a few glasses to guests, got a view of the dancing. She searched among the bobbing and turning peasants and pirates, vagabonds and princes, faeries and soldiers, but then an astonishing sight made her pause. There was a woman dressed as a basket of fruit complete with handle and it seemed that all she was wearing was the wicker, stockings, fruit, flowers, ribbons, and a toy rabbit. To make the already extraordinary sight yet more absurd, her arms were pinioned inside the wicker cylinder, causing her partner, a pharaoh in dancing pumps, to hold her in the most awkward manner while virtually shunting her about the room. Then Queen Elizabeth sailed into view with Minkov firmly attached. In all her life, not once had Sophie ever considered how proficient a dancer Beethoven may have been or in what style he danced, if he had danced at all. At a guess, she would have said he was a slow dancer and probably not very interesting. What she witnessed was so far removed from that. Minkov was very accomplished, and his imaginative interpretation of Beethoven's technique was so intensely passionate that good Queen Bess might not have had to worry about the line of succession for much longer. But this was the good Mayoress Mrs Gosling pretending to be Bess, and she was laughing, laughing, and playing up to Minkov without a care.

Sophie came away wondering why dancing altered people's normal behaviour beyond all recognition. Had either Minkov or the Mayoress behaved in the street the way they were now, the police would have cautioned or possibly arrested them.

Broadbent-Wicks was the first to get a message to Ada. He had overheard Clive, supposedly the Scarlet Pimpernel, with powdered face, wig, and employing the affectation of an eyeglass through which he scrutinized people, talking to a man in evening dress meant to be a policeman, but with only a helmet identifying him as such. The message was that whatever was going to be done to Lord Eldred would happen at about ten o'clock and when practicable. Ada, by signals, called Sophie to her and passed the message on. Sophie then told Flora. They were already vigilant, but now took steps to identify as many Londoners and Mundays by their costumes before whatever was to come came.

The room grew hot, so Surridge had the French doors opened. The guests ate, drank, and danced in the room and on the terrace outside. After only an hour, Basil Munday, pleased by the signs of widespread enjoyment, already considered the night a success. Lord Gerald had danced twice more, but was now seated within the colonnade — his nurse, dressed as a nun, standing discreetly several steps behind him. Lord Gerald beckoned Broadbent-Wicks over to his side.

"Come closer. I don't want to shout."

"Yes, my Lord."

"Listen carefully. I'm sending me nurse away about ten. So be on hand at five to. Got it?"

"Yes, me Lord, *my* Lord, I mean."

"I've got me bathing costume on underneath me toga."

"Have you really, my Lord? You're such a good old sport."

"Eh? What did you say?"

"Nothing, my Lord."

"As I said, I might swim, I might not, we'll see. Five to ten — remember that, and bring a towel with you just in case. Now, go away before she suspects anything."

"Yes, my Lord. I'll stuff the towel under my jacket."

271

Ada, at the buffet, spent her time either mute or repeatedly answering the same questions. She soon detected differences between the classes.

"What is in *those* sandwiches?" asked Little Bo-peep, the wife of a senior partner in a law firm.

"Salmon and cucumber, madam."

"Oh. I don't like salmon. What else do you have?"

"Well, look at this here," said a Dickensian character, probably meant to be Mr Micawber. "I never seen the loike in my loife. If it ain't too much trouble, miss, may I ax, what's in them sammidges?"

"Salmon and cucumber, sir."

"Is that so? They're a bit dainty with the crusts off... How many am I allowed?"

Ada leaned forward to speak quietly, "They can make plenty more, so you can fill your plate if you like, but you never heard that from me."

"Roight, you are." He winked, then took a handful. "Lord Munday's a good man for doin' all of this for everyone, and you can tell him I said so."

"I will, if I get the chance. What name shall I give?"

"Cordery. He knows who I be. Others are famished, so I'd best move along. Thank you, miss."

"Might I enquire as to what is contained in the sandwiches?" asked Beethoven.

"Best Scottish salmon and cucumber, sir."

"Thank you."

Minkov was helping himself when Clare Munday stood in the space next to him.

"Good evening, Toshko."

"*Clare*... You look divine... and as for your dancing..." He shrugged, conveying his feelings were beyond expression.

"I feel anything but *divine*. In fact, I just need to catch my breath and have a snack." She picked up a plate. Despite her words, she visibly warmed to his compliment.

Ada unobtrusively took a step back, then turned away before they noticed her. At close range, in her brilliant costume and flushed with exertion, for she had been dancing continuously and watched by many, Clare seemed larger than life — as though a famous actress or royalty had stepped down from on high to walk among the public.

"Surely you will dance again. I had hoped…"

"My dance card isn't full," she said archly. "In fact, I reserved a space for you at Basil's request."

"I claim it now, and a second, if I may be so bold."

"You certainly are bold, Toshko. We shall see."

They had both taken food and moved away from the table. Ada stepped forward and could just hear them if she concentrated, shutting out the surrounding noise by sheer willpower.

"Basil mentioned you like dancing, but failed to say how accomplished you are," said Clare. "Were you ever a professional?"

"Only an ardent amateur. In my youth, several friends were musicians. To earn money, they played in the town square or at banquets. My father also had many banquets. There was dancing. Therefore, I often danced to keep away the boredom. Soon, I became enthusiastic. In a small competition, my partner and I won a silver medal. As you can appreciate, I was good, but not so *very* good."

"How interesting… I should go. There are several people I must meet."

"Your time is valuable, and here I am, talking only of myself."

"And what would you rather talk about?"

"You. Us."

"Why does your answer not surprise me? They will lower the lights soon and, while dancing, we may explore the subject."

"When?"

"I've promised my next three, but the fourth is yours. You'll find me by *that* pillar."

"I will be ready."

She smiled and was about to go, but then asked,

"Are you aware of anything planned against Lord Eldred?"

"Such as what?" Minkov asked with great concern.

"Well, I'm not sure. There appears to be a lot of whispering in corners going on, and I believe it is about him. It's not surprising, I suppose, considering."

"I am not aware of any plotting." He looked up and saw Basil coming towards them. "Your husband approaches."

Clare turned to Basil and smiled before saying something.

Ada had caught almost every word, but then a clown dressed in white with a conical hat spoke to her. It was Dr Hurst.

"The salmon in those sandwiches — fresh or tinned?"

A gentleman asked Flora to dance, convinced she was a guest in the fancy dress of a maid. He was put out when she politely explained his mistake. She had taken two steps when she saw Pruney, dressed as Cleopatra.

"Miss Prunella," said Flora, attracting her attention so that the woman turned. "Would you like some ice-cold *champers*?"

"Champers! Would I *ever*, darling. Oh, it's you. The calamine girl."

"I was happy to help, miss. I notice your shoulders are much better."

"They hardly bother me at all now, thanks."

"Are you enjoying the Ball, miss?"

"I am. Why do you ask?"

Flora whispered, "Because I think something's going on."

"And you're right!" Pruney laughed.

"I'd love to know what it is."

"I'm sure you would, but I'm *not* supposed to tell."

"Would you like another glass? I might not be back this way for a while."

"I really shouldn't." Pruney suddenly drained her glass. "Why not?" She took another from the tray.

"You see, miss, the police are still outside, and the family wouldn't like any trouble."

"Oh! We hadn't thought of that."

"It might be all right, if I knew what it was."

"It's only a silly prank... Very well. Promise me you won't say anything."

"I promise, miss, I shall never utter a word."

"What do you think of this, then? We're going to carry Lord Eldred down to the pool and throw him in." Pruney's face glowed.

"Oh, how exciting! Excuse me, but that doesn't sound wrong to me. I can't see why the police should get involved because of a *joke*."

"That's exactly what I think. Now, be sure to watch later, and remember your promise."

"Yes, miss, I most certainly will."

Flora beat a path to the buffet table to tell Ada.

Edward Eldred, in flowing white robes, was on his way to becoming a minor sensation. He was rather wooden at the beginning of his first dance. His partner was his mother, and they were both conscious of there being many eyes upon them. Perhaps it was the sight of Madame de Pompadour turning about the room with Lawrence of Arabia, perhaps it was because they were Eldreds — she with a title and he the heir — but, whatever it was, they soon forgot the scrutiny and laughed. Edward's stiff formality relaxed. Afterwards, and feeling emboldened, he approached an aged aunt of the Mundays sitting by herself. He politely asked if she would dance. This exceptional move was only possible because of Edward's ignorance about the true state of affairs. The old lady, slightly aghast because she knew about the feud all too well, hesitated, but then said yes. Now his confidence rose, and he proved very considerate to the aunt. Everyone stared at them. During this exhibition, Edward catapulted from being a relatively unknown and not much of a person in his own right to being someone to watch. For his next dance, Edward approached Violet and, after his severely formal bow, took her by the hand onto the Ballroom floor. During this waltz, and while conversing agreeably with Violet, Edward flowed, much to Violet's delight, although she was taller than he. Later, now being widely referred to as young Master Edward, as if everyone had known all about him all along, he glided around the room with lady after lady and was rapidly becoming a favourite.

Edward, setting aside the difficulties of being nearly fourteen, took upon himself the mission of approaching every woman sitting unasked, regardless of age, rank, and disposition. Although his ulterior motive was to work his way towards Julia, whom he had yet to find in the press, he found it inexpressibly sad that a woman should dress in her best and yet go unasked. There was not a wallflower he could pass, but that he had to stop and ask politely if she were engaged. His zeal did not go unnoticed. Some females, even several of those who were popular, hoped he would ask them next, because to dance with young Master Edward had rapidly become a noteworthy notch on the gunstock of society's achievements.

In another corner of the Ballroom, Julia was equally active. The slender girl wore the chiton of ancient Greece in pale yellow silk chiffon, cunningly folded, draped, and fastened. Her hair was restrained by a golden circlet and she wore a pair of tiny golden wings fastened by gold cords. Julia did not want for partners but, whereas Edward had choices, and made them without fear or favour, an endless succession of Mundays petitioned her. She danced with her father, her brothers, her uncles, and cousins — some twice. It was as if her male relatives had deliberately conspired to keep her dance card full, and the only reason for them to do so that she could see was to keep her away from the astonishing Mr Beethoven-Minkov. Julia observed him stepping beautifully, but he was also having a strange effect upon those with whom he danced. She had noticed several ladies strangely delighted to be in his arms, and she put that down to how closely he held them, which she believed was too close.

It was her opinion that Edward was a near-perfect exponent of the dance steps suitable for the music the orchestra played. Twice had their paths crossed on the floor. Each time, he had briefly smiled and then nodded to her in an old-fashioned way. It crossed her mind that if she wanted to dance with Edward, she must somehow put herself in his way before a dance began.

Sophie was painstaking in her pretense of cleaning a vacated table to one side of a pillar. By moving little and barely breathing, she could just overhear Basil Munday conversing with Lord Eldred on the other side.

"I've spoken to father," began Basil, "and explained your proposition to him. We consulted with the others and agree..."

Sophie missed what came next because some passing people were talking loudly. She breathed while she had the chance. They paused for several seconds before moving on. She held her breath again.

"So it will finally settle the business?" asked Lord Eldred.

"Everything ends when you sign the papers. Of course, we must still meet at the old place. It will be entirely fitting..."

The song ended, and a small crush of people surged between the columns to find refreshments. Sophie waited until the clamour abated but, by then, both Lord Eldred and Basil Munday had gone.

Chapter 23

And the Band Played On

After a hectic start, the Ball settled into a maintenance phase. Many guests now preferred sitting and talking; consequently, the lounge area became busy. Those comfortable spectators with a ring-side seat could sip a drink or nibble a canapé as they commented on those in motion — who had the best costume, who really needed lessons, and who was barking up the wrong tree with a view to matrimony. The orchestra had played a tango, then a foxtrot. Now came another waltz, and the spectators forgot to sip, nibble, or whisper, because Beethoven in a dark blue coat with the Gypsy in red and pink now glided before them. A space opened around the pair. People further back within the colonnade came forward to watch.

They had not rehearsed, but it looked as though they had. Unusually, they slowly swayed forward and backward as they travelled, and Clare's dress swirled like a Catherine wheel. Across the floor they glided. Minkov, dancing differently now, tenderly held Clare, allowing her complete freedom of movement within the confines of his formal embrace. She blossomed there, and could only flourish because of his assiduous care. With perfect easy stepping, without hesitation or error, they swept slowly around the room. When they had finished, they were applauded, and laughingly they took a bow. Even while people clapped, uppermost in more than one mind was, what does Mr Basil think of it? Basil, it turned out, was unperturbed. He kissed his wife on the cheek when she returned to him and he shook Minkov's hand.

While the dance had been ongoing, Edward, noticing Julia standing by herself, seized the opportunity and went up to her.

"Good evening, Miss Julia."

"Good evening, Master Edward."

"Allow me to say that your mother is the finest of dancers."

"Yes, she is rather good, thank you. I take after her, so everyone says."

"I think they're right. Has she ever danced professionally?"

"It's complicated. She always wanted to join a corps de ballet, but said she was denied the chance because she married young. She also said that having children ruined her figure, and the only way to prevent herself from becoming a complete wreck was by devoting herself to dance in any way that she still could. Daddy said she was talking *nonsense*, dancing was *silly*, and Mummy was *obsessed*. They were having one of their arguments, and that's how I found out."

"Oh, I see."

"I've said all that in the strictest confidence, of course."

"Of course, I'm a gentleman… Who is the Beethoven chap, though? He's rather good. Is *he* a professional dancer?"

"I really couldn't say. Mr Minkov has lots of coal and he's Bulgarian."

"Is he? He was on the wrong side during the war."

"I know. No one's told *me* anything about *that*. All I was told was to be nice to Mr Minkov. But I don't particularly care for his type."

"Why?"

"Because he ignores me."

"The cad."

"Thank you for being so sympathetic. He also ignores Audrey, who behaved like a silly goose, until she went off him. And she thinks I don't know... What are your sisters like?"

"I'm not really sure. They're very nice sometimes," said Edward. He then became most formal. "Miss Julia, would you honour me with your hand in the next dance?"

"I wonder if I'm free?" She put a hand to her brow. "Yes, lucky for you, I believe I am."

"That's settled. May I say, how splendid you look in your costume? Are you somebody in particular?"

"Oh, yes. I'm Iris, messenger to the gods."

"So that's why you have wings. It's all very jolly. Who do you think I am?"

"Let me see... The name is on the tip of my tongue... It's... It's... What's the first letter?"

"X."

"No, it isn't."

"I didn't know you were Iris, and you didn't know that I'm Lawrence of Arabia."

"I *knew* that's who you were. Aren't you hot under all of that?"

"A little. After our dance, shall we have lemonade? Then we could sit outside and cool off."

"Yes, but we must take a blanket and some chocolate cake, too."

Their chance to test their skills soon came, with the result that they were both delighted by their own performances and were therefore agreeably pleased with each other's. Being hotter than ever, they found the things they needed and went outside.

They were sitting on a blanket on a patch of lawn in a quiet spot. The night was warm, and they stared at the stars and the full moon.

"You're a wonderful dancer," said Edward. "Absolutely the best."

"Do you really think so, or are you just being kind?"

"Kind? What rot. You're easily the leading lady at the ball."

"Better than Mother?"

"I haven't danced with her."

"Then don't. Keep it the way it is, thank you."

"You have a funny way... I rather like it. Shall we dance again?"

"Master Edward, you are altogether too forward, but as you insist... yes. And as we are being *totally* honest, I also think you're rather splendid. Where did you learn?"

"Oh, picked it up, don't you know... This cake's very good."

They ate and drank in silence.

"What is this Roman Pool business I've heard about?" asked Edward.

"Grandfather wanted it built. If he hadn't, he was going to tear the place down and build another Dumond Hall. You should have heard them. They were arguing away about money. Only Daddy was calling everything an 'unnecessary expense,' so as not to be *really* and *unutterably* rude to Grandfather."

"Mother and Father talk about money sometimes, but they never argue. They only look sad, go into a room, and shut the door before speaking... So, it's your Grandfather's pool, is it?"

"Yes, and he hopes to go swimming tonight while avoiding his nurse, Dr Hurst, and Daddy. They all tell him he might drown if he's not supervised. He says they're making a big fuss and should mind their own business. Grandfather has been plotting like mad. Now he's even got a footman involved in his scheme. It's so obvious and we all know what he's up to... Except for his nurse."

"Lord Munday sounds very lively. I'd like to see this pool."

"It's around that corner and is all lit up. It is lovely. I'll show you it later."

They fell silent again. The lawn was bright under the moon, and while the outer leaves on the trees ten yards away stood out in clear detail, everything beyond and beneath lay in shadow so dark that it hid everything. In the stillness, the children suddenly became alert. They watched a man stealing out from the house no more than twenty-five yards away. He entered the line of trees and disappeared. Within seconds, he came back into view. The children turned puzzled faces to one another and there was just enough light for them to see that each felt the same. A moment later, they heard a faint rustling in the dark under the trees. There followed the muffled click of a snapping twig, and then the stealthy sounds died away.

"What are they doing?" asked Julia.

"I don't know... and I don't like it. Let's go in."

In the Ballroom, Basil was speaking to the guests, asking people to clear a space in front of the orchestra. When satisfied, he signalled to the orchestra leader to play. The music had a faster tempo than before. Although a few couples further away kept going, most watched as Clare and Minkov took up their position in the middle of the space. They gave a performance of such clever, effortless gaiety that it was worth stopping to see. Without practise, missteps were to be expected, and when twice they came, Clare and Minkov laughed them off, recovering quickly, and delighting their audience as if they had been made privy to an intimate joke. Lady Shelagh looked around for Lord Eldred, to see if he was also enjoying the spectacle, but she could not find him.

Broadbent-Wicks pushed the wheelchair carefully along the stone path. Barely visible, except as a grey shape in the twilight created between the glowing pool and the lights from the house, the lord and the servant seemed hardly to be moving at all.

"Sorry about being so slow, my Lord."

Lord Gerald did not answer; his attention was fixed upon the lighted area ahead.

Broadbent-Wicks kept going, peering at the bumpy path where the soft raking light had turned the small imperfections between the stones into miniature gaping, wheelchair-overturning chasms. BW mused over several things. One was settled. If his lordship started drowning or even only struggling, he would jump in and save him. Whatever heroism he might display, someone would get annoyed with him. If it wasn't Lord Gerald, then it would be somebody else, such as the doctor, the nurse, the family, and Miss King. They might *all* be annoyed with him. Still, he would not let the old boy drown, come what may. But what to do with a soggy lord? Dry him off, wrap him in his toga, take him back to the house, bundle him into bed, and make a hot toddy. He thought that should do it.

"Do you prefer brandy or whisky, my Lord?"

"Eh? What was that you said?"

"Oh, nothing really, my Lord."

BW thought that if Lord Gerald was chilled enough, he wouldn't care what spirit he poured down his gullet. The bigger problem was the nurse. She would blab, no doubt of that, and give the show away. Then his lordship would be under a permanent watch and very unhappy.

The ground rose, causing the threat of the viscount being pitched from the chair to diminish. They passed by the statues and halted at the side of the pool.

"Will you look at that, my Lord," said BW in awe of the mysterious water in its classical setting. The statues looked down upon Lord Gerald in his moment of triumph.

"It's turned out far, far better than I had hoped," said Lord Gerald. "During the day, you can see the imperfections, but the pool still looks good enough... but at night... That's when you can dream, and believe you've gone back in time... I'm putting in more columns — not too many, mind you, or it will ruin the effect. Then there's Diana's Templet... I'll show you the drawings of that little beauty... To the changing rooms!" He pointed with a walking stick.

As they turned to go, neither saw the figure emerge from the dark to step over the low wall by the side of a statue. They did not hear the swift approach of rubber-soled shoes. They could not have foreseen that an armed assailant could ever have got into position and be standing behind them. After the blow landed, Broadbent-Wicks fell down behind the wheelchair and was aware of nothing further.

Lady Shelagh had been speaking for some time to several people, but they now left her sitting alone. In the next couple of minutes, she became increasingly concerned over where her husband had got to. Then she saw him approaching, and the relief she felt made her realize just how tense she had been about his absence and their being present at Dumond Hall.

"Where have you been, Pass?"

"There was some important business requiring my attention." He forced a smile. "It's all done now... Did you miss me?"

"Miss you! That's a fine thing to say. It made me most uncomfortable to be left here on my own under these circumstances."

"I'm sorry for deserting you. The matter took longer than I had thought." He frowned slightly, then sat down. He smiled again, saying,

"You do look lovely, madame."

"Oh, get away with you," said Shelagh. Then she laughed and changed the subject. "They're foine dancers." She pointed towards Clare and Minkov.

"Yes, they are... Have you seen my hat?" asked Pascoe. He looked under the table.

"You had the great ugly thing before we danced," said Shelagh.

"I'm sure it will turn up... A servant must have taken it."

"Are you all right, Pass?"

"Yes, of course, I am."

"You're brooding about summat. What is it?"

"It will keep for later." He smiled. "Now, tell me, are you glad you came?"

"Yes... It's not as bad as I feared. People are polite and it all looks so lovely. But what I want to know, and he hasn't told me, is where did Edward learn to dance so well? You should see him with the ladies... He's not at all abashed about axing them. Where'd he learn that? Will you have a word with him, or shall I?"

"You speak to him. Undoubtedly, Edward has had lessons, and I imagine he'll be more forthcoming with you."

Flora, stationed with a tray just behind the Eldreds, saw Mr Surridge approaching and had to move away.

Clare and Minkov took a bow to loud applause. Minkov then presented Clare and applauded her himself. She took a second bow. Even though there were cries of 'Encore! Encore!' Clare declined. After a suitable pause, the orchestra began the next number, and the ball resumed.

Chapter 24

Under the Cover of Darkness

Ada was trying to read Luke Munday's lips, but it proved to be a useless exercise. Forced to remain at the buffet tables, she had nothing to do. The food in front of her was diminishing, but the demand for it had slackened. She knew there would be a rush later, between ten-thirty and midnight, as there always was. The kitchen would bring more dishes and a different array of desserts. She turned away from Luke Munday to see the two children hurrying towards her.

"Nancy! Nancy!" called Julia, with Edward close behind.

"Whatever is it?" asked Ada, noticing their excitement.

"You've got to help us," said Julia, "simply *got* to. Old Surrey's busy, Daddy's dancing, and Luke told me not to be silly, so there's only you. This is Master Edward Munday, my very good friend."

"Pleased to meet you, Master Edward."

"Good evening, Nancy. What Julia is trying to say is that there's a prowler in the grounds."

"Oh, is there, indeed!"

"He was outside the Ballroom in the bushes," pleaded Julia, "and someone from the house met him. We must *do* something, Nancy!"

Ada looked about. "Have you seen Miss King anywhere? We need to find her first."

"What can she do? She only serves in the dining room," said Julia.

"She'll do something all right... There she is. Come with me."

They rushed towards Sophie, who had returned from unsuccessfully searching Minkov's room. Forewarned by Archie, Sophie had searched for a trap, and found Minkov had indeed set one — a tiny fold of paper wedged low between the door and jamb. Sophie had replaced the paper, but if he had set a second trap, she had missed it.

"Ah, good evening, Miss Julia and Master Edward." Sophie smiled pleasantly while giving the children a welcoming and kindly look.

"There's a bloke in the bushes outside, miss," said Ada. "He's up to no good, but we don't know what."

"Is this true? And you two saw him?"

"Yes," said Julia.

Storm clouds rapidly gathered on Sophie's brow.

"Nancy, find BW and send him outside immediately. Tell Flora to cover for us as best she can. If you can get away from the buffet, you come, too."

"Right, miss." Ada shot away.

"Show me *exactly* where this took place." Sophie hurried off.

The children looked at each other and then chased after her.

"I say," said Edward, when he had caught up. "Shouldn't we get some chaps to help?"

"They're all jigging about, and we need to act immediately if this person is up to no good... It was a man, I take it?"

"We don't really know. We didn't see the one in the bushes, but it was a man who came from the house and returned to it."

"They were meeting in the dark," said Julia. "Supposing they're robbers, Miss King?"

"Then we shall be careful. What did the man from the house look like? Did either of you recognize him?"

"It was difficult to see properly, but he was quite tall," said Edward.

"And he wore a hat or a cap," said Julia.

"That's right. Leastways, he had *something* on his head."

"Keep a sharp lookout for him when we come back, then."

"You think he's a guest?" asked Julia.

"Or one of the staff?"

"He must be," said Sophie.

They stepped outside, and Edward showed her the way.

"So, the man used the door we just passed through?"

"That's correct, Miss King."

"Do you remember anything else about him? Was he in fancy dress, for example?"

"I don't believe so," replied Julia.

They arrived at the place where the children had sat — close to the bushes by the corner of the Ballroom. Sophie switched on her torch and played the beam beneath the trees.

"Oh, I say. You carry a torch," said Edward.

"Yes. The cover is quite sparse, so the person relied solely on the darkness for concealment... There was also a prowler on the estate last night." Sophie gave Edward a searching look, wondering if he had heard that the mayor had identified his father, Lord Eldred, as the prowler. She saw he knew nothing. "It must be the same person. He's a man who has some familiarity with the layout of the house and grounds."

"Crikey," said Edward. "Are you a detective?"

"No. I'm a maid, and please don't say otherwise to anyone. I just happen to find this interesting. Now, I'm going to search under the trees. The fellow has gone, but stay posted here. Julia, you watch the lawn. Edward, you stand on the other side of these bushes to see if anyone approaches from the other terrace. Don't stare at any lights or you'll lose your night vision. Any signs of trouble, call out, and for goodness' sake, stay close to one another and get back to the house. Neither of you must wander about."

"Yes, Miss King," said Julia and Edward.

When she was under the trees examining the ground, Sophie took the blackjack from her pocket — just in case.

"As soon as this dance ends," said Luke Munday, "we'll grab him."

"Do you think it will make the papers?" asked Pruney.

"No," said Kit. "We're in the provinces, so they'll hush it up — too embarrassing for the locals. Eldred shan't make a fuss, because it draws attention to himself, which he *won't* want."

"But he might start murdering us," said Pruney.

"Don't you worry your pretty head," slurred Clive, who was unsteady. "Just let him try," he sneered. "We'll be ready for him."

Sophie returned from the dark line of trees.

"Did you find anything?" asked Julia.

"No... Go back inside. I'll look around the pool. If you see Nancy or a young footman named Broadbent-Wicks, tell them where I've gone."

She walked away, but the children followed. She turned an enquiring face to them.

"Can't we come, too?" asked Edward. "I haven't seen the pool yet."

"Oh... very well, but be quiet and *no* talking."

They set off, passing the terrace outside of the Ballroom where two men were smoking. They glanced at the little party with scant interest. Music came through the open French doors. Rounding the corner of the house, the glowing pool in its serene magnificence lay before them.

"It's beautiful," whispered Edward.

"Shh," said Sophie.

No one was about. As they drew closer, Sophie noticed a dark shape in the water, and could not make sense of it at first. Then, through the gap in the low wall, she saw the foot of someone lying on the ground. She gasped, stopped, and turned, then abruptly seized Julia by the arm while deliberately blocking her view.

"Go back to the house. *Now!* Go on and *don't* look back."

"What is it?" asked Julia.

"There has been an accident. Edward, take her away, then raise the house. Send Dr Hurst."

"She's right. Come with me, Julia. Come on."

As soon as they started walking back, Sophie ran to the pool.

"Who is it?" asked Julia. "What's happened? Tell me."

"There's been an accident..." replied Edward. "I saw enough for both of us. I'll take you to your mother and explain then."

Sophie's heart raced, and she struggled to clamp down the rising panic she felt by telling herself she could not give way now. She half-guessed what had happened and dreaded what she would see. Under the lights, she went first to Broadbent-Wicks, because she could do nothing for the still body floating in the water. Sophie wanted to scream when she saw the blood on Broadbent-Wicks' neck and in his hair. Wishing she knew first aid, Sophie felt for a pulse and, in moving his hand, he groaned. She sighed audibly from the intense relief she felt.

Within a minute, Ada joined her. She glanced at the body in the pool, and put her hand to her mouth, then joined Sophie.

"Oh, my *godfathers*," said Ada quietly, in a shaken voice. "He's not dead an' all, is he?"

"No, unconscious with a nasty head wound... He looks bad."

"I'd say. He's gone the colour of raw pastry. What do we do, miss? Should we try an' get him up, or leave him for the doctor?"

"I'm not sure. I think with head wounds, we should keep the patient still. Dr Hurst will be here soon."

"Oh... And they've killed Lord Munday... What dreadful goings on... Poor old BW... Do you know, an uncle of mine was in an argument and got hit with a brick, and ever since he gets 'eadaches off and on. He was back at work the next day but ain't never touched a drop of drink since. Says it makes him feel funny. Sorry, miss, that's all I know about 'ead wounds."

They made BW more comfortable and used a cushion from the wheelchair as a pillow.

"Did you see that hat in the water?" asked Ada.

"I saw something."

"It's Lord Eldred's Nelson hat."

"Good grief..."

Loud noises coming from the direction of the house caught their attention, so they stood up. A compact rabble, shouting, jeering, and laughing, was approaching. In their midst, they carried someone.

"This is awful." Sophie was appalled by the noisy mob baying and bawling while their host floated dead in the water. "They can't have heard about Lord Munday."

"Just look at 'em. They've got Lord Eldred on their shoulders like a sack."

"I wasn't going to interfere," said Sophie. "I see I must now. Stay here and look after BW."

A crowd followed the young men bearing Lord Eldred, but a woman was running ahead of them all. It was Flora, and she reached the pool first.

"This is hideous," she said breathlessly. "I've just heard what's happened to Lord Munday and BW. How is he?"

"He's very poorly, and not conscious," said Ada. "We're ever so worried about him."

"The doctor will be here soon," said Flora. "He's getting his bag from the car."

"Thank goodness," said Sophie. "Why has Basil Munday not stopped their outrageous behaviour?"

"Phoebe, he's *letting* them do it!"

"No! I don't believe it... Here, take my police whistle. Summon the constables from the end of the drive. If they don't come immediately, then fetch them or there'll be another murder. There's no telling what this drunken mob will do when they discover Lord Gerald's body."

"Right!" Flora ran off towards the front of the house.

The mob came closer and now the floodlights illuminated the leaders. Pruney was dancing about like a demented spirit, laughing, calling out — urging them on. Sophie caught sight of Basil Munday walking by the side of those who carried Eldred. He was smiling. She stepped into the entrance to block their path and shone her torch in their faces.

"Put that gentleman down!" she shouted.

"Get that torch out of my bloody eyes!" cried Kit.

"Stop where you are!"

"Ignore her. It's only a maid."

"You will not throw Lord Eldred in the pool!"

The rabble and Sophie were face to face now.

"Get her out of the way," said Clive.

"Maybe she's right, though," said someone at the back.

"Coward," said Kit.

"Come on," said Clive. "We'll throw her in the pool, too."

"Yes!" cried Pruney.

The rabble laughed and moved forward.

"Lord Munday is dead!" Sophie shouted above the din. "He is *dead*!"

Some heard and balked, others at the back did not and pressed on, causing Lord Eldred to slip off their shoulders. Pruney lunged at Sophie, who side-stepped and tripped her over on the lawn.

"What did you say?" asked Basil, who came to the front.

"Your father has drowned in the pool," said Sophie.

The mob fell silent and released Lord Eldred. He put his costume in order, although his wig had gone. The men who had roughly handled him drew back. If a Munday was dead, then an Eldred had killed him — they were a mob, and they reasoned as a mob. The murderer stood there in their midst and could not escape. In the dreadful moment of silence that had descended, the mob would only have needed to hear a single urging voice to turn violent. What they *did* hear was the unmistakable sound of a distant police whistle.

Chapter 25

It's all over

The music ended. No one danced. The Ball was over, and the night transitioned from bright gaiety into a dull series of ragged, overlapping phases that were like scenes in a nightmare. First came the shared horror over the violent death of Lord Munday in his Romanesque pool. After the body was retrieved and after a brief examination, it was Dr Hurst's opinion that his lordship had been beaten senseless with a blunt, heavy instrument before being dropped into the water to drown. Cautious, as medicos are wont to be in such circumstances, he stated that only after an autopsy would anything definite be known, but that foul play was certainly indicated. Those eighty or so who had viewed the body while it bobbed in the water held the same opinion.

For most guests, a lesser and subsidiary concern was the plight of an unconscious servant. However, the fact that someone who was not a Munday or an Eldred had been a victim of the same attack perpetrated upon Lord Gerald widened, broadened, and deepened the sense of disquiet. Many wondered who next? The danger had come closer to everyone, which caused speculation to run riot.

Police ineptitude marked the beginning of the second general phase, as those tokens of civil authority, the two constables at the gate, were flung unprepared into the middle of a murder investigation. Everyone could see they were totally inexperienced in such serious crime and were floundering accordingly. The officers did their best — telephoning the local station for help and by keeping the crime scene intact after the area around the pool had already been thoroughly trampled. However, they did well when they discovered an old police truncheon where it had fallen or been thrown behind a statue. In the handle were the crudely scratched initials P. E. The two constables could not be everywhere and so just awaited reinforcements. This left the guests, family, and servants with a great deal of latitude in their actions, the most notable being the departure of the Eldred family.

After the outrage perpetrated upon Lord Pascoe's dignity, it was intolerable for them to stay. Eldred, angry and distracted, spoke to no one. Lady Shelagh first gave their condolences to Basil Munday, and then, with some heat, ventured her own opinion. She held him responsible — if not for the orchestration of the attempt to throw her husband in the pool, at least for his abject failure to prevent it. Lord Gerald's death had disturbed and saddened her, resulting in fear and agitation manifesting itself in her sharpness of tongue — a personal quality hitherto unknown to her husband and son.

The short car ride home was a silent one. Lady Shelagh worried over what would come next. Lord Pascoe was so bemused it was as if he had not merely lost his tongue, but also his wits.

Neither parent considered what Edward might be experiencing. They did not possess the capacity to put themselves in the child's place because their own thoughts were so deeply fixed elsewhere. Even if they had the capacity, they could not have realized the profound changes he had undergone that night.

Edward had started the evening off apprehensively — a young boy with a modest hope at his first big social gathering. At the Ball, he was soon enjoying himself, and had made friends. His dancing had improved — better than he would have believed possible. Next was the night's crowning glory — his dance and subsequent blossoming friendship with Julia. A detective adventure followed, which showed much promise. Then the entire dreamlike edifice crashed down about him. He had learned that his father, his loving, kind, patient father, was hated by many people, who soon made it apparent that he himself also was despised by virtue of his being his father's son. In all of this confusion and horror, the image that stayed with him the most was Julia's tear-stained face. She had cried because her grandfather was gone, and that troubled Edward over and above the fact that a sudden death had occurred. Most galling was how they had deliberately removed her from him. He did not know their names, only their silence, cold shoulders, and disdainful backs, but they had pulled Julia from the room only to separate her from him. There was no explanation given, no goodbye, and no chance of petition. All he saw was Julia's hurried backward glance. This hurt Edward, piercing him, as much as when his old dog had died, which was when he had first learned the meaning of grief.

The third phase was when the guests realized they were trapped until the police said they could go, and no one knew when that was likely to be. Some had left early out of fear, or fear of getting involved, but most had stayed out of interest or a sense of duty. When Inspector Haddock arrived with reinforcements, and with escape denied, those who had voluntarily remained could see the night would be a long one.

The feud had come home in every sense. It never would be considered in the same way again. No longer a tradition, a strange competition between two families, and of perennial interest, it was now, and for the first time, truly a police matter. Neither the Eldreds nor the Mundays controlled events anymore. The authorities had intervened at last. Everyone might believe Lord Pascoe Eldred had killed Lord Gerald Munday, but it was now up to the police to prove it.

The Munday women gathered in the drawing room. Flora and Ada served tea to them. Clare, despite her own sorrow, had to console Violet and Julia, her distraught daughters. Several other women were similarly affected. Audrey, dry-eyed yet greatly upset, although too independent to seek her mother's help, was at a loss to know what to do. She stalked restlessly about the room until an aunt, Clare's sister, spoke to her.

"It's up to the police now, dear."

"No."

"Yes, there can be no more. It's far too dangerous to continue. They'll catch him, and that will be that."

"No, I don't believe it can *ever* end."

"Are you saying... You *surely* can't mean that little boy? He knows nothing about anything."

"We should drop it," said Audrey. "Sorry to be rude, but this isn't the time."

In a small, dimly lit upstairs bedroom, the nurse and Sophie sat talking quietly. Broadbent-Wicks was in bed, resting his bandaged head. His eyes were closed. Servants had carefully carried him into the house, where he was as much under Sophie's care as Dr Hurst's. When first picked up, he regained consciousness, but his speech was slurred. Since then he had improved, but his head hurt him. Doctor Hurst, still in his white clown suit, although he had removed his conical hat, had strictly admonished everyone that the patient must get rest and the room was to be kept dark and quiet. Broadbent-Wicks said he felt fine apart from a sore head and the doctor promptly forbade him to speak or move.

"I looked everywhere for him... *Everywhere*," whispered the nurse, referring to Lord Gerald. She still held a handkerchief, but her duties and the presence of a physician had forced her to pull herself together instead of indulging in the weeping she longed for.

"I know you did," said Sophie.

"Sorry... My fault," murmured Broadbent-Wicks.

"Shh," said both women.

"Don't speak," said Sophie.

"No, I won't, Miss King."

"Not another word. I mean it." She spoke softly and kindly to him.

The women paused and waited for him to settle before they resumed. Once more, the nurse bitterly reproached herself for letting Lord Gerald out of her sight. Again, Sophie had to remind the woman that the attack was not her fault, and Lord Munday had planned to evade her. She took her leave of the nurse shortly afterwards.

It was difficult for her to get Flora and Ada alone but, when she did, she told them of BW's improving condition.

"Where is everyone?" asked Sophie.

"Most of them are still in the Ballroom," said Ada. "That Inspector Haddock is in a room next to the study interviewin' some of the gentlemen, and Sergeant Gowers has arrived."

"Has he? I'm supposed to meet him in half an hour... I wonder if Elizabeth will be at the rendezvous."

"I'm sure she will," said Flora. "By the way, Minkov, who's also in the study, was observing you earlier. He didn't see me watching him watching you."

"I *thought* he was. Do you think he's remembered me from the cruise ship?"

"Even if he hasn't, I believe he suspects you're from the police."

"Oh, *blast* it. What can I do?"

"Stay out of his way, miss. He don't suspect us. We was discussin' it, and we reckon he wouldn't think that we're police, 'cause he believes he's the only one being followed, and wouldn't think we was after anyone else. So, he'd never guess the police would send four to follow him, but only the one, meanin' you. Do you see what we mean, miss?"

"Yes. Hopefully, that's the correct view for us to take. What are the ladies doing?"

"Indulging in tea, tears, and restorative brandies," said Flora. "They're very upset, though. Audrey looks like she could kill someone."

"Yes, she does, an' all, miss."

"Right... I'll see Sergeant Gowers first, then meet Elizabeth, and after that, I'm not sure what to do."

"Who do you think done it?"

"Nelson's hat being in the pool and the truncheon with the initials point to Lord Eldred. Motive, opportunity — *everything* points to Lord Eldred."

"We think the same," began Flora, "but don't see how he hoped to get away with it, especially after dropping his hat. You know, when they grabbed him, he was just standing next to Lady Shelagh, minding his own business. What murderer would do that?"

"It certainly seems all wrong, somehow," said Sophie.

"What about the two men who were seen outside by Julia and Edward?" asked Ada.

"Hmm... Let's consider where they might fit in. The man who left the house, possibly Lord Eldred, met another man, the prowler. He who was hiding could not have been Lord Eldred. The prowler is most likely to be Lord Munday's murderer. The person from the house is either a confederate or in charge. However, yesterday the same or another prowler was identified as Lord Eldred. It's absurd that there should be two prowlers, although it is possible. As far as tonight's prowler is concerned, as we said, he's highly likely to be the murderer, but can't be Lord Eldred. So, how did Nelson's hat get in the pool?"

They were silent for a moment.

"I know! I know!" said Flora. "The man from the house gave it to the prowler."

"Ooh, that's an intriguing thought."

"Then Lord Eldred had nothing to do with it?"

"It seems impossible for him to behave like that... I wish we had more time to think this through." Sophie began pacing.

"Well, look," said Flora, "when the murderer left Wilfred Munday's body in the road, he fired shots only to draw attention. All of that was totally unnecessary."

"Yes... Wait a minute! The car... the car. Lord Eldred was seen driving while wearing his straw hat. The two old gentlemen who saw him often sit in the same place at the same time and are always there when the weather's fine. Someone who knows their habits set them up as witnesses against Lord Eldred."

"Obviously, he's being *framed*," said Flora with her eyebrows raised.

"It has to be something like that."

"Miss, I know this talking is important, but we ought to get back to work."

"You're right. It will keep for a little while. I'll find Sergeant Gowers first, then leave at ten minutes to midnight."

On the way to resuming their duties, Ada said,

"But the mayor saw Lord Eldred yesterday."

"Or someone pretending to be him," replied Sophie.

"You said they got the mayor tipsy," said Flora. "Ah! Then the framer must be..."

Mrs Lester came around a corner.

"Uh, where are you going?" Her voice was lifeless, and she looked very pale.

"Miss Walton and Miss Carmichael are returning to the drawing room. I was about to go to the kitchens."

"You may carry on," said Mrs Lester to Flora and Ada. "Go to the Ballroom instead, Miss King, in case anything further is required there for the general guests. I am retiring for the night, so if you need instruction, find Mr Surridge... I believe that's everything."

"I'm very sorry for what happened to Lord Munday. I'm sure the loss under such deplorable circumstances must be dreadful for you."

"I can't bring myself to believe it... Such a tragedy, but what can one do when they... No matter. It doesn't matter now." She sighed heavily. "How is Mr Broadbent-Wicks?"

"He's resting quietly and seems to improve. Dr Hurst is concerned, but hopeful."

"That's something to be thankful for. Good night."

Sophie found Sergeant Gowers in the Ballroom interviewing a married couple, so she went to the buffet to see what state it was in. Much of the food had been eaten or cleared away. In examining a large tea urn, she found it had been recently filled. Sophie tidied the area and went over to the bar, where a footman was staring into space. While there speaking to him, a few of the orchestra and the musicians from London began playing softly to fill in the time — not recognizable pieces, but improvisations.

"Hello, Miss King," said Gowers. "Mind if I interview you next?" He then whispered, "Minkov's not here."

"Of course not, Sergeant."

They found out-of-the-way seats in the lounge area and sat down. Gowers took out his notebook.

"First, how is Mr Broadbent-Wicks?"

"He's comfortable, thank you, and Doctor Hurst believes he will be back to normal within the week, but tonight is a critical time. Fortunately, he did not detect a fracture during his examination."

"That's a relief. He's a willing young man, and I'd hate for anything to happen to him." He smiled. "Don't you worry, Miss King. He'll be up on his feet in no time."

"We all hope so."

"Do you mind giving me your report?"

Sophie recounted all that had occurred since they met last, including the mayor's sighting of Lord Eldred in the grounds the night before, which Gowers had not heard about.

"Something's wrong here," said Gowers. "I'm not *entirely* convinced, but I'm of a similar opinion to yours. Eldred's being framed."

"Where is he now?"

"A sergeant and a constable have gone to fetch him... Quite a few members of the Munday family are baying for his blood."

"I can imagine they are."

"Now here's something you don't know, and he's given me the liberty to tell you." Gowers glanced around the room and lowered his voice. "Mr Drysdale is outside. Only no one knows except you and me."

"What on *earth* is he doing here?"

"It's all that palaver with Minkov who, apparently, has an agent working for him. They're up to something. Mr Drysdale reckons the chap in Swindon is the same man who received the telegram from the ship."

"How interesting... What can they be up to?"

"He doesn't know, but then he doesn't know yet about this prowler."

"No... Do you think the prowler and Minkov's agent are one and the same?"

"It's a possibility, Miss King; one of several." He turned to a specific page in his notebook. "I wonder if you can help me. I have a timeline of events up to when they were about to throw Lord Eldred in the pool."

"I'd love to hear what you have. We've tried making a timeline ourselves, but can't get it straight."

"That's because no one was paying attention to clocks. If they were, well, that would look suspicious and as if they had been involved, so they'd keep mum about it. This is what I have so far, and it doesn't include Lord Eldred's statement, of course." He politely cleared his throat and began reading.

"About 9:50 p.m., Lord Munday sent away his nurse to dance so he could go down to the pool. Broadbent-Wicks approaches Lord Munday approximately two minutes later, and off they went. Around the same time, Lord Eldred left the room, and was absent for approximately twenty to twenty-five minutes…"

"He was gone that long? Oh, dear."

"Several remarked his long absence at the critical time, including Basil Munday. They believe Lord Eldred went to the study to use the telephone — if they're not amongst those who are accusing him outright of murder. We'll confirm all of that when he arrives. Either he has an alibi, or he murdered Lord Munday, or, as we're now thinking possible, someone has framed him.

"Lord Munday was murdered between 10:05 and 10:15 p.m. Doctor Hurst said his lordship died within an hour of being examined, but we already knew it had only been a matter of minutes after they left the Ballroom. During this critical time, at five past ten, to be precise, Clare Munday began dancing with Minkov. Basil Munday was present to watch them. That lets those three out. I heard they put on quite an exhibition."

"I missed it, although Gladys said they were rather brilliant."

"I'd liked to have seen that. I don't know how those types make it look so easy. For myself, and having policeman's feet, if I make it through a number without stepping on my fiancée's toes, well, I've done all right."

Sophie laughed. "I can understand that completely, because I'm not very good at dancing, either."

"I find that hard to believe, so I'll have to take your word for it. Now, according to my notes, Lord Eldred returned to the Ballroom between 10:10 and 10:15. No later than 10:15, eight or nine chaps grab hold of him. In that group were Luke and Clive Munday, a young man called Farley Peters who is a cousin of theirs, and the rest were London gentleman, one of whom was supposedly masquerading as a policeman, but he only had the helmet. It was a stolen one, so I charged him, mainly because he was getting noisy and I didn't like his attitude. That soon shut him up, though."

"My goodness, I hadn't even considered that."

"Young London gentleman in their drink often do that sort of thing for a lark. We policemen take a different view, of course." He consulted his notes. "They paraded Lord Eldred around on their shoulders for a bit, and then headed towards the pool, arriving there no later than 10:20. You were already present... How long were you there, would you say?"

"Oh, only two or three minutes. In the minute or two it took to cross the lawn with the pool in view, I didn't see anyone. Then the mob turned up several minutes later... About five minutes, I should think."

"Yes, that's good." He wrote a note. "Then you having the crime scene in view for three to five minutes confirms what we know so far. The mob arrived at the pool at about 10:18... Allowing that puts the time of death at approximately 10:08... You must have just missed the murderer."

"If only I had been a little earlier... Where is Inspector Haddock?"

"With the gentlemen in the study. They need cossetting, you see. There's a Wiltshire detective and a few uniforms interviewing everyone else. I can't do that officially, because it's not my patch. They're feeding me information, though, and it's been fairly consistent so far. Either the witnesses saw nothing or, if they did, their statements agreed. Makes life so much easier in one way. But then we come to you, and the other agents, and now we've got something else going on — a chap in the undergrowth meeting with someone from the house. It would be a great favour if you could fit in those times with what I have, because we can't interview either child until tomorrow — one's left and the other's too upset."

"Certainly. I noticed Edward and Julia dancing and that must have been about 9:15, but I didn't see them again until they and Nancy approached me at about ten. I got the sense that they had witnessed the meeting with the prowler only within the previous ten minutes. They were still too excited for it to have been much longer than that."

"About 9:50 for the meeting, then. That means three things happened at approximately the same time. Lord Eldred goes to the study, *maybe*. Lord Munday goes to the pool, and the chap from the house meets the prowler... I wonder in what order they actually occurred."

"Hmm... If Lord Eldred is being framed, I would say the person from the house handed over the hat first and gave the go ahead for the murder; Lord Munday going to the pool second because the timing of that was a variable beyond the framer's control; and the third, Lord Eldred's going to the study, was very much dependent upon the timing of the second."

"How *did* the framer get his lordship in the study, though?"

"Who do you think it is?"

"Same as you, I reckon," said Gowers.

"Ah. It's so dreadful and senseless... Possibly by sending Lord Eldred to sign the papers he mentioned. He then asked him to wait for some reason or other — to speak to Lord Gerald, perhaps."

"That would do it. Whatever it was, it had to be important enough to keep Lord Eldred hanging about on his own for nearly twenty-five minutes while there's a party going on... If he's innocent, he's sunk, as it stands. He'll be arrested once he turns up here."

"Surely, not."

"Inspector Haddock's got no choice. If I were in his place and what with the evidence, I'd do the same. He's a decent fella and wants a word with Lord Eldred first to give him a chance, but, really, no matter what he says, Haddock will have to lay charges. It's the hat and the truncheon that do it. It was wiped clean of prints, by the way. The only thing that'll save him is if someone can identify the man from the house who met the prowler."

"I see... Whoever it was took a chance on getting hold of the hat."

"Not really, Miss King. It's true that Lord Eldred would have lost his hat once they started carrying him about, but it would have been too late to use by then. So, they probably had something else ready to plant belonging to Lord Eldred, but used the hat because it so happened that he could get it easily and it was much more suitable."

"Such as a monogrammed handkerchief?"

"Yes, that sort of thing."

"They could have taken a personal effect from Lord Eldred's room at any time."

"That's it, Miss King."

"Ah... It's all so wicked."

"*If* the theory is correct."

Sophie glanced at her watch. "Good grief. I have to meet Elizabeth."

"I nearly forgot. I told her the meeting was off. There was no point in it with my being here."

"Of course, and that makes perfect sense. I should get back to work anyway, though."

"Thank you very much for your help."

A constable approached and asked to speak to Gowers privately. Sophie waited in case it was important. After he left, Gowers said to her,

"That was the constable who went to Capel House. Lord Eldred's done a runner."

Chapter 26

A Quick Change of Plan

Sophie crept away from the house, knowing full well that, despite Sergeant Gowers having cancelled the meeting, Miss Elizabeth would still be waiting at the rendezvous. The spring night was sultry, more like August than May, and her light coat made her hot as she hurried.

There were now fewer cars parked along the dark drive. Sophie had to pass one cautiously because a man was sleeping in the driving seat. Out of the moonlit areas in the shadow of trees, her path was dark, but she hesitated to use her torch for fear of being observed. Upon reaching the gate, she almost jumped out of her skin when a low whistle sounded out from the darkness right next to her.

"Could you recommend a good beer?"

"Oh, *Archie*, how could you! You frightened the life out of me."

"Sorry, Soap. Where are you off to? Isn't Gowers inside?"

"I'm meeting Elizabeth... What are you doing lurking? Come out at once."

She could barely see him, even when he was only a yard away.

"I'll walk with you a little way... To answer your question, I'm here to find out what Minkov and his agent are up to."

"Don't you know yet?"

"We all know where Minkov is, but the agent has vanished. Despite your inestimable help, we lost him. More particularly, I lost him. He left the hotel before I got there."

"That *is* a shame. You poor dear, I am sorry."

"Your words are like balm to my wounded vanity... So, being at a loose end in Swindon, I thought loitering near Wynbourne and waiting for the misplaced agent to turn up was a wonderful idea. Sadly, I am told, we lost Viscount Munday tonight."

"Oh, it was *dreadful*, Archie, and Mr Broadbent-Wicks has been injured, too."

Sophie explained the salient points of what had happened. When she had finished, Archie said,

"So, you believe... There's a car coming from the house. Let's get off the road."

They hid in the shadows behind a large tree. The big car passed them at speed. They stepped back onto the road when it had gone.

"Who was that?" asked Archie.

"That was Basil Munday's car and, by the size of the driver, it was he who was driving."

"Where do you think he's off to?"

"I can't imagine... His place should be with his family."

"He's up to something... So, you believe *he's* behind all these killings?"

"I'm rather muddled still, but I think there are three involved. The man Gavin Nuttall or Graham Nye pretended to be Lord Eldred by wearing a straw hat on the day of Wilfred Munday's death. Wilfred Munday was already dead and Nuttall propped up his body in the passenger seat. It's likely the murder took place somewhere here on Loxie Lane, or in an outbuilding on the estate, while Farmer Cordery was using his tractor. That noise covered the sound of the shots, or they may have muffled them some other way."

"He could have used a silencer or a cushion," said Archie. "Even without them, the result would have been a couple of dull bangs coming from a shed in a rural area — easily assumed to be hammer blows. The tractor noise would completely cover the sound. Please continue."

"Thank you. It means Basil Munday is ultimately behind it, because Minkov wasn't even in the country then."

"As you well know. But it was *his* telegram which sent Nuttall, or Nye, into action."

"Yes, that's true. Minkov's involved somehow. It might have been he the children saw coming from the house, mistaking his full head of Beethoven hair for a hat."

"That's too speculative to be useful."

"I know... Did you ever discover what his telegram meant? That message still annoys me."

"If you recall, and if I remember it correctly, it was, Unaccompanied enfreighted agreeable meeting urgentest redirect obliterate. As you rightly surmised, unaccompanied meant no one aboard ship following me. Enfreighted — I have the package, which almost certainly contained money. Agreeable meeting proved to mean, yes, we will meet at the British Museum as planned. We discovered it was the British Museum because we followed Minkov there late in the morning after he had landed. Urgentest redirect probably meant there was a change to a plan, and the plan with changes had to be carried out at once. I think we can now assume the objective was the demise of Lord Munday, and Nuttall had to go to Wynbourne via Swindon immediately after the meeting. Obliterate. Destroy the message, but likely also to mean leave where you are staying and do so without trace."

"Then someone saw Nuttall?"

"No — at least, not to recognize him again. We think Minkov passed the money along with new instructions to Nuttall in a crowd in front of an exhibit at the museum. Minkov never did speak to anyone that we could see."

"Does that mean Nuttall is also a spy?"

"Yes, and he's good at his job. I had a faint hope of finding him here tonight. Alas, he got to Lord Munday and away again without my seeing him. He must have gone across the fields."

"What a terrible pity. Are Minkov and Nuttall involved just for the murders — my goodness, how awful it is to say such a thing — or are they plotting something else?"

"So far, we cannot identify an espionage angle. What eludes me completely is why Minkov has involved himself in this wretched feud business. It's quite far outside his usual line... Oh, look. We have glow-worms to light our path."

"They're so cheerful. Perhaps Minkov needs the money."

"No, it can't be that. He has substantial interests in several industries, particularly coal."

"So, I understand."

"We've discovered that Basil Munday and Minkov are currently selling and will continue to sell coal to the Royal Navy for the duration of the miners' lockout. They stand to make a lot of money."

"Then I'm under a misapprehension. I thought his father ran the family business. Minkov often telephones him."

"It would be a miracle if he did. Father Minkov died in 1917 under the suspicious circumstances of a burglary where very little was taken."

"That's the year Minkov and Basil met in Marseille, and the year Viscount Ian Eldred died in France... Good grief!"

"Soap, my dear old darling, allow me to kiss you — in a very chaste and cousinly fashion, of course."

Smiling, she presented her cheek to him, and he planted a kiss.

"What are you going to do?" she called, because, immediately after the kiss, he started walking back to the house.

"Have Minkov arrested and check everyone's passports, don't you know. We'll worry about charges later. Sorry to leave you on a dark deserted lane in the middle of nowhere, but that's to be expected when one is a spy!"

"*Aha!* You said, spy!"

"Agent! I meant to say agent!"

Sophie quickened her steps. The conspiracy plan was becoming clearer to her by the time she met Elizabeth at the rendezvous. She explained everything while they stood outside Rabbit and Sophie observed her friend undergo the same emotions as they all had experienced when learning of the murder of Lord Munday and Broadbent-Wicks' injury.

"How much petrol is in the tank?"

"It's quite full, Miss King, and so is the petrol can. Do you intend driving somewhere?"

"I don't know… I'm *really* in two minds about it. I may as well explain where things stand. After everything that's happened, and with all the fabricated evidence and suspicious behaviour of certain parties, I am prepared to believe that Lord Eldred is innocent, and that Basil Munday, Minkov, and Nye-Nuttall have conceived a wicked plan to frame him. What I don't yet see is why they are doing it at all. To top everything, Lord Eldred has disappeared, and now Basil Munday has gone off to who-knows-where. Is that about the feud? It makes me think they might fight a duel… By the Pagoda at Kew, if can you believe it? Basil mentioned the 'old place' and that's the only place that comes to my mind. Am I going mad, Elizabeth?"

"Not at all, Miss King. For them to duel at Kew would be quite fitting in a way, according to the rather bizarre reasoning surrounding this whole affair. May I make a suggestion about what motivates Basil Munday? I have no opinion on Mr Minkov's reasons."

"Of course, you may."

"Thank you. This occurred to me only this morning, while I was reviewing my notes and, after yesterday, when you cast doubt upon Lord Eldred being a murderer. Basil Munday's brothers were both older than he. The eldest, Bartholomew, when he was killed in London was survived by two daughters, neither of whom can inherit the title or the estate. The inheritance, after Lord Gerald's death, would have then passed to the middle brother, Wilfred, who was a bachelor. From local newspaper accounts, I have gleaned that he may have had an, um, *understanding* with a woman fifteen years his junior. Her name was mentioned several times in connection with his at recent events. Perhaps, if it's not altogether too far-fetched, Wilfred contemplated matrimony after suddenly finding himself next in line to the title. If this potential union produced a male heir, Wilfred's son would be next in line, ahead of Basil and his son, Luke."

"I must be a complete dunce. I really should have a proper cap made up."

"Please don't blame yourself, Miss King. I should have seen this earlier. The fact is that the feud colours all one's thoughts."

"That is so true... But if I had understood it was all about inheritance from the first, perhaps Lord Gerald would still be alive."

"I doubt it. Unless you gave convincing and timely evidence to the police, there was nothing to prevent Basil Munday carrying out his plans."

"Everything's coming to an end, it seems. Lord Eldred might still hang despite Minkov's arrest, because of the evidence and opinion against him. Minkov has not even been connected with the murder, and everything against Basil is only inference and conjecture, while the prosecution will need the strongest evidence in court. They must overcome the fact that he was in the Ballroom when his father died."

"I can see that, Miss King. What can we do?"

"I wish I knew... All I can think is to go up to Kew on the off-chance, to stop them from killing each other."

"Oh... Miss King, if you decide to go, would you mind my accompanying you? I could help with the driving and the maps. It is seventy miles or more."

"Bless you, Elizabeth. Of course, you can. Evidence will still be needed, though."

"Then, if I might make another suggestion... Perhaps Miss Carmichael and Miss Walton could find such evidence during the night. That would be rather an exciting task, too."

"Perfect! They can at least try. Do you need to get anything from the hotel?"

"No, I don't think so... If I might make yet another suggestion. A flask of coffee and some sandwiches would be very useful."

"Indeed, they would. Let's get going."

"We have to do what, miss?" asked Ada. They were sitting in their bedroom.

"She said find evidence," said Flora.

"You'll know it when you see it," said Sophie.

"How can we know that we will know it when we see it? You must be more precise, Phoebe."

"Lord Eldred signed papers tonight. Look for them. Also, correspondence, telegrams, rough notes, diaries, journals — go through everything."

"So, we're to do this while the police are in the house?" asked Ada.

"If you can."

"We're going to get caught," said Flora. "They'll catch us — the Surridge, the Lester, and the police will see us dragging box-loads of papers along the hall. Bring some oranges and a nice bar of soap when you visit us in prison."

"And some packets of cigarettes so we can trade with the warders," said Ada.

"Is that what they do?" asked Flora.

"Oh, yes. I could tell you stories, but they'll keep for when we're inside."

"If you don't want to do it..."

"We didn't say that, Phoebe," said Flora. "Of course, we'll do it — we only want to exercise our right to complain because we're doomed, you see. We'll be up all night burrowing in the Mundays' drawers until the police arrest us."

"I think your complaint needs rephrasing," said Sophie, "but I see what you mean. The study and Basil's room are the best places. If he has a safe..." Sophie looked at Ada.

"I can't do safes, miss, 'cause I never learned, but I'll have a go if there is one."

"Oh, *do* try," said Flora. "Safecracking will make our charge sheets so much more dignified."

They all laughed.

"You two are terrible," said Sophie. "I must go. Good luck."

"Don't get in any trouble, miss," said Ada.

"I shan't, and neither shall you, I'm sure."

"Famous last words," said Flora. "Be very careful, though."

Chapter 27

Running Rabbit, Flying Dragon

The unlit, unsignposted narrow lanes around Wynbourne were the slowest part of the journey. Once on the main road to Reading, the going was faster. It was warm inside Rabbit and, to offset the heat from the engine, Sophie and Elizabeth had the windows down, which then made it noisy.

"Is that Maidenhead?" asked Sophie, seeing the glow of streetlamps ahead.

"Yes," said Elizabeth, studying a folded map by torchlight. "We're two-thirds of the way to Kew. It's a quarter to four and sunrise is in an hour and twenty minutes."

"Twenty-odd miles to go. We just have enough time. The roads in London will be much slower."

"And we must watch out for the police," said Elizabeth, for the third time.

"If they meet at dawn, we will be ready and waiting for them. To be honest, I hope I'm mistaken about there being a duel. The worst result will be if we're correct about that, but mistaken in the choice of venue."

"All we can do is try, Miss King... I find driving at night to be quite pleasurable."

"Yes... Although that deer gave us a fright."

"I can't understand what possessed it to just stand in the road like that. At least it didn't leap out at us."

"One would think the lights and engine noise would scare it away... The hooter certainly did."

"We have plenty of fuel." Elizabeth read the gauge and gave an update because the amount left in the tank was of perpetual concern to her. "Rabbit is quite economical in her habits."

"Thankfully, yes, and she's no trouble at all."

No sooner had the words left Sophie's mouth than a tyre blew, causing Rabbit to swerve sharply. Sophie hung on to the wheel. The car came to a halt on a dark stretch of empty road between streetlamps. On one side stood a high wall on top of a bank. On the other was an equally tall hedgerow.

"Blast it!" said Sophie.

They got out of the car and into a silence made more profound by the so recent noise of the engine and the roar of air blowing through the windows. Elizabeth lit a warning lamp and put it by the side of the road. They dug out the tools and began the laborious process of jacking up the car to change the wheel.

After several vehicles and a lorry had passed them, the road was empty for some time while they worked. Another car roared past.

"What an idiot!" exclaimed Sophie. "Did you see how close he came?"

"*Far* too close, and he didn't even slow down!" Elizabeth, in charge of the torch, came nearer to being annoyed than Sophie had ever seen before.

A minute later, a large car coming from London slowed to a halt. They could barely see the upper-class speaker through the open window.

"Hello. Having a spot of bother?"

"Yes. A punctured tyre."

"Can I be of any assistance?"

"That's kind of you, but we've changed the wheel."

"Excellent. Then I bid you a good night for what's left of it and safe motoring."

"And safe motoring, to you, too. Good night."

They set off shortly afterwards, with Elizabeth driving this time.

At four in the morning, and after everyone in Dumond Hall was in bed, two tired maids stole silently from their room and crept down the stairs. Ada was leading.

"We'll be fit for nothing tomorrow... today," whispered Flora.

"I know... What do we say if we get caught?" asked Ada.

"If it's in the study, we'll say we're after Minkov because he's a spy. If it's in Basil's dressing room, then we'll say it's because he's a murderer."

"They won't believe none of that."

"I know, and they'll ask why we didn't go to the police, but at least it will get Superintendent Penrose or others involved in our plight — those who can put in a good word for us."

"Sounds dodgy to me... Shh. The copper's comin'."

At twenty to five, the sky began brightening.

"Could you step on it, please," said Sophie tersely.

"We're in a built-up area, and I fear that if the police stop us, they will detain us and we'll be too late to do anything."

"If we go this slowly, we shall also be too late."

"I'll see what I can do, Miss King."

317

When they were on Kew Bridge, the sun crested the horizon. Some light Sunday traffic was about, but Rabbit was now stuck behind a covered cart pulled by a horse that was in no particular hurry.

"I hope he goes in a different direction," said Sophie. "We're almost out of time." She looked at her watch. "Can't you go around him?"

"Yes. There's a gap in the oncoming traffic... Here we go."

They passed the cart and were soon driving through Kew Green, heading for Kew Road. Elizabeth took the turning, and both women were stunned by what they saw.

"I forgot every word about it," said Sophie. "I've been here twice, and I simply forgot."

"So had I."

They had forgotten that Kew Gardens was completely enclosed by a ten-foot-high wall, and it cost a penny to get in during visiting hours.

"What shall we do?" asked Elizabeth.

They stopped outside a pair of tall, wrought-iron gates which led to a courtyard surrounded by old buildings.

"Um... We can't get in here... Drive on to the next gate. The Pagoda is at the far end, anyway."

Kew Road was desolate. The sun was just beginning to strike the dun bricks of the old thousand-yard wall, turning them a pale, glowing tan. Majestic trees in the gardens beyond already gloried in the new day. Birds called and darted purposefully across the road. Two rabbits ran off at the approach of the car.

"These are rather delightful houses," said Elizabeth, referring to the attractive villas opposite the wall.

"Very spacious and well-kept... Although this is not exactly the time for us to be looking at houses. Here's another entrance."

Sophie got out and tried the wooden door, but it was locked.

"The sign said they open at ten," said Sophie when she got back in.

"That is discouraging."

They drove to Victoria Gate, identifiable at a distance by the nearby Italian-style bell tower called the Campanile.

"I've never been up that before," said Sophie.

"You can't go up it, Miss King. It's the chimney for the Palm House boilers."

Sophie laughed. "Is it really? How clever of them to beautify an otherwise ugly thing… Those gates are padlocked." She sighed, then sighed again when finding the next entrance was also locked.

Lion Gate, the last gate, was still two hundred yards away when a man, the first pedestrian they had seen, crossed the road ahead of them and disappeared through the wall.

"Quick," said Sophie.

Elizabeth stopped across from the pedestrian's entrance, which had a low turnstile.

"I'll go in while you park Rabbit," said Sophie.

"Here is the pistol."

"Thank you. Follow as best you can."

Sophie got out and glimpsed the top of the Great Pagoda standing some little distance inside. She charged across the road, putting the pistol in her coat pocket. The turnstile was locked, and the box for the pennies had been removed for the night, so she climbed over and left her penny admission on the top. Then she ran.

Elizabeth followed a minute later but, at her age, to climb a turnstile proved beyond her capabilities. Distraught by this unexpected obstacle, she returned to the car to think over what she could do.

At a quarter past five, Lord Eldred approached the turnstile and saw a penny sitting on top. He climbed over and also left a penny.

The park was empty and, with the Great Pagoda sited in a corner so distant from the glasshouses and other features, this part was likely to remain unfrequented until the gardens were officially opened. Inside the park, Sophie moved cautiously, standing behind a tree until she was sure she could reach the next bit of cover unobserved. While by a hundred-and-fifty-year-old elm, she was surprised she could not now see anything of the Pagoda. Bushes screened the base and tree canopies hid its height, so she was uncertain exactly where the tower lay. She chose another tree and ran towards it.

Basil Munday stood on the flagstones with his back to the Pagoda just behind him. The sun rose slowly, marking its progress by the inching reclamation of each storey, revealing to the day the tower's dilapidation and faded red paint. Most of the wooden dragons on the rooves had long since rotted and been removed. However, the bricks and roof tiles and dull red trim shone nobly at the top, while everything below in the morning's shadows awaited the awakening kiss of the sun. He impatiently looked at his watch before glancing towards the Lion Gate entrance. An old briefcase lay on a bench against the wall. Munday paced with his hands behind his back. He turned, paced, and turned again. The still air was damp yet warm, causing him to unbutton his tweed jacket and fan himself with his cap. He paced once again and then took off his jacket to fling it next to the bag. The white shirt he wore clung to him. He cooled himself with the cap, then threw it on top of his jacket. Eldred had arrived.

"You're late," said Munday.

"A minute, no more," replied Eldred as he stepped between the red columns of the lowest storey.

"We haven't got all day."

"It's certain one of us hasn't... Were you behind that stupid idea to throw me in the pool?"

"I knew of it. Does it matter?"

Eldred did not answer. Presented with a clear plan of action, some of his self-possession had returned. He was calm, in contrast to Munday's obvious nervousness. In a way, he appeared to be the stronger of the two, although he was the smaller man.

"As I mentioned yesterday evening, I could not bring my revolver because the police have it. So, I would be obliged if I may borrow the one you offered... Unless, of course, your intention is to shoot me down like a dog despite our agreement."

"Naturally, I shall keep my word. The ground is flattest on the western side."

"That will be suitable. I'm afraid my knowledge of duelling is rather limited. Back-to-back, take ten paces, turn, present, fire — is that more or less it?"

"So, I believe... Will you choose your revolver?" Munday moved his jacket and cap to one side, then indicated the briefcase on the bench. He opened the case and motioned again for Eldred to step forward, which he did.

The delay agitated Sophie. Wood pigeons made their cooing calls but, although those most peaceful of natural sounds echoed among the trees, they did not quell her distress. Had she missed the pagoda completely? She retraced her steps and went around the other side of a great cedar whose branches swept the ground. She was in an avenue now. One way led further into the gardens, the other led to the Great Pagoda, sitting atop a slight knoll. She could see two men and knew who they were before she recognized them. She jumped back into the cover of the trees and hurried forward.

Although now knowing where to go, she found her near-panic undiminished. Where was Elizabeth? Were they really going to shoot at each other to kill, or to wound? How could they choose such a pretty place? The absurdity and emptiness of violence stood exposed for her in those moments. Were two mature, reasonable men going to slaughter each other... and for what grand reason would they do it? Tradition, jealousy, greed, money? There was no sense to it, whatever the reason might be. As with all violence, there was never any underlying rational sense, and the awareness of this fact becoming now starkly apparent to her made her hands tremble.

She reached the ring of low trees and bushes surrounding the towering structure. Ten oriental storeys, in such an elegant style so far from home, set in an English parkland cleverly devised by gentlemen much concerned with proportions, symmetry, and vistas — it was there, before this monument to culture and good taste, that a slaughter was about to occur. Sophie hesitated and swallowed. She could think of no easy way to interfere. It was not her place to tell men of standing what to do. These were viscounts — Basil now entitled with the death of his father. This old affair was theirs, not hers. In their eyes, she was a servant and, if that were not sufficient reason for their outrage, she was a woman meddling in the proceedings of men. Many different thoughts and questions jostled in her mind. If one man was foully motivated against another, what of it? They knew what they were doing and were settling the matter in their own way, and it was not her place to intervene. It was illegal and senseless, and she could easily judge them for their folly, but it was their business. She suddenly missed sensible, reliable Elizabeth. The sheer enormity of the thought that she should now act by stepping between them had her paralyzed.

Eldred looked into the bag, then pulled out an unloaded Webley service revolver. He broke it open and tried the action by pulling back the hammer, revealing the claw-like firing pin. He pulled the trigger and gently lowered the hammer.

"It works better when loaded," said Eldred, in a low, wry tone.

"Yes," said Munday, who now seemed more relaxed. He reached in for an identical revolver. "There's a box of cartridges in the briefcase, too."

"Is there?" Eldred looked inside.

He rummaged among holsters and other paraphernalia for the box. While his attention was on the contents, a man appeared at the side of the Pagoda. Munday violently seized Eldred around the neck. There ensued a frantic struggle before the two men together bore Eldred to the ground. Munday sat on Eldred's chest and pinioned his arms, while the man, kneeling beside them and wearing gloves, loaded the revolver Eldred had handled.

"I should have known," said Eldred. "I did know, really… Remember, Munday, with my death, the feud ends."

"It ends for you, yes. If the papers you signed pass muster and I buy your property, then your son will live to a ripe old age."

"I suppose you killed your brothers. Your father, too?"

"No, I couldn't bring myself to go *that* far. This gentleman dealt with Father for me." He nodded to the other man and said, "Make sure you don't shoot my knee off."

"I won't," said the man. He then spoke to Eldred. "It'll be over in a second, matey. All you'll feel is a little touch and then nothing."

Eldred struggled and jerked his head away, making it difficult for the man to aim.

"I'm holding a pistol," said Sophie, standing behind the engrossed group. "If that gun goes off, there will be three dead bodies for the police to find."

Everyone froze as though in a tableau entitled 'Justice Surprises the Banditti at Their Vile Work.' Eldred stared up at her from the ground. Munday slackened his grip but did not otherwise move. The other man, completely still, was very aware. His revolver's barrel was motionless, but he was looking sideways at Sophie. Then he slowly turned around. Sophie blindly fired a shot into the air.

"I mean it," she said, levelling the pistol at the unknown man.

Her shot had knocked something heavy off the pagoda. It bounced and noisily slithered on the roof tiles of every storey. They all jumped with surprise, and Sophie jumped the highest, when a decayed wooden dragon's head with a protruding tongue landed with a thump only inches from Eldred's ear.

"As you can see, I am an expert shot," said Sophie, recovering mendaciously and fast. "Put that weapon down, my man, or I shall shoot without warning."

He complied, but the revolver lay within his reach.

"You get up first. Do so slowly. Munday, you'll stay put until I tell you to move."

The man got to his feet but was as tense as a coiled spring.

"Put your hands up."

She kept the pistol aimed at him while quickly retrieving both revolvers and the briefcase, removing all to a safe distance.

"Sit down on that bench and don't make a move."

When he had sat down, she turned, and Munday saw her face for the first time.

"But you're the dining room maid!?"

"Be quiet you, you... odious *creature!*" She briefly pointed the pistol at him. "You're now my prisoner." She took a step back so she could cover both men more easily. "Get over there with him... What is your name?" she asked the man on the bench.

He did not answer. Munday got up and joined his accomplice. Both men looked unhappy. Munday looked puzzled and sat slumped with all vigour gone out of him, because his plans were ruined and there was no escape, while the other was morose yet all too vigilant.

"Are you all right, my Lord?" asked Sophie when Lord Eldred got up.

"Nothing serious. Bruises, a banged elbow, and my neck hurts like blazes, but I'm alive and only because of your timely intervention. They were making it as though I had committed suicide... I'm forever in your debt. Thank you."

"I'm relieved you're no worse off."

After having said this, she realized what her unspoken implication meant, that Eldred could have died, and she shuddered.

"Oi! Stay where you are!" shouted a policeman.

Sophie turned. Three gardeners and a constable wheeling a bicycle were quickly approaching via the long avenue. A noise made her look back. The man on the bench was off and running. She raised the pistol but hesitated and he reached the trees. Munday attempted to follow the example, but he was slow. Eldred caught him and punched him on the jaw. Munday staggered and collapsed, being defeated in his purpose rather than knocked out.

The constable and gardeners closed the gap. They had seen much of what had happened.

"Constable. I am Viscount Eldred. Apprehend that man," he pointed towards Lion Gate. "He's wanted for the murder of Viscount Munday. This one is also a murderer," he pointed at Basil, "but he's not going anywhere."

"Has anyone been shot?" asked the constable.

"No. You'd better be quick. He doesn't have a gun, but may have a car."

"It's all true, officer," said Sophie, still holding the pistol. "Superintendent Penrose at Scotland Yard can vouch for me."

"Penrose, eh?" He stared at the pistol.

"Quick, man!"

"Yes, my Lord."

The constable pushed his bike at a run, jumped onto the saddle, and pedalled like mad towards the entrance.

The gardeners stared at the man on the ground; they stared at the viscount; they stared at the young woman, and they finished by staring fixedly at the pistol she held.

"Good morning," said Sophie awkwardly, while putting the weapon in her pocket. "I left a penny on top of the turnstile. I hope nobody's taken it."

Chapter 28

The Cautious and the Cautioned

Miss Elizabeth Banks was in a quandary. Miss King had hopped over the turnstile, but when Elizabeth tried to follow, she could not raise her leg high enough and there was nothing for her to step on. She considered hurling herself over but was sure she would either fail or worse — land on her head. Frustrated, she acknowledged defeat, and sadly reflected that the decades had taken their toll. Her spirit was willing, though. To be in Kew Gardens when she shouldn't was something she had childishly looked forward to with glee. To apprehend murderers was her more mature ambition. Stuck outside on an empty road, she did not have a clue what to do next, so she returned to where she had parked Rabbit on a side street.

Boredom is a godsend. It means the afflicted party has an excess at their disposal of that most precious of commodities — time. How the bored use that spare time is entirely their responsibility. They can remain afflicted, they can complain, or they can become inventive and creative. Add to boredom a sense of missing out on some desirable activity, either depression threatens, complaints turn to whining, or a stunning idea presents itself.

Elizabeth had returned to and sat in the car because she could not stand about in the street. She could not stay in the car because, being tired, she would certainly fall asleep. Therefore, she cogitated, and continued cogitating until a smile came. She checked her pocket, and the box of matches was still there from when she had lit the warning lamp.

She got out to examine Rabbit's bonnet for signs of dew. Taking off a glove that needed cleaning, she put her hand on the metal. It was warm. Elizabeth looked along the sideroad and counted nine other parked cars. She went to see what she could find.

Upon hearing the noise of an approaching vehicle, she ducked out of sight behind an old Ford covered in dew. The car pulled up, and she watched a man get out. He hurried towards the entrance and climbed over the turnstile. It's Lord Eldred, she thought, having recognized him from a newspaper photograph. She stood still for some seconds and then resumed her walk.

The next car's bonnet still felt warm. It was a blue car — a two-door Morris Cowley — travel-stained, and not in the best state of repair. Elizabeth remembered from the police reports that a similar car had been seen in Wynbourne at the time of Wilfred Munday's murder. Sophie's reports also came to mind, in which she had mentioned the old men in the beer tent discussing a noisy tyre. Elizabeth examined the wheels. All the tyres looked worn, but one at the rear had a patched hole in the cover, which caused the tyre to be out of round. She took out a match and bent down. While depressing the inner tube's valve pin with the matchstick, she heard a satisfying hiss. Next, she went to the back and let the air out of the spare tyre. She had only gone a few steps when a man came out of his house.

"Good morning," he said.

"Good morning, and what a glorious one it is, too."

Elizabeth had barely returned to Rabbit and seated herself when a pistol shot sounded. Out she got, alarmed and dithery.

"Oh, dear me."

She looked about for a policeman or to see if anyone else had heard the shot. A young woman dressed for church left another house, but she gave no sign of having heard anything out of the ordinary. Elizabeth waited, fearful and imagining the most dreadful things. She crossed Kew Road and leaned over the turnstile. For two minutes, she searched the trees and bushes for any movement and listened for the slightest sound. She heard a shout and could not think what it meant. In searching for activity, the last thing that she expected was that a man should come hurtling towards her at top speed.

"Argh!" she cried in horror.

Stepping to one side, she held her breath and put a hand to her throat, gaping at close range as a tall, thin man scrambled over the turnstile, his features so distorted he seemed like a hunted animal. He was gone soon enough — fleeing down the side road opposite. He ran and then jumped into the car with flat tyres. Elizabeth now peered to see what would happen next.

"Stand aside!" cried a man behind her.

She spun around at the shout to see a burly policeman with a bicycle on his shoulder running up to the turnstile.

"Allow me to assist you, constable," said Elizabeth.

She took hold of the handlebars. Between them, they got the bicycle over. The policeman came next.

"He's down there," she pointed. "He's trying to drive away in a blue Morris Cowley with a flat tyre."

"Is he? Thanks."

The policeman mounted his bicycle and set off but, almost at once, he had to swerve out of the path of the veering Morris Cowley as it lurched onto Kew Road. The car headed towards Richmond, with the cycling policeman in hot pursuit.

Elizabeth stared after them. Sophie joined her.

"Will he get away?"

"Oh, Miss Burgoyne! Thank goodness you're safe!"

They hugged each other.

"To answer, no he won't, Miss King. I let the air out of his tyre. You see, without the protective barrier provided by the pneumatic inner tube, the rim will eventually distort, and that will lead to the wooden spokes breaking... May I ask what happened?"

"Oh, well *done*, Elizabeth! Let's find somewhere to have a cup of tea, and I shall tell you all about it."

"What a good idea, Miss King. I'm dying for some tea, myself!"

Lord Eldred joined them with his face noticeably white and pinched. He asked,

"Did he get away?"

"The constable has gone after him," said Sophie. "But he won't get far, because Miss Banks... May I present Miss Banks, Lord Eldred?"

"Please to meet you, Miss Banks," said Eldred.

"It is a great honour to meet you, my Lord," said Elizabeth.

"Yes," said Sophie. "So, Miss Banks let the air out of his tyre."

"Well done... How is it you both come to be here?"

"We can't really say, because those for whom we work have sworn us to secrecy. But we know a lot about the feud. Did Basil Munday say much to you? I heard him when he said he got that man to murder his father."

"That he killed his brothers. I stated it, and he agreed."

"They were Bartholomew and Wilfred," said Elizabeth.

"Yes," said Sophie. "But what about his uncle Allan in Scotland?"

"I can't help you there. All I can tell you is that it wasn't me... I'm very sorry, I'm not feeling very well."

"Strain, I should imagine," said Sophie. "We all need some tea to settle our nerves."

"The gardeners have taken Munday to the main office. Perhaps we could get some tea there."

"That's an excellent idea. Can we offer you a lift?"

"Thank you, but I'll take my car. It would be a long walk back, otherwise."

It was just after seven. In the study at Dumond Hall, Sergeant Gowers was talking quietly to Inspector Haddock by a window, while Flora and Ada sat on a settee looking like two naughty little girls uncomfortably awaiting a decision upon their punishment.

"They were caught in the act of stealing," whispered Inspector Haddock so as not to be overheard by the two women. "The housekeeper walked in on them and screamed."

"Technically, that's true, and very unfortunate. They should not have done what they did, and I'm sorry. But looking at it another way, they found some incriminating evidence against Basil Munday. Surely you can see what he's up to? He's framing and blackmailing Lord Eldred. The paper they found is set up as a codicil to the man's will so that Basil Munday has the right to purchase Capel House. I don't know about the values and all that, but it's worth a lot more money than I'll ever see."

"Me, too."

"So why did Lord Eldred get it signed and witnessed yesterday? — the same day as Lord Munday was killed by him, as you think, or by an unknown assailant, as I believe. Whichever it turns out to be, it looks very fishy."

"Look here, Sergeant. I'm agreeable to discussin' theories with you, but Mrs Lester has complained that those two were in Basil Munday's dressing room, going through his papers, and with a handful o' the same already secreted about their persons... What am I to say to her? I can tell the constable to drop it, an' he'll be foine about that. But Mrs Lester will talk to Mrs Clare Munday as soon as she's up, an' then she'll get on the loine a-wanting to speak to the Chief Constable. If he hears I swept everything under the rug, so to speak, there'll be the devil to pay, and it's me who'll do the payin', not you."

"I understand your position, Inspector, and I'm not saying it's an easy one. But *you* know something's not right, what with Minkov under arrest and taken up to London. He was Munday's guest, not anyone else's."

"All that's out of my league. Who was that fellow Drysdale?"

"Foreign Office, as everyone knows, but he has a great deal of pull, and he's smart. He had Minkov arrested on a smuggling charge, but he's the type who won't get out of bed in the morning for anything as small as that. There's a lot more going on there than meets the eye."

"Spy, is he?"

"You didn't hear me say it."

"Interesting... Still, that's all a bit too rarefied, an' don't answer for the situation we have on hand."

"How about this..."

"Can I say something in our defence?" called Flora from the settee.

"No, you cannot!" said Gowers. He lowered his voice again. "They're not going to re-offend, because they're not criminals. They were helping us, if you recall, although they overstepped the mark..."

The telephone rang, and the inspector went to the desk to pick it up.

"Inspector Haddock here... London call? Yes, put it through..." While he waited, he absent-mindedly pushed Ada's confiscated lock-picking tools about on the desk. "Good morning, Superintendent Penrose... Yes... Yes... Oh, I see... At Kew Gardens... Yes... Papers?" Haddock cleared his throat. "Yes, sir. We found some *very* interesting things... Oh, you know. Just glad we could help, sir... Yes... Goodbye, bye."

He replaced the receiver. "I'm sure you can guess what that was about. Basil Munday and an accomplice were arrested for attempted murder this morning. Other charges are pending."

"Then all's well that ends well," said Gowers.

"Hooray!" called Flora. "You can let us go now. We're starving and ever so tired, Inspector."

"Get along with you," he said. "And stay out of trouble."

Flora approached him, and Ada followed. "We would just like to say how terribly, terribly sorry we are. We are truly despondent, devastated, and distressed." She put a hand on his arm, and her voice became husky. "We promise *never* to do anything like it again, unless *absolutely* necessary."

"You should leave before I change my moind."

"Then, goodbye!" said Flora.

"Goodbye, sir," said Ada.

Ada and Flora bolted from the room.

He laughed. "By them opening that strongbox, they saved us getting a warrant."

"That was a good lock on it, too," said Gowers.

"Are you sure they're not criminals?"

"Yes, I'm sure."

"Now, seeing as they were your responsibility, I have a little job that wants doin'. Go and explain matters to Mrs Lester." Inspector Haddock smiled triumphantly.

"I had a feeling that was coming, sir," said Gowers, who then left.

The Inspector shook his head, pleased with himself. He was about to leave and so he reached for the lock-picks, but they had disappeared.

The following morning, Sophie was summoned to Scotland Yard to meet Superintendent Penrose. She could go, because

Burgoyne's had been ejected from Dumond Hall, and so she never returned to the place. Ada, Flora, and a much-recovered Broadbent-Wicks, still sporting a bandage on his head, had returned to London, bringing Sophie's things with them. The agency was to have left shortly anyway, but that Burgoyne's had been thrown out, with its honour impugned, nettled her a great deal. She also very much doubted that the Mundays would pay her bill without a court action, a step she would avoid for fear of too much truth being revealed and written in the court records.

"The case now stands like this," said Penrose. "We caught the chap in Richmond. Robert Townsend's his name, and he didn't get far because he lost a wheel in the High Street only forty yards from the police station. That was very thoughtful of him and handy for us. We've charged him and Basil Munday with attempted murder. They'll both go down for that. Townsend's intelligent, so he's playing a game with us. He could tell us a lot more about Munday and other things but won't co-operate unless we drop charges against him. Of course, we can't, because he killed Viscount Munday, as we well know, but cannot prove at present. Both Munday and Townsend are keeping quiet about all the other murders by pleading ignorance. Would you believe Munday is trying to pass off the business at Kew as a practical joke?"

"No, I don't believe it."

"Well, he is, but taking that tack won't do him any good. Now, neither man had mentioned Minkov as being involved. Yesterday, Mr Drysdale interviewed both and specifically mentioned Minkov. That rattled Munday, but he hasn't said anything further. Townsend says he knows things about Minkov, and a lot more besides, that would be of use to Mr Drysdale. He feels his hand's strengthened by what he knows, but that won't last long. Now that the Wiltshire police are on the right track, they'll find evidence, I'm sure."

"All of that doesn't seem very satisfactory, somehow," said Sophie.

"I wouldn't say that. We found a straw trilby hat in Townsend's car."

"Did you? That's marvellous!"

"He doesn't yet know that we're on to him about that little ruse in the Wilfred Munday case. Then there are the two witnesses who saw the car. Seeing the actual vehicle might jog their memories. So, we're getting somewhere, but it takes time."

"I see. What about Minkov?"

"Hasn't said a word, and probably won't. They're all getting lawyers involved, which slows the process, and rightly so. We'll get there in the end, but Minkov's involvement will be harder to prove. Basil Munday can't mention him, or he'll destroy whatever hope he thinks he has, while Townsend is all too ready to talk but only if he benefits. That's about it for the moment."

They stared at each other.

"Did you bring it, Miss Burgoyne?" He put his unlit pipe in his mouth.

"I did."

She placed the automatic in front of him and then sat as demurely as if butter would not melt in her mouth. He picked up the pistol and removed all the cartridges.

"FN 1910... That there is the same model o' automatic pistol as was used to kill Archduke Ferdinand. Started the Great War, it did." He removed his pipe.

"I suppose it did," said Sophie.

"If I said you were in a lot of trouble, would you believe me?"

"Of course, I would."

"Let me see." He held up his meaty fingers and gripped each with his other hand to count. "For starters, you have an unlicensed firearm. Two, you discharged said firearm in a public place in a manner likely to cause harm to others..."

"I simply forgot that by firing in the air, the bullet had to come down somewhere."

"You shot a dragon. Now that's a rare feat but seein' as it was made o' wood and quite rotten, and your shot dislodged it from where it had lain hidden for a century and a half, we can pass over that one."

"Thank you," said Sophie.

"Don't thank me yet, because it gets a lot worse."

"I thought it would."

"Did you purchase this pistol, or was it a gift?"

"I found it," said Sophie.

"And I know where," said Penrose. "Theft, *and* concealing evidence... Look at that, I'm running out o' fingers."

"I'm very sorry."

"Only because I've caught you. That you pointed the firearm at two murderous individuals and threatened to shoot them, I'm inclined to ignore, but *only* because it suits me to do so."

"What can I say?"

"Nothing, Miss Burgoyne, because it's me who's doing the saying. How many times have we talked over this matter? How often have I explained that if you want to purchase a firearm and register it, you have every right to do so? But, oh no, you couldn't bring yourself to do that. You think behaving like a normal person is unnecessary because you believe you're above the law."

"I certainly do *not*!" said Sophie. "You won't believe this, but I was going to register it this week."

He stared at her. "Why are we having this interview?"

"Do you really want to know?"

"Arh."

"You won't think it silly or get cross?"

"I'm cross already."

"Well... It's such a dear little pistol. You know where and when I acquired it, and it was needed at the time for protection. I thought it might come in handy in the future. I knew I should turn it in but, by that time, I had named it, so I couldn't."

"You named it?"

"Yes. You see that it has the letters FN on the handle? Well, they reminded me of a *really* good friend of mine. We were at school together and her name is Freda Nicholls. So, I named the pistol Freda after her. Once having done that, how could I ever part with it?"

"That's ridiculous."

"No, it isn't... I can't help myself. I get attached to certain things and give them names. I've always done it."

He kept his eyes on Sophie while taking out his tobacco pouch. She got up and opened the window wider, then returned to her chair. He lit his pipe.

"Will you purchase a pistol?"

"It's likely I shall. I'll need to train with it, of course, but I don't know how to do that... What will happen to Freda?"

"Never you mind."

Penrose picked up a pen and began writing a note. When he had finished, he folded the paper and held it out between two fingers.

"You'll take this note to the sergeant on duty at Cannon Row. He'll help you fill out the license application, and you'll pay him the five shillings. Be back here in two hours or I'll issue a warrant for your arrest. Don't you go thinking I'm joking, because I'm not. When you come back, I'll arrange for you to get training. We have a shooting range in the basement." He waved the note, and she took it.

"Thank you." She rose to leave.

"Don't forget Freda."

He offered the pistol by holding the barrel. Sophie took it by the handle.

"I don't know how to thank you."

"I do. There's a job coming up at the end of this month or beginning of next. You'll take it without question, and that will be the end of this business."

"Yes," said Sophie.

"Better hurry. The clock's ticking."

On Wednesday afternoon, Nick, the office boy, found the address he was seeking in Dalston. He knocked on the door of a semi-detached house, a package in his hand. The door swung open, and a smell of stew and floor polish assailed his nose. The large lady filling the doorway wore mourning and had dark, curled hair. What puzzled him were her many jangling bracelets. Her face was heavily powdered, and she wore a long imitation pearl necklace. Her lipstick was orange, as though she had kissed one and the colour had come off.

"Yes?"

"Good morning, Mrs Edwards. I have a package for Mr Broadbent-Wicks." He decided right then that a little compliment or two might go a long way.

"Oh, it's for Mr Wicksy, is it? I can give it to him." Her voice had a spread of three and a half classes, from the one in which she was born to the one to which she aspired.

"I'm ever so sorry, but I was instructed to deliver it personal and get him to sign for it."

"Oh?"

"It's from his work, and they'd like to know how he's doing after being bonked on the head."

"The window cleaning?" She looked baffled.

"No, Mrs Edwards. The domestic business, Burgoyne's Agency."

"Oh, I *see*. You'd better come in. Wipe your feet."

Nick entered. "Is that Irish stew?" he asked.

"No, Lancashire hotpot."

"Smells lovely. My mum made it once, but the spuds went like rubber, so we've never had it again."

"I've never had that trouble... How do you know my name?"

"Because Mr Broadbent-Wicks says you're the best landlady in the world. I'm Nick, by the way."

"Does he?" She gave her widest smile of delight. "He's such a dear boy, and now he's been so dreadfully wounded. I'm sick with worry, I am. Absolutely *sick*! To think that anyone would do such a thing."

"What happened?"

"Don't you *know*? He was attacked in the street and robbed of his money. And to think the police are doing nothing about it. The rates are so 'igh, but we get no value for them and now no safety *neither*. I don't know what things think they are coming to." She put a hand to her forehead, her bracelets crashing like little cymbals.

"I s'pose you're right," said Nick. "So, the robbers took all his money, eh?"

"That's correct, and I'm still waiting on last week's rent. He's usually such a *regular* gentleman. All my guests are regular. But there, the poor fellow must get his strength back before he can resume work and earn something. I wish he'd 'urry up."

"I'm sure he will soon, and your hotpot will help do the trick nicely. It's a pity there aren't more landladies as understanding as you."

"I don't know what to *say*… Would you like some tea?"

"Yes, I would, thank you kindly, but I have other deliveries, and I should see Mr Broadbent-Wicks."

"Yes, of course. His room is this way. You must speak quietly to him, Nick — his head is *h*ever so delicate."

Outside the closed door of a back bedroom, Mrs Edwards called in a cheerful falsetto, "Mr Wicksy! There's a visitor for you by the name of Nick."

"Thank you, Mrs E. Send him in." BW's voice was faint and weary.

Nick entered and shut the door. They said hello in the dim room and waited for the landlady to descend the stairs.

"Hello, Mr Wicksy," said Nick with a grin.

"Please, don't say that. I'm an invalid." His voice was normal. BW was wearing vivid red striped pyjamas and a bandage while propped up in bed.

"Is it bad? Turn round so I can have a butcher's."

BW took off his bandage and turned. "It's almost healed up."

"I can see it was a nasty crack, but you look fit. Why aren't you back at work?"

"My head doesn't really hurt, but I can tell I'd get dizzy at the top of a ladder. Otherwise, I'm fine. The dizziness is already going and another couple of days' rest should do it. Mrs E. is the *real* problem. If I got up and dressed, she would think I'm a malingerer, and drone on and on about the rent. That's why I'm in bed. My trouble is, I don't have the readies, and I'm a week behind. You didn't happen to bring anything with you?"

"Mr Broadbent-Wicks..."

"Call me BW, please. I'm training everyone to use it, although Mrs E. is proving difficult."

"BW, your worries are over. I've brought your pay."

"*Oh, it's like the relief of Mafeking.* You've bucked me up no end... How do you know it's my pay?"

"Never mind that. There's a note in the package, your wages, and an extra tenner from Miss Burgoyne to make you feel better."

"How *wonderful*... That is so kind of her. Isn't she splendid?"

"Yes. I don't know what the gift is — a scarf or socks or something."

"You'll get into trouble if you carry on like that."

"Maybe. I'm going to be a spy, so I need to practise." Nick got up and looked out of the window. "If you're hard up, why don't you get another job?"

"Because I enjoy spying, too. Window cleaning doesn't pay that well, but it's very healthy, and allows me to do the other work. It's a shame there's not more of the *other*. If there were, then I'd be in the pink."

"Oh... What about your getting attacked?"

"The rotter sneaked up on me. You'd better believe that I shan't, absolutely shall *not*, get caught like that again. Then he murdered the dear old boy, and I could have stopped the plague spot given half a chance. I've been thinking of *nothing* else while lying here."

"Yeah, that must be hard on you." Nick came back from the window. "Here, let me tell you something. There's a big job in the works. Mr Drysdale and old Penrose came round to the office together. Then Lord Laneford from the Home Office with another geezer came round the next day. Home Office has never visited before, so that means it's big. Miss Burgoyne didn't bring in Ada or Miss Flora to talk about it, so that means it's still in the works."

"How extraordinarily clever of you. I would have missed all of that."

"Only takes practise," said Nick airily. "I've got to go, and I hope you get well soon."

"Kind of you to come and do give my heartfelt thanks to Miss Burgoyne. It will be such a relief to pay the rent and walk past Mrs E. holding my unbandaged head high."

Nick paused at the door. "Her downstairs. What's her tea like?"

"Not bad. If you like it sweet, don't let her put the sugar in — put your own in when she's not looking — she guards *everything*. Also, she slices the cake abominably thin."

"You've got Lancashire hotpot tonight."

"No! Not that again." He put his bandage back on.

Chapter 29

Archie ties a bow

At seven on Friday evening, Archie Drysdale was in high spirits when he arrived at White Lyon Yard. Hawkins, the butler, admitted him, and took care of his coat and top hat while deferentially offering his congratulations.

"Archie!" Sophie rushed down the stairs and threw herself into his arms. "I'm so happy for you both!"

"Steady on, old thing, but thank you kindly."

"Come on," she said as she took him by the hand. "We saw it in the newspaper today." They entered the drawing room where Aunt Bessie was waiting.

"Archibald, my dear, dear boy." They kissed each other on the cheek. "Where's Victoria? You should have brought her."

"Not tonight, Bessie."

"Then I insist you both come to dinner soon. Where is she now?"

"She's been in meetings this morning and only arrived in London two hours ago. The steel business has been impacted by the coal shortage and all the industries *dependent* on steel are anxious, of course."

"Ah… Hawkins, the sherry… Come along, sit down and tell us all about it."

"Was it a romantic setting?" asked Sophie.

"You'll have to be the judge of that. It was at Euston Station..."

Archie explained how, when, and where he became engaged to Miss Victoria Redfern.

"And what is the word from her father?" asked Aunt Bessie.

"So far, there has only been ominous silence. Redfern will keep his word and cut Victoria out of his will. She has a good salary, and an allowance, but he's also threatened those in the past... We await his severest judgment."

"It's obvious the man's an imbecile," said Aunt Bessie. "That he should insult our family... Who does he think he is?"

"A wealthy man who likes to get his own way."

"Don't discuss all that now," said Sophie. "This is a day for celebration. Where are you going this evening?"

"A night on the town... I'll tell you about it afterwards if there's time. As promised, I'm here to explain how things stand, but I must be quick, or I'll be late."

"Sit down and have your sherry," said Bessie.

"Thank you. As Minkov is my specific interest in this whole affair, I'll tell you about him first. We still don't know what game he was playing when he passed the money that he smuggled into the country, and we still don't know where it went. He's not talking, of course, but we didn't expect him to. That case Minkov gave to the diplomat almost certainly contained a large sum of money — far more than was necessary to pay off Robert Townsend. This slippery agent of Minkov was the one who murdered Lord Gerald and was also an accomplice in the murder of Wilfrid Munday. However, the police are hopeful that Lord Basil Munday will name Minkov as a co-conspirator, because I'm told that he is now behaving erratically, seeming to be more concerned for his son, Luke, than he does for himself.

"Robert Townsend has a police record for minor offences. He sees that the game is up and is bartering to save his neck. He hinted that a foreign power — Germany, we believe — has several dormant agents stationed in Britain, either left over from the war or newly recruited. Townsend says he can give us their names, but he wants all charges against him dropped. When I questioned him about Minkov, he merely shrugged, and said I'd caught a big fish. Really, he shouldn't have said that much, because he's further confirmed our suspicion that Minkov is still an active agent — again, probably for Germany."

"Will you turn Minkov into a double agent?" asked Sophie. "Even if he's a murderer?"

"No. Even if he weren't, he's too untrustworthy. He'll be tried for smuggling and will eventually be deported after a term in prison. If Munday or Townsend name him in a murder case, then that's a different story. If a conspiracy can be proved, he'll stand trial for murder. Despite the communications you intercepted, the evidence against Minkov is weak. The police are looking for other exchanges he made with Townsend, but I'm not sure they'll find anything useful.

"By the way, we had a serious talk with the diplomat who carried Minkov's case through customs. The man is incompetent, to say the least — so much so that he's highly unlikely to be passing secrets to anyone. Minkov had met him at a hotel bar in Malta, and there groomed him for the job by telling him it was the family's jewels. Minkov also paid him a hundred pounds. Their plan was in place before they boarded the Rangoon. If Minkov pleads guilty to smuggling, the diplomat will probably not be charged or appear in court. His career is over, though."

"Who is this diplomat?" asked Aunt Bessie.

"I'm keeping his name private."

"Do you mean I know him?"

"Shall we move on, or shall I stop altogether?"

"Don't be irritating," said Aunt Bessie.

Archie looked at the clock. "I'll give you as much as I can about the murders. Viscount Major Ian Eldred was likely killed by Minkov or Luke Munday; we don't know which one, but I'll come to that in a moment.

"Allan Munday was killed in Scotland. He was quite wealthy, so Basil's motive may have been the five-thousand-pound legacy he received. Acquaintances and business associates have provided Basil with a partial alibi for the crucial period, because he *was* legitimately conducting business in the north of England. However, there are significant gaps, which may or may not be filled in later. One gap occurs after he was in Harrogate, and that was as near as he is known to have come to the Trossachs."

"What is the distance from Harrogate?" asked Sophie.

"Oh, about two hundred and fifty miles. Not exactly close, but then he's rarely as far north as Harrogate, which makes it intriguing."

"Basil Munday would need three days clear for that journey and to carry out the murder," said Sophie.

"So it would seem, but, as I say, the police have not interviewed everyone yet. That one is likely to be a dead end anyway, unless someone saw him near the murder scene."

"Why don't they get on with it?" said Aunt Bessie.

"They're going as fast as they can. Please allow me to continue. Next is the Bartholomew Munday case. A re-examination of the facts and fresh interviews while investigating Basil Munday as potentially being his brother's murderer has so far revealed he was absent from the estate for four days at the critical time. This allowed him plenty of opportunity for travelling and for killing his brother. When asked about this absence, Basil Munday remembered very little, although he was certain he was not in London the night of the murder. He maintains he left the estate for business reasons, and several witnesses confirm this. His diary yielded no information. Again, with nothing to tie him to the murder scene, he will not be charged with Bartholomew's death, either."

"Well, if there's nothing else, there's definitely a pattern," said Sophie. "When there was a murder out of the area, Basil was away. When Wilfred was murdered in the area, Basil was at home."

Archie sipped his sherry, then looked at his watch.

"Sorry, I'll have to go faster. Another murder has cropped up, and we have a theory that ties them all together. What partially substantiates the theory is Miss McMahon and Miss Dane's discovery of a forged Swiss passport in an assumed name containing Munday's photograph. They found it in a secret compartment of the desk in the study. His erratic behaviour, that I mentioned just now, stems from the moment the police questioned him about possessing such a document.

"Basil Munday entered France on the 23rd of June 1917, using his British passport. His son, Luke, was on leave because his unit had been rotated out of the front lines, so they met in Paris on the twenty-fifth. Luke Munday was back at the front on the twenty-ninth. Later, he was stationed about ten miles distant from where Major Ian Eldred was murdered on the third of July. Luke Munday maintains that the meeting with his father was innocent and innocuous. Basil, when questioned about why he was in France, says it was for sightseeing and searching for business opportunities. Upon reaching Marseille, he stayed at a hotel for eight days, from the thirtieth of June to the seventh of July. Minkov had arrived two days earlier but left the same day Basil did. There's no evidence they knew each other before Marseille, and Basil says Minkov was one of many business agents he met.

"Now it becomes a tale of two passports. Munday lands in Algiers on the ninth of July using his British passport. He's there, supposedly looking for cheap sardines. On the thirteenth, he uses his Swiss passport to enter Greece. On the nineteenth, he crosses from Greece into Bulgaria. Those countries were on different sides during the war, and they still don't particularly care for each other, so it is quite remarkable how that was managed. Minkov must have very good contacts in the area. Anyway, Minkov's father was killed on the twenty-second. Minkov was in Bulgaria then and remained there until August. We can't tell when Munday left or what route he took, but he arrived in Malta using his British passport on the twenty-eighth."

"Perhaps they were using a friend's private yacht," said Sophie.

"What a marvellous idea. We can check that with the Harbour Master's records on the Maltese end of things."

"Archibald, I'm sure you find passports fascinatin', but I don't. What is the wretched theory?" Aunt Bessie was visibly impatient.

"Minkov was a German agent during the war. He was in Marseille recruiting contacts among the French. Munday happened along. Remember, either Basil or Luke planned to kill Major Eldred. Minkov and Munday had a few drinks and got chummy. Somewhere within their discussions of business and trade, they each express a wish that their respective fathers — and brothers, in Munday's case — would soon die so that they might receive their inheritances. Munday also conceives a plan to remove all intervening heirs to the title. They decide that each will kill the other's father. At some point, Minkov arranges for Munday to get a fake passport.

"To establish trust and protect Luke from prosecution, Munday asks and probably pays Minkov to kill Major Eldred. The tip about sardines was probably a goodwill gesture on Minkov's part. He had to earn his keep at the time; Basil was looking for food to import; they both wanted their fathers out of the way, so they settled matters like two good men of business."

"As you say," began Sophie, "it could have been Luke or Minkov who killed Ian Eldred. But didn't Minkov's passport reveal anything?"

"Unfortunately, he renewed it in nineteen. Let us not also forget, he certainly used a forged passport to get into France. Perhaps Munday knew Minkov was using an assumed identity, in which case he would have known he was dealing with a foreign agent. Alternatively, and I believe this to be the more likely scenario, Minkov saw Munday as a potential source for business dealings and so used his actual name when introducing himself."

"I wonder if they had already agreed to the murdering of each other's father?" mused Sophie. "If so, then Basil Munday would have no scruples over fake passports and identities. Perhaps Minkov was selling forged documents on commission — he must have got one for Munday readily enough."

"That's all quite conceivable, but we'll never know... As ever, Bessie, your sherry is superb."

"I'm glad you enjoy it."

"For theoretical purposes, we shall assume Minkov kills the Major, otherwise I cannot see what would have induced Munday to take the stupendous risk he does in travelling to Bulgaria during the war on a forged passport. Anyway, he does take the risk and stabs Minkov's father in a supposed burglary attempt that has gone wrong. That's according to the Bulgarian police and the accounts in the newspapers. The Bulgarian authorities, of course, knew nothing of Basil Munday's involvement, although they do now.

"Minkov was present in that country at the time but had the strongest of alibis — a dozen independent and unimpeachable witnesses. The two conspirators then go their separate ways, with a promise to do business in the future. Minkov is prepared to come to England to kill Viscount Munday whenever it is convenient.

"The war deferred the plan. In his spying capacity, Minkov answered to others, and perhaps it was too risky for him to enter England without their permission. That scenario could have gone wrong for him in several ways, but I digress.

"Regarding his own family, what did Basil do? He may have killed Uncle Allan Munday in Scotland. He almost certainly killed brother Bartholomew in London. He definitely killed brother Wilfred. Lord Eldred's testimony concerning Munday's admission confirms he was behind three murders. But direct evidence is also mounting. The Wiltshire police found bloodstains on the earthen floor of a shed at Dumond Hall. Someone had tried removing the affected soil but dropped a small clump and left a disturbed area. Clare Munday remembers hearing shots while Farmer Cordery was running his tractor, and the farmer said he saw Basil Munday near the shed that morning — only because he was now being asked about the man's movements, although he maintains he didn't hear any shots while on the tractor. They laid charges for Wilfred's murder today."

"If only we had known to suspect Basil Munday! We could have found that evidence and saved Lord Gerald!" exclaimed Sophie.

"Hindsight's such a wonderful thing. So, now we come to the end of this theoretical tale. Minkov was perfectly capable of killing Lord Munday, but realized he would become a suspect in short order unless he had an alibi. A foreign national, with a past he wants concealed, does not like to be the subject of a police enquiry. Therefore, he employed an agent, and Basil Munday was agreeable to this move. At the idea of shifting the blame for the murders to Lord Eldred, Basil became enthusiastic because he foresaw the chance to acquire the Eldreds' estate — something the Mundays have always wanted to do. When Lord Eldred tried to negotiate an end to the feud, Munday probably could not believe this stroke of luck. Undoubtedly, Basil would have had some other reason lined up to get Eldred out of the room at the crucial time. However, he seized the fortuitous opportunity by having Eldred go to the study to sign the papers and arranging for two servants to witness the signatures. The source for this part is, of course, Lord Eldred. With everything signed, Basil then left Eldred in the study, saying Lord Gerald wanted to talk to him. However, Viscount Munday would not be coming to talk with anyone because he was about to be killed."

"His own father," said Aunt Bessie in a sepulchral voice. "I have never heard of anything so callous and hideous."

"Munday has a complete disregard for the sanctity of life," said Sophie. "Knowing his father has just been killed, he blithely goes out and arranges the dance between his wife and Minkov. Do you believe Munday meant to get those papers signed all along?"

"No, I don't believe so. Like the businessman he is, he saw a chance and took it. Basil Munday *may* have been trying to implicate Lord Eldred beforehand. If so, he had done a poor job. Because of the unusual history of the feud, Minkov crafted a plan to fabricate evidence and confirm everyone's belief that Lord Eldred was the murderer. Minkov employed Townsend, an agent known to him and one whom he trusted. This permitted the charade of the supposed Eldred driving through Wynbourne with Wilfred's dead body. Munday killed Wilfred. Then he and Townsend must have taken the body from the shed to the hidden car while Farmer Cordery was out of sight.

"What is surprising is the boldness of it all. Even though there were weaknesses in the scheme that could raise questions once probed, such as accounting for Lord Eldred's own movements at the critical moment, they were relying on the fact that no one would take any notice of Basil Munday.

"Finally, we come to Lord Gerald's murder. The alibi is perfect — Minkov danced with Clare while Basil looked on in the middle of the crowded Ballroom. Then, with it being arranged that Eldred should be out of the room at the precise moment Lord Munday was killed, opinion would solidify about all the murders — Munday is forever innocent, Eldred is forever guilty, and Minkov's a non-starter. And that, my dears, is all I have time for. Victoria is summoning me. I hear her calling."

"Are you this long-winded with her?" asked Aunt Bessie.

"She hangs on my every word, as I do on hers. You can't score off me tonight, Bessie."

"The idea of it." Aunt Bessie smiled. "Don't keep her waiting and thank you for coming to explain things. Once again, congratulations."

Archie kissed her on the cheek and left the room. Sophie went with him.

"I hope you have a lovely evening, and do say hello to Victoria for me. Tell her I'm thrilled to bits that you're engaged."

"Thank you, and I will convey your message word for word. Good night."

Sophie waved to him as he went off to find a taxi. Then she closed the door and returned to the drawing room.

"It's a pity about Redfern," said Aunt Bessie. "What an obstinate, unfeeling brute of a man he must be."

"I have many ideas on how to change his mind, but none of them very good."

"Perhaps he'll thaw in time. You know Archibald mentioned a diplomat? Well, I believe I might know him."

"I know who it is."

"You do? Then what is his name?"

"No, I can't say. I'm sworn to secrecy."

"Nonsense. Tell me at once."

"I'm not a little girl, and there is such a thing as the Official Secrets Act. Archie shouldn't have said half the things he did. Allow him this one secret."

"Do you mean to say, when my friend Dot Callan sits in this very room and asks me who the diplomat is, I'm to answer that I don't know because Sophie is not a little girl? What will she think? It's preposterous."

"You know I can't tell you. So don't go through your bag of tricks of trying to get it out of me."

"Bag of tricks! Now look, I have been very patient..."

The butler entered the room.

"What is it, Hawkins?" asked Aunt Bessie sharply.

"A telephonic communication, my Lady. Mr Yardley wishes to speak to Miss Burgoyne."

Sophie was out of her chair in a flash, throwing an "Excuse me, Auntie" over her shoulder. She entered the study and picked up the receiver.

"Sinjin," she said softly. As she listened, she traced a finger along the curling marquetry of the desktop.

Epilogue

The spring and summer of '21 were the driest seasons anyone could remember. A drought is always bad, but to see crops fail in the growing season was hard to endure. Every county was affected — some more than others.

Lord Pascoe Eldred inspected his fields daily. If worrying caused plant growth, everything he had would have been ten feet tall. By the end of May, he and Lady Shelagh knew they could not save everything, so they abandoned the fields more distant from the river and those areas on slopes where the soil was thinner. They ignored the stunted plants with deformed buds that did not blossom. Then they tried to ignore them as they wilted and lay flat on the ground. After that, they took no notice of the brown tufts in the cracked dust that was their land.

Around the little pools, life hung on. Everything the family could think to do to conserve water, they did. Hope stayed long with them. When they saw a fifth of the crops had died, they told themselves they would get through it; they would survive somehow. When only a fifth of the crops precariously remained, they knew they had lost, and the hope that had sustained them thus far was gone for good. Yet they kept working, whether in anger, irritation or despondency.

Towards the end of June, the River Wynnet ran very low. It was never a gushing stream, nor was it wide or deep, but it always ran reliably. This year it might stop altogether. Pascoe and his men had dug channels and filled buckets beyond counting. Now they sank holes in the riverbed to see if something could be pumped out. He walked upstream, making a survey of suitable places to pump water.

Across the river was the Munday estate, now only unused fields of dead grass dotted about with tall green weeds that could tolerate the heat and lack of moisture. Pascoe did not know how Farmer Cordery was faring, because those fields that the farmer worked on the estate were not visible from the Eldred property.

He reached the Tongue, the little acre in the forks of the Wynnet. It was less blighted than elsewhere — a small, green remnant in a land turning brown. Then he stopped and stared and saw a sight he had never seen before. His branch of the Wynnet, skirting the Tongue, had disappeared. He saw no water and there had obviously been none for a while because tall grasses and weeds were growing in the dry bed. There was not so much as an isolated pool, but just some patches of damp earth not easily seen. He ran further along, and the growth was denser. He crossed to the Tongue and pushed his way past bushes that caught at his clothes until he found the Munday branch of the river. It was down but still flowing well in its channel.

"To the river," he murmured. This was the term the ancient deeds had used when describing and measuring the acreages of and division between the Eldred and Munday lands. No one had ever made sense of the measurement in this one particular part of the boundary, and both families deemed them inaccurate. An idea gripped Pascoe. He leapt to the assumption that, in the year the deeds were drawn up, there had been a drought. The surveyor had referenced only the Munday branch of the Wynnet and not the Eldred branch, because that was all there was for him to have seen. The dried-up branch must have been missed altogether!

Excited for a moment, he was suddenly dismayed. The Tongue was his, but whether he could prove the claim in court was another matter. The Tongue was Eldred land, after all. This meant the feud had been unnecessary, and arose simply because the deeds had never been interpreted properly. The futile nature of the disputes struck him. He considered the senseless long struggle, the enduring enmity, and all the wasted lives. A gulf-like sense of loss hit him, so sudden and so hard it hurt his soul, yet he quickly resolved to check the documents. He ran to tell Shelagh.

The next day, Pascoe visited Dumond Hall. Surridge opened the door and, suppressing whatever beliefs he held or emotions he experienced in that moment, admitted Lord Eldred with all due courtesy. Pascoe asked if he could speak to Lady Clare. While he waited, Audrey came to the top of the staircase and stared down at him. Her hostility was plain for him to see.

"Good morning," he said.

She swept away.

Luke Munday walked across the hall. His manner was both stiff and wary.

"Mother is not receiving visitors today, Lord Eldred. What do you want?"

"An important thing has happened, and you should see it. The Wynnet has dried up."

"Oh... Not surprising under the circumstances."

"Yes, but it is my branch that is affected. Your branch still flows."

"Um... What of it?"

"The deeds... They say, 'to the river.' If the land were to be surveyed today using that criterion... Well, the Tongue..."

"Strewth! You mean it's *yours*?"

"I'm not come to lay claim to it, you understand," he said hurriedly, "but I think you should take a look for yourself."

"Allow me to change my shoes."

When Luke returned, he hesitated.

"I'm not armed," said Pascoe, who opened his light summer jacket to prove his point.

"Dashed awkward, what? I'll take your word for it."

The two men set off and, by paths skirting the desiccated fields, reached the Tongue.

"We can't cross without getting wet," said Pascoe, "but if we go downstream a little, we will see it."

At the fork itself, Luke scanned for the Eldred branch of the Wynnet. It had disappeared to the extent it seemed only to be a low point in the sloping bank, and the growth within the bed made it look as though flowing water had never been present.

Luke slowly nodded. They stood in silence in the sun's glare, each alone with his thoughts while looking across to the Eldred fields. Pascoe lifted his straw hat and mopped his brow with a handkerchief.

"Are you wiped out?" asked Luke.

"Yes, we're finished," said Pascoe.

"I'm sorry for that… For many things… What happens now?"

"I don't know. I just wanted someone to see it." He realized his hope must sound pathetic.

"Yes… You must understand how difficult things are for us at present."

"I do."

"I'll inform Mother of this."

"As I say, I'm not making a claim… I'm not really concerned about the Tongue."

Luke looked at Pascoe. His initial thoughts flew to his father in prison. Then it occurred to him, for the first time, that he was the viscount-in-waiting and here was a land matter to be settled with a neighbour. The duties of a squire suddenly challenged his urbane London habits and attitudes. It confused him.

"This needs some consideration."

"That's understandable. Lawyers will want to look into the matter, anyway. I should get back..."

Luke's gaze flickered again towards Eldred's fields, and he received a foretaste of that duty of care which would eventually devolve upon himself.

"Yes, of course."

The rains came. It was already July, and they came too late. Just before they arrived, the police laid charges against Minkov and Townsend. Basil Munday named them when he confessed to the murders of Wilfred and Lord Gerald. The Bulgarian police also issued warrants for the arrest of Basil Munday and Todor Minkov.

Lord Basil Munday could not disclaim his hereditary peerage and had to remain a viscount until the day he died. Dumond Hall, substantial monies even after inheritance tax, and several other assets, went with the title following Lord Gerald's death. However, the tangible parts of the inheritance were governed by separate legal instruments — unrestricted except by the terms contained within them. Lawyers were set to work, their labours dominated by the guiding principle that time was of the essence. *Just* in time, the estate transferred to Luke, with provisions being established for Clare and the remaining children. Lord Basil became a landless, penniless peer.

Luke Munday, only days before he was ennobled and only weeks before the Eldreds would have failed, purchased the Tongue from Pascoe Eldred for the most extraordinary, life-saving sum of three thousand pounds. The feud was over.

When first observed riding on horseback together over the bridge, the sight of Julia Munday and Edward Eldred, now aged seventeen, caused a momentous stir. Tongues wagged and speculation ran from the settle outside the Swan to the church door and back again. Over time, the village accepted the oft-seen riders, and the sight of them together became just another part of Wynbourne life.

Late Tuesday morning, 24th of May, 1921, Sophie sat in the office of Superintendent Penrose at Scotland Yard. The office could have done with being a little larger, because also crammed in there, besides Penrose, were Lord Laneford, Archie Drysdale, Inspector Morton, Sergeant Gowers, and another man by the name of Maxwell Handley.

"Thank you for coming, Miss Burgoyne," said Penrose.

The others murmured a chorus of thanks.

"We have a delicate situation."

"Most delicate," added Lord Laneford.

"This is the job I mentioned a few days ago," said Penrose. "It's become urgent."

"In the extreme," said Archie.

"It must be urgent," said Sophie, "for all you busy gentlemen to be present. I know that Lord Laneford and Mr Drysdale have been much concerned recently over Burgoyne's ability to provide staff on certain dates. Concerned enough to visit me." She smiled. "Would this be the same matter?"

"Yes," said the chorus.

"Oh."

"Where to begin?" said Penrose. "We've had a bit of trouble at the docks, although nothing outside of ordinary police work, or so we believed. Something has come to light with far-reaching consequences... Far reaching, meaning Whitehall, and," he hesitated awkwardly, "Buckingham Palace."

"Good grief."

"Indeed. Now I'll explain what it is we'd like your staff to do. All these gentlemen will fill in the details as we go along. The arrangements have to be settled today, because... they simply *must*."

"May I take notes?"

There was an exchange of significant glances which silently elected Archie as spokesman.

"Only if they're in code and you do not identify any names, dates, or places."

Inspector Morton and Lord Laneford nodded their agreement. Penrose began his introduction and Sophie's pencil point flew across the page of her notebook, forming the mysterious and arcane symbols of shorthand.

OTHER BOOKS BY G J BELLAMY

IF YOU HAVE ENJOYED THIS BOOK, PLEASE HELP BY LEAVING A GOOD REVIEW. IT IS GREATLY APPRECIATED.

SOPHIE BURGOYNE SERIES
Secret Agency
Lady Holme
Dredemere Castle
Chertsey Park
Primrose Hill
An Old Affair
Royal Fright (coming soon)
Royal Menace (coming soon)

BRENT UMBER SERIES
Death between the Vines
Death in a Restaurant
Death of a Detective
Death at Hill Hall
Death on the Slopes
Death of a Narcissist

Printed in Great Britain
by Amazon